CLASSICS
OF
RUSSIAN
LITERATURE

ЛЕВ ТОЛСТОЙ

ДЕТСТВО · ОТРОЧЕСТВО · ЮНОСТЬ

Издательство Литературы
на иностранных языках
Москва

LEV TOLSTOI

CHILDHOOD
BOYHOOD
YOUTH

*Foreign Languages
Publishing House
Moscow*

TRANSLATED FROM THE RUSSIAN

DESIGNED BY D. BISTI

C. 1

Левъ Толстой

CONTENTS

CHILDHOOD

BOYHOOD

YOUTH

CHILDHOOD

Chapter I

THE TUTOR, KARL IVANICH

On the 12th of August 18—, the third day after my tenth birthday, when I had received such wonderful presents, Karl Ivanich woke me at seven o'clock in the morning by slapping at a fly directly above my head with a flapper made of sugar-paper and fastened to a stick. He did it so awkwardly that he entangled the image of my angel, which hung upon the oaken head-board of the bed, and the dead fly fell straight upon my head. I peeped out from under the coverlet, steadied the image, which was still rocking, brushed the dead fly on to the floor, and regarded Karl Ivanich with angry and still sleepy eyes. But attired in his motley wadded dressing-gown, girded with a belt of the same material, a red knitted skull-cap with a tassel, and soft goat-skin shoes, he pursued his course along the walls, taking aim and flapping away.

"Suppose I am little," I thought, "why should he disturb me? Why doesn't he kill the flies round Volodya's bed? There are heaps of them there. No, Volodya is older than I, I am the youngest of all, and that is why he torments me. He thinks of nothing else in life," I whispered, "except how he may do unpleasant things to me. He knows quite well that he has waked me up and fright-

ened me; but he pretends not to see it—the hateful man!
And his dressing-gown, and his cap, and his tassel—how
disgusting!"

As I was thus mentally expressing my vexation with
Karl Ivanich, he approached his own bed, glanced at the
watch hanging above it in a slipper embroidered with
glass beads, hung his flapper on a nail, and turned
towards us, evidently in the most agreeable frame of
mind.

"*Auf, Kinder, auf ... s'ist Zeit. Die Mutter ist schon
im Saal!*"* he cried in his kindly German voice; then he
came over to me, sat down at my feet, and pulled his
snuff-box from his pocket. I pretended to be asleep. First,
Karl Ivanich took a pinch of snuff, wiped his nose,
cracked his fingers, and then turned his attention to me.
He began to tickle my heels, laughing the while. "Come,
come, lazybones," he said.

Much as I dreaded tickling, I neither sprang out of bed
nor made any reply, but buried my head deeper under
the pillow, kicked with all my might, and used every
effort to keep from laughing.

"How good he is, how he loves us, and yet I could
think so badly of him!"

I was vexed at myself and at Karl Ivanich; I wanted
to laugh and to cry: my nerves were upset.

"*Ach, lassen Sie*, Karl Ivanich!" I cried, with tears in
my eyes, thrusting my head out from beneath the pillow.
In surprise Karl Ivanich left off tickling me, and began
anxiously to inquire what was the matter with me: had
I had a bad dream? His kind German face, the sympathy
with which he strove to divine the cause of my tears,
made them flow more abundantly. I was ashamed; and
I could not understand how, a moment before, I could
have hated Karl Ivanich, and thought his dressing-gown,

---

* Karl Ivanich generally speaks in German.—*Tr*.

cap, and tassel disgusting; now, on the contrary, they all seemed to me extremely pleasing, and even the tassel appeared a plain proof of his goodness. I told him that I was crying because I had had a bad dream—I had dreamed that Mamma was dead, and they were carrying her to be buried. I invented all this, for I really did not know what I had been dreaming that night; but when Karl Ivanich, touched by my tale, began to comfort and soothe me, it seemed to me that I actually had had that dreadful dream, and my tears flowed from another cause.

When Karl Ivanich left me, and, sitting up in bed, I began to draw my stockings over my little legs, my tears ceased in some measure; but gloomy thoughts of the fictitious dream did not leave me. *Dyadka** Nikolai came in—a smart, neat little man, who was always serious, precise, and respectful, and a great friend of Karl Ivanich. He brought our clothes and shoes; Volodya had boots, but I still had those intolerable shoes with ribbons. I was ashamed to cry before him; besides, the morning sun was shining cheerfully in at the window, and Volodya was imitating Marya Ivanovna (my sister's governess), and laughing so loudly and merrily as he stood over the wash-basin, that even grave Nikolai, with a towel over his shoulder, the soap in one hand and a hand-basin in the other, smiled as he said: "Enough, Vladimir Petrovich, please wash yourself."

I became quite cheerful.

"Are you nearly ready?" called Karl Ivanich's voice from the school-room.

His voice was stern, and had no longer that kindly accent which had moved me to tears. In the school-room Karl Ivanich was a different man altogether: he was the tutor. I dressed quickly, washed, and still brushing my wet hair, I entered the school-room.

---

* Children's valet.—*Tr*.

Karl Ivanich, with his spectacles on his nose, and a book in his hand, was sitting in his usual place between the door and the window. To the left of the door were two shelves of books: one was ours—the children's; the other was Karl Ivanich's particular property. On ours were piled all sorts of books—school-books and others: some standing upright, others lying down. Only two big volumes of *Histoire des Voyages*, in red bindings, were properly placed against the wall; then came a jumble of long, thick, big, and little books—covers without books, and books without covers. We used to cram everything in there topsy-turvy when we were ordered to tidy up the library, as Karl Ivanich called this shelf, before our play-hour. The collection of books on his private shelf, though not as large as ours, was even more miscellaneous. I remember three of them—a German pamphlet on the manuring of cabbage-gardens, without a cover; one volume of the *History of the Seven Years' War*, in parchment, burned at one corner; and a complete *Course of Hydrostatics*. Karl Ivanich spent the greater part of his time reading, and even injured his eyesight thereby; but he never read anything except these books and *The Northern Bee*, a popular magazine.

Among the articles which lay on Karl Ivanich's shelf, there was one which recalls him to me more than all the rest. It was a round cardboard shade on a wooden stand that could be moved up and down by means of wooden pegs. On the shade was pasted a caricature of a lady and a hairdresser. Karl Ivanich was very skilful at making such things, and had himself invented and made this shade to protect his weak eyes from the bright light.

I seem to see before me now his long figure, in its wadded dressing-gown, and the red cap beneath which his thin grey hair is visible. I see him sitting at a little table, his lamp-shade with the figure of the hairdresser on it, casting a shadow on his face; he holds a book in one hand, the other rests on the arm of the chair; before him lie his watch, with the huntsman painted on the face, his checked handkerchief, his round black snuff-box, his green spectacle-case, and the snuffers on the dish. The very orderliness with which each object lies neatly and precisely in place leads one to conclude that Karl Ivanich's conscience is clear and his mind at rest.

Sometimes, after running about downstairs in the hall until I was tired I would steal upstairs on tip-toe to the school-room to find Karl Ivanich sitting alone in his arm-chair, reading some one of his beloved books, with a calm, grave expression on his face. Sometimes I would come upon him at a moment when he was not reading but just sitting there with his spectacles drooping over his nose, his blue half-closed eyes gazing before him with a peculiar expression, and a melancholy smile on his lips. The room would be quite still but for the sound of his even breathing, and the ticking of the hunter watch.

Often he would not notice me, and I would stand in the doorway, thinking: Poor, poor old man! There are many of us and we can play together and enjoy ourselves—but he is all alone and there is nobody to be kind to him. He is an orphan, he told us himself. And the story of his life is so terribly sad! I remember him telling Nikolai about it: it is dreadful to be in such a position!

And I would feel so sorry for him that I would go to him, take his hand, and say, "*Lieber* Karl Ivanich!" He must have liked me say that; for he would always pet me, and it was plain that he was touched.

On another wall hung maps, nearly all of them torn, but skilfully repaired by the hand of Karl Ivanich. On the third wall, in the middle of which was the door leading downstairs, hung two rulers: one was all hacked up—that was ours; the other—the new one—was his own private ruler, and used more for "ruling" us than our copy-books. On the other side of the door was a black-

15

board, upon which our major misdeeds were designated by circles, and the lesser ones by crosses. To the left of the board was the corner where we were made to kneel when we were punished.

How well I remember that corner! I remember the damper, and the hole in it to let the warm air through, and the noise this made when it was turned. I would stand in that corner until my knees and back ached, thinking that Karl Ivanich had forgotten all about me. "It's all very well for him sitting comfortably in his soft arm-chair, and reading his hydrostatics; but what about me?" And then to remind him of my existence, I would softly open and shut the damper, or peel some plaster off the wall; but if too big a piece suddenly fell noisily to the floor, the fright alone was worse than the whole punishment. I would peep round at Karl Ivanich, but he sat, book in hand, as though he had not noticed anything.

In the middle of the room stood a table, covered with a torn black oil-cloth, through which the edge of the table, cut in many places with penknives, could be seen. Around the table were several unpainted stools, polished with long use. The last wall was taken up by three windows. They looked out upon the road, every hollow, pebble and rut of which had long been familiar and dear to me; on the other side of the road was an avenue of clipped lime-trees, through which a wattled fence peeped. Beyond the avenue one could see a meadow with a barn on one side of it and a wood on the other; the watchman's little cottage was visible in the distance. The window to the right overlooked a part of the terrace where the grown-ups generally sat before dinner. If you looked in that direction while Karl Ivanich was correcting your page of dictation, you could catch a glimpse of Mamma's dark head, and of someone's back, and hear faint sounds of conversation and laughter; and you would grow vexed that you could not be there, and think, "When shall

I ever be grown up and stop learning lessons, so that I might sit always with those I love instead of with these dialogues?" Vexation would change to grief, and all sorts of strange thoughts would fill your head so that you would not even hear Karl Ivanich scolding you for your mistakes.

At last Karl Ivanich took off his dressing-gown, put on his blue swallow-tailed coat, with humps and folds upon the shoulders, arranged his cravat before the glass, and led us downstairs to say good-morning to Mamma.

Chapter II

MAMMA

Mamma was sitting in the parlour, pouring out the tea: in one hand she held the tea-pot, in the other the tap of the samovar, from which the water flowed over the top of the tea-pot on to the tray. But though she was gazing steadily at it, she did not preceive it, nor that we had entered.

So many memories of the past arise when one tries to recall the features of a beloved being, that one sees them dimly through these memories, as through tears. These are the tears of imagination. When I try to recall my mother as she was at that time, nothing appears to me but her brown eyes, which always expressed love and kindness; the mole on her neck just below where the little curls grow; her white embroidered collar; her cool, soft hand, which caressed me so often, and which I so often kissed: but her image as a whole escapes me.

To the left of the sofa stood the old English grand piano; my dark-complexioned sister Lyuba sat at it, playing Clementi's studies with obvious effort, her little fingers rosy with just having been washed in cold water. She was eleven. She wore a short linen dress with white lace-trimmed pantalettes, and could only manage an octave in arpeggio. Beside her, half-turned away, sat Marya Ivanovna, in a cap with rose-coloured ribbons and a blue jacket. Her face, red and angry, grew still more severe when Karl Ivanich entered. She threw him a black look and, without responding to his bow, went on counting and beating time with her foot, *un*, *deux*, *trois—un*, *deux*, *trois*, more loudly and commandingly than before.

Karl Ivanich, paying no attention whatever to this, went up to my mother and greeted her as usual in German. She started, shook her head as though to chase away her painful thoughts, gave her hand to Karl Ivanich, and kissed him on his wrinkled temple as he bent to kiss her hand.

"*Ich danke, lieber* Karl Ivanich," she said. And continuing to speak in German, she inquired:

"Did the children sleep well?"

Karl Ivanich was deaf in one ear, and now heard nothing at all on account of the noise from the piano. He bent nearer to the sofa, resting one hand on the table and standing on one foot; and with a smile which seemed to me then the height of refinement, he raised his cap, and said:

"Will you excuse me, Natalya Nikolayevna?"

Karl Ivanich never took off his red cap for fear of catching cold, but each time he entered the drawing-room he begged permission to keep it on.

"Keep it on, Karl Ivanich. . . . I asked you if the children slept well?" said Mamma, moving nearer to him, and speaking louder.

But again he heard nothing and stood with his red cap on his bald head, and smiled more amiably than ever.

"Stop a moment, Mimi," said Mamma to Marya Ivanovna, with a smile: "we can hear nothing."

Beautiful as was Mamma's face, it became incomparably more lovely when she smiled, and seemed to enliven everything about her. If in life's trying moments I could catch but a glimpse of that smile, I should not know what grief is. It seems to me that what is called beauty lies in the smile alone: if the smile enhances the charm of a face, that face is beautiful; if the smile does not change it, the face is plain; if the smile spoils it, the face is ugly.

When she greeted me, Mamma took my head in both her hands, and bent it back, looked intently at me, and said:

"You have been crying this morning?"

I made no reply. She kissed my eyes, and asked in German:

"Why were you crying?"

When she spoke pleasantly to us, she always addressed us in German, which she knew to perfection.

"I cried in my sleep, Mamma," I said, recalling my fictitious dream in all its details, and I involuntarily shuddered at the thought.

Karl Ivanich confirmed my words, but said nothing about the dream. Having talked a little about the weather, in which conversation Mimi also took part, Mamma laid six pieces of sugar on the tray for some of the favoured servants, and went to her embroidery-frame which stood by the window.

"Now, go to your father, children, and tell him that he must come to me without fail before he goes to the threshing-floor."

The music, the counting, and black looks were resumed, and we went to Papa. Passing through the room which had been known as the butler's pantry ever since Grandfather's time, we entered the study.

Chapter III

PAPA

He was standing by his desk, pointing to some envelopes, papers, and bundles of bank-notes, and speaking sharply with Yakov Mikhailov, the steward, who stood in his usual place between the door and the barometer, with his hands behind him, nervously turning and twisting his fingers.

The angrier Papa grew, the faster the fingers moved, and on the contrary, when Papa ceased speaking, the fingers also stopped moving; but when Yakov began to speak himself, his fingers betrayed the greatest agitation, and jumped wildly about. It seemed to me that Yakov's secret thoughts might be guessed from their movements. His face, on the other hand, was always calm; it expressed a sense of dignity and at the same time of subordination, as if saying, "I am right, but you may do as you like!"

When Papa saw us, he merely said:

"Wait a minute," and motioned to us to shut the door.

"Merciful God! What's the matter with you today, Yakov?" he continued, addressing the steward, and twitching his shoulders, which was a habit of his. "This envelope with eight hundred rubles in it...."

Yakov moved his abacus, counted off eight hundred rubles, fixed his gaze on some indefinite point, and waited to hear what would come next.

"... is for the expenses of the farming during my absence. Do you understand? From the mill you are to receive one thousand rubles: right? You are to receive eight thousand worth of loans from the treasury; for the hay, of which, according to your own calculation, you can sell seven thousand poods*—at forty-five kopeks, say—

---

* A pood is about forty pounds.—*Tr.*

20

you will get three thousand; now, how much money will you have in all? Twelve thousand: is that right?"

"Quite right, sir," said Yakov.

But I saw by the quick movement of his fingers, that he was about to contradict, when Papa interrupted him.

"Now then, out of this money, you will send ten thousand rubles to the Council, for Petrovskoye. The money which is in the office," continued Papa (Yakov removed the twelve thousand, and counted off twenty-one thousand), "you will bring to me, and charge to expenses dating from today." (Yakov shook up his abacus again, and turned it over, perhaps indicating thereby that the twenty-one thousand would disappear in the same manner.) "This envelope containing money you will transmit for me to the address given."

I was standing near the table, and I glanced at the inscription. It read: "Karl Ivanich Mauer."

Papa must have noticed that I had seen what I had no business to see; for he laid his hand on my shoulder, and with a slight movement indicated that I was to go away from his table. I did not know whether it was a caress or a reproof; but, whatever it meant, I kissed the large, sinewy hand which rested on my shoulder.

"Yes, sir," said Yakov. "And what are your orders with regard to the Khabarovka money?"

Khabarovka was a village belonging to Mamma.

"Leave it in the office, and on no account make use of it without my permission."

Yakov was silent for a few moments, then his fingers suddenly began to move with increased rapidity, and altering the look of servile stupidity with which he had listened to his master's orders, to the sly, keen look which was natural to him, he drew the abacus towards him, and began to speak.

"Permit me to report, Pyotr Alexandrovich, sir, that it is impossible to pay the Council on time. You said,"

21

he continued, speaking with deliberation, "that we are to receive money from the loans, from the mill, and from the hay." As he mentioned these items, he told them off on the abacus. "I am afraid we're a bit out in our reckoning," he added, after a pause, glancing sharply at Papa.

"Why?"

"Permit me to explain, sir: about the mill—the miller has been to me twice to ask for delay, and swears that he has no money. He is here now. Will you please to talk with him yourself?"

"What does he say?" asked Papa, signifying by a motion of his head that he did not wish to speak with the miller.

"The same old story. He says there's been no work; that what little money he had was spent on the dam. If we turn him out, sir, will it be of any advantage to us? Now with regard to the loans, as you were pleased to mention them, I think I have already reported that our money is sunk there, and we shall not be able to get at it very soon. I sent a load of flour to the city a few days ago, to Ivan Afanasich, with a note about the matter; he replied that he would be glad to render Pyotr Alexandrovich a service, but the affair is not in his hands, and you will hardly receive your quittance under two months. You were pleased to speak of the hay: suppose we do sell it for three thousand...."

He marked off three thousand on his abacus, and remained silent for a moment, looking first at the abacus and then into Papa's eyes, as much as to say:

"You see yourself how little it is. Besides, we'll be selling at a loss if we sell now, as you know yourself..."

It was obvious that he had a great fund of arguments ready; it must have been for that reason that Papa interrupted him.

"I shall make no change in my arrangements," he said, "but if any delay should actually occur in receiving

22

this money, then there is nothing to be done; you will take what is necessary from the Khabarovka funds."

"Yes, sir."

It was evident from the expression of Yakov's face and from his fingers that this last order afforded him the greatest satisfaction.

Yakov was a serf, and a very zealous and devoted man. Like all good stewards, he was extremely parsimonious on his master's account, and entertained the strangest possible ideas as to what was in his master's interest. He was eternally fretting over the increase of his master's property at the expense of that of his mistress, and tried to demonstrate that it was necessary to invest all the revenue from her estate in Petrovskoye (the village in which we lived). At this moment he was triumphant, because he had gained his point.

Papa greeted us, and said that it was time to put a stop to our idleness: we were no longer babies, and we must begin to study in earnest.

"I daresay you already know that I am going to Moscow tonight, and I shall take you with me," he said. "You will live with your grandmother, and Mamma will remain here with the girls. And you know that she will have but one consolation—to hear that you are studying well, and that your tutors are pleased with you."

Although we had been expecting something unusual from the preparations which had been going on for several days, this news came as a shock to us. Volodya turned red, and repeated Mamma's message in a trembling voice.

"So that is what my dream foretold," I thought. "Please God let there be nothing worse!"

I was very, very sorry for Mamma; and, at the same time, the thought that we were grown up afforded me pleasure.

"If we are going away tonight, we surely shall have no lessons. That's splendid," I thought. "But I'm sorry

23

for Karl Ivanich. He is certainly going to be dismissed. That was why that envelope was prepared for him. No, it would be better to go on studying for ever, and not go away, and not part from Mamma, and not hurt poor Karl Ivanich's feelings. He is so very unhappy!"

As these thoughts flashed through my mind, I stood motionless staring down at the black ribbons in my slippers.

After speaking a few words to Karl Ivanich about the fall of the barometer, and ordering Yakov not to feed the dogs so that he might go out after dinner and make a farewell trial of the young hounds, Papa, contrary to my expectations, sent us back to our lessons, comforting us, however, with a promise to take us on the hunt.

On the way upstairs I ran out on the terrace. Papa's favourite greyhound, Milka, lay blinking in the sunshine at the door.

"Milochka," I said, patting her and kissing her nose, "we are going away today; good-bye! We shall never see each other again."

Overcome with emotion, I burst into tears.

Chapter IV

LESSONS

Karl Ivanich was very much out of sorts. This was evident from his frowning brows, and from the way he flung his coat into the wardrobe, his angry manner of tying his girdle, and the deep mark which he made with his nail in the conversation-book to indicate the passage we were to memorize. Volodya studied diligently; but I was so upset that I positively could do nothing. I gazed long and stupidly at the conversation-book, but I could not read for the tears which gathered in my eyes at the

24

thought of the parting before us. When the time came for me to repeat the passage to Karl Ivanich, who listened with his eyes half shut (a bad sign), just at the place where one says, "*Wo kommen Sie her?*" and the other answers, "*Ich komme vom Kaffe-Hause*," I could no longer restrain my tears, and sobs prevented me from saying, "*Haben Sie die Zeitung nicht gelesen?*" When it came to writing, I made such blots with my tears falling on the paper, that I might have been writing with water on wrapping-paper.

Karl Ivanich became angry; he sent me into the corner, declared that it was obstinacy, a puppet comedy (this was a favourite expression of his), threatened me with the ruler, and demanded that I should beg his pardon, although I could not utter a word for my tears. At last he must have felt that he was unjust, for he went into Nikolai's room and slammed the door.

The conversation in Nikolai's room was audible in the school-room.

"Have you heard, Nikolai, that the children are going to Moscow?" said Karl Ivanich as he entered.

"Yes, indeed I have," Nikolai replied in a respectful tone.

He must have made a motion to rise, for Karl Ivanich said, "No, don't get up, Nikolai!" and then he shut the door. I emerged from the corner, and crept over to the door to listen.

"However much good you do to people, however much you are attached to them, you need not expect gratitude, it seems, Nikolai," said Karl Ivanich, with feeling.

Nikolai, who was sitting by the window at his shoe-making, nodded his head affirmatively.

"I have lived in this house twelve years, and I can say before God, Nikolai," continued Karl Ivanich, raising his eyes and his snuff-box to the ceiling, "that I have loved them, and taken more interest in them than if they had been my own children. You remember, Nikolai, when Volodya had the fever, how I sat by his bedside, and never closed my eyes for nine days. Yes! Then I was 'good, dear Karl Ivanich'; then I was necessary. But now," he added, with a bitter smile, "now *the children are grown up; they must study in earnest*. Just as if they were not studying here, Nikolai!"

"They study as much as can be, if you ask me," said Nikolai, laying down his awl, and drawing out his thread with both hands.

"Yes, I am no longer needed, I must be sent away. But where are their promises? Where is their gratitude? I love and revere Natalya Nikolayevna, Nikolai," said he, laying his hand on his breast. "But what is she? Her will is of no more consequence in this house than that!" and he flung a scrap of leather on the floor with an expressive gesture. "I know whose doing this is, and why I am no longer needed; because I don't flatter or ingratiate myself like *some people*. I have always been accustomed to speak the truth to everyone," said he, proudly. "Let God be their judge! They won't be any the richer for getting rid of me; and with God's will I shall manage to earn my bread ... shall I not, Nikolai?"

Nikolai raised his head and looked at Karl Ivanich, as though wishing to assure himself that he really would be able to earn a living; but he said nothing.

Karl Ivanich spoke a great deal more in this vein. He said his services had been far better appreciated at the house of general so-and-so, where he had formerly lived (I was much pained to hear it). He spoke of Saxony, of his parents, of his friend Schönheit, the tailor, and so forth.

I sympathized with his sorrow, and it pained me that Papa and Karl Ivanich, whom I loved almost equally, did not understand each other. I went back to my corner again, crouched down on my heels, and pondered how I might bring about an understanding between them.

Presently Karl Ivanich returned to the school-room. He ordered me to get up and prepare my copy-book for writing from dictation. When all was ready, he seated himself majestically in his arm-chair, and in a voice which appeared to issue from some great depth, he began to dictate in German:

" 'Of all pas-sions the most re-volt-ing is,' have you written that?" Here he paused, slowly took a pinch of snuff, and continued with renewed energy—" 'the most revolting is In-gra-ti-tude' . . . a capital *I*."

I looked up at him after writing the last word, expecting more.

"Period," said he, with a barely perceptible smile, and motioned to me to give him my copy-book.

He read this apothegm, expressive of his innermost feelings, several times, with various intonations and with the greatest satisfaction. Then he set us a lesson in history, and seated himself by the window. His face was not so morose as it had been; it expressed the delight of a man who has taken a proper revenge for an injury dealt him.

It was a quarter to one; but Karl Ivanich seemed to have no intention of dismissing us; instead, he continued to give out new lessons.

Ennui and hunger increased in equal measure. With the greatest impatience, I noted all the signs which betokened the approach of dinner. There came the woman with her mop to wash the plates; then I could hear the dishes rattle on the sideboard. I heard them move the table, and place the chairs; then Mimi came in from the garden with Lyubochka and Katenka (Katenka was Mimi's twelve-year-old daughter); but nothing was to be seen of Foka, the butler, who always came and announced that dinner was ready. Then only could we throw aside our books without paying any attention to Karl Ivanich, and run downstairs.

Now footsteps were heard on the stairs, but that was not Foka! I knew his step by heart, and could always recognize the squeak of his boots. The door opened, and a figure totally unknown to me appeared.

Chapter V

THE PILGRIM

Into the room walked a man of about fifty, with a long, pale, pock-marked face, long grey hair and a sparse reddish beard. He was so tall that in order to pass through the door he was obliged to bend not only his head, but his whole body. He wore a ragged garment which resembled both a kaftan and a cassock, and in his hand he carried a huge staff. As he entered the room he smote the floor with it with all his might; opening his mouth, and wrinkling his brows, he laughed in a terrible and unnatural manner. He was blind in one eye, and the white pupil of that eye hopped about incessantly, imparting to his ugly countenance a still more repulsive expression.

"Aha! I've found you!" he shouted, and running up to Volodya with little steps, he seized his head, and began a careful examination of his crown. Then, with a perfectly serious expression, he left him, walked up to the table, and began to blow under the oil-cloth, and to make the sign of the cross over it. "O-oh, what a shame! o-oh, how sad! They'll fly away," he said in a voice quivering with tears, gazing feelingly at Volodya; and he began to wipe away the tears, which were actually falling, with his sleeve.

His voice was harsh and rough; his movements hasty and jerky; his talk was senseless and incoherent; but his intonations were so touching, and his ugly yellow face assumed at times such a sincerely sorrowful expression, that, listening to him, it was impossible to repress a mingled feeling of pity, fear, and grief.

This was the pilgrim Grisha.

Where did he come from? Who were his parents? What had induced him to adopt the life of a pilgrim? No one knew. I only knew that he had passed since the age of fifteen as a fool who went barefoot winter and summer, visited the monasteries, gave little images to those who struck his fancy, and uttered mysterious words which some people accepted as prophecy; that no one had ever known him in any other aspect; that he occasionally went to Grandmother's; and that some said he was the unfortunate son of wealthy parents, and a pure and saintly soul; while others held that he was just a good-for-nothing peasant.

At length the long-wished-for and punctual Foka arrived, and we went downstairs. Grisha, still sobbing and talking his nonsense, followed us, and pounded every step on the stairs with his staff. Papa and Mamma entered the drawing-room arm-in-arm, conversing in low tones. Marya Ivanovna sat primly in one of the arm-chairs, symmetrically arranged at right angles to the divan, admonishing the girls who sat beside her in a low, stern voice. She looked up when Karl Ivanich entered the room, but immediately turned away, and her face assumed an expression which might have been interpreted to mean, "You are beneath my notice, Karl Ivanich." It was plain from the girls' eyes that they were very anxious to impart to us some extremely important news as soon as possible; but it would have been an infringement of Mimi's rules to jump up and come over to us. We must first go to her and say, "*Bonjour*, Mimi!" and give a scrape with the foot; only then was it permissible to enter into conversation.

What an intolerable creature that Mimi was! It was impossible to talk about anything in her presence: she considered everything improper. Moreover, she was constantly exhorting us to speak French, and that, as if out of malice, just when we wanted to chatter in Russian; or at dinner—you would just begin to enjoy a dish, and want to be let alone, when she would infallibly say, *"Mangez donc avec du pain,"* or *"Comment ce que vous tenez votre fourchette?"*—"What business is it of hers?" you would think. "Let her teach her girls—we have our Karl Ivanich to see to us." I fully shared his hatred for *some people.*

"Ask Mamma to take us on the hunt," whispered Katenka, catching me by my jacket, when the grown-up people had passed into the dining-room.

"All right: we will try."

Grisha also ate in the dining-room, but at a small table apart; he did not raise his eyes from his plate, made fearful grimaces, sighed occasionally, and muttered to himself: "It's a pity ... she has flown away ... the dove will fly to heaven.... Oh, there's a stone on the grave!" and so on.

Mamma had been in a troubled state of mind ever since the morning; Grisha's presence, his words, and his behaviour evidently increased this perturbation.

"Oh, yes, I nearly forgot to ask you about one thing," she said, handing Papa a plate of soup.

"What is it?"

"Please have your dreadful dogs shut up; they nearly bit poor Grisha when he passed through the yard. And they might attack the children."

Hearing himself mentioned, Grisha turned towards the table, and began to exhibit the torn tails of his garment and to speak with his mouth full.

"Wanted to bite to death.... God would not let them.... It's a sin to set the dogs on! Don't beat, *bolshak....** Why beat? God will forgive.... Times are different now."

"What is he saying?" asked Papa, gazing sternly and intently at him. "I don't understand a word."

"Well—I do," answered Mamma: "he is saying that some huntsman set his dogs on him, on purpose, as he says, 'that they might bite him to death,' and he begs you not to punish the man for it."

"Ah! that's it," said Papa. "How does he know that I mean to punish the huntsman? You know that I'm not overfond of these gentlemen," he added in French, "and this one in particular does not please me, and ought—"

"Ah, do not say that, my dear," interrupted Mamma, as if frightened. "What can you know about him?"

"I think I have had sufficient opportunity to learn these people's ways by heart: enough of them come to you. They're all alike. The same story over and over again."

It was plain that Mamma held a totally different opinion on this point, but she would not dispute.

"Please give me a patty," she said. "Are they good today?"

"It annoys me," went on Papa, taking a patty in his hand, but holding it just beyond Mamma's reach; "it annoys me to see sensible and cultivated people fall into the trap."

And he struck the table with his fork.

"I asked you to hand me a patty," she repeated, reaching out her hand.

"And they do well," continued Papa, moving his hand farther away, "when they arrest such people. The only good they do is to upset the weak nerves of certain individuals," he added, with a smile, perceiving that the con-

---

* Elder of a village, family, or religious community.—*Tr.*

31

versation greatly displeased Mamma, and gave her the patty.

"I have only one thing to say on the subject: it is difficult to believe that a man who, in spite of his sixty years, goes barefoot summer and winter, and wears chains weighing two poods, which he never takes off, under his clothes, and who has more than once rejected a proposal to lead an easy life—it is difficult to believe that such a man does all this merely from laziness."

"As for prophecy," she added, with a sigh, after a pause, "*Je suis payée pour y croire*; I think I have told you how Kiryusha foretold the very day and hour of Papa's death."

"Oh dear, what have you done to me!" exclaimed Papa, in mock dismay, smiling and putting his hand to his mouth on the side where Mimi sat. (When he did this I always listened with strained attention in the expectation of something amusing.) "Why have you reminded me of his feet? I have looked at them, and now I shall not be able to eat anything."

The dinner was nearing its end. Lyubochka and Katenka winked at us incessantly, fidgeted in their chairs, and showed great restlessness. The winks, of course, signified, "Why don't you ask them to take us hunting?" I nudged Volodya with my elbow; Volodya nudged me, and finally summoned up his courage: he explained, at first in a timid voice, but afterwards quite firmly and loudly, that, as we were to leave on that day, we should like to have the girls taken to the hunt with us in the carriage. After a short consultation among the grown-up people, the question was decided in our favour; and, what was still more delightful, Mamma said that she would come too.

Chapter VI

PREPARATIONS FOR THE HUNT

During dessert Yakov was summoned, and given orders with regard to the carriage, the dogs, and the saddle-horses—everything being specified in the greatest detail, and every horse called by name. Volodya's mount was lame: Papa ordered a hunter to be saddled for him. This word "hunter" always sounded strange to Mamma's ears: it seemed to her that it must be something in the nature of a wild beast, and that it would infallibly run away with Volodya and kill him. In spite of all Papa's and Volodya's assurances—Volodya declaring stoutly that it was quite all right, he liked it when the horse ran away—poor Mamma insisted that she would be in torments during the whole of the excursion.

Dinner came to an end; the grown-ups went to the library to drink their coffee, while we ran into the garden, to scrape our feet along the paths covered with rustling yellow leaves, and to talk about Volodya's riding the hunter, and how shameful it was that Lyubochka could not run as fast as Katenka, and what fun it would be to see Grisha's chains, and so on. Not a word was said about our separation. Our talk was interrupted by the arrival of the carriage, a servant boy perched on each of its springs. Behind the carriage came the huntsmen with the dogs, followed again by Ignat, the coachman, on the horse intended for Volodya, and leading my old nag by the bridle. We rushed to the fence, to get a sight of all these interesting things and then we flew upstairs, shouting and stamping our feet, to dress ourselves as much like huntsmen as possible. One of the chief means to this end was tucking our trousers into our boots. We lost no time in doing this and rushed out on to the porch to feast our eyes on the dogs and horses, and chat with the huntsmen.

The day was hot and white clouds of fanciful shapes had been hovering all the morning on the horizon; later on a light breeze began to drive them nearer and nearer, so that they obscured the sun from time to time. But black and frequent as were these clouds, it was plain that they were not destined to gather into a thunder-storm and spoil the pleasure of our last day. Towards evening they began to disperse again: some grew pale, lengthened out, and fled to the horizon; others, just overhead, turned into white transparent scales; only one large black cloud lingered in the east. Karl Ivanich always knew where every sort of cloud went; he declared that this cloud would go to Maslovka, that there would be no rain, and that the weather would be fine.

Foka, in spite of his advanced years, ran down the steps in a very sprightly manner, cried "Drive up!" and, planting his feet far apart, took up a stand in the middle of the entrance, between the spot to which the carriage should be brought and the threshold, in the attitude of a man who does not need to be reminded of his duty. The ladies followed, and after a brief dispute as to who should sit on which side, and whom they should cling to (although it seemed to me quite unnecessary to hold on at all), they seated themselves, opened their parasols, and drove off. When the *lineika** started, Mamma pointed to the hunter and asked the coachman in a trembling voice:

"Is that the horse for Vladimir Petrovich?"

And when the coachman replied in the affirmative, she made a little gesture with her hand and turned away. I was very impatient: I mounted my horse, looked straight between his ears, and went through various evolutions in the court-yard.

"Please, be careful not to run over the dogs," said one of the huntsmen.

* A particular sort of four-seated droshky.—*Tr.*

"Don't worry—I've been on horseback before," I answered proudly.

Volodya mounted the hunter, not without some quaking in spite of his resolute character, and asked several times as he patted him:

"Is he gentle?"

He looked very handsome on horseback—just like a grown-up person. His thighs sat so well on the saddle that I envied him—particularly because so far as I could judge from my shadow, I was far from presenting so fine an appearance.

Then we heard Papa's step on the stairs: the overseer of the young dogs drove up the scattered hounds; the huntsmen with greyhounds called in theirs, and began to mount. The groom led the horse to the steps; Papa's dogs, which had been lying about in various picturesque attitudes, sprang up and ran to him. After them came Milka, in her bead collar, its iron bit jingling merrily. She always greeted the other dogs when she came out; some she played with, some she sniffed and growled at, on others she hunted fleas.

Papa mounted his horse, and we set out.

Chapter VII

THE HUNT

The huntsman-in-chief, who was called Turka, rode in front on a dark-grey horse; he wore a shaggy cap, a huge horn over his shoulder, and a knife in his belt. From the man's fierce and gloomy exterior, one would sooner imagine that he was going to some deadly conflict than on a hunting expedition. At his horse's heels ran the hounds, clustered together in a many-hued, undulating pack. It was pitiful to see what happened to the unfortunate dog who took it into his head to linger behind. He would have to drag his leash-mate with him, and no sooner had he done so than one of the whippers-in riding in the rear would crack at him with his whip, saying, "To the pack with you!"

When we emerged from the gates, Papa ordered us and the servants to ride along the road, while he himself turned into a field of rye.

The grain harvest was in full swing. The shining yellow field, extending farther than the eye could reach, was on cne side closed in only by a lofty blue forest, which seemed to me then a very distant and mysterious place, behind which the world came to an end, or some uninhabited region began. The whole field was dotted with shocks of sheaves and with people. Here and there along the reaped lanes, the bent back of a reaper might be seen amidst the swinging ears of corn as she took them between her fingers, or some other woman bending over a cradle placed in the shade, or scattered sheaves upon the stubble strewn with corn-flowers. Farther on, peasants in long shirts, stood on carts, loading the sheaves and raising clouds of dust on the dry, scorched fields. The starosta, in high boots, and with his *armyak** thrown on over his shoulders, and tally-sticks in his hand, perceiving Papa in the distance, took off his lamb's-wool cap, wiped his reddish head and beard with a towel, and shouted at the women. The sorrel horse which Papa rode trotted along at a light, playful pace, now and then bending his head, pulling at the bridle, and with his heavy tail swishing away the gnats and flies which clung thirstily to him. Two greyhounds, their tails curved like sickles, bounded gracefully over the tall stubble, behind the horse's heels; Milka ran in front, with her head turned back expectantly. The hum of voices, the noise of the horses and carts, the merry

---

* A long, wide coat worn by peasants.—*Tr.*

whistle of the quail, the buzzing of insects which hung in motionless swarms in the air, the scent of wormwood, straw, and horse sweat, the thousands of varying hues and shadows cast by the burning sun over the bright yellow stubble, the blue of the distant forest and the pale lilac of the clouds, the white gossamer threads which floated through the air or lay upon the stubble—all this I saw, heard, and felt.

When we reached Kalinovo woods we found the carriage already there, and, beyond all our expectations, a cart, on which sat the butler. A samovar peeped from under the straw; a tub with ices, and diverse other exciting-looking hampers and baskets. There was no mistaking these signs: we were going to have tea, ice-cream, and fruit in the open air. We shouted for joy at the sight of the cart, for it was considered a great treat to drink tea in the woods on the grass, and especially in a place where nobody had ever drank tea before.

Turka came to this little wood, halted, listened attentively to Papa's minute directions as to the way they were to draw up and where to sally forth (although he never followed these directions, and did exactly as he chose), unleashed the dogs, arranged the straps in a leisurely manner, mounted his horse, and disappeared behind the young birches. The hounds wagged their tails with joy on being released, shook themselves, sniffed the ground, and, still wagging their tails, scampered off in various directions.

"Have you a handkerchief?" asked Papa.

I pulled one from my pocket, and showed it to him.

"Well, tie it to this grey dog."

"Zhiran?" I inquired, with a knowing air.

"Yes; and run along the road. When you come to a little meadow, stop and look about you; don't come back to me without a hare."

I wound my handkerchief about Zhiran's shaggy neck, and set off at breakneck speed for the appointed place. Papa laughed and called after me:

"Hurry up, hurry up, or you'll be too late."

Zhiran kept stopping, pricking up his ears, and listening to the sounds of the hunt. I pulled at him with all my might, but I could not make him move until I shouted: "Tally-ho! halloo!" Then he tore away with such force that I could hardly hold him, and I fell more than once before I reached my post. Selecting a shady and level place at the root of lofty oak, I lay down on the grass, made Zhiran lie down beside me, and waited. My imagination, as always happens in such cases, far outstripped reality. In fancy I was already coursing my third hare when the first hound was giving tongue. Turka's voice rang louder and clearer through the forest; a hound whimpered and the sound was repeated again and again. Another deeper voice joined in, then a third and a fourth. These voices now died down, now rose again drowning each other out. The sounds grew gradually louder and louder until at length they merged in one continuous tumultuous baying. As the huntsmen would say, the forest had found its tongue, the hounds were in full cry.

I stiffened at my post. Fixing my eyes upon the edge of the woods, I smiled foolishly; I was dripping with perspiration, and although the drops tickled me as they ran down my chin, I did not wipe them off. It seemed to me that nothing could be more decisive than this moment. This attitude of expectancy was too tense to last long. The hounds' cry came now from the edge of the woods, now receded, but there was no hare. I looked about me. Zhiran was in the same state; at first he tugged and whimpered, then lay down beside me, put his nose upon my knees and became quiet.

Around the bare roots of the oak-tree under which I sat, ants swarmed in countless numbers over the grey, parched earth, amid the withered oak-leaves, acorns, dry moss-grown sticks, yellowish-green moss, and the thin green blades of grass. They hurried one after another along the track they had made for themselves, some heavily laden, others without any burden at all. I picked up a twig and obstructed their path. It was curious to see how some, scorning all danger, climbed over it, while others, especially those who had loads, seemed puzzled and did not know what to do; they halted, and hunted for a way around, or turned back, or crawled up the twig to my hand, with the intention, apparently, of getting under the sleeve of my jacket. I was diverted from these interesting observations by a butterfly with yellow wings, which was fluttering alluringly before me. No sooner had I directed my attention to it than it flew away a couple of paces, circled about a nearly wilted head of wild white clover, and settled upon it. I do not know whether it was warming itself in the sun or drawing the sap from this weed, but it was evident that it was enjoying itself. Now and then it fluttered its wings and pressed closer to the flower, and at last became perfectly still. I propped my head on both hands and gazed at it with pleasure.

All at once Zhiran began to howl, and gave such a violent tug that I nearly fell over. I looked up. Along the edge of the woods skipped a hare, one ear drooping, the other raised. The blood rushed to my head, and, forgetting everything else for the moment, I uttered a wild cry, let the dog go, and ran after it. But a moment later I was sorry I had—the hare squatted, gave a leap, and I saw it no more.

But what was my mortification when, following the hounds, who came baying down to the edge of the woods, Turka appeared from behind a bush! He had seen my mistake (which consisted in not having waited), and, glancing scornfully at me, he said: *"Ekh, barin!"** That

* Master.—*Tr.*

was all, but his tone made me wish he had rather hung me to his saddle like a hare.

I stood for a long time on the same spot in the deepest despair. I did not call the dog, and I could do nothing but beat my thighs, and repeat over and over again: "Oh dear, what have I done!"

I heard the hounds coursing in the distance; I heard them give tongue on the other side of the wood and kill the hare, and Turka summoning the dogs with his long whip: but still I did not stir from the spot.

Chapter VIII

GAMES

The hunt was over. A carpet was spread under the shadow of the young birches, and the whole company gathered round. Gavrilo, the butler, trampling the lush green grass under his feet, wiped the plates, and emptied the baskets of plums and peaches wrapped in leaves. The sun shone through the green branches of the young birches, and cast round quivering beams upon the patterns of the carpet, upon my feet, and even upon Gavrilo's bald perspiring head. A cool refreshing breeze fluttered through the leaves, and played upon my hair and my steaming face.

When we had finished the ices and fruits there was nothing more to keep us on the carpet; and, in spite of the oblique but still hot rays of the sun, we rose and went off to play.

"Now, what shall it be?" said Lyubochka, blinking in the sun, and skipping about on the grass. "Let's play Robinson!"

"No, it's tiresome," said Volodya, rolling lazily on the turf and chewing a leaf: "We're always playing Robinson! If you must play at something, let's build an arbour."

Volodya was clearly putting on airs: it must have been because he was proud of having ridden the hunter, and he pretended to be very much tired; or, perhaps, he had too much good sense, and too little imagination to fully enjoy a game of Robinson. This game consisted in acting various scenes from *Robinson Suisse*,* which we had read not long before.

"Oh, please ... just to please us!" persisted the girls. "You shall be Charles, or Ernest, or the father, whichever you like," said Katenka, trying to pull him from the ground by the sleeve of his jacket.

"I really don't want to: it's so tiresome," said Volodya, stretching himself and smiling in a self-satisfied manner.

"It would have been better to stay at home if nobody wants to play," declared Lyubochka through her tears.

She was a dreadful cry-baby.

"Come along, then; only please don't cry. I can't stand it."

Volodya's condescension gave us very little satisfaction: on the contrary, his bored, lazy air spoiled all the charm of the play. When we sat down on the ground and, imagining that we were setting out on a fishing expedition, began to row with all our might, Volodya persisted in sitting with folded arms, in anything but a fisherman's posture. I told him so, but he retorted that we should gain nothing however much we waved our arms, and certainly not travel any farther. Unwillingly I agreed with him. When I made believe to go hunting, and set off for the woods with a stick on my shoulder, Volodya lay down flat on his back, with his hands under his head, and told me to pretend he was going too. Such speeches and behaviour

---

* The Swiss Family Robinson.—*Tr.*

cooled our interest in the game, and were extremely unpleasant; the more so, since we could not help feeling that Volodya was right.

I knew myself that it was impossible to fire at a bird with my stick, let alone kill it. It was only a game. If you reasoned in that fashion, you could not ride on chairs either; but, thought I, Volodya himself must remember how, on long winter evenings, we covered an arm-chair with a cloth, and made a calash out of it, while one mounted as coachman, the other as footman, and the girls sat in the middle, with three chairs for a troika of horses, and we set out on a journey. And how many exciting adventures we had on the way! And how merrily and swiftly the winter evenings passed! If you go by reality, there would be no games. And if there are no games, what is left?

Chapter IX

SOMETHING LIKE FIRST LOVE

Lyubochka, pretending to be plucking some American fruits from a tree, tore off a leaf with a huge caterpillar on it, dropped it on the ground in terror, raised her hands, and sprang back as though she feared that it might spurt some poison at her. The play ceased, and we all stooped to examine this curiosity, our heads pressed close together.

I looked over Katenka's shoulder as she tried to pick the worm up on a leaf which she placed in its way.

I had observed that many girls had a way of twitching their shoulders, to bring their low-necked frocks, which had slipped down, back into place. I remember that this motion always made Mimi angry: *"C'est un geste de femme de chambre,"* she said. Katenka made this motion as she bent over the worm, and at the same moment the wind raised the kerchief off her white neck. Her little shoulder was within two fingers' length of my lips. I no longer looked at the worm: I stared and stared at Katenka's shoulder, and then I kissed it with all my might. She did not turn round, but I noticed that her neck and even her ears turned red. Volodya, without raising his head, said scornfully:

"What tenderness!"

But my eyes were full of tears.

I could not take my eyes off Katenka. I had long been used to her fresh little face, and I had always loved it. But now I began to observe it more attentively, and I liked it still better.

When we rejoined the grown-ups, Papa announced, to our great joy, that, at Mamma's request, our departure was postponed until the following day.

We rode home with the carriage. Volodya and I galloped alongside it, vying with each other in our exhibition of horsemanship and daring. My shadow was longer than before, and, judging from it, I imagined that I looked like a very fine horseman; but that feeling of self-satisfaction was soon destroyed by the following circumstance. Wishing to completely fascinate all who rode in the carriage, I fell behind a little; then, with whip and spur I set my horse at a gallop and assumed an attitude of careless grace with the intention of dashing past them like a whirlwind on the side where Katenka sat. But just as I was trying to decide whether it would be better to gallop by in silence or to shout as I passed by, the nasty horse stopped so unexpectedly when he came up with the carriage-horses, that I flew over the saddle on to his neck and almost tumbled off his back.

Chapter X

WHAT KIND OF A MAN WAS MY FATHER?

He was a man of the past century, and his character was that indefinable mixture of chivalry, enterprise, self-assurance, gallantry and debauchery common to the youth of that period. He looked with scorn at the present generation; and this view proceeded as much from innate pride as from a secret resentment at being unable to wield the influence or enjoy the successes in our time which he had enjoyed in his own. The governing passions of his life were cards and women. In the course of his life he had won millions at cards and had had liaisons with innumerable women of all classes.

A tall, stately figure, a strange mincing gait, a habit of shrugging his shoulders, small eyes which were always smiling, a large aquiline nose, irregular lips rather oddly though pleasantly compressed, a lisp, and a bald head—such was my father's appearance from the time I first recollect him, an appearance with which he not only managed to earn the reputation of a man *à bonnes fortunes*, as indeed he was, but to make himself liked by everyone without exception—people of all classes and stations, and especially those whom he desired to please.

He knew how to get the upper hand over everybody. Though he had never belonged to the *very highest society*, he had always moved in those circles, and contrived to be respected by all. He knew the exact degree of pride and self-confidence which, without offending others, would raise him in the estimation of the world. He was original, though not always, and he used his originality at times as a substitute for breeding or wealth. Nothing in the world could arouse in him a sensation of wonder: however brilliant his position, he seemed born to it. One could not but envy his ability to hide from others, and put away from himself, the darker side of life, with all its petty vexations and annoyances.

He was a connoisseur of all things which afford comfort or pleasure, and knew how to make the most of them. He prided himself on his brilliant connections, which he had formed partly through his marriage with my mother and partly through the companions of his youth, against whom he bore a secret grudge, because they had all risen in rank, while he had remained a retired lieutenant of the Guards. Like all ex-officers, he did not know how to dress fashionably; nevertheless, his dress was original and elegant. His clothes were always very loose and light, his linen of the finest quality, his large cuffs and collars turned back. Indeed everything he wore suited his tall, muscular figure, his bald head, and his calm, self-confident movements. He was sensitive, and even easily moved to tears. Often, when he came to a pathetic passage while reading aloud, his voice would begin to tremble, the tears would come; and he would drop the book in vexation. He loved music, and sang, to his own piano accompaniment, romances written by his friend A—, some Gipsy songs, and a few opera tunes; but he did not care for serious music, and would say frankly, in defiance of public opinion, that Beethoven's sonatas sent him to sleep; and that he knew nothing finer than *Wake Not the Maid*, as sung by Madame Semenova, and *None but Thee*, as the Gipsy woman Tanyusha sang it. His nature was one of those to whose good deeds a public is indispensable, and he only valued or esteemed that which was valued or esteemed by the world. Whether he had any moral convictions it is difficult to say. His life was so full of impulses of every sort that he had no time to think about them, and he was so happy in his life that he saw no necessity for doing so.

As he grew older he acquired a set outlook on life and a stern code of behaviour, which, however, was purely practical. Those deeds and that manner of life which procured him happiness and pleasure, he considered good; and he believed that every one was bound to follow them. He spoke eloquently and this quality, it seems to me, heightened the flexibility of his principles: he was capable of depicting the same action as a charming prank or as a piece of downright villainy.

Chapter XI

IN THE STUDY AND THE DRAWING-ROOM

It was already dark when we reached home. Mamma seated herself at the piano, and we children fetched our paper, pencils, and paints, and settled ourselves about the round table at our drawing. I had only blue paint; nevertheless, I undertook to depict the hunt. I very quickly painted a blue boy mounted on a blue horse, and some blue dogs, but I was not quite sure whether I could paint a blue hare, and I ran to the library to consult Papa. Papa was reading; and he answered to my question, "Are there any blue hares?" without raising his head, "Yes, my dear, there are." I went back to the round table, and painted a blue hare; then I found it necessary to turn the blue hare into a bush. The bush did not please me either; I turned it into a tree, and the tree into a haystack, and the haystack into a cloud; and finally I made such a mess of my whole paper with blue paint that I tore it up in vexation, and went off to have a nap in the big arm-chair.

Mamma was playing the Second Concerto of Field— who had been her teacher. I dreamed, and bright, phantom dream-shapes arose in my imagination. Then she played Beethoven's Sonata Pathétique, and my memories became gloomy and sorrowful. As Mamma often played those two pieces, I can well remember the feeling they aroused in me. It was like a remembrance—but of what, I did not know. It almost seemed as if I remembered what had never been.

Opposite me was the door of the study, and I saw Yakov enter, and some long-bearded men in kaftans. The door immediately closed behind them. "Now business has begun!" I thought. It seemed to me that nothing in the world could be more important than the business which was transacted in that study; this idea of mine was confirmed by the fact that all who entered the study door did so on tip-toe and spoke in whispers. Through the door came the sound of Papa's loud voice, and the smell of cigars which always excited me, I know not why. Dozing in the arm-chair I was surprised to hear a familiar squeaking of boots in the butler's pantry. Karl Ivanich, with a look of grim determination on his face, and carrying some papers in his hand, tip-toed over to the door and knocked gently on the panel. He was admitted, and the door was slammed again.

"I do hope nothing bad is going to happen," I thought. "Karl Ivanich is angry; he is ready for anything."

And again I fell into a doze.

But no misfortune occurred. In about an hour the same squeaking boots woke me up. Karl Ivanich came out of the study, drying his eyes—which I saw were full of tears—with his handkerchief, and went upstairs, muttering to himself. Papa came out after him, and entered the drawing-room.

"Do you know what I have just decided to do?" he said gaily, laying his hand on Mamma's shoulder.

"What, my dear?"

"I shall take Karl Ivanich with the children. There is room for him in the britchka. They are used to him, and he seems very much attached to them; seven hundred rubles a year is not much: *et puis au fond c'est un très bon diable!*"

I could not understand why Papa should speak so disrespectfully of Karl Ivanich.

"I am very glad," said Mamma, "both for the children's sake and for his: he is a good old man."

"If you could only have seen how much affected he was when I told him that he might keep the five hundred rubles as a gift! But the most amusing thing of all is this account which he has just handed me. It's worth looking at," he added, with a smile and handed her a list in Karl Ivanich's handwriting: "It is delightful."

This was what the list contained:

"Two fish-hooks for the children, seventy kopeks.

"Coloured paper, gilt border, a press and glue for making boxes for presents, six rubles fifty-five kopeks.

"A book and a bow, presents to the children, eight rubles sixteen kopeks.

"Trousers for Nikolai, four rubles.

"A gold watch promised me by Pyotr Alexandrovich, to be brought by him from Moscow in 18—, one hundred and forty rubles.

"Total due Karl Mauer, besides his salary, one hundred and fifty-nine rubles seventy-nine kopeks."

Anyone reading this list, in which Karl Ivanich required to be paid not only for the money he had spent on presents, but even for the gift promised to himself, would think that Karl Ivanich was nothing more than a grasping, hard-hearted egoist—and he would be very much mistaken.

When he entered the study with this account in his hand, and a speech ready prepared in his head, he had intended to set forth eloquently before Papa all that he had endured in our house; but when he began to speak in that touching voice, and with those feeling intonations which he usually employed when dictating to us, he was so much affected by his own eloquence that when he reached the place where he had to say, "Painful as it is for me to part from the children," he broke down, his voice trembled, and he was forced to pull his checked handkerchief from his pocket.

"Yes, Pyotr Alexandrich," he said, through his tears (this passage did not occur in the prepared speech), "I have become so used to the children that I do not know what I shall do without them. Let me stay without salary," he added, wiping away his tears with one hand and presenting the bill with the other.

Knowing Karl Ivanich's kindness of heart I can vouch for his sincerity; but how he reconciled that account with his words still remains a mystery to me.

"If it is painful for you, it would be still more painful for me to part with you," said Papa, tapping him on the shoulder. "I have changed my mind."

Shortly before supper Grisha entered the room. From the moment he had come to the house he had not ceased to sigh and weep; and that, in the opinion of those who believed in his power of prophecy, was a sure sign that some evil was to befall us. At last he took his leave, saying that he intended to depart the next morning. I winked at Volodya, and left the room.

"What is it?"

"If you want to see Grisha's chains, let's go upstairs. Grisha sleeps in the second room. We shall be able to see everything from the lumber-room."

"Splendid! Wait here; I'll call the girls."

The girls ran out, and we went upstairs. After some discussion as to who should go first, we entered the dark garret and settled down to wait.

Chapter XII

GRISHA

The darkness weighed down on all of us: we huddled together, and did not speak. Grisha entered his room almost immediately with his noiseless steps. In one hand he carried his staff, in the other a tallow candle set in a brass candlestick. We held our breaths.

"Lord Jesus Christ! Most Holy Mother of God! Father, Son, and Holy Ghost!" he repeated over and over again, with the various intonations and abbreviations peculiar to those only who repeat these words often.

Still praying, he placed his staff in the corner, inspected his bed, and began to undress. He unfastened his old black belt, removed his tattered nankeen smock, folded it carefully, and hung it over the back of a chair. His face did not now wear its usual expression of haste and stupidity. On the contrary, it was composed, melancholy, and even majestic. His movements were deliberate and thoughtful.

Clad in his underclothes, he sank gently down upon the bed, made the sign of the cross over it on all sides, and with an evident effort (for he frowned) he adjusted the chains beneath his shirt. After sitting there a while and carefully examining several rents in his linen, he rose, lifted the candlestick to the level of the shrine in the corner, which contained several images, and saying a prayer, crossed himself before them, and turned the candle upside down. It sputtered and went out.

The moon, which was almost full, shone in through the window, overlooking the forest. Its pale, silvery light fell on one side of the long white figure of the fool; the other side was in deep shadow, which, merging with the shadows cast by the window-frames on the floor and walls, reached all the way up to the ceiling. The watchman's rattle sounded in the court-yard below.

His huge arms folded upon his breast, his head bent, Grisha stood in silence before the images sighing heavily and ceaselessly; then he knelt with some difficulty, and began to pray.

At first he softly recited the familiar prayers, merely accentuating certain words; then he repeated them, but in a louder voice, and with greater animation. He began to use his own words, endeavouring, with evident effort, to express himself in Slavonic language. His words were incoherent, but touching. He prayed for all his benefactors (as he called those who gave him shelter), among them Mamma, and us; he prayed for himself, besought God to forgive him his grievous sins, and said, "O God, forgive my enemies!" He rose with a groan, and, repeating the same words over and over, he fell to the ground again, and again rose, notwithstanding the weight of the chains, which made a rasping sound as they struck the floor.

Volodya pinched my foot hard, but I did not even look round: I merely rubbed the spot with one hand, and continued to follow Grisha's every word and gesture with a feeling of childish wonder, pity, and reverence.

Instead of the fun and laughter I had expected when I entered the lumber-room, I felt a trembling and sinking at my heart.

Grisha remained for a long time in this state of religious exaltation and extempore prayer. He repeated *"Lord, have mercy,"* several times in succession, but each time with fresh force and expression. Or, *"Forgive me, Lord; teach me what to do; teach me what to do, Lord!"* with an expression as though he expected an immediate response to his words; at times only mournful lamentations were heard. Presently he rose to his knees, crossed his hands upon his breast, and was silent.

Noiselessly I thrust my head in at the door, and held my breath. Grisha did not stir; heavy sighs rent his breast; a tear stood in the dim pupil of his blind eye, glistening in the moonlight.

"Thy will be done!" he cried suddenly, with an indescribable expression, fell with his forehead to the floor, and sobbed like a child.

Much time has passed since then; many memories of the past have lost all significance for me, and have become blurred and indistinct, like dreams; even the pilgrim Grisha has long since ended his last pilgrimage; but the impression he made upon me, the feeling he awakened in me, will never die out of my memory.

Oh, great Christian Grisha! Your faith was so strong that you could feel the nearness of God; your love was so great that the words poured from your lips of themselves—you did not control them with your reason. And how well did you glorify his greatness when, finding no words, you flung yourself to the ground and wept!

The emotion with which I listened to Grisha could not last long; in the first place, because my curiosity was satisfied, and, secondly, because my legs were stiff with sitting in one position, and I wanted to join in the general whispering and movement which was audible behind me in the dark. Some one caught my hand and said, "Whose hand is this?" It was perfectly dark, but by the touch and the whispering beside me I knew it to be Katenka.

Quite unconsciously I grasped her arm, with its sleeve reaching only to the elbow, and raised it to my lips. Katenka must have been surprised, for she jerked her hand away and in doing so she struck it against a broken chair which stood in the room. Grisha raised his head, looked around, saying a prayer, and began to make the sign of the cross over all the corners of the room. We ran noisily out of the garret whispering loudly among ourselves.

Chapter XIII

NATALYA SAVISHNA

About the middle of last century a little girl called Natashka, ragged and barefoot but plump, rosy-cheeked and always merry, used to run about the court-yards in the village of Khabarovka. My grandfather had *taken her upstairs*, that is to say, made her one of Grandmother's female servants, in recognition of the services of her father Savva, a serf clarionet player, and at his request. As a maid, Natashka was distinguished for her gentleness of nature and her zeal; when Mamma was born and a nurse was required, this service was entrusted to Natashka; and in this new career she won both praises and rewards for her industry, faithfulness, and attachment to her young mistress.

But the powdered head, stockings, and bickles of the stout young butler Foka, who, in virtue of his office, was often brought in contact with Natalya, won her simple but loving heart. Emboldened by her love, she went herself to Grandfather and asked permission to marry Foka. Grandfather looked upon her request as ingratitude, turned her away, and punished the poor girl by sending her away to a village he owned in the steppes, to work as cowherd. But within six months, since no one could fill her place, Natalya was restored to her former duties. On her return she went to my grandfather, threw herself at his feet, and besought him to restore her to favour and affection, and to forget her folly, and which she swore would never recur. And she kept her word.

From that day Natashka became Natalya Savishna, and wore a cap. All the treasures of love which she possessed she lavished upon her young mistress.

When, later on, a governess took her place, she was made housekeeper, and all the linen and provisions were given into her charge. She fulfilled these new duties with the same love and zeal. She only lived for her master's property; she saw waste, ruin, robbery on every hand, and considered it her bounden duty to counteract them.

When Mamma married, desiring to reward Natalya Savishna for her twenty years' service and attachment to the family, she summoned her, and, expressing in the most flattering terms her love and gratitude, handed her an official document, which declared that Natalya Savishna was a free woman;* and added that she was to receive a yearly pension of 300 rubles, whether she continued to serve in our house or not. Natalya Savishna listened to all this in silence; then taking the document in her own hands, she examined it angrily, muttered something between her lips, and flew out of the room, slamming the door behind her. Puzzled by this strange behaviour, Mamma went to Natalya's room. She found her sitting on her chest, her eyes streaming, twisting her handkerchief in her fingers, and intently regarding the tattered fragments of her emancipation paper, which were scattered over the floor before her.

"What is the matter, dearest Natalya Savishna?" asked Mamma, taking her hand.

"Nothing, my dear mistress," she replied. "I must be repulsive to you in some way since you want to drive me out of the house. Well, I will go."

She pulled away her hand, and, with difficulty restraining her tears, was about to leave the room, but Mamma detained her, embraced her, and they both wept in company.

Ever since I can recollect anything, I remember Natalya Savishna, her love and tenderness; yet only now

_____

* It will be remembered that this was in the days of serfdom.—*Tr*.

am I able to appreciate their worth—at that time it never entered my mind to think what a rare and wonderful being that old woman was. Not only did she never speak about herself, but she seemed never even to think of herself: her whole life was love and self-sacrifice. I was so accustomed to her tender, unselfish love for us that I did not even imagine it otherwise; was not in the least grateful to her, and never paused to ask myself whether she was happy or content.

Often, on some pretext or other, I would run away from my lessons to her room and begin to weave fancies aloud, not in the least embarrassed by her presence. She was always busy with something: she was either knitting a stocking, or tidying the chests with which her room was filled, or taking account of the linen, and as she worked, she listened to all the nonsense which I uttered; how, "when I got to be a general, I would marry a great beauty, buy myself a sorrel horse, build a crystal house, and send for all Karl Ivanich's relatives from Saxony," and so on; she would say, "Yes, my dear, yes." Generally, when I rose and prepared to take my departure, she would open a blue chest—on the inside of whose cover, as I now remember, there were pasted a picture of a Hussar, a picture from a pomade-box, and a drawing by Volodya—and take from it a stick of incense, lighted it, and say, as she waved it about:

"This, my dear, is Ochakov incense. When your late grandfather—God rest his soul!—went to war against the Turks, he brought it back from there. This is the last bit," she would add, with a sigh.

The chests that filled Natalya Savishna's room contained absolutely everything. If ever anything was needed, we would say, "We must ask Natalya Savishna"; and, indeed, after a little rummaging, she always found the article required. "It's well that I hid it away," she would say. In those chests were thousands of things which nobody in the house, except herself, ever knew or troubled themselves about.

Once she made me very angry. This is how it was. I dropped the decanter while pouring myself some *kvass* at dinner, and stained the table-cloth.

"Call Natalya Savishna, let her see what her favourite has done," said Mamma.

Natalya Savishna came, and on seeing the mess I had made, she shook her head; then Mamma whispered something in her ear, and she went out, shaking her finger at me.

After dinner I was on my way to the hall, skipping about in the most cheerful frame of mind, when all at once Natalya Savishna sprang out from behind the door, with the table-cloth in her hand, caught me, and, in spite of my desperate resistance, began to rub my face with the wet part of the cloth, crying, "Never dirty the table-cloth, never dirty the table-cloth!" I was so offended that I roared with rage.

"How dare she strike me in the face with a wet table-cloth, as if I were a servant-boy!" I said to myself, as I walked up and down the room and gulped down my tears. "How awful!"

As soon as she saw that I was crying, she ran off, leaving me pacing to and fro, considering how to take revenge on that impudent Natalya for the insult which she had inflicted on me.

In a few minutes Natalya Savishna returned, approached me timidly, and tried to pacify me.

"There now, my dear, don't cry. Forgive me, I am an old fool. It's my fault. You will forgive me, my darling will you not? Here, this is for you."

From under her kerchief she drew a red paper packet, in which were two caramels and a fig, and gave it to me with a trembling hand. I could not look the kind old woman in the face; I turned away, took her gift, and my tears flowed afresh—not from anger now, but from love and shame.

Chapter XIV

PARTING

At twelve o'clock on the day following the events which I have described, the calash and britchka stood at the door. Nikolai was dressed for travelling—that is to say, his trousers were tucked into his boots, and his old coat was tightly belted. He stood by the britchka, packing the overcoats and cushions under the seat; when the pile seemed to him too high, he seated himself on the cushions, and jumped on them to press them down.

"For Heaven's sake, Nikolai Dmitrich, can't we put the master's box in?" said Papa's valet, quite out of breath, leaning out of the calash, "it won't take up much room."

"You should have said so before, Mikhei Ivanich," answered Nikolai, quickly and angrily, flinging a parcel with all his might on the floor of the britchka. "O Lord, my head is going round, and here you come with your box!" he added, pulling off his cap and wiping the big drops of perspiration from his sun-burned brow.

Men-servants in coats, kaftans, shirts, without hats, women in striped petticoats and striped dresses, with children in their arms, and barefooted children, stood about the porch, stared at the equipages, and talked among themselves. One of the coachmen—a bent old man in a winter cap and *armyak*—held in his hand the pole of the calash, tested it carefully, and thoughtfully surveyed its action; the other, a good-looking young fellow, in a white smock with shoulder-gussets of red fustian and a black lamb's-wool cap, which he tilted first over one ear and then over the other as he scratched his blonde curls, placed his *armyak* on the box, flung the reins there also, and, cracking his braided knout, gazed now at his boots, now at the coachmen who were greasing the britchka. One of them was straining himself to lift a wheel; another was bending over it and carefully greasing the axle, and even smearing the rim from below in order that none of the grease on his cloth should be wasted. At the fence the overworked post-horses of various colours stood brushing away the flies with their tails—some of them planted their shaggy, swollen legs far apart, closed their eyes, and dozed; others, tired of standing still, rubbed against each other or plucked the leaves and stalks of the dark-green ferns which grew beside the porch. Several greyhounds lay panting in the sun; others walked about in the shade under the carriages, and licked the tallow around the axles. The whole atmosphere was filled with a kind of dusty mist; the horizon was of a greyish lilac hue, but there was not so much as a tiny cloud in the sky. The strong west wind raised pillars of dust from the roads and fields, bent the crests of the lofty lindens and the birches in the garden, and carried away the faded yellow leaves. I sat by the window, impatiently awaiting the completion of all these preparations.

When all were assembled around the large table in the drawing-room, in order to spend a few minutes together for the last time, it did not occur to me that a painful moment was awaiting us. The most trivial thoughts wandered through my brain. I tried to guess which coachman would drive the calash, and which the britchka; who would travel with Papa, and who with Karl Ivanich, and why must I be bundled up in a scarf and a long wadded overcoat.

"Am I so delicate? I shall not freeze. I wish they would get through this as quickly as possible! I want to get in and ride off."

"To whom shall I give the list of the children's linen?"

Natalya Savishna, coming in with tear-swollen eyes and the list in her hand, asked Mamma.

"Give it to Nikolai, and come and say good-bye to the children."

The old woman tried to say something, but suddenly paused, covered her face with her handkerchief, and left the room with a wave of the hand.

My heart contracted with pain when I saw that motion; but impatience to start was stronger than that feeling, and I continued to listen indifferently to Papa's conversation with Mamma. They talked of things which evidently interested neither of them: what was it necessary to purchase for the house; what was to be said to Princess Sophie and Madame Julie; and would the travelling be good.

Foka entered and, halting on the threshold, announced, "The carriages are ready," in exactly the same tone with which he announced, "Dinner is served." I noticed that Mamma shuddered and turned pale at this announcement, as though she had not expected it.

Foka was ordered to close all the doors of the room.* I thought it very funny, "as if we were all hiding from somebody."

When all sat down, Foka also seated himself on the edge of a chair; but no sooner had he done so than a door squeaked, and all glanced round. Natalya Savishna hastily entered and, without raising her eyes, sat down near the door on the same chair with Foka. I seem even now to see Foka's bald head and wrinkled, immovable face, and the kind, bent form in the cap beneath which the grey hair was visible. They were crowded together on the one chair, and both felt awkward.

I remained unconcerned and impatient. The ten seconds during which we sat there with closed doors seemed a

---

* An old Russian custom: to shut all the doors and sit for a while before starting off on a long journey.—*Tr.*

whole hour to me. At length we all rose, crossed ourselves, and began to take leave. Papa embraced Mamma, and kissed her several times.

"Enough, my dear," said Papa. "We are not parting for ever."

"It is painful, nevertheless," said Mamma, in a voice which quivered with tears.

When I heard that voice, and beheld her trembling lips and her eyes filled with tears, I forgot everything, and felt so sad and miserable and so terrified that I would much rather have run away than have said good-bye to her. At that moment I realized that when she embraced Papa she had already taken leave of us.

She kissed and crossed Volodya so many times that, supposing she would now turn to me, I stepped forward. But she continued to bless him and to press him to her bosom. Finally I embraced her and, clinging to her, I wept without a thought beyond my grief.

When we went out to get into the carriage the tiresome servants stepped forward in the anteroom to say farewell. Their "Your hand, please, sir," their noisy kisses on our shoulders, and the smell of the tallow on their heads, aroused in me a feeling akin to that of disgust. Under the influence of this feeling I kissed Natalya Savishna very coldly on her cap when, bathed in tears, she bade me farewell.

It is strange that I can even now see the faces of all those servants, and I could draw them with all the most minute details, but Mamma's face and attitude have utterly escaped my mind; perhaps because during all that time I could not once summon up courage to look at her. It seemed to me that if I did so, her sorrow and mine must increase to the bounds of impossibility.

I rushed to the calash ahead of the others and sat down on the back seat. As the back was up, I could see nothing, but some instinct told me that Mamma was still there.

"Shall I look at her again or not? Well, for the last time, then!" I said to myself, and leaned out of the calash towards the porch. At that moment Mamma had come to the other side of the carriage with the same intent, and called me by name. When I heard her voice behind me I turned round, but I did it so abruptly that we bumped our heads together. She smiled mournfully, and kissed me long and warmly for the last time.

It was only after we had driven several yards that I dared to look at her. The breeze raised the blue kerchief which was tied about her head; with bowed head, her face covered with her hands, she was slowly climbing the steps. Foka was supporting her.

Papa sat by my side in silence. Tears choked me, and there was such a lump in my throat that I was afraid I should stifle. As we reached the highway we saw a white handkerchief which someone was waving from the balcony. I waved mine, and this movement calmed me somewhat. I continued to cry, and the thought that my tears proved my tender-heartedness afforded me pleasure and consolation.

After we had travelled a verst or so I calmed down a little, and proceeded to fix my attention on the object nearest to my eyes—the hind quarters of the piebald horse running on my side of the calash. I observed how the animal flourished his tail, how he set one foot down after the other, how the post-boy's braided knout reached him, and his feet began to leap together. I noticed how the harness leaped about on him, and the rings on the harness; and I gazed until the bands were covered at places near the tail with foam. I began to look about me—at the waving fields of ripe rye, at the dark fallow land, on which here and there one could see a peasant with a plough, or a mare with a foal beside it; at the milestones; I even glanced at the carriage box to see which coachman was driving us; and the tears were not dry on my face, when my thoughts were already far from the mother whom I had left perhaps for ever, yet every recollection led me to the thought of her. Then I suddenly recalled the mushroom which I had found the day before in the birch alley, and remembered that Lyubochka and Katenka had disputed as to who should pluck it, and I remember how they had wept at parting from us.

How sad I felt to be leaving them, and Natalya Savishna, and the birch alley, and Foka. Even the malicious Mimi. I would miss them all. And poor dear Mamma? The tears again filled my eyes, but not for long.

Chapter XV

CHILDHOOD

Happy, happy childhood, that blissful time never to be recalled! How can I help loving it and cherishing its bright memories? Those memories refresh and elevate my soul, they are a source of never-ending joy to me.

Tired out with running about I sit at the tea-table in my high chair; I have drunk my cup of milk and sugar long ago; though sleep glues my eyes together, I do not stir from the spot—I sit and listen. Mamma is talking with some one, and the sound of her voice is sweet. That sound alone says so much to my heart! My eyes dimmed with drowsiness, I gaze upon her face, and all at once she becomes small, so small—her face is no bigger than a little button, but I see it just as plainly still. I see her look at me and smile. I like to see her so small. I draw my eyelids still closer together, and she is no larger than the little boys one sees in the pupils of the eyes; but I move, and the illusion is destroyed. I screw up my eyes, twist about, and try in every way to reproduce it, but in vain.

I get up, climb into an easy-chair, and make myself comfortable.

"You will go to sleep again, Nikolenka," says Mamma; "you had better go upstairs."

"I don't want to go to bed, Mamma," I reply, and sweet, misty dreams fill my brain; the healthy sleep of childhood closes my lids, and in a moment I lose consciousness, and sleep until they wake me. In my dreams I feel somebody's soft hand touching me; I recognize it by that touch alone; and, still sleeping, I seize it and press it warmly, so warmly, to my lips.

Every one has already departed: one candle only burns in the drawing-room. Mamma has said that she would wake me: it is she who has sat down on the chair in which I am sleeping, and strokes my hair with her wonderfully soft hand, and in my ears resounds the dear, familiar voice.

"Get up, my darling; it is time to go to bed."

There are no cold glances to embarrass her, she does not fear to pour out upon me all her tenderness and love. I do not move, but kiss her hand passionately.

"Get up, my angel."

She puts her other hand around my neck, and her slender fingers tickle me. It is quiet in the room and almost dark. My nerves are excited by the tickling and by being roused from sleep. Mamma sits close to me, she touches me, and I am conscious of her perfume and her voice. I spring up, throw my arms around her neck, press my head to her bosom with a sigh, "Oh, dear, dear Mamma, how I love you!" I say.

She smiles her sad, bewitching smile, takes my head in both her hands, kisses my brow, and sets me on her knees.

"So you love me very much?" She is silent for a moment, then speaks: "You will always love me, won't you, and never forget me? When Mamma is no more, you will not forget her? You will not forget her, Nikolenka?"

She kisses me more tenderly still.

"Oh please, don't say that, dearest mother!" I cry, kissing her knees; and the tears stream from my eyes—tears of love and rapture.

After that, on going upstairs to my room, and standing before the images in my little wadded dressing-gown, how earnestly would I repeat the words: "God bless Papa and Mamma!" In repeating the prayers which my childish lips had first learned to lisp after my beloved mother, the love of her and the love of God were united, in some strange fashion, in one feeling.

Having said my prayer, I wrap myself in my little blanket, with a spirit light and joyous; one dream follows another, but what are they all about? They are intangible, but full of pure love, and hopes of happiness. And then I think of Karl Ivanich and his bitter lot—the only unhappy man I know—and I feel so sorry for him, I love him so, that tears fill my eyes, and I say to myself, "God grant him happiness, give me the power to help him, to lighten his sorrow; I am ready to sacrifice everything for him." Then I thrust my favourite toys—a china dog or a hare—into the corner of the downy pillow, and it pleases me to think how warm and comfortable it will be there. I pray again, that God will grant happiness to all, that every one may be content, and that the weather tomorrow may be good for walking. I turn on the other side; my thoughts and dreams mingle confusedly, and I fall asleep quietly, calmly, with my face still wet with tears.

Will that freshness, that light-heartedness, that necessity for love, that strength of faith which one possessed in childhood, ever return? What better time can there be than that when the two greatest of virtues—innocent gaiety and unbounded thirst for love—are the only impulses in life?

Where are those burning prayers? Where is that best gift of all, those pure tears of emotion? The angel of solace used to come and wipe away those tears with a smile and instil sweet visions in the pure imagination of infancy.

Has life laid such a heavy burden on my heart that those tears and raptures have deserted me for ever? Do the memories alone abide?

Chapter XVI

VERSES

Nearly a month after our arrival in Moscow I was sitting upstairs in Grandmamma's house, writing. On the other side of the big table sat the drawing-master, making the final corrections in a pencil-sketch of the head of a Turk. Volodya was standing behind the master, craning his neck, to look over his shoulder. This head was Volodya's first pencil drawing, and it was to be presented to Grandmamma that day, which was her saint's day.

"Aren't you going to put a little more shading here?" said Volodya, rising on tip-toe and pointing at the Turk's neck.

"No, it is not necessary," said the teacher, putting his pencil and drawing-pen into the case. "It is just right now, and you need not do anything more to it. Well, and you, Nikolenka," he added, rising, and continuing to gaze at the Turk from the corner of his eye: "Won't you reveal your secret to us? What are you going to give your grandmother? I think another head just like this would be the best gift. Good-bye, gentlemen," said he, and, taking his hat and register, he departed.

I had been thinking myself at the moment that a head would be better than what I was working at. When it had been announced to us that Grandmamma's name-day was near at hand, and that we must prepare gifts for the occasion, the idea of writing a verse occurred to me, and I immediately made up two couplets, hoping that the rest would soon come to my mind. I really do not know how the idea—so strange for a child—entered my mind; but I remember that it pleased me greatly, and that to all questions on the subject I replied that I would certainly give Grandmamma a present but that I would not tell anyone what it was.

Contrary to my expectations, and in spite of all my efforts, I could not compose any more than the two couplets which I had thought up on the spur of the moment. I began to read the poems in our books; but neither Dmitriev nor Derzhavin could help me. Quite the reverse: they only convinced me more thoroughly of my own incapacity. Knowing that Karl Ivanich was fond of copying poetry, I rummaged among his papers on the sly, and found, besides German poems, also a Russian one, which must have been the product of his own pen:

To Madame L.

Remember near,
Remember far,
For ever remember me—
Aye, still beyond the grave, remember
That I have well loved thee.

Petrovskoye, 1828, June 3   *Karl Mauer*

This poem, transcribed in a handsome round hand, on a thin sheet of note-paper, pleased me because of the touching sentiment with which it was inspired. I immediately learned it by heart, and resolved to take it for a pattern. After that, progress was rapid. By the name's-day my twelve verses of congratulation were ready, and I sat down in the school-room to copy them out on vellum paper.

Two sheets of paper were soon ruined; not because I wanted to change anything in my verses—they seemed to me very fine—but from the third line on the ends would go on curving upwards more and more, so that it was evident, even at a distance, that the whole thing was written crookedly, and was fit for nothing.

The third sheet was askew like the others; but I was determined not to do any more copying. In my poem I congratulated Grandmamma, wished her many years of health, and concluded thus:

> *To comfort thee we shall endeavour,*
> *And love thee like our own dear Mother.*

It seemed to be very good, yet the last line offended my ear strangely.

"And love thee like our ... own ... dear ... moth ... er," I kept repeating to myself. "Now what rhyme could I use instead of 'mother'? 'bother'? ... 'feather'?... Well, never mind. It's better than Karl Ivanich's, anyway."

So I transcribed the last line. Then I read my whole composition over aloud in the bedroom, with feeling and gesticulations. The verses were entirely lacking in rhythm or measure, but I did not pause over them; the last line, however, struck me still more powerfully and unpleasantly. I sat down on the bed and began to think.

"Why did I write *like our own dear mother*? She's not here, and it was not necessary to mention her. I love Grandma, it's true; I respect her, but still she is not the same. Why did I write that? Why did I write a lie? What if it is poetry, I shouldn't have done it all the same."

At this moment the tailor entered with my new jacket.

"Well, let it go," I said in great vexation as I thrust my verses under my pillow and ran to try on my new clothes.

They were very fine indeed. The cinnamon-brown half-coat, with its bronze buttons, was made to fit snugly, not as they made them in the country. The black trousers were also tight; it was wonderful to see how well they showed the muscles, and concealed the shoes.

"At last I've got some trousers with real straps," I thought, quite beside myself with joy as I surveyed my legs on all sides. Although the new garments were very tight, and it was hard to move in them, I concealed the fact from everybody, and declared that, on the contrary, I was extremely comfortable, and that if there was any fault about the clothes, it was that they were, if anything, a little too loose. After that I stood for a long time before the glass, brushing my copiously pomaded hair: but, try as I would, I could not make the tuft on the crown lie flat; as soon as I ceased to press it down with the brush, in order to see if it would obey me, it rose and projected in all directions, making my face look ridiculous.

Karl Ivanich was dressing in another room, and his blue swallow-tailed coat and underlinen were carried through the school-room to him. I heard the voice of one of Grandmamma's maids at the door which led downstairs. I went out to see what she wanted. In her hand she held a stiffly-starched shirt-front, which she told me she had brought for Karl Ivanich; she vowed she had not slept all the previous night to have it ready for him. I undertook to deliver it, and asked if Grandmamma had risen.

"Oh yes, sir! She has already had her coffee, and the priest has arrived. What a fine young gentleman you are!" she added, glancing at my new suit with a smile.

Her remark made me blush. I whirled round on one foot, snapped my fingers, and gave a leap. I wanted her to see that she did not thoroughly appreciate, as yet, how grand I was.

When I brought the shirt-front to Karl Ivanich, I found that he no longer needed it; he had put on another one, and, bending over before the little glass which stood on the table, he was holding the magnificent knot of his cravat with both hands, and moving his clean-shaven chin up and down in it to make sure that it fitted. After smoothing our clothes down on all sides, and requesting Nikolai to do the same for him, he led us to Grandmamma. I laugh now when I remember how strongly we three smelt of pomade as we descended the stairs.

Karl Ivanich carried a little gift box of his own making, Volodya had his drawing, and I, my verses; each one had upon his tongue the greeting with which he intended to present his gift. Just as Karl Ivanich opened the drawing-room door the priest was putting on his robes, and the first words of the service resounded.

Grandmamma was already in the drawing-room: she was standing by the wall, her arms resting on the back of a chair, and was praying devoutly with bent head; beside her stood Papa. He turned towards us and smiled as he saw us hide our gifts in haste behind our backs, and halt just inside the door, endeavouring to escape being seen. The whole effect of unexpectedness upon which we had counted was ruined.

When the time came to go up and kiss the cross, I was suddenly seized by an overpowering paralyzing fit of shyness, and, feeling that I should never have the courage to present my gift, I hid behind Karl Ivanich, who, having congratulated Grandmamma in the choicest language, shifted his box from his right hand to his left, handed it to her, and retreated a few paces in order to make way for Volodya. Grandmamma appeared to be delighted with the box, which had gilt strips pasted on the edges, and smiled to express her gratitude with the warmest of smiles. Yet it was evident that she did not know where to put the box, and perhaps that was why she gave it to Papa, asking him to note how skilfully it was made.

After satisfying his curiosity, Papa handed it to the priest, who seemed exceedingly pleased with this trifle. He dandled his head, and gazed curiously now at the box, and again at the artist who could make such a beautiful object. Volodya produced his Turk, and he also received the most flattering praise from all quarters. Now it was my turn: Grandmamma turned to me with an encouraging smile.

Those who have suffered from shyness know that it is a feeling which increases in direct proportion to delay, while resolution decreases in similar measure: that is to say, the longer the sensation lasts, the more unconquerable it becomes and the less decision there is left.

The last remnants of courage and determination forsook me when Karl Ivanich and Volodya presented their gifts, and my shyness reached its climax; I felt that the blood was incessantly rushing from my heart to my head; I turned alternately pale and red, and great drops of perspiration broke out upon my nose and forehead. My ears burned; I felt a shiver and a cold perspiration all over my body; I shifted from foot to foot, and did not stir from the spot.

"Come, Nikolenka, show us what you have—a box or a drawing," said Papa. There was nothing to be done. With a trembling hand, I presented the crumpled, fateful scroll; but my voice failed me completely, and I stood before Grandmamma in silence. I could not bear the thought that, in place of the drawing which was expected, my worthless verses would be read before every one, including the words, *like our own dear mother*, which would clearly prove that I had never loved Mamma and had forgotten her. How can I describe my sufferings when Grandmamma began to read my poem aloud, and when, unable to decipher it, she paused in the middle of a line and glanced at Papa with what then seemed to me a mocking smile; when she did not pronounce to suit me; and when, owing to her feeble eyesight, she gave the paper to Papa before she had finished, and begged him to read it all over again from the beginning? It seemed to me that she did so because she did not care to read such stupid and crookedly-written verses, and yet she wanted Papa to read for himself that last line which proved so clearly my lack of feeling. I expected that he would rap me on the nose with those verses, and say, "You wicked boy to forget your mother—take that!" But nothing of the sort happened; on the contrary, when all was read, Grandmamma said, "Charming!" and kissed me on the forehead.

The little box, the drawing, and the verses were laid out in a row, beside two cambric handkerchiefs and a snuff-box with a portrait of Mamma, on the movable table attached to the arm-chair in which Grandmamma always sat.

"Princess Varvara Ilyinichna," announced one of the two huge footmen who accompanied Grandmamma's carriage.

Grandmamma gazed thoughtfully at the portrait set in the tortoise-shell cover of the snuff-box, and made no reply.

"Will your excellency receive her?" repeated the footman.

Chapter XVII

PRINCESS KORNAKOVA

"Show her in," said Grandmamma, settling herself in her arm-chair.

The Princess was a woman of about forty-five, small, frail, dry and bitter, with disagreeable greyish-green eyes, whose look plainly belied the unnaturally amiable expression which sat on her lips. Beneath her velvet bonnet, adorned with an ostrich plum, her light reddish-tinted hair was visible; her eyebrows and lashes appeared still lighter and redder against the unhealthy pallor of her face. Yet, for all that, her unconstrained manners, her tiny hands, and a peculiar dryness of feature, imparted some-thing aristocratic and energetic to her general appearance.

The Princess talked a great deal, and by her volubility belonged to the class of people who always speak as though some one were contradicting them, though no one has uttered a word: she alternately raised her voice and lowered it gradually, and then began all at once to speak with fresh animation, glancing around at all present even if they took no part in the conversation, as though en-deavouring to obtain their support.

Although the Princess kissed Grandmamma's hand, and called her *ma bonne tante* incessantly, I observed that Grandmamma was not pleased with her; she twitched her brows in a peculiar manner while listening to her excuses why Prince Mikhailo could not call in person to congratu-late Grandmamma, in spite of his ardent desire to do so, and replied in Russian to the Princess's French.

"I am very much obliged to you, my dear, for your at-tention," she said, with a singular drawl, "and as for Prince Mikhailo not coming, pray do not mention it. He's always so busy; besides, what pleasure could he find in coming to see an old woman like me?" And without giv-ing the Princess time to contradict her, she asked: "How are your children, my dear?"

"Thank God, *ma tante*, they are growing well, and studying and playing pranks, especially Etienne. He is the eldest, and he is becoming such a scapegrace, that we don't know what to do with him; but he's clever—a prom-ising boy. Just imagine, *mon cousin*," she continued turn-ing to Papa, because Grandmamma, who took no inter-est in the Princess's children, and wished rather to boast of her own grandchildren, had taken my verses from the box with great care and was beginning to unfold them— "just imagine, cousin, what he did the other day." And the Princess leaned over to Papa, and began to relate some-thing with great animation. When she had finished her tale, which I did not hear, she laughed, and looking inquiringly at Papa, said:

"What do you think of that, *mon cousin*? He deserved a whipping; but his prank was so clever and amusing that I forgave him, *mon cousin*."

And, fixing her eyes on Grandmamma, the Princess went on smiling, but said nothing.

"Do you *beat* your children, my dear?" inquired Grandmamma, raising her brows significantly, and laying a special emphasis on the word *beat*.

"Alas, *ma bonne tante*," replied the Princess in a good-natured tone, with a swift glance at Papa, "I know your opinion on that point; I am sorry but I must disagree with you in this particular matter: in spite of all I have thought and read on the subject; in spite of all the advice I have taken, experience has led me to the conviction that children must be governed by fear. Fear is requisite in order to make something out of a child. Is it not so, *mon cousin*? Now, *je vous demande un peu*, do children fear anything more than the rod?"

With this she glanced inquiringly at us, and I confess I felt rather uncomfortable at that moment.

"Whatever you may say, a boy of twelve, or even of fourteen, is still a child. A girl, of course, is quite another matter."

"How lucky," I thought to myself, "that I am not her son!"

"Yes, that's all very fine, my dear," said Grandmamma, folding up my verses and placing them under the box, as though, after that, she considered the Princess unworthy of hearing such a production: "that's all very fine, but tell me, pray, how can you expect any delicacy of feeling in your children after that?"

And considering this argument unanswerable, Grandmamma added, in order to put an end to the conversation:

"However, every one has a right to his own opinion on that subject."

The Princess made no reply, but smiled condescendingly, thereby giving us to understand that she pardoned these strange prejudices in an individual whom she so much respected.

"Pray introduce me to your young people," she said, glancing at us, and smiling graciously.

We rose, fixed our eyes on the Princess's face, but did not in the least know what we ought to do in order to show that the acquaintance had been made.

"Kiss the Princess's hand," said Papa.

"You will love your old aunt, won't you?" she said, kissing Volodya on the hair; "I am only a distant aunt, but I value friendly relations far more than blood relationship," she added, directing her remarks chiefly to Grandmamma; but Grandmamma was still displeased with her, and answered:

"Ah! my dear, does such relationship count for anything nowadays?"

"This one will be a young man of the world," said Papa, pointing to Volodya; "and this is the poet," he added, just as I was kissing the Princess's dry little hand, and imagining, with exceeding vividness, that the hand held a rod, and beneath the rod was a bench, and so on, and so on.

"Which?" asked the Princess, detaining me by the hand.

"This little fellow with the tuft on his crown," answered Papa, smiling gaily.

"What does my tuft matter to him? Is there nothing else to talk about?" I thought, and retreated into a corner.

I had the strangest conceptions of beauty. I even considered Karl Ivanich the handsomest man in the world; but I knew very well that I was not good-looking, and on this point I was not mistaken: hence any allusion to my personal appearance offended me deeply.

I remember very well how once—I was six years old at the time—they were discussing my looks at dinner and Mamma was trying to discover something handsome about my face: she said I had intelligent eyes, and an agreeable smile, and at last, yielding to Papa's arguments and to ocular evidence, she was forced to confess that I was plain; and then, when I thanked her for the dinner, she fondled my cheek and said:

"Remember, my darling, that no one will love you for your face. So you must try to be good and clever, will you?"

These words not only convinced me that I was not handsome, but also that I was bound to become good and clever.

Yet I often had moments of despair: I fancied that there was no happiness on earth for a person with such a wide nose, such thick lips, and such small grey eyes as I had; I besought God to work a miracle, to make me handsome, and all I had in the present, or might have in the future, I would give in exchange for a handsome face.

Chapter XVIII

PRINCE IVAN IVANICH

When the Princess had heard the verses, and had showered praises upon the author, Grandmamma relented, began to address her in French, ceased to call her *you** and *my dear*, and invited her to call again in the evening, with all her children, to which the Princess consented; and after staying a little longer, she took her departure.

So many visitors came that day with congratulations that carriages stood in the court-yard near the entrance all the morning.

* That is to say, she called her *thou.—Tr.*

"Bonjour, chère cousine," said one of the guests, as he entered the room and kissed Grandmamma's hand.

He was a man about seventy years of age, of lofty stature, dressed in a military uniform, with large epaulets, from beneath the collar of which a large white cross was visible, and with a calm, frank expression of countenance. The freedom and simplicity of his manners surprised me. His face was still notably handsome, in spite of the fact that only a thin semi-circle of hair was left on the nape of the neck, and that his sunken upper lip betrayed the lack of teeth.

Toward the end of the last century Prince Ivan Ivanich had made a brilliant career while he was still very young, thanks to his noble character, his handsome person, his remarkable courage, his distinguished and powerful family, and, especially, to his good luck. He remained in the service, and his ambition was very speedily so thoroughly gratified that there was nothing left for him to wish for in that direction. From his earliest youth he had conducted himself as if preparing to occupy that exalted station in the world in which fate eventually placed him. Hence, although he encountered some failures and disappointments in his brilliant and somewhat vainglorious life, such as all people undergo, his calm disposition, his lofty manner of thought, his well-grounded principles of religion and morality had never failed him, and he had won universal respect less by his brilliant position than by his firmness and consistency. He was not a man of distinguished intellect; but, thanks to a position which permitted him to look down upon all the vain bustle of life, his cast of thought was elevated. He was by nature kind and sensitive, but in manner he appeared cold and somewhat haughty; this sprang from the fact that being placed in a position in which he could be of use to many people, he endeavoured by his cold demeanour to protect himself against the incessant petitions and appeals of persons who only wished to take advantage of his influence. But this coldness was softened by the condescending politeness of a man of *the very high society.*

He was cultivated and well read; but his cultivation stopped at what he had acquired in his youth—that is to say, at the close of the last century. He had read everything of note which had been written in France on the subject of philosophy and eloquence during the eighteenth century; he was thoroughly acquainted with all the best products of French literature, so that he was able to quote passages from Racine, Corneille, Boileau, Molière, Montaigne and Fénelon, and was fond of doing so; he possessed a brilliant knowledge of mythology, and had studied with profit the ancient masterpieces of epic poetry in the French translations; he had acquired a sufficient knowledge of history from Ségur; but he knew nothing at all of mathematics beyond arithmetic, nor of physics, nor of contemporary literature; he could maintain a polite silence or utter a few commonplaces about Goethe, Schiller, and Byron, but he had never read them. In spite of this French and classical education, of which so few examples still exist, his conversation was simple, and this very simplicity concealed his ignorance of various things, and at the same time imparted to his speech an air of tolerance and good taste. He hated eccentricity of every kind, declaring that it was a device of the vulgar. Society was a necessity to him, wherever he might be living; whether in Moscow or abroad, he always lived generously, and on certain days received all the town. His standing in society was such that an invitation from him served as a passport to all drawing-rooms, and many young and pretty women willingly presented to him their rosy cheeks, which he kissed with seemingly paternal feeling; and many, to all appearances, very important and respectable people were delighted to be admitted to the Prince's parties.

Very few people were now left who, like Grandmamma,

had been members of the same circle, of the same age, the same education, the same views; and for that reason he especially prized his old friendship with her, and always showed her the greatest respect.

I could not gaze enough at the Prince. The respect which every one showed him, his huge epaulets, the particular joy which Grandmamma manifested at the sight of him, and the fact that he alone did not fear her, treated her with perfect ease, and even had the daring to address her as *ma cousine*, inspired me with a reverence for him which equalled, if it did not excel, that which I felt for Grandmamma. When she showed him my verses, he called me to him, and said:

"Who knows, *ma cousine*, he may be another Derzhavin?"

Thereupon he pinched my cheek so hard that if I did not cry out it was because I guessed that it was intended as a caress.

The guests departed. Papa and Volodya went out, too. The Prince, Grandmamma, and I remained in the drawing-room.

"Why did not our dear Natalya Nikolayevna come?" asked Prince Ivan Ivanich suddenly, after a few moments' silence.

. "Ah! *mon cher*," replied Grandmamma, bending her head and laying her hand upon the sleeve of his uniform, "she would certainly have come had she been free to do as she wished. She writes to me that *Pierre* proposed that she should come, but that she had refused because they had had no income at all this year; and she writes: 'Moreover, there is no reason why I should move to Moscow this year with the whole household. Lyubochka is still too young; and as for the boys who are to live with you, I am more easy about them than if they were to live with me.' All that is very fine!" continued Grandmamma, in a tone which showed very plainly that she did not consider it fine

78

at all. "The boys should have been sent here long ago, in order that they might learn something and become accustomed to society. What kind of education was it possible to give them in the country? Why, the eldest will soon be thirteen, and the other eleven. You have observed, *mon cousin,* that they are perfectly untamed here; they don't know how to enter a room."

"But I don't understand," replied the Prince; "why these constant complaints of straitened circumstances? *He* has a very handsome property, and Natasha's Khabarovka, where I played in the theatricals with you once upon a time, I know as well as the palm of my own hand. It is a splendid estate and it ought to bring in a handsome revenue."

"I do not mind telling you, as a true friend," broke in Grandmamma, looking sad: "it seems to me that all these excuses are invented simply for the purpose of allowing *him* to live here alone, to lounge about at the clubs, at dinners, and to do God knows what else. But she suspects nothing. You know what an angel she is; she believes in *him* implicitly. He assured her that it was necessary to bring the children to Moscow, and to leave her alone with that stupid governess in the country, and she believed him. If he were to tell her that it was necessary to whip the children as Princess Varvara Ilyinichna does, she would probably believe that too," said Grandmamma, turning about in her chair with an expression of thorough contempt. "Yes, my friend," pursued Grandmamma, after a momentary pause, taking one of her two handkerchiefs to wipe away the tear which had come to her eye, "I often think that *he* can neither value her nor understand her, and that, in spite of all her goodness and love for him, and her efforts to conceal her grief—I know it very well— she cannot be happy with him; and, mark my words, if he does not—"

Grandmamma covered her face with her handkerchief.

"Ah, *ma bonne amie*," said the Prince reproachfully, "I see that you have not grown any wiser. You are always distressing yourself over some imaginary sorrow. Come, are you not ashamed of yourself? I have known him for a long time, and I know him to be a good, attentive, and excellent husband, and, what is the principal thing, a perfectly honest man."

Having involuntarily overheard a conversation which I ought not to have heard, I took myself out of the room, on tip-toe, in a state of violent agitation.

Chapter XIX

THE IVINS

"Volodya! Volodya! The Ivins!" I shouted, catching sight from the window of three boys in blue overcoats, with beaver collars, who were crossing from the opposite side-walk to our house, headed by their young and dandified tutor.

The Ivins were related to us, and were of about our own age; we had made their acquaintance soon after our arrival in Moscow and were now intimate friends.

The second son, Seryozha, was a dark-complexioned, curly-headed boy, with a turned-up little nose, very fresh red lips, which rarely closed over his white and rather prominent upper teeth, fine dark-blue eyes, and a remarkably alert expression. He never smiled, but either looked very serious, or laughed heartily with a clear, ringing, and very infectious laugh. His unusual beauty struck me at first sight. I felt irresistibly attracted to him. To see him was enough to make me quite happy; and at that time all my soul was in that one wish. If three or four days chanced to pass without my having seen him, I began to feel dull and sad even to tears. All my dreams, both waking and sleeping, were of him: when I lay down to sleep, I longed to dream of him; when I shut my eyes, I saw him before me, and cherished the vision as the greatest delight. So precious was this feeling that I could not have confided it to anyone. He obviously preferred to play and talk with Volodya rather than with me, possibly because it annoyed him to feel my restless eyes constantly fixed upon him, or simply because he felt no sympathy for me. But nevertheless I was content; I desired nothing, demanded nothing, and was ready to sacrifice everything for him. Besides the passionate attachment with which he inspired me, his presence aroused another feeling in a no less powerful degree—a fear of hurting, of offending him in any way, or of displeasing him. I felt as much fear for him as love, perhaps because his face had a haughty expression, or because, despising my own appearance, I valued beauty too highly in others, or, what is most probable of all, because this is an infallible sign of love. The first time Seryozha spoke to me, I lost my wits to such a degree at this unexpected bliss that I turned pale, blushed, and could make no reply. He had a bad habit when he was thinking, of staring fixedly at some object blinking incessantly, and twitching his nose and eyebrows at the same time. Everyone agreed that this habit was an ugly one but I thought it so charming that I involuntarily acquired it myself. A few days after our first acquaintance Grandmamma inquired whether my eyes pained me, that I was blinking like an owl. Not one word of love was ever uttered between us; but he felt his power over me, and exercised it unconsciously but tyrannically in our childish intercourse. As for me, though I yearned to pour out my heart to him, I was too much afraid of him to speak plainly; I endeavoured to seem indifferent, and submitted to him without a murmur. At times his influence appeared to me oppressive, intolerable; but it was not in my power to escape from it.

It saddens me to think of that fresh, beautiful feeling of unselfish and unbounded love, which died away without having found vent or met with a return.

Why is it that when I was a child, I strove to be like a grown-up person, and when I ceased to be a child, I so often longed to be like one?

How often did this desire not to seem like a child in my relations with Seryozha restrain the feeling which was ready to pour forth, and cause me to dissimulate! Not only did I never dare to kiss him, which I very much wanted to do at times, to take his hand, to tell him that I was glad to see him, but I did not even dare to call him Seryozha, and kept strictly to the more formal Sergei. Every expression of feeling was considered childish, and to indulge in such show of feeling merely proved that one was still a *little boy*. Without having, as yet, gone through those bitter trials which lead adults to caution and coldness in their intercourse with each other, we deprived ourselves of the pure enjoyment of tender, childish affection, simply through the strange desire to imitate *grown-up* people.

I met the Ivins in the anteroom, exchanged greetings with them, and then flew headlong to Grandmamma. I announced their arrival with as much delight as if this news must render her completely happy. Then, without taking my eyes off Seryozha, I followed him into the drawing-room, watching his every movement. While Grandmamma was telling him that he had grown a great deal, regarding him with her piercing eyes, I experienced that sensation of fear and hope which a painter must experience when awaiting the verdict upon his work from a judge whom he respects.

Herr Frost, the Ivins' young tutor, with Grandmamma's permission, went into the front garden with us, seated himself on a green bench, crossed his legs picturesquely, placing between them a cane with a bronze head, and began to smoke his cigar with the air of a man who is very well satisfied with his own conduct.

Herr Frost was a German, but a German of a very different sort than our good Karl Ivanich. In the first place, he spoke Russian correctly, spoke French with a bad accent, and generally enjoyed, especially among the ladies, the reputation of being a very learned man; in the second place, he wore a red moustache, a big ruby pin in his black satin cravat, the ends of which were tucked through his braces, and light blue trousers with spring bottoms and straps; in the third place, he was young, had a handsome, self-satisfied exterior, and a pair of remarkably fine muscular legs. It was evident that he was particularly proud of the latter; he considered them irresistible for the opposite sex, and perhaps that was why he tried to exhibit them as much as possible, and, whether standing or sitting, always put his calves in motion. He was a type of the young Russian German, who aspires to be a gay fellow and a lady's man.

We were very merry in the garden. Our game of robbers could not have been more successful; but one circumstance came near ruining everything. Seryozha was the robber; as he was hastening in pursuit of the travellers he stumbled, and struck his knee against a tree so violently that I thought he must have broken it. In spite of the fact that I was the gendarme, and that it was my duty to capture him, I approached, and sympathetically inquired if he was hurt. Seryozha got angry with me; he clenched his fists and stamped his foot and in a voice which showed plainly that he was badly hurt, he shouted:

"Well, what of it? You're spoiling the whole game! Come on, catch me! Why don't you catch me?" he repeated several times, glancing sideways at Volodya and the elder Ivin, who, as the travellers, were racing down along the path; and all at once he gave a shriek, and rushed after them with a loud laugh.

I cannot describe how impressed I was by this heroic conduct. In spite of the terrible pain, he not only did not cry, but he did not even show that he was hurt, and never for a moment forgot the game.

Shortly after this, when Ilenka Grap also joined our company, and we went upstairs to play till dinner-time, Seryozha once again astounded and delighted me by his remarkable courage and firmness of character.

Ilenka Grap was the son of a poor foreigner who had once lived at my grandfather's, was indebted to him in some way, and now considered it his imperative duty to send his son to us very often. If he supposed that our acquaintance would afford any honour or satisfaction to his son, he was entirely mistaken; for we not only did not make friends with Ilenka, but we only noticed him when we wanted to make fun of him. Ilenka Grap was a tall, thin boy of thirteen, with a pale, bird-like face and a good-naturedly submissive expression. He was very poorly dressed, but his hair was always so excessively greased that we declared that, on sunny days, Grap's pomade melted and trickled down under his jacket. As I recall him now, I find that he was very obliging, gentle and kind; but at that time he appeared to me as a contemptible creature, whom it was not necessary to pity or even to think of.

When the game of robbers came to an end we went upstairs, and began to cut capers and to show off various gymnastic tricks before each other. Ilenka watched us with a timid smile of admiration, and when we proposed that he try in his turn, he refused, saying that he was not strong enough. Seryozha looked wonderfully charming. He had taken off his jacket. His cheeks and eyes were blazing; he laughed incessantly, and invented all sorts of new tricks; he leaped over three chairs placed in a row, executed cart wheels, stood on his head on Tatishchev's lexicon, which he placed in the middle of the room for a pedestal, and at the same time cut such funny capers with his feet that we could not help laughing. After this last performance he pondered for a moment—blinking his eyes as usual—and went up to Ilenka with a perfectly sober face. "Now, you do that; it really is not difficult." Grap, perceiving that general attention was directed to him, turned red, and declared, in a faint voice, that he could not possibly do it.

"What's the matter with the fellow? Why won't he do anything? You'd think he was a girl! He's *got* to stand on his head!"

And Seryozha took him by the hand.

"Yes, yes, on your head at once!" we all shouted, surrounding Ilenka, who at that moment was visibly terrified, and had turned quite pale. We seized his arms, and dragged him to the lexicon.

"Let me go; I'll do it myself! You'll tear my jacket," cried the unhappy victim. But these cries of despair merely excited us the more; we were choking with laughter; the green jacket was cracking in every seam.

Volodya and the eldest Ivin bent his head down and placed it on the dictionary; Seryozha and I seized the poor boy's thin legs, which he flourished in all directions, rolled his trousers up to the knee, and roaring with laughter, held his legs high up in the air, while the youngest Ivin tried to balance the rest of his body.

Suddenly our noisy laughter subsided and we all fell silent, and it was so quiet ˙n the room that the unfortunate Grap's breathing alone was audible. At that moment I was by no means certain that all this was so very laughable and amusing.

"There's a fine fellow now," said Seryozha, slapping him.

Ilenka remained silent, and in his endeavour to free himself flung his legs out in all directions. In one of these desperate movements he struck Seryozha in the eye with his heel so painfully that Seryozha instantly released the leg, clasped his own eye, from which the unbidden tears were streaming, and pushed Ilenka with all his might. Ilenka, being no longer supported by us, crashed heavily to the floor, and all he could utter for his tears was—

"Why do you torment me so?"

The woeful figure of poor Ilenka, with his tear-stained face, disordered hair, and his tucked-up trousers, under which his dirty boot-legs were visible, sobered us, and we stood silent, forcing ourselves to smile.

Seryozha was the first to recover himself.

"You silly snivelling cry-baby," he said, pushing him lightly with his foot; "Can't take a joke. That's enough now. Get up."

"You are a nasty, wicked boy!" said Ilenka angrily, and turning away, he sobbed loudly.

"What! First you kick me, and then you call me names!" shouted Seryozha, seizing the lexicon and swinging it over the head of the wretched boy, who never thought of defending himself, and only covered his head with his hands.

"Take that! And that! Let's leave him alone, if he can't understand a joke. Let's go downstairs," said Seryozha, with a forced laugh.

I gazed with sympathy at the poor fellow, who lay on the floor, hiding his face on the lexicon, and crying so that it seemed as if he would die of the convulsions that shook his whole body.

"Oh, Sergei!" I said to him, "why did you do that?"

"That's a good one! I didn't cry, did I, when I cut my knee nearly to the bone today."

"Yes, that's true," I thought; "Ilenka is nothing but a cry-baby. Seryozha now, there's a brave fellow for you!"

I had no idea that the poor boy was crying not so much from physical pain as from the thought that five boys, whom he probably liked, had all joined, without any cause, in hating and persecuting him.

I really cannot explain to myself the cruelty of my own conduct. Why did I not go to him, defend him, comfort him? What had become of the compassionate feelings which had made me cry violently at the sight of a young raven which had fallen out of its nest, or a puppy which was to be thrown out, or a chicken which the cook was carrying off for soup?

Had this beautiful feeling been overshadowed by love for Seryozha, and the desire to appear as manly in his sight as he was himself? If so, that love and that desire to appear manly were not enviable qualities. They are the only dark spots in the pages of my childish memories.

Chapter XX

WE HAVE VISITORS

Judging by the unusual activity in the pantry, the brilliant illumination, which imparted a new and festive aspect to objects in the drawing-room and *salon* which had long been familiar to me, and especially by the fact that Prince Ivan Ivanich had sent his musicians to our house, a large number of guests were expected that evening.

I ran to the window at the sound of every passing carriage, pressed my nose to the glass and peered out into the street with impatient curiosity. Through the darkness, which at first concealed all objects from the window, there gradually appeared, across the way, the familiar shop with a lantern beside it; the large house with two lighted windows on the lower floor further down; in the middle of the street some poor cabby with two passengers, or an empty calash returning home at a foot-pace. But now a carriage drove up to the porch, and in the full conviction that it was the Ivins, who had promised to come early, I ran down to meet them in the anteroom. Instead of the Ivins, two ladies appeared behind the liveried servant who opened the door: one was tall, and wore a blue cloak with a sable collar; the other, who was small, was all wrapped up in a green shawl, beneath which her little feet, shod in fur boots, alone were visible. Paying no attention to my presence in the anteroom—although I thought it my duty to make them a bow—the little one went up to the big one and halted in front of her. The big one unwound the kerchief which covered the little one's head, unbuttoned her cloak, and when the liveried footman took charge of these things and pulled off her little fur boots, there appeared from all these wraps a beautiful little girl of about twelve, dressed in a low-necked white muslin frock, white pantallettes, and tiny black slippers. There was a black velvet ribbon on her little white neck; her head was a mass of dark chestnut curls, which suited her lovely face admirably, and fell upon her white shoulders so charmingly that I would not have believed Karl Ivanich himself if he had told me that they curled so because they had been twisted up in bits of the *Moscow Gazette* ever since the morning and pinched with hot irons. She seemed to have been born with that curly head.

A striking feature of her face was her unusually large, prominent, half-closed eyes, which formed a strange but agreeable contrast to her tiny mouth. Her lips were tightly closed; and her eyes had such a serious look, and the general expression of her face was such that you would not look for a smile on it; and that made her smile all the more enchanting.

I slipped in the hall, endeavouring to remain unperceived, and began to walk back and forth, pretending to be deep in thought and unaware that guests had arrived.

When they reached the middle of the room I started, made my bow, and informed them that Grandmamma was in the drawing-room. Madame Valakhina, whose face pleased me extremely, especially because I discerned in it a strong resemblance of her daughter Sonechka, nodded graciously to me.

Grandmamma appeared to be very glad to see Sonechka: she called her over to her, smoothed away a curl that had fallen over her forehead, and, gazing attentively at her face, she said, "*Quelle charmante enfant!*" Sonechka smiled and blushed so prettily that I blushed too as I looked at her.

"I hope it will not be dull for you here, my child," said Grandmamma, taking her chin and raising her little face. "Pray enjoy yourself and dance to your heart's content. So we have one lady and two gentlemen already," she added, turning to Madame Valakhina, and touching me with her hand.

This bringing us together pleased me so much that I blushed again.

Conscious that my shyness was increasing, and hearing the sound of carriage wheels, I withdrew. In the anteroom I found Princess Kornakova with her son and an incredible number of daughters. The daughters were all exactly alike—they resembled the Princess, and were ugly; not one of them was worth looking at. As they took off their cloaks and shook out their trains, they all began to talk in shrill voices, fussing and laughing at something—probably at the fact that there were so many of them. Etienne was a tall, fleshy lad of fifteen, with a bloodless face, sunken eyes with blue circles beneath them, and hands and feet which were enormous for his age: he was awkward, had a gruff and disagreeable voice, but appeared very well satisfied with himself, and according to my views he was precisely the sort of boy who gets whipped with a switch.

We stood for a while facing each other without uttering a word, examining each other attentively. Then we approached a little nearer, apparently intending to kiss each other, but we changed our minds for some reason or other after we had looked into each other's eyes. When the dresses of all his sisters rustled past us, I inquired, for the sake of beginning the conversation, whether they had not been very crowded in the carriage.

"I don't know," he answered carelessly, "for I never ride in the carriage, because it makes me feel sick, and Mamma knows it. When we go anywhere in the evening I always sit on the box. It's much jollier, you can see everything; Philip lets me drive, and sometimes I take the whip, too. Sometimes, you know, the passers-by catch it," he added, with an expressive gesture: "it's great fun!"

"Your excellency," said the footman, entering the anteroom, "Philip wants to know where you were pleased to put the whip?"

"Why, I gave it to him, of course."

"He says that you did not."

"Well, then, I hung it on the lantern."

"Philip says that it is not on the lantern; and you had better say that you took it and lost it, or Philip will have to pay for your pranks out of his own money," continued the footman, his anger rising.

The footman, who seemed to be a respectable but sullen man, appeared to take Philip's side, and was resolved to clear up this matter at any cost. With an involuntary show of tact I stepped aside, as though I had observed nothing. But the lackeys who were present behaved quite differently; they came nearer, and gazed approvingly at the old servant.

"Very well, then I lost it, what of it?" said Etienne, evading further explanations. "I'll pay him what this whip is worth. This is amusing!" he added, approaching me and leading me towards the drawing-room.

"Excuse me, sir, how are you going to pay? I know you have been eight months paying Marya Vasilyevna twenty kopeks, and it's the same in my case, and it's two years since Petrushka—"

"Hold your tongue!" shouted the young Prince, turning pale with rage. "I will tell."

"You'll tell, you'll tell!" mocked the footman. "For shame, your excellency," he added feelingly as we entered the drawing-room, and he went to the wardrobe with the cloaks.

"That's right, that's right!" said an approving voice behind us in the anteroom.

Grandmamma had a peculiar gift for expressing her opinion of people when she so wished, by using the singular and plural pronouns of the second person with particular emphasis. She employed *you* and *thou* in exactly the opposite sense to that generally accepted, and with her the words acquired an entirely different significance. When the young Prince approached her, she at first addressed a few words to him, calling him *you,* and regarding him with such an expression of scorn that had I been in his place I should have been utterly abashed. But evidently Etienne was not a boy of that stamp: he not only paid no heed to Grandmamma's reception, but even to her person, and saluted the whole company, if not gracefully, at least without constraint.

Sonechka occupied all my attention. I remember that when Volodya, Etienne, and I were talking together in a part of the room from which we could see Sonechka, and she could see and hear us, I talked with pleasure; when I had occasion to utter what seemed to me an amusing or manly remark, I spoke loudly and glanced at the drawing-room door; but when we changed to another place from which it was impossible to be seen or heard from the drawing-room, I fell silent and found no further pleasure in the conversation.

The drawing-room and *salon* gradually filled with guests. As always happens at children's parties, there were several older children among the number, who were not willing to miss an opportunity of dancing and making merry, but pretended to do so merely for the sake of pleasing the hostess.

When the Ivins arrived, instead of the pleasure which I generally experienced at meeting Seryozha, I was conscious of a curious feeling of vexation at the thought that he would see Sonechka, and she would see him.

Chapter XXI

BEFORE THE MAZURKA

"I see you are going to have dancing," said Seryozha, coming from the drawing-room and pulling a pair of new kid gloves from his pocket; "I must put on my gloves."

"What shall we do—we have no gloves," I thought; "I must go upstairs and hunt for some."

But although I rummaged in all the drawers, all I found was our green travelling mittens and one kid glove, which was of no use whatever to me—in the first place because it was very old and soiled, in the second because it was too large for me, and especially because the middle finger was missing, having been cut off long ago, probably by Karl Ivanich for a sore hand. Nevertheless, I put this remnant of a glove upon my hand, and stared at the place on my middle finger which was always stained with ink.

"If Natalya Savishna were here, she would surely find me some gloves." It was impossible to go downstairs without them, because, if they asked me why I did not dance, what could I say? To remain here was equally impossible, because I was sure to be missed. What was to be done?

"What are you doing here?" asked Volodya, running in; "Go and engage your lady, the dancing will begin directly."

"Volodya," I said despairingly, showing him my hand with two fingers thrust into the dirty glove, "Volodya, you have forgotten this."

"What?" said he impatiently. "Ah! gloves," he added, carelessly. "That's true, we have none. We must ask Grandmamma what she thinks about it." And, without pausing to reflect, he ran downstairs.

Reassured by his coolness on a point which seemed to me so weighty, I hastened to the drawing-room, completely forgetting that I still wore the torn glove on my left hand.

Cautiously approaching Grandmamma's arm-chair, and touching her mantle lightly, I said in a whisper:

"Grandmamma, what are we to do? We have no gloves!"

"What, my dear?"

"We have no gloves," I repeated, drawing nearer and nearer, and laying both hands on the arm of her chair.

"And what is this?" she said, all at once seeing my left hand. "*Voyez, ma chere,*" she went on, turning to Madame Valakhina, "this young man has made himself elegant in order to dance with your daughter."

Grandmamma held me firmly by the hand, and gazed gravely and inquiringly at her guests until the curiosity of the whole company was satisfied and the laugh had become general.

I should have been very much upset if Seryozha had seen me at the moment when, frowning with shame, I vainly endeavoured to tear my hand free; but I was not at all discomfited by the presence of Sonechka, who laughed until her eyes were filled with tears and all her

93

curls fluttered about her flushed face. I saw that her laugh was too hearty and natural to be mocking; on the contrary, we laughed together, and that seemed to draw us nearer to each other. This episode of the glove, although it might have ended badly, gained me the advantage of putting me at my ease in the circle which had always seemed to me most terrible—the drawing-room circle; I no longer felt the slightest shyness as I entered the ball-room.

The sufferings of shy people come from their uncertainty as to the opinion which people have formed of them; as soon as this opinion bad or good, is clearly expressed, the suffering ceases.

How charming Sonechka Valakhina was as she danced opposite me in the French quadrille with the clumsy young Prince! How sweetly she smiled when she gave me her little hand in the chain! How prettily her golden curls waved in measure, how naïvely she brought her tiny feet together! When, in the fifth figure, my partner left me and went to the other side, and I waited for the beat in preparation for my solo, Sonechka closed her lips seriously and looked aside. But her fear for me was unnecessary. I boldly made my *chassé* to the front, *chassé* to the rear, and my glide; and when I approached her I playfully showed her my glove with my two fingers sticking out. She burst out into peals of laughter, and her little feet tripped about upon the waxed floor more bewitchingly than ever. I still remember how, when we formed a circle and all joined hands, she bent her little head and, without removing her hand from mine, scratched her little nose with her glove. I can still see all this as though it were directly before my eyes, and I still hear the quadrille from *The Danube Maid,* to whose music all this took place.

The second quadrille I danced with Sonechka herself. Yet when we went to sit down together during the interval I felt extremely awkward and did not know in the least what to say to her. When my silence had lasted too long I began to fear that she would take me for a fool, and I resolved to rescue her from any such error on my account at any cost. "*Vous êtes une habitante de Moscou?*" I said to her, and after receiving an answer in the affirmative I went on: "*Et moi je n'ai encore jamais fréquenté la capitale,*" reckoning particularly on the effect which the word "*fréquenté*" would produce. Yet, I felt that although this was a very brilliant beginning, and fully proved my knowledge of the French language, I was incapable of continuing the conversation in this strain. Our turn to dance would not come very soon, and silence fell again. I glanced at her uneasily, anxious to know what impression I had produced, and waiting for her to help me. "Where did you find such a funny glove?" she inquired suddenly to my greatest pleasure and relief. I explained that the glove belonged to Karl Ivanich, talked rather ironically about Karl Ivanich himself, telling her how funny he looked when he took off his red cap, and how once, dressed in his green overcoat, he had fallen off his horse right into a puddle, and so forth. The quadrille passed off without our perceiving it. It was all very pleasant; but why had I made fun of Karl Ivanich? Should I have lost Sonechka's good opinion if I had described him with the love and respect which I felt for him?

When the quadrille came to an end, Sonechka said "Thank you," with as sweet an expression as though I had really deserved her gratitude. I was beside myself with joy, and did not know myself whence I had obtained such daring, confidence, and even boldness. "Nothing can abash me," I thought, walking carelessly up and down the ball-room; "I am ready for anything."

Seryozha asked me to be his *vis-à-vis*. "Very well," said I; "I have no partner, but I will find one." Casting

95

a decisive glance about the room, I perceived that all the ladies were engaged save one—a young lady standing at the parlour door. A young man was approaching her with the intention, as I concluded, of inviting her to dance; he was within a couple of paces of her, while I was at the end of the hall. In the twinkling of an eye I flew across the intervening space, sliding gracefully over the polished floor, and, with a scrape of my foot and in a firm voice, I invited her for the dance. The young lady smiled patronizingly, gave me her hand, and the young man was left partnerless.

I was so conscious of my power that I paid no heed to the young man's vexation though afterwards I learned that he inquired who that frowsy boy was who had jumped in front of him and taken away his partner.

Chapter XXII

THE MAZURKA

The young man whom I had robbed of his lady danced the mazurka in the first pair. He sprang to his feet, took his lady by the hand, and, instead of making the *pas de Basques,* as Mimi had taught us, he simply ran forward. When he had reached the corner he halted, cracked his heels, turned around, and went skipping on farther.

As I had no partner for the mazurka, I sat behind Grandmamma's high chair and looked on.

"Why does he do that?" I pondered. "That's not the way Mimi taught us at all. She always said that everybody danced the mazurka on their toes, moving their feet in a round gliding motion; but it turns out that they don't dance that way at all. And there are the Ivins and Etienne all dancing, and none of them doing the *pas de Basques*. Even Volodya has picked up the new fashion!

It's not bad! And how lovely Sonechka is! There she goes!"

I was very merry.

The mazurka was nearing its end. Several elderly ladies and gentlemen came up to take leave of Grandmamma and departed. The lackeys, skilfully keeping out of the way of the dancers, brought the dishes into the back-room. Grandmamma was evidently tired, and seemed to speak unwillingly, and very slowly; the musicians lazily began the same tune for the thirtieth time. The young lady with whom I had danced caught sight of me as she was going through a figure, and, smiling treacherously—she must have wanted to please Grandmamma— she led Sonechka and one of the innumerable princesses up to me. "Rose or nettle?" said she.

"Ah, so you are here!" said Grandmamma, turning round in her chair. "Go and dance, my dear."

Although at that moment I would much rather have hid my head under Grandmamma's chair than emerge from behind it, how could I refuse? I stood up and said "Rose," as I glanced timidly at Sonechka. Before I could recover myself, some one's hand in a white kid glove rested in mine, and the Princess started forward with a pleasant smile, without the least suspicion that I did not in the least know what to do with my feet.

I knew that the *pas de Basques* were unsuitable, improper and could even disgrace me; but the well-known sounds of the mazurka acting upon my ear communicated a familiar movement to the acoustic nerves, which in turn communicated it to my feet, and the latter, quite involuntarily, and to the amazement of all beholders, began the fatal circular gliding step on the tips of the toes. As long as we proceeded straight ahead we got on after a fashion; but when we turned I observed that, unless I took some precautions, I should certainly get in advance. In order to avoid such a catastrophe I stopped short,

with the intention of making the same swift turn which
the young man in the first couple had done so beautifully.
But at the very moment when I separated my feet and
was preparing to spring, the Princess, circling hastily
around me, looked down at my feet with an expression
of stupified curiosity and amazement. That look finished
me. I lost my self-possession to such an extent that
instead of dancing I stamped my feet up and down in one
spot in the strangest fashion, and finally came to a dead
standstill. Every one stared at me, some with surprise,
others with curiosity, with amazement, or sympathy;
Grandmamma alone looked on with complete indifference.

"You should not dance if you do not know how," said
Papa's angry voice in my ear; and thrusting me aside
with a light push, he took my partner's hand, danced a
turn with her in the old-fashioned way to the vast delight
of the lookers-on, and led her to her seat. The mazurka
immediately came to an end.

Lord, why dost Thou punish me so terribly?

. . . .

Everybody despises me, and will always despise me.
The paths to everything—love, friendship, honour—are
closed to me. All is lost! Why did Volodya make signs
to me which every one saw, and which were of no use
to me? Why did that hateful Princess look at my feet like
that? Why did Sonechka—she was lovely, but why did she
smile just then? Why did Papa turn red, and seize my
hand? Was even he ashamed of me? Oh, this was frightful! If Mamma had been there she would not have blushed
for her Nikolenka. And my fancy bore me far away
to this sweet vision. I recalled the meadow in front of
the house, the tall lime-trees in the garden, the clear
pond over which the swallows fluttered, the blue sky in
which hung transparent white clouds, the perfumed stacks
of fresh hay; and many other joyous, soothing memories
were borne in upon my distracted imagination.

Chapter XXIII

AFTER THE MAZURKA

At supper the young man who had danced in the first couple sat down at the children's table with us and paid special attention to me, which would have flattered my vanity not a little if I had been capable of feeling anything at all after the catastrophe which had occurred to me. But the young man seemed determined to cheer me up. He jested with me, called me a fine fellow; and when none of the grown-up people were looking, he helped me to wine from various bottles and pressed me to drink. At the end of the supper, when the butler poured me only a quarter of my little wine glass of champagne from his napkin-wrapped bottle, and the young man insisted that he should pour it full, and made me swallow it at one gulp, I felt an agreeable warmth through all my body and a special kindliness towards my jolly protector, and I laughed gaily.

All at once the sounds of the "Grandfather" dance resounded from the ball-room, and the guests began to rise from the table. My friendship with the young man immediately came to an end; he went off to the grown-ups, while I, not daring to follow, approached with a curiosity to hear what Madame Valakhina was saying to her daughter.

"Please just half an hour more," Sonechka entreated.

"Impossible, my angel."

"Oh please, for my sake," she coaxed.

"Will it make you happy if I am ill tomorrow?" said Madame Valakhina, and was so imprudent as to smile.

"Then we may stay? Yes?" cried Sonechka, dancing with joy.

"What am I to do? Very well, go and dance. Here's a partner for you," she said, pointing at me.

Sonechka gave me her hand, and we ran into the ball-room.

The wine which I had drunk, Sonechka's presence and gaiety, made me quite forget my miserable scrape in the mazurka. I cut amusing capers with my feet; I imitated a horse, and went at a gentle trot, lifting my legs proudly, then I stamped on one spot like a ram provoked by a dog, and laughed heartily, without caring in the least what impression I might produce upon the spectators. Sonechka, too, never ceased to laugh: she laughed when we circled round hand-in-hand, she laughed when she looked at some old gentleman who lifted his feet with care and stepped over a handkerchief, pretending that it was very difficult for him to do it, and she nearly died with laughter when I leaped almost to ceiling in order to display my agility.

As I passed through Grandmamma's study I glanced at myself in the mirror: my face was bathed in perspiration, my hair was in disorder, the tuft on the crown of my head stood up worse than ever; but my general expression was so merry, kind, and healthy, that I was even pleased with myself.

"If I were always like this," I thought, "I might yet be able to please."

But when I glanced again at the lovely little face of my partner, I saw there, besides gaiety, health, and freedom from care which had pleased me in my own, so much gentle and elegant beauty that I was vexed with myself; I understood how stupid it was of *me* to hope to attract the attention of such a wonderful being to myself.

I could not hope to be loved in return, and, indeed, I did not think of it: my soul was overflowing with happiness. I could not imagine that, in return for the love which filled my soul with joy, one might ask for any greater happiness or desire anything more than that this feeling might never end. I was happy. My heart fluttered like a dove, the blood poured into it incessantly, and I wanted to cry.

When we went through the corridor, past the dark store-room under the stairs, I glanced at it and thought: What bliss it would be if I could live for ever with her in that dark store-room, and if nobody knew that we lived there!

"Isn't it jolly tonight?" I said in a quiet, trembling voice, and hastened my steps, frightened not so much at what I had said, but at what I had been minded to say.

"Yes, very," she replied, turning her little head towards me with such a frank, kind expression that my fears vanished.

"Especially after supper. But if you only knew how sorry (I wanted to say *unhappy*, but did not dare) I am that you are going away so soon, and that we shall not see each other any more!"

"Why shall we not see each other?" said she, regarding intently the toes of her slippers, and drawing her fingers along the grated screen which we were passing. "Mamma and I go to the Tverskoi Boulevard every Tuesday and Friday. Don't you ever go for walks?"

"I shall ask permission to go next Tuesday; and if they won't let me, I'll run away alone, without my hat even. I know the way."

"Do you know what I have just thought of?" said Sonechka suddenly, "I always say *thou* to the boys who come to our house; let us call each other *thou*. Dost thou agree?" she added, throwing back her little head and looking me straight in the eye.

At this moment we entered the ball-room, and the second lively part of "Grandfather" was beginning. "I agree with ... you," I said thinking that the noise and music would drown my words.

"Say *thee*," corrected Sonechka, with a laugh.

"Grandfather" ended, and I had not managed to utter a single phrase with *thou*, although I never ceased inventing such as would allow of several repetitions of that pronoun. I had not sufficient courage. "Wilt thou?" resounded in my ears and produced a kind of intoxication. I saw nothing and nobody but Sonechka. I saw her locks tucked away behind her ears, disclosing portions of her brow and temples which I had not seen before; I saw her being wrapped up in the green shawl so closely that only the tip of her little nose was visible; indeed if she had not made a little opening near her mouth with her rosy little fingers she would surely have suffocated; and I saw how she turned quickly towards us, as she descended the stairs with her mother, nodded her head, and disappeared through the door.

Volodya, the Ivins, the young Prince, and I were all in love with Sonechka, and we followed her with our eyes as we stood on the stairs. I do not know to whom in particular she nodded her little head, but at that moment I was firmly convinced that it was to me.

As I took leave of the Ivins I talked and shook hands quite unconstrainedly, and even rather coldly, with Seryozha. If he understood that on that day he had lost both my love and his power over me, he was surely sorry for it, though he endeavoured to appear quite indifferent.

For the first time in my life I was unfaithful to my love, and for the first time I experienced the sweetness of that feeling. It delighted me to exchange a worn-out sentiment of familiar affection for the fresh feeling of a love full of mystery and uncertainty. Moreover, to fall out of love and into love at the same time means loving with twice the previous fervour.

Chapter XXIV

IN BED

"How could I love Seryozha so passionately and so long?" I meditated as I lay in bed. "No, he never understood me, he was unable to appreciate my love, and was never worthy of it. And Sonechka? What a darling! 'Wilt thou?' 'It is thy turn to begin.'"

I sprang up in bed as I vividly pictured to myself her little face, covered my head with the coverlet, tucked it under me on all sides, and when no opening remained anywhere I lay down and, with a pleasant sensation of warmth, buried myself in sweet visions and memories. Fixing my gaze immovably upon the lining of the wadded quilt, I saw her as clearly as I had seen her an hour before; I conversed with her mentally, and that conversation, though utterly lacking in sense, afforded me indescribable delight, because the pronoun *thou*, to *thee*, with *thee* and *thine* occurred in it constantly.

These visions were so clear that I could not sleep for sweet emotion, and I wanted to share my superabundance of bliss with some one.

"The darling!" I said almost aloud, turning abruptly on the other side. "Volodya! are you awake?"

"No," he replied in a sleepy voice; "what is it?"

"I am in love, Volodya. I am decidedly in love with Sonechka."

"Well, what of it?" he answered, stretching himself.

"Oh, Volodya! you cannot imagine what is going on within me: here I was just now lying tucked up in the coverlet, and I saw her so plainly, so plainly, and I talked with her; it was simply marvellous! And, do you know, when I lie thinking of her I feel so sad, that I could cry."

Volodya moved.

"There's only one thing I wish," I went on; "that is, to be always with her, to see her always, and nothing else. And are you in love? Tell me the truth, Volodya!"

It's odd, but I wanted everybody to be in love with Sonechka, and I wanted them all to talk about it.

"What is that to you?" said Volodya, turning his face towards me; "perhaps."

"You don't want to sleep; you are only pretending!" I cried, perceiving by his shining eyes that he was not thinking of sleep in the least; and I flung aside the coverlet. "Let's talk about her. She's a darling, isn't she? So sweet that if she were to say to me, 'Nikolenka! jump out of the window, or throw yourself into the fire,' I swear I should do it at once," said I, "and with joy. Ah, how bewitching she is!" I added, as I called her before me in imagination, and in order to enjoy myself in this manner to the fullest extent, I rolled abruptly over on the other side and thrust my head under the pillow. "Oh, I want to cry dreadfully, Volodya!"

"What a fool!" said he, smiling, and then was silent for a while. "I don't feel a bit like you: I think that, if it were possible, I would rather sit beside her and talk."

"Ah! so you are in love too?" I interrupted.

"And then," continued Volodya, smiling tenderly, "then I would kiss her little fingers, her eyes, her lips, her nose, her tiny feet—I would kiss her all over."

"Nonsense!" cried I from under the pillow.

"You don't understand anything about it," said Volodya contemptuously.

"Yes, I do understand, but you don't, and you're talking nonsense," I said through my tears.

"Well, there's nothing to cry about. What a cry-baby you are!"

Chapter XXV

THE LETTER

On the 16th of April, nearly six months after the day just described, Father came upstairs to us, during our lesson hour, and told us that we were going to the country with him that night. My heart contracted at this news, and my thoughts at once turned to my mother.

The following letter was the cause of our unexpected departure:

Petrovskoye, 12th April

"I have just received your dear letter of 3rd April, at ten o'clock in the evening, and, as usual, I answer it immediately. Fyodor brought it from town last night, but, as it was late, he gave it to Mimi. And Mimi, since I was ill and nervous, kept it from me all day. I really have been a little feverish, and, to tell the truth, this is the fourth day that I have been in bed.

"Pray do not be alarmed, my dear; I feel quite well, and, if Ivan Vasilich permits me, I think of getting up tomorrow.

"On Friday I took the children for a ride; but the horses stuck in the mud close to the entrance to the highway, near that very bridge which has always frightened me. The day was very fine, and I thought I would go as far as the highway on foot, while they pulled the calash out. When I reached the chapel I had to sit down, I was so tired; and in this way about half-an-hour elapsed while they were summoning people to pull the carriage out. I felt cold, particularly in my feet, for I had on thin-soled shoes, and they were wet through. After dinner I felt feverish, but I did not go to bed, and after tea as usual sat down to play a duet with Lyubochka. (You would not recognize her, she has made such progress!) But imagine my surprise when I found that I could not count the time. I began to count several times, but my head was all dizzy, and I felt a strange noise in my ears. I counted one, two, three, then all at once eight and fifteen; and most curious thing was that I knew that I was talking nonsense and could not help it. Finally Mimi came to my assistance, and put me to bed, almost by force. There, my dear, you have a detailed account of how I became ill, and how I myself am to blame. The next day I had quite a high fever, and our good old Ivan Vasilich came; he has not left us since, and promises to put me on my feet again very soon. What a wonderful old man he is! When I had the fever and was delirious, he sat up by me all night and now, as he knows that I am writing, he is sitting with the girls, and from my bedroom I can hear him telling them German stories, and them dying with laughter as they listen.

"*La belle Flamande*, as you call her, has been staying with me for two weeks past, because her mother has gone off visiting somewhere, and she is most attentive and attached to me. She intrusts me with all the secrets of her heart. If she were in good hands, she might turn out a very fine girl, with her beautiful face, kind heart, and youth; but she will be utterly ruined in the society in which she lives, judging from her own account. It has occurred to me that, if I had not so many children, I should be doing a good deed in taking charge of her.

"Lyubochka wanted to write to you herself; but she has already torn up the third sheet of paper, and says, 'I know what a scoffer Papa is; if you make a single mistake, he'll show it to everybody.' Katenka is as sweet as ever, Mimi as good and boring.

"Now I will talk to you about serious matters. You write that your affairs are not going well this winter, and that you are obliged to take the income from Khabarovka. It surprises me that you should even ask my consent to that. Surely what belongs to me belongs equally to you.

"You are so kind and good that you conceal the real state of things for fear of troubling me: but I guess that you have probably lost a great deal at cards, and I assure you that I am not angry at you; therefore, if you can only tide over this crisis, pray do not think too much of it, and do not worry yourself needlessly. I have become accustomed not to count upon your winnings as regards the children, not even (forgive me) upon your whole estate. Your winnings cause me as little pleasure as your losses cause pain; the only thing which does pain me is your unhappy passion for gambling, which robs me of part of your tender attachment, and forces me to tell you such bitter truths as I tell you now—and God knows how this hurts me! I shall not cease to pray God for one thing, that He will save us—not from poverty (what is poverty?)—but from that frightful situation when the interests of the children, which I am bound to protect, shall come into conflict with ours. Hitherto the Lord has fulfilled my prayer: you have not passed the line beyond which we must either sacrifice our property—which no longer belongs to us, but to our children—or—it is terrible to think of, yet this dread misfortune continually threatens us. Yes, it is a heavy cross which the Lord has sent to both of us.

"You write about the children, and return to our old dispute: you ask me to consent to send them to some educational institution. You know my prejudices against such education.

"I do not know, my dear friend, whether you will agree with me; but nevertheless I beseech you to promise, for my sake, that never as long as I live, nor after my death, if it shall please God to part us, to do this.

"You write that you must go to St. Petersburg to attend to our affairs. Christ be with you, my friend; go, and return as speedily as possible. It is so wearisome for all of us without you! The spring is wonderfully beautiful. The balcony door has already been taken down, the paths to the hothouse were perfectly dry four days ago, the peach-trees are in full bloom, the snow lingers in a few spots only, the swallows have come, and now Lyubochka has brought me the first spring flowers. The doctor says I shall be quite well in three days, and may breathe the fresh air and warm myself in the April sun. Now, *au revoir*, dear friend: pray do not worry about my illness, nor about your losses; finish your business as speedily as possible, and come to us with the children for the whole summer. I am making great plans for the summer, and your presence alone is lacking for their fulfilment."

The remaining portion of the letter was written in French, in a cramped and uneven hand, on a second scrap of paper. I translate it word for word:

"Do not believe what I wrote to you about my illness; no one suspects how serious it is. I alone know that I shall never rise from my bed again. Do not lose a moment: come, and bring the children. Perhaps I may be able to embrace them once again, and bless them: that is my last wish. I know what a terrible blow I am dealing you; but sooner or later you would have had to receive it either from me or from others. Let us try to bear this misfortune with firmness, and trust in God's mercy. Let us submit to His will.

"Do not think that what I write is the raving of a delirious imagination; on the contrary, my thoughts are remarkably clear at this moment, and I am perfectly composed. Do not console yourself either with vain hopes that these are but the vague and false presentiments of a timid soul. No, I feel, indeed, I know because God was pleased to reveal this to me—that I have not long to live.

"Will my love for you and the children end with this life? I know that this is impossible. At this moment I am too full of love to think that this feeling, without which I cannot conceive of existence, could ever be annihilated. My soul cannot exist without its love for you; and I know that it will exist for ever, by this alone, that such a love as mine could never have been, were it not destined to live for ever.

"I shall not be with you, but I am firmly convinced that my love will never leave you; and this thought is so comforting to my heart that I await my fast approaching death calmly and without fear.

"I am calm, and God knows that I have always regarded death, and still regard it, as a passage to a better life, yet why can I not keep back my tears? Why must my children be deprived of the mother they love? Why deal you so heavy, so unlooked-for a blow? Why must I die, when your love has made my life so infinitely happy?

"May His holy will be done!

"I can write no more for tears. Perhaps I shall not see you. I thank you, my beloved, for all the happiness with which you have surrounded me in this life; I shall pray God that He will reward you. Farewell, dearest one; remember, when I am no more, that my love will never abandon you, wherever you may be. Farewell Volodya, my angel; farewell my little Benjamin, my Nikolenka.

"Can it be that they will forget me?"

This letter enclosed a note in French, from Mimi, which read as follows:

"The sad forebodings of which she speaks are but too well confirmed by the doctor. Last night she ordered me to take this letter to the post at once. Thinking she was delirious, I waited until this morning, and then made up my mind to open it. No sooner had I done so than Natalya Nikolayevna asked me what I had done with the letter, and ordered me to burn it if it had not been sent. She keeps speaking of it, and declared that it will kill you. Do not delay your coming, if you wish to see our angel before she leaves us for ever. Excuse this scrawl. I have not slept for three nights. You know how I love her!"

Natalya Savishna, who had passed the entire night of the 11th of April in Mamma's chamber, told me that, after writing the first part of the letter, Mamma laid it on the little table beside her and went to sleep.

"I confess," said Natalya Savishna, "that I dozed in the arm-chair myself, and my stocking fell from my hands. But about one o'clock I heard in my dreams that she seemed to be talking with some one; I opened my eyes and saw her sitting up in bed, my little dove, with her little hands folded like this, and tears streaming from her eyes. 'So it's all over?' she said, and buried her face in her hands. I sprang up to my feet and asked: 'What is the matter with you?'

" 'Ah, Natalya Savishna, if you only knew what I have just seen!' she said.

"But no matter how I begged her to answer me she would say no more; she only told me to bring the little table, wrote something more, made me seal the letter then and there, and send it off immediately. After that, she grew worse and worse."

Chapter XXVI

WHAT AWAITED US IN THE COUNTRY

On the 18th of April we alighted from our carriage at the porch of the Petrovskoye house. Papa had been very thoughtful when we left Moscow, and when Volodya asked him whether Mamma was ill, he looked sadly at him and nodded in silence. During the journey he seemed to grow calmer; but as we approached home his face assumed a more and more mournful expression, and when, on alighting from the calash, he asked Foka, who ran panting out, "Where is Natalya Nikolayevna?" his voice was not firm, and there were tears in his eyes. Good old Foka glanced at us, dropped his eyes, and opening the door of the anteroom, he turned aside and answered:

"It is the sixth day, sir, that she has not left her room."

Milka, (who, as I afterwards learned, had not ceased to howl mournfully since the day Mamma was taken ill) sprang joyously at Papa, leaped upon him, whined, and licked his hands; but he pushed her aside and went through the drawing-room into the boudoir, from which a door led directly into the bedroom. As he approached the room he grew more and more agitated, as was evident by his every movement: he entered the boudoir on tip-toe, hardly daring to breathe, and crossed himself before he could make up his mind to grasp the handle of the closed door. At that moment Mimi, dishevelled and tear-stained, ran in from the corridor. "Ah, Pyotr Alexandrovich," she said in a whisper, with an expression of genuine despair, and then, observing that Papa was turning the handle, she added almost inaudibly, "Not here. That door is locked. The entrance is through the maids' room."

Oh, how sadly all this affected my childish imagination, attuned to sorrow by a dread foreboding!

We went to the maids' room. In the corridor we encountered Akim, the little fool, who always amused us with his grimaces; but at that moment I saw nothing droll about him—indeed nothing struck me so painfully as his senseless, indifferent face. In the maids' room two maids, who were sitting over their needle work, rose to bow to us with such a sorrowful expression that it frightened me. Passing through Mimi's room next, Papa opened the door of the bedroom, and we entered. To the right of the door were two windows hung with shawls; at one of them sat Natalya Savishna, with her spectacles on her nose, knitting a stocking. She did not kiss us, as she generally did, but merely rose, looked at us through her spectacles, and the tears streamed down her cheeks. It upset me to see people, who had always been calm and self-possessed, begin to cry as soon as they looked at us.

At the left of the door stood a screen, and behind the screen the bed, a little table, a little cabinet full of medicines, and the big arm-chair, in which dozed the doctor; beside the bed stood a young and extremely beautiful girl with very fair hair. The sleeves of her white morning dress turned back, she was applying ice to Mamma's head, but Mamma herself I could not see. This girl was *la belle Flamande* of whom Mamma had written, and who later on played such an important part in the life of our whole family. As soon as we entered she removed her hand from Mamma's head, arranged the folds on the bosom of her gown, and then said in a whisper, "She is unconscious."

I was very wretched at that moment, but I involuntarily noted all these trifles. It was nearly dark in the room, it was hot, and there was a mingled odour of mint, eau de Cologne, camomile, and Hoffmann's drops. This odour impressed me to such a degree that when I smell it, or when I even recall it, my fancy instantly carries me back to that dark, stifling chamber, and reproduces every detail, even the most minute, of that terrible moment.

Mamma's eyes were open, but she saw nothing. I shall never forget that dreadful look. It was so full of suffering.

They led us away.

When I afterwards asked Natalya Savishna about Mamma's last moments, this is what she told me:

"After you were taken away, my dear one was restless for a long time, as though something oppressed her, then she dropped her head on her pillow and dozed as quietly and peacefully as an angel from heaven. I went out to see why they did not bring her drink. When I returned my darling was awake again and was beckoning your Papa to her; he bent over her, but her strength failed her and she could not say what she wished to; she could only open her lips and groan, 'Oh God! Lord! The children, the children!' I wanted to run and fetch you, but Ivan Vasilich stopped me and said, 'It will excite her more; it is better not.' After that she only raised her hand and dropped it again. What she meant by that, God alone knows. I think that she was blessing you in your absence. The Lord did not grant her to see her little ones before the end. Then my little dove raised herself, made this motion with her hand, and spoke in a voice which I cannot bear to think of, 'Mother of God, do not desert them!' Then the pain must have reached her heart. We could see from her eyes how dreadfully the poor thing was suffering; she fell back on the pillows, caught the bed-clothes in her teeth, and her tears flowed and flowed."

"And then?" I asked.

But Natalya Savishna could say no more; she turned away and wept bitterly.

Mamma died in terrible agony.

Chapter XXVII

SORROW

Late in the evening of the following day I wanted to see her once more. I overcame the involuntary feeling of terror, opened the door gently, and entered the hall on tip-toe.

The coffin stood on a table in the middle of the room, and around it stood lighted candles in tall silver candlesticks. In a distant corner sat the chanter reading the Psalms in a low, monotonous voice.

I paused at the door and gazed; but my eyes were so weak with weeping, and my nerves were so unstrung, that I could see nothing. Everything ran together in strange fashion—lights, brocade, velvet, the great candelabra, the rose-coloured pillow bordered with lace, the cap with ribbons, and something waxlike and transparent. I climbed upon a chair in order to see her face, yet where it should have been I could see the same waxlike transparent something. I could not believe it to be her face. Yet as I stood gazing at it, little by little I began to recognize the familiar, dearly-loved features. I shuddered when I realized that it was she. But why were the closed eyes so sunken? Why that dreadful pallor and the blackish spot beneath the skin on one cheek? Why was the expression of the whole face so stern and cold? Why were the lips so pale and their outline so very beautiful, so majestic, and so expressive of an unearthly calm that a cold shudder ran down my back and through my hair when I looked upon it?

As I gazed I felt that some incomprehensible, irresistible power was drawing my eyes to that lifeless face. I did not take my eyes from it, and imagination sketched me pictures of blooming life and happiness. I forgot that the dead body which lay before me, and upon which I stupidly gazed, as upon an object which had nothing in common with my dreams, was *she*. I fancied her again as I had so often seen her, alive, gay, smiling. Then all at once some feature in the pale face upon which my eyes rested struck me. I recalled the terrible reality, shuddered, but did not cease my gaze. And again visions would replace reality, and again the consciousness of the reality would put them to flight. At length imagination grew weary, and ceased to deceive me; the consciousness of reality also vanished, and I lost my senses. I do not know how long I remained in this state, or in what it consisted; I only know that I lost for a time all consciousness of my existence and experienced an exalted, ineffably pleasant and sorrowful delight.

Perhaps, in flying hence to a better world, her beautiful soul gazed sadly back upon that in which she left us; she perceived my grief, took pity upon it, and descended to earth on the pinions of love, with a heavenly smile of compassion, in order to comfort and bless me.

The door creaked, a chanter entered the room to relieve the first. This noise roused me; and the first thought which occurred to me was that, since I was not crying, and was standing on a chair in an attitude which had nothing touching about it, he might take me for an unfeeling boy who had climbed on the chair out of pity or curiosity. I crossed myself, bowed my head, and began to cry.

As I now recall my impressions, I find that that moment of self-forgetfulness was the only one of genuine grief. Before and after the burial I never ceased to weep, and was sad; yet I am ashamed to recall that sadness, because a feeling of self-love was always mingled with it; at one time a desire to show that I was more afflicted than anybody else; again, concern as to the impression which I was producing upon others; at another time, an aimless curiosity which caused me to make observations upon Mimi's cap and the faces of those present. I despised myself, because the feeling I experienced was not exclusively one of sorrow, and I tried to conceal all others; for this reason my grief was insincere and unnatural. Moreover, I experienced a sort of pleasure in knowing that I was unhappy. I tried to arouse my consciousness of unhappiness; and this egotistical feeling, more than all the rest, stifled genuine grief within me.

After passing the night in a deep and quiet sleep, as is always the case after great sorrow, I awoke with my tears dried and my nerves calm. At ten o'clock we were summoned to the mass for the dead, which was celebrated before the body was taken away. The room was filled with weeping house-servants and peasants, who came to take leave of their mistress. During the service I cried quite enough, crossed myself, and made reverences to the earth; but I did not pray in spirit, and was rather cold-blooded. I was worrying because my new half-coat, which they had put on me, was tight under the arms. I thought about not soiling the knees of my trousers too much; and I took observations, on the sly, of all those who were present. My father stood at the head of the coffin. He was as pale as his handkerchief, and restrained his tears with evident difficulty. His tall figure in its black coat, his pale, expressive face, his movements, graceful and assured as ever, when he crossed himself, bowed, touching the ground with his hand, took the candle from the hand of the priest, or approached the coffin, were extreme-ly effective. Yet I do not know why that very ability to appear so effective at such a moment was precisely what did not please me. Mimi stood leaning against the wall, as though she could hardly stand. Her dress was crumpled and flecked with down, her cap pushed on one side; her swollen eyes were red; her head shook. She never ceased to sob in a heart-rending manner, and was constantly burying her face in her hands and her handkerchief. I imagined that she did this in order to hide her face from the spectators, and to rest for a moment after her hypoc-ritical sobs. I remembered her telling Papa, the day be-fore, that Mamma's death was such a terrible shock to her that she had no hope of living through it; that it deprived her of everything; that that angel (as she called Mamma) had not forgotten her before her death, and had expressed a desire to secure her future and Katenka's for ever from care. She shed bitter tears as she said this, and perhaps her grief was genuine, but it was not pure and exclusive. Lyubochka, in her black frock, with mourning trimmings, her face wet with tears, stood with bent head, glancing at the coffin from time to time with an expres-

116

sion of childish terror. Katenka stood beside her mother, and, in spite of her sad expression, was as rosy as ever. Volodya's frank nature was frank even in his grief. He stood at times with his thoughtful, immovable glance fixed on some object; then his mouth began suddenly to twitch, and he hastily crossed himself and bowed in reverence. All the strangers who were present at the funeral were intolerable to me. The phrases of consolation which they uttered to Father, that she would be better off there, that she was not for this world, aroused a kind of anger in me.

What right had they to speak of her and mourn for her? Some of them in speaking of us called us *orphans*. As if we did not know without their assistance that children who have no mother are called by that name! It evidently pleased them to be the first to bestow it upon us, just as they generally make haste to call a young girl who has just been married *Madame* for the first time.

In the far corner of the hall, almost concealed by the open door of the pantry, knelt and bowed a grey-haired woman. Hands clasped and eyes raised to heaven, she did not weep but prayed. Her soul aspired to God, and she besought Him to let her join the one whom she loved more than all on earth, and she confidently hoped that it would be soon.

"There is one who loved her truly!" I thought, and I was ashamed of myself.

The mass came to an end; the face of the dead woman was uncovered, and all present, with the exception of ourselves, approached the coffin one by one and kissed it.

One of the last to draw near and take leave of her was a peasant woman leading a beautiful five-year-old girl, whom she had brought hither, God only knows why. At that moment I unexpectedly dropped my moist handkerchief and stooped to pick it up. But I had no sooner bent over than a frightful piercing shriek startled me; it was so full

117

of terror that if I live a hundred years I shall never forget it, and when I recall it a cold chill always runs all over my body. I raised my head: on a stool beside the coffin stood the same peasant woman, holding in her arms with difficulty the little girl, who, beating the air with her tiny hands, and straining her frightened face away stared wildly at my dead mother's face and uttered a succession of fearful shrieks. I too screamed in a voice perhaps still more terrible than the one which had startled me, and rushed out of the room.

It was only at that moment that I understood whence came that strong, heavy odour which, mingling with the odour of the incense, filled the room; and the thought that that face which a few days before had been full of beauty and tenderness, that face which I loved more than anything in the world, could excite terror, seemed for the first time to reveal to me the bitter truth, and filled my soul with despair.

Chapter XXVIII

THE LAST SAD MEMORIES

Mamma was no longer with us, but our life pursued its usual course. We went to bed and got up at the same hours, and in the same rooms; morning and evening tea, dinner, supper, all took place at the usual time; the tables and chairs stood in the same places; nothing was changed in the house or in our manner of life, only—she was no more.

It seemed to me that, after such unhappiness, all must change—our ordinary manner of life appeared to me an insult to her memory, and recalled her absence too vividly.

After dinner, on the evening before the funeral, I wanted to go to bed; and I went to Natalya Savishna's room, intending to install myself on her soft feather-bed, and beneath the warm wadded coverlet. When I entered, Natalya Savishna was lying on her bed and was probably asleep; hearing my footsteps, she rose, flung aside the woollen cloth which protected her head from the flies, and, adjusting her cap, seated herself on the edge of the bed.

I used to come to her room rather often to have a nap after dinner, and as soon as I entered the room, she immediately understood, why I had come.

"So you've come to rest here a little, have you? Lie down, then, my dear," she said.

"Oh no, Natalya Savishna!" I said, holding her hand. "That is not it at all. I thought I'd just come. You are weary yourself; you had better lie down."

"I have slept enough, dear," she said (I knew that she had not slept for three days), "and besides, who could think of sleep now," she added, with a deep sigh.

I wanted to talk with Natalya Savishna about our misfortune. I knew how sincerely she had loved Mother, and it would have been a comfort to me to weep with her.

"Natalya Savishna," I said, seating myself on the bed after a brief silence, "did you expect it?"

The old woman looked at me in amazement and curiosity, probably because she did not understand why I asked her that.

"Who could have expected this?" I repeated.

"Ah, my dear," said she, casting a glance of the tenderest sympathy upon me, "even now I can hardly believe it. I am an old woman, my old bones ought to have been laid to rest long ago, yet the old master, Prince Nikolai Mikhailovich, your grandfather (Lord rest his soul!), my two brothers, and my sister Annushka have all been buried before me, though all younger than myself, and now, for my sins evidently, it is my fate to outlive her. His holy will be done! He took her because she was worthy, and he wants good souls there."

119

This simple thought comforted me, and I moved nearer to Natalya Savishna. She folded her hands on her bosom and looked upwards; her sunken, tearful eyes expressed great but quiet suffering. She cherished a firm hope that God would not long part her from the one upon whom she had for so many years concentrated all the power of her love.

"Yes, my dear, it does not seem long since I was her nurse, and dressed her, and she called me Nasha. She would run to me, putting her little arms around me and begin to kiss me and to say, 'My Nashik, my beauty, my sweet one!' And I would say in jest, 'No, my dear, you do not love me; wait, you grow up, and marry, and forget your Nasha.' She would turn thoughtful. 'No,' she would say, 'I'd rather not marry if I cannot take Nasha with me; I will never leave Nasha.' And now she has left me, and has not waited for me. And how she loved me! And, in truth, who was there that she did not love? You must never forget your Mamma, my dear, she was not an ordinary mortal, she was an angel from heaven. When her soul reaches the kingdom of heaven, it will love you there, and rejoice over you."

"Why do you say when she reaches the kingdom of heaven, Natalya Savishna?" I asked. "I think she is there now."

"No, my dear," said Natalya Savishna, lowering her voice, and sitting closer to me on the bed: "her soul is here now," and she pointed upwards. She spoke almost in a whisper, and with so much feeling and conviction that I involuntarily raised my eyes and stared at the cornice in search of something. "Before the soul of the just goes to paradise it undergoes forty changes, my dear, and it can stay in its home for forty days."

She talked long in this strain, and with as much simplicity and faith as though she were relating the most everyday occurrences which she had witnessed herself, and which it would never enter any one's head to doubt. I held my breath as I listened to her; and although I did not understand very well what she said, I believed her entirely.

"Yes, my dear, she is here now; she is looking at us; perhaps she hears what we are saying," said Natalya Savishna in conclusion.

She bent her head and became silent. She wanted a handkerchief to wipe her falling tears; she rose, looked me straight in the face, and said, in a voice which trembled with emotion:

"The Lord has brought me many steps nearer to Him through this. What is left for me here now? Whom have I to live for? Whom have I to love?"

"Don't you love us?" I said reproachfully, hardly restraining my tears.

"God knows how I love you, my darlings; but I have never loved any one as I loved her, and I never can love any one in that way."

She could say no more, but turned away and sobbed loudly.

I no longer thought of sleeping: we sat opposite each other in silence and wept.

Foka entered the room; but on seeing our condition and probably not wishing to disturb us, he glanced at us timidly and in silence, and paused at the door.

"What do you want, my good Foka?" asked Natalya Savishna, wiping her eyes.

"A pound and a half of raisins, four pounds of sugar, and three pounds of rice, for the *kutya.*"*

"Yes, in a moment," said Natalya Savishna, taking a hasty pinch of snuff; and she went to her cupboard with brisk steps. The last traces of the grief called forth by our conversation had vanished when she set about her duty, which she considered as extremely important.

---

* A dish partaken of by the mourners at a Russian funeral.—*Tr.*

"What do you want with four pounds?" she grumbled, as she took out the sugar and weighed it in the scales. "Three and a half will be enough," and she took several bits from the scales. "And how can you need more rice? I gave out eight pounds of rice yesterday! No offence to you, Foka Demidich, but I can't let you any more rice. That Vanka is glad because the house is upside down: he thinks no one will notice. No, I won't have any trifling with my master's property. Eight pounds! Whoever heard of such a thing!"

"What is to be done? He says that it's all gone."

"Well, there, take it, then! Let him have it!"

I was surprised at this transition from the affecting sentiment with which she had talked with me to this grumbling and petty calculation. Thinking about it later, I saw that, in spite of what was going on in her soul, she retained sufficient presence of mind to busy herself with her affairs, and the force of habit drew her to her customary duties. Her grief was too strong and too genuine to require any pretence of being unable to busy herself with trivial things, nor would she have understood that such an idea could occur to anyone.

Vanity is a feeling which is utterly incompatible with genuine grief, yet so strongly interwoven with the nature of many that even the deepest woe rarely expels it. Vanity exhibits itself in sorrow by the desire to appear sad, or unhappy, or firm; and these low desires, which we do not acknowledge, but which rarely forsake us, even in the deepest trouble, deprive it of force, dignity, and truth. But Natalya Savishna was so deeply wounded by her unhappiness that no desire lingered in her soul at all, and she went on living purely by habit.

After giving Foka the provisions he had asked for, and reminding him of the pasty which must be prepared for the entertainment of the clergy, she dismissed him, took her stocking, and seated herself beside me again.

The conversation turned again upon the same subject as before; and again we wept together.

These conversations with Natalya Savishna were repeated every day; her quiet tears and calm, devout words brought me comfort and consolation.

But at last we had to part. Three days after the funeral the whole household removed to Moscow, and I was fated never to see her again.

Grandmother only received the terrible news on our arrival, and her grief was intense. We were not allowed to see her, because she lay unconscious for a whole week, and the doctor feared for her life, the more so as she not only would not take any medicine, but would speak to no one, did not sleep, and took no nourishment. Sometimes as she sat alone in her chamber, in her arm-chair, she would suddenly break into a laugh, then begin to sob without tears, or else relapse into convulsions, screaming out frightful, incoherent words. It was the first real sorrow which she had known in her life, and it threw her into despair. She felt the need of blaming some one for her misfortune; and she would say terrible things, speak to some invisible person with unusual energy, spring from her chair, pace the room in long and rapid strides, and then fall senseless.

I entered her room on one occasion. She was sitting in her arm-chair as usual, and was calm to all appearances, yet her glance startled me. Her eyes were very wide open, but their gaze was wavering and vacant; she looked straight at me without seeing me. Her lips began a slow smile, and she spoke in a voice of touching gentleness: "Come here, my dear; come here, my angel." I thought that she was addressing me, and approached nearer; but she did not look at me. "Ah, if you only knew, my love, what torments I have suffered, and how glad I am that you have come!" Then I understood that she fancied she saw Mamma, and halted. "They told me you were dead," she went on, with a frown. "What nonsense! Could you die before me?" and she gave a dreadful hysteric laugh.

Only people who are capable of loving deeply can also suffer great sorrow; yet this same necessity of loving serves to counteract their grief, and heals them. For this reason the moral nature of man is more tenacious than the physical and grief never kills.

After the lapse of a week Grandmamma could weep, and her condition improved. Her first thought when she came to herself was of us, and her love for us increased. We never left her arm-chair; she cried softly, spoke of Mamma, and tenderly caressed us.

It could not enter the mind of any one who looked upon Grandmamma's grief that she was exaggerating it, and the expressions of that grief were deeply moving; yet I do not know why I sympathized more with Natalya Savishna, and to this day I am convinced that no one loved and mourned Mamma so purely and so sincerely as that simple, affectionate creature.

The happy days of childhood ended for me with Mamma's death, and a new epoch began—the epoch of boyhood; but as my recollections of Natalya Savishna, whom I never saw again, and who exercised such a powerful and beneficient influence over my career and the development of my sensibility, belong to the first epoch, I will say a few words more about her and her death.

After our departure, as we were afterwards informed, she remained in the country, and found the time hang heavy on her hands from lack of occupation. Although all the clothes-presses were still under her charge, and she never ceased to turn over their contents, hang things up and pack them away again, yet she missed the noise and bustle of the master's presence in the house, for she had been accustomed to this from her childhood. Grief, the change in her manner of life, the absence of responsibilities, speedily developed an old complaint to which she had long been inclined. Just a year after Mamma's death she developed dropsy and took to her bed.

It was hard, I think, for Natalya Savishna to go on living—still harder, to die alone in the great empty house at Petrovskoye, without relatives or friends. Every one in the house loved and revered Natalya Savishna; but she had formed no friendships and was proud of it. She considered that, in her position of a housekeeper who enjoyed the confidence of her master and had in her charge so many chests filled with all sorts of property, a friendship with any one would infallibly lead to partiality and culpable condescension. For that reason, or possibly because she had nothing in common with the other servants, she held herself aloof from all, and said that she had neither kinsmen nor cronies in the house, and would permit of no exceptions with regard to her master's property.

She sought and found consolation by confiding her feeling to God in fervent prayer; yet sometimes in those moments of weakness to which we are all subject, when man finds his best comfort in the tears and sympathy of a living being, she put her little dog on her bed (it licked her hand, and fixed its yellow eyes upon her), talked to it, and wept softly as she petted it. When the poodle began to howl piteously she endeavoured to quiet it, and said, "Enough, enough! I know, without your telling me, that my time is near."

A month before her death she took from her chest some white calico, white muslin, and pink ribbons; with the assistance of her maid she made herself a white dress and a cap, and arranged everything which was requisite for her funeral, down to the most minute detail. She also sorted over the chests belonging to her master, wrote out an exact inventory of the contents and transferred them to the steward. All that she kept was two silk dresses, an old shawl which Grandmamma had given her at some time or other, and Grandfather's military uniform, which

125

had also been given to her for her own. Thanks to her care, the embroidery and galloon on the uniform were perfectly fresh, and the cloth had not been touched by the moths.

Before her death she expressed a wish that one of these dresses, the pink one, should be given to Volodya for a dressing-gown or jacket, and the other, the brown checked one, to me for the same purpose, and the shawl to Lyubochka. The uniform she bequeathed to whichever of us should first become an officer. All the rest of her property and her money, with the exception of forty rubles which she laid aside for her funeral and masses, she left to her brother. Her brother, who had received his freedom long before, led a very dissipated life in some distant province, hence she had had no intercourse with him during her lifetime.

When Natalya Savishna's brother presented himself to receive his inheritance, and the deceased's entire property proved to consist of twenty-five rubles in notes, he would not believe it, and said that it could not be that the old woman, who had lived for sixty years in a wealthy family, and had had sole charge of the household, had always led a miserly existence, and fretted over every scrap, had left nothing. Yet this was actually the case.

Natalya Savishna suffered for two months from her complaint, and bore her pain with truly Christian patience; she did not grumble or complain, but merely prayed incessantly, as was her custom. An hour before the end came she made her confession, received the last sacrament and extreme unction with quiet joy.

She begged forgiveness of all the house-servants for any injuries which she might have done them, and besought her priest, Father Vasili, to say to all of us that she did not know how to express her thanks for all our kindness, and prayed us to pardon her if she had pained any one by her stupidity; "but I never was a thief, and I

can say that I never cheated my masters out of a thread."
This was the only quality in herself which she valued.

Dressed in the wrapper and cap which she had prepared, and propped up on the pillows, she never ceased
until the moment of death to converse with the priest. She
remembered she had left nothing for the poor, gave him
ten rubles, and begged him to distribute it in the parish.
Then she crossed herself, lay back, sighed for the last
time, and uttered the name of God in a joyous tone.

She quitted life without regret; she did not fear death,
but accepted it as a blessing. This is often said, but how
rarely is it true! Natalya Savishna could not fear death,
because she died firm in the faith and fulfilling the law
of the Gospels. Her whole life had been pure, unselfish
love and self-sacrifice.

What if her creed might have been more lofty, if her
life might have been devoted to higher aims? Is this pure
soul any the less deserving of love and admiration on that
account?

She accomplished the best and grandest deed in this
life: she died without regret or fear.

She was buried, in accordance with her wish, not far
from the chapel which stood upon Mamma's grave. The
hillock, overgrown with nettles and burdock, beneath
which she lies is enclosed within a black iron paling; I
never forget to go from the chapel to that railing and bow
reverently to the ground.

Sometimes I pause silent midway between the chapel
and that black fence. Painful memories arise in my mind.
The thought comes to me: Did Providence connect me
with these two beings merely in order that I might be
made to mourn them for ever?

BOYHOOD

Chapter I

A JOURNEY WITHOUT RELAYS

Again two carriages are brought round to the porch of the Petrovskoye house: one is a coach, in which Mimi, Katenka, Lyubochka, and the maid take seats with our clerk Yakov on the box; the other is a britchka, in which Volodya and I are to travel with the footman Vasili, who was recently brought back to rent-service.

Papa, who is to follow us to Moscow in a few days, stands hatless in the porch and makes the sign of the cross upon the window of the coach and the britchka.

"Christ be with you! Away you go!" Yakov and the coachmen (we are travelling in our own carriages) take off their hats and cross themselves. "God be with us! Gee-up, gee-up!"

The carriage and britchka begin to jolt over the uneven road, and the birches along the great drive fly past us one by one. I am not at all sad; my mind's eye sees not what I am leaving, but what awaits me. As the objects connected with the painful memories which have filled my mind until this moment retreat into the distance, those memories lose their force, and give place to an exquisite consciousness that life is full of strength, freshness and hope.

9*   131

Rarely have I spent days so—I will not say merrily, for I was still rather conscience-stricken at the idea of yielding to merriment—but so agreeably, so pleasantly, as the four days our journey lasted.

No longer do my eyes see the closed door of Mamma's room, which I could not pass without a shudder; nor the closed piano, which nobody dared look at, let alone open, without a sort of fear; nor the mourning garments (we are all in simple travelling suits), nor any of those things which, vividly reminding me of my irrevocable loss, made me recoil from any show of life lest I should offend *her* memory in some way. Here, on the other hand, new and picturesque places and objects catch and hold my attention, and the spring nature awakens in my soul a cheering sense of contentment with the present and bright hope in the future.

Early, very early in the morning, the pitiless Vasili, who is overzealous as people always are in new situations, pulls at the blanket and announces that it is time to set out and that everything is ready. Snuggle and rage and contrive as you will to prolong even for another quarter of an hour your sweet morning slumber, you see by Vasili's determined face that he is inexorable and prepared to pull away the blanket twenty times: so you jump up and run out into the court to wash yourself.

The samovar is already boiling in the anteroom, and Mitka, the outrider, is blowing it until he is as red as a lobster. It is damp and misty out of doors, as though the steam were rising from a reeking dung-heap; the early sun diffuses a bright, cheerful light over the eastern sky and the thatched roofs of the ample sheds around the court-yard, which glisten with dew. Beneath them we can see our horses, tied to mangers, and hear their regular champing.

A shaggy black dog that curled itself up on a heap of dry manure before dawn stretches lazily, and trots gently across the yard, wagging its tail the while. The bustling housewife opens the creaking gates, drives the meditative cows into the street, from which already come the tramp, lowing, and bleating of herds, and exchanges a word or two with her sleepy neighbour. Philip, with his shirt-sleeves rolled up, draws the bucket of shining, splashing water out of the deep well and pours it into an oaken tub, around which the ducks are already having the morning dip in a pool; and I gaze with pleasure upon Philip's handsome face, his luxuriant beard, and at the thick sinews and muscles which stand out on his bare, powerful arms when he makes any exertion.

Sounds of movement come from behind the partition-wall where Mimi and the girls sleep, and over which we conversed in the evening. Masha, their maid, keeps passing in and out with various objects which she endeavours to conceal from our curiosity with her dress; finally she opens the door and calls us to drink our tea.

Vasili, in a fit of superfluous zeal, continually runs into the room, carrying out first one thing, then another, winking to us, and doing his best to persuade Marya Ivanovna to set out as early as possible. The horses are harnessed, and show their impatience by jingling their bells every now and then; the trunks, chests, caskets, and dressing-cases are again packed away, and we take our seats. But each time we find a mountain of luggage inside the britchka instead of seats so that it is impossible to understand how it was all arranged the day before and how we are going to sit now. One walnut tea-caddy, with a triangular cover, which is placed under me in the britchka, enrages me particularly. But Vasili says it will settle down, and I am forced to believe him.

The sun has just risen above the dense white clouds which veil the east, and all the country round is illuminated with a restful cheery light. All is so very beautiful about me, and I am so tranquil and light of heart.

The road winds away in front, wide and unconfined, amid fields of dry stubble and green grass sparkling with dew. Here and there by the roadside we come upon a gloomy willow, or a young birch with small lush leaves, casting a long, motionless shadow upon the dry loamy ruts and the short green grass of the highway. The monotonous sound of the wheels and bells does not drown the song of the larks hovering close to the road. The smell of moth-eaten cloth, of dust, and a certain sourish smell that clung to our britchka, is lost in the fragrance of the morning; and I feel a joyous uneasiness in my soul, a desire to do something, which is a sign of true enjoyment.

I did not manage to say my prayers at the post-house; but as I have more than once observed that some misfortune happens to me on the day when, for some reason or other, I forget to fulfil this rite, I try to make good my omission. I take off my cap, turn to the corner of the britchka, recite my prayers, and cross myself under my jacket so that no one may see it. Yet a thousand different objects distract my attention, and I absent-mindedly repeat the same words of the prayer several times over.

On the footpath which winds beside the road some slowly moving figures come into view: they are pilgrims. Their heads are covered with soiled kerchiefs; on their backs are birch-bark scrips; their feet are wrapped in dirty, tattered foot-bands, and shod in heavy bast shoes. Swaying their staves in unison, and hardly glancing at us, they plod slowly along in single file. Where are they going to, I wonder, and why? Will their journey last long? And will the slender shadows which they cast upon the road soon unite with the shadow of the willow on their path? Here a calash with four post-horses comes rapidly to meet us. Another two seconds, and the faces which looked at us with smiling curiosity within an arm's reach have already flashed past; it seems incredible that these faces are those of complete strangers and that I shall probably never set eyes on them again.

Next comes a pair of shaggy, perspiring horses galloping along the side of the road in their halters, with the traces knotted to the breech strap, while behind rides a post-boy drawling a melancholy song, his lamb's-wool cap cocked to one side, his long legs in their huge boots dangling on the sides of a horse with a *duga** and bells which jingle faintly now and then. His face and attitude are expressive of so much lazy, careless content that it seems to me it would be the height of bliss to be a post-boy, to ride the horses home, and sing melancholy songs. Yonder, far beyond the ravine, a village church with its green roof detaches itself against the bright blue sky; yonder is a hamlet, the red roof of a gentleman's house, and a green garden. Who lives in that house? Are there children in it, father, mother, tutor? Why should we not drive up to it and make the acquaintance of the owner? Here comes a long train of cumbersome waggons harnessed to troikas of well-fed, thick-legged horses which we are obliged to go off the road to pass. "What are you carrying?" Vasili inquires of the first carter, who, with his big feet hanging from the board which forms his seat, rivets on us a long vacant gaze, waves his whip, and makes some sort of reply only when he is too far for us to hear him. "What are your wares?" Vasili asks, turning to another team, upon whose railed-in front lies another carter beneath a new straw-matting. A blonde head with a ruddy face and a reddish beard, is thrust out from beneath the straw-matting for a moment; it casts upon us a glance of scornful indifference, and disappears again; and the thought occurs to me that these carters surely cannot know who we are and where we are going.

---

* Arch over the middle horse of a troika, or three horses harnessed abreast.—*Tr.*

I am so engrossed in my various observations that for an hour and a half I do not notice the crooked numbers inscribed upon the verst-posts. But now the sun begins to burn my head and back, the road becomes more dusty, the triangular lid of the tea-caddy begins to discommode me greatly, and I change my position several times. I am beginning to feel hot and uncomfortable and bored. My whole attention is directed to the verst-posts and the figures on them. I make various mathematical calculations as to the time it will take us to reach the next stage.

"Twelve versts are one-third of thirty-six, and it is forty-one to Lipets; consequently we have travelled one-third and something of the way?" and so forth.

"Vasili," I say, when I notice that he is beginning to nod upon the box, "let me sit on the box, that's a dear." Vasili agrees: we change places. He immediately begins to snore and sprawls so that there is no room left for anybody else in the britchka. Before me, from my new perch, the most delightful picture presents itself—our four horses, Neruchinskaya, Deacon, Lyevaya, the pole-horse, and Apothecary, all of whom I know so well down to the most minute details and shades of the qualities of each.

"Why is Deacon on the near side today instead of the off side, Philip?" I inquire rather timidly.

"Deacon?"

"And Neruchinskaya is not pulling at all," I say.

"You can't harness Deacon on the off," says Philip, paying no attention to my last remark. "He is not the kind of horse for that; there you need the kind of horse that—well, a real horse, and Deacon's not that sort."

And with these words Philip bends over to the right, and, pulling on the reins with all his might, he begins to whip poor Deacon on the tail and legs, in a peculiar manner, from below; and despite the fact that Deacon strains every muscle, so that the britchka swerves, Philip does not desert from his stratagem until he feels the need to rest and to tip his hat over to the side, although it was square and firm on his head before. I take advantage of this favourable opportunity, and beg Philip to let me drive. Philip gives me first one rein, then another; and finally all six reins and the whip are transferred to my hands, and I am perfectly happy. I endeavour to imitate Philip in every detail and ask him whether I am doing well: but he is generally dissatisfied; he says that one horse is pulling a great deal, and that another is not pulling at all, and leans over and takes the reins away from me. It is getting hotter and hotter. The little fleecy clouds begin to puff up higher and higher, like soap-bubbles, merging and taking on a dark grey tint. A hand holding a bottle and a little package emerges from the coach window. Vasili leaps from the box with wonderful agility while we are in motion, and brings us little cheese-cakes and *kvass*.

We all alight from the carriages at a sharp descent, and have a race to the bridge, while Vasili and Yakov put on the brakes, and support the coach on both sides with their hands as though they could hold it up in case it upset. Then, with Mimi's permission, either Volodya or I get into the coach, and Lyubochka or Katenka takes the place in the britchka. These changes afford the girls great pleasure, because, as they rightly think, it is jollier in the britchka. Sometimes, when it is hot and we are passing through the woods, we linger behind the coach, tear off green boughs, and build an arbour in the britchka. This moving arbour overtakes the coach, and Lyubochka pipes up in the most piercing of voices, which she never forgets to do on any occasion which affords her pleasure.

But here is the village where we are to dine and rest. We have already smelt the village, the smoke, tar, and baking. We have heard the sound of voices, steps, and wheels; the horses' bells no longer sound as they did in the open fields; and on either side we pass cottages with thatched roofs, carved wooden porches, and little windows with red and green shutters, between which a curious woman's face peeps out. Little peasant boys and girls, clad only in smocks, their eyes wide open, their hands thrown out in surprise stand rooted to the spot, or nimbly pick their way through the dust, with their little bare feet and try to climb upon the trunks behind the carriages, in spite of Philip's menacing gestures. Ginger-haired inn-keepers hasten up to the carriages from every direction, and endeavour, with alluring words and gestures, to entice the travellers away from one another. Whoa! the gate creaks, the splinter-bar catches on the gate-posts, and we enter the court-yard. Four hours of rest and freedom!

Chapter II

THE THUNDER-STORM

The sun declined towards the west and burned my neck and cheeks intolerably with its hot, slanting rays. It was impossible to touch the scorching sides of the britchka. A thick dust rose over the road and filled the air. There was not the slightest breeze to carry it away. The tall dusty body of the coach swayed in rhythm always at the same distance in front of us, and occasionally above it we caught sight of the whip as the coachman waved it, his hat and Yakov's cap. I did not know what to do with myself; neither the dust-blackened face of Volodya dozing beside me, nor the movements of Philip's back, nor the long oblique shadow of our britchka hot in our pursuit afforded me any diversion. All my attention was focussed on the verst-posts, which I observed in the distance, and on the clouds, which had before been scattered over the sky, and were now gathering into one dark menacing mass. From time to time distant thunder rumbled. This last circumstance, more than all the rest, increased my impatience to reach the post-house. Thunder-storms inspired me with an indescribably oppressive sensation of fear and sadness.

It was still ten versts to the nearest village, but the great, dark-purple cloud, which had arisen from I knew not where for there was not the slightest breeze, was moving swiftly upon us. The sun, not yet hidden by the clouds, brightly lit up its sombre mass and the grey streaks which stretched from it to the very horizon. Lightning flashed from time to time in the distance and a low rumble was heard which gradually became louder as it approached and merged into broken peals embracing the heavens. Vasili got upon the box, and raised the hood of the britchka. The coachmen put on their *armyaks,* at every thunder clap they removed their hats and crossed themselves. The horses pricked up their ears, puffed out their nostrils as if smelling the fresh air which was wafted from the approaching thunder-cloud, and the britchka rolled faster along the dusty road. An uncanny feeling came over me. I was conscious of the blood pounding in my veins. Presently the first clouds veiled the sun; for the last time it peeped forth, cast a last gleam of light over the glowering horizon, and vanished. The entire landscape suddenly changed and assumed a gloomy aspect. The aspen coppice quivered; the leaves take on a greyish tint, and clearly stood out against the purple cloud—and rustled and fluttered; the tops of the tall birches rocked, and tufts of dry grass whirled across the road. Swift and white-breasted swallows came circling around the britchka and swooping under the horses' chests as though they wanted to stop us; daws with ruffled wings flew sideways in the wind; the edges of the leather apron, which we had fastened over us, fluttered up, letting in gusts of moist wind, and flapped and beat against the body of the carriage. The lightning seemed to flash in the britchka itself, blinding us and lighting up for a moment the grey cloth with its braid border, and Volodya's figure cowering in a corner. At the same moment, a majestic peal boomed directly above our heads, and seemed to rise ever higher and higher and to spread ever wider and wider, in a vast spiral, gradually swelling, until it burst in a deafening crash, which sent a shudder through us and forced us to hold our breath. The wrath of God! How much poetry there is in that popular notion.

The wheels whirl faster and faster. I can see by the backs of Vasili and Philip, who keeps on flourishing his reins, that they too are afraid. The britchka rolls swiftly down the hill and thunders over the wooden bridge. I dare not move, in the fearful expectation that any minute will bring destruction to us all.

Whoa! the trace is broken, and, in spite of the unceasing deafening claps of thunder, we are forced to halt upon the bridge.

I lean my head against the side of the britchka and hold my breath, despair clutching at my heart as I watch the movements of Philip's fat black fingers. He slowly ties a knot, straightens out the traces and strikes the side horse with palm and whip-handle.

The distressful feelings of sadness and terror increased within me as the storm gained in strength; but when the majestic silence set in which generally preceded the thunder-clap, those feelings reached such a pitch that, had the situation lasted a quarter of an hour longer, I am convinced I should have died of excitement. Just then there appeared from beneath the bridge a human form clothed in a dirty, ragged shirt, with a bloated, senseless face, a bare, shaven, wagging head, crooked, nerveless legs, and in place of a hand a shining red stump, which he thrust right into the britchka.

"For the love of Christ, help a cripple!" said the beggar in a tremulous voice, crossing himself at every word and bowing deeply.

I cannot describe the terror that chilled my soul at that moment. A shudder ran through my hair, and my eyes were riveted on the beggar in a stupor of fright.

Vasili, who bestowed the alms on the journey, was giving Philip directions how to strengthen the trace; and only when all was ready, and Philip, gathering up the reins, had climbed upon the box, did he begin to fumble in his side pocket. But we had no sooner set out again than a blinding flash of lightning filled the whole ravine for a moment with its fiery glare and brought the horses to a stand; it was accompanied, without the slightest interval, by such a deafening clap of thunder that it seemed as though the whole vault of heaven were crumbling down upon us. The wind became still stronger; the manes and tails of the horses, Vasili's cloak, and the edges of the apron all fluttered wildly in the same direction under the bursts of the raging gale. A large drop of rain fell heavily upon the leather hood of the britchka, then a second, a third, a fourth; and all at once it beat upon us like a drum, and the whole landscape resounded with the regular patter of falling rain. I noticed by the movement of Vasili's elbow that he was untying his purse; the beggar, still crossing himself and bowing, was running close to the wheel, so that it seemed he would be crushed. "For the love of Christ!" At last a copper flew past us; the wretched creature halted, hesitating in the middle of the road, swaying in the wind, his rain-sodden smock clinging to his lean limbs, and then disappeared from our sight.

The slanting rain, driven by the fierce wind, was pouring down in torrents; streams trickled down the back of Vasili's frieze coat into the puddle of dirty water which had collected on the apron. The dust, which at first had been beaten into pellets, was now liquid mud, through which the wheels splashed; the jolts became fewer, and turbid brooks flowed in the ruts. The lightning flashes grew broader and paler; the thunder-claps were no longer so startling above the pitter-patter of the rain.

The rain no longer fell so heavily; the thunder-cloud began to disperse; light appeared where the sun must be, and a rift of clear azure was almost visible through the greyish-white edges of the cloud. Yet a moment, and a timid ray of sunlight gleamed in the pools on the road, in the fine, straight streaks of rain which fell as if through a sieve, and upon the shining, newly-washed green of the wayside grass.

The black thunder-cloud stretching over the opposite portion of the sky was no less sinister, but I no longer feared it. An unutterably delightful feeling of hope in life had come over me, dispelling my oppressive sensation of fear. Like Nature, my soul smiled, refreshed and enlivened.

Vasili turned down his coat-collar, took off his cap and shook it. Volodya flings off the apron. I leaned out of the britchka, and eagerly drank in the fresh, fragrant air. The shining, well-washed body of the coach, with its cross-bar and trunks, goes rocking along in front of us; the backs of the horses, the breeching and reins, the tyres of the wheels, everything is wet, and glitters in the sun as though covered with lacquer. On one side of the road a boundless field of winter wheat, scarred here and there by shallow gullies, gleams with damp earth and verdure and spreads in a carpet of varying tints to the very horizon; on the other side an aspen grove, with an undergrowth of hazel-nut and wild cherry, stands unruffled as rapt in bliss, slowly shedding bright rain-drops from its storm-washed branches upon last year's dry leaves. Crested larks soar on all sides with joyous song and quickly fall again, while from the wet bushes comes the sound of bustling little birds and the note of the cuckoo rings clear from the heart of the wood. So enchanting after this spring storm was the fragrance of the wood—the scent of the birches, violets, dead leaves, mushrooms and wild cherries—that I could not sit still in the britchka, but jumped from the step, ran to the bushes, and, in spite of the shower of rain-drops, plucked sprigs of bird-cherry, and switched my face with them, drinking in their wondrous perfume.

Heedless of my boots, clodded with mud, and of my stockings, long soaked through, I splashed through the mud at a run to the window of the coach.

"Lyubochka! Katenka!" I shouted, handing up a few branches of cherry blossom, "look how lovely it is!"

The girls gasped and squeaked in alarm. Mimi shouted to me to go away, or I would certainly be run over.

"But just you smell how sweet it is!" I shouted.

Chapter III

NEW VIEWS

Katenka was sitting beside me in the britchka, and, her pretty head bent, was thoughtfully watching the dusty road as it flew past beneath the wheels. I gazed at her in silence, and wondered at the sad, unchildlike expression which I saw for the first time on her rosy face.

"We shall soon be in Moscow now," said I. "What do you think it is like?"

"I do not know," she answered unwillingly.

"But what do you think? Is it bigger than Serpukhov or not?"

"What?"

"Oh, nothing."

But through that instinct by which one person divines the thoughts of another, and which serves as a guiding thread in conversation, Katenka understood that her indifference pained me: she raised her head and turned towards me.

"Your Papa has told you we are to live with Grandmamma?"

"Yes; Grandmamma insists on our living with her."

"And we are all to live there?"

"Of course: we shall live upstairs in one half of the house, you in the other half, and Papa in the wing; but we shall all dine together downstairs with Grandmamma."

"Mamma says that your grandmother is awfully dignified—and bad-tempered."

"Oh no, she is not! She only seems so at first. She is dignified, but not at all bad-tempered; on the contrary, she is very kind and cheerful. If only you had seen what a ball we had on her name-day!"

"Still, I am afraid of her; and besides, God knows if we shall—"

Katenka stopped suddenly, and again fell into thought.

"What is the matter?" I asked uneasily.

"Nothing."

"There is, you said, 'God knows—'"

"And you said, 'What a ball we had at Grandmamma's!'"

"Yes, it's a pity you were not there: there were ever so many guests—hundreds of them, and music, and generals—and I danced." Suddenly I paused in the middle of my description: "Katenka, you are not listening."

"Yes, I am; you were saying you danced."

"Why are you so dull?"

"One can't be gay all the time."

"But you have changed so much since we returned from Moscow. Tell me honestly," I added, with a look of determination as I turned towards her: "What has made you so queer?"

144

"Am I queer?" replied Katenka, with an animation which showed that my remark interested her. "I am not. Not at all."

"You are not like you used to be," I went on. "It used to be quite plain that you felt the same as we did about everything, that you regarded us as relatives, and loved us, just as we loved you; but now you have become so serious, you are so offish—"

"No, I'm not...."

"Let me finish," I interrupted, already conscious of a slight tickling in my nose—the forerunner of tears which always rose to my eyes when I gave vent to a long-repressed, heart-felt thought. "You keep away from us; you talk with nobody but Mimi, as though you wanted to ignore us."

"Well, you can't always be the same; you must change some time," replied Katenka, who had a habit of explaining everything by a kind of fatal necessity when she did not know what to say.

I remember how once, after quarrelling with Lyubochka, who called her a *stupid thing*, she answered, "Everybody can't be wise; some people must be stupid." But this reply, that you had to change sometimes, did not satisfy me, so I went on with my questions.

"Why must you?"

"Why, we won't always live together," Katenka answered, blushing slightly and staring at Philip's back. "My Mamma could live with your dead Mamma, because she was her friend; but God knows whether she will get along with the Countess, who they say is so bad-tempered. Besides, we must part some day, in any case. You are rich, you have Petrovskoye; but we are poor, my Mamma has nothing."

You are rich; we are poor! Those words, and the ideas connected with them, seemed very strange to me. In those days I thought only beggars and muzhiks could be poor, and this idea of poverty I could never link in my imagination with pretty, graceful Katya. It seemed to me that since Mimi and Katya had always lived with us, they would go on living with us and getting their share of everything. It could not be otherwise. But now a thousand new, undefined thoughts concerning their lonely situation dawned on me; I was so ashamed that we were rich and they poor that I blushed, and could not make up my mind to look Katenka in the face.

"What does it mean," I thought: "we are rich and they are poor? And how does it follow that we must part? Why cannot we share what we have equally?" But I understood that it was not a thing I should speak to Katenka about; and some practical instinct which ran contrary to these logical deductions already told me that she was right, and that it would be out of place to explain to her what I thought.

"Is it true that you will leave us?" I asked. "How shall we be able to live away from one another?"

"How can we help it? It hurts me too; but if it does happen I know what I shall do."

"You will become an actress! What nonsense!" I broke in, knowing that it had always been her dream to be an actress.

"No; I said that when I was very small."

"What will you do, then?"

"I'll become a nun and live in a monastery, and go about in a black gown and a velvet hood."

Katenka burst into tears.

Has it ever happened to you, reader, to notice all at once, at a certain period of your life, that your view of things has entirely changed; as though all the objects which you had seen hitherto had suddenly turned to you another side of which you were not aware! A moral change of this kind first took place in me during our journey. From that time I date the beginning of my boyhood.

For the first time it came home to me that we—our family—were not alone in this world; that we were not the centre around which all interests revolve; and that there was another life—of people who had nothing to do with us, who cared nothing for us, and even had no idea that we existed. No doubt I had known all this before, but I had not known it as I knew it now. I did not feel it.

An idea becomes a conviction only in a definite way, often entirely unexpected and different from the way in which other minds arrive at the same conviction. The conversation with Katenka, which affected me powerfully, and made me ponder her future situation, was the way for me. When I looked at the villages and towns through which we drove, in every house of which lived at least one family such as ours; at the women and children who gazed with momentary curiosity after our carriages, and vanished for ever from sight; at the shopkeepers and the peasants, who not only did not greet us as I was accustomed to see them do in Petrovskoye, but did not honour us with so much as a glance—the question entered my mind for the first time: what could occupy them if they cared nothing for us? And from this question arose others: how and by what means do they live? how do they bring up their children? do they instruct them or let them play? how do they punish them? and so forth.

Chapter IV

IN MOSCOW

On our arrival in Moscow the change in my views of things, people, and my own relations to them, became still more perceptible. When at my first meeting with Grandmamma I saw her thin, wrinkled face and dim eyes, the feeling of abject reverence and terror which I had entertained for her changed to one of sympathy. And when, pressing her face on Lyubochka's head, she sobbed as though she were gazing on the corpse of her beloved daughter, my sympathy even changed to love. It made me uncomfortable to see her sorrow at meeting us. I saw that we of ourselves were nothing in her eyes; that we were dear to her as memories. I felt that there was but one thought expressed in every one of the kisses with which she covered my cheeks: "She is gone; she is dead; I shall never see her any more."

Papa, who had next to nothing to do with us in Moscow, and, his face perpetually worried, came to us only at dinner-time in a black coat or dress-suit, lost a great deal in my eyes, as did also his big flaring collars, his dressing-gown, his stewards, his clerks, his walks to the threshing-floor, and his hunting. Karl Ivanich, whom Grandmamma called *dyadka*, and who had suddenly taken it into his head, God knows why, to exchange his respectable and familiar baldness for a red wig with a parting almost in the middle of his head, seemed to me so strange and ridiculous that I wondered how I could have failed to notice it before.

Some invisible barrier also arose between the girls and us. They had their secrets and we had ours. They seemed to put on airs before us over their petticoats, which grew longer, and we were proud of our trousers with footstraps. And Mimi appeared at the first Sunday dinner in such an elegant gown and with such ribbons on her head that it was at once apparent that we were not in the country, and that everything was to be different now.

Chapter V
THE ELDER BROTHER

I was only a year and some months younger than Volodya: we had grown up together, and parted neither at lessons nor games. The distinction of elder and younger had never been made between us. But just about the time of which I am speaking I began to realize that I was not Volodya's equal either in years, inclinations, or abilities. I even began to fancy that Volodya was aware of his superiority, and was proud of it. This conviction, possibly an erroneous one, aroused my self-love, and wounded it at every encounter with him. He was my superior in everything—in games, in studies, in quarrels, and in the knowledge of how to conduct himself, and all this estranged him to me and caused me moral torments I could not understand. If, on the first occasion when Volodya put on a linen pleated shirt, I had said plainly that I was vexed at not having the same, I am sure it would have made it easier for me, and I would not have had the impression every time he adjusted his collar that he did it solely in order to hurt my feelings.

What tormented me most of all was that Volodya saw through me, as it seemed to me at times, but tried to hide it.

Who has not noticed those mysterious, wordless relations which are disclosed in a barely perceptible smile, a motion or a glance, between people who always live together—brothers, friends, husband and wife, master and servant, particularly when these people are not in every respect frank with each other! How many unuttered desires, thoughts, and fears—of being understood—are expressed in one casual glance when eyes meet timidly and irresolutely!

But possibly I was deceived on this point by my excessive sensitiveness and tendency to analysis; perhaps

Volodya did not feel at all what I did. He was impetuous, frank, and inconstant in his impulses. He was carried away by the most diverse objects, and he gave himself up to them with his whole soul.

At one time a passion for pictures took possession of him: he took to drawing himself, spent all his money on it, begged of his drawing-master, of Papa, and of Grandmamma; then it was a passion for articles with which he decorated his table, and he collected them from all parts of the house; then a passion for novels, which he procured on the sly and read day and night. I was involuntarily carried away by his hobbies; but I was too proud to follow in his footsteps, and too young and too dependent on others to choose my own way. But there was nothing which I envied so much as Volodya's happy, frank, and noble character, which was revealed with particular clearness when we quarrelled. I felt that he behaved well, yet could not bring myself to imitate him.

Once when his passion for curios was at its height I went up to his table and accidentally broke an empty little multi-coloured smelling-bottle.

"Who gave you leave to touch my things?" said Volodya, as he entered the room and perceived the havoc which I had wrought in the symmetry of the varied ornaments on his table; "and where's that little smelling-bottle? You always—"

"I dropped it by accident and it broke. Where's the harm?"

"Please never *dare* to touch my things," he said, putting the bits of the broken bottle together and contemplating them sorrowfully.

"And you please don't *order* me," I retorted. "It's broken and that's that. What's the use of making a fuss?"

And I smiled, although I had not the least desire to smile.

"Oh, it may mean nothing to you, but to me it means a great deal," Volodya went on, with a shrug of his shoulders which he had from Papa: "you go and break my things and then you laugh. You nasty little boy!"

"I am a little boy, but you're as stupid as you're big."

"I've no intention of quarrelling with you," said Volodya, giving me a slight push; "get away from here!"

"Don't you push me!"

"Get away!"

"Don't you push me, I tell you!"

Volodya took me by the hand and tried to drag me away from the table; but I was boiling with rage. I caught hold of the leg of the table and brought the porcelain and cut-glass ornaments with a crash to the floor. "There!"

"You disgusting little brat!" yelled Volodya, trying to save some of his falling treasures.

"Now it's all over between us," I thought, as I left the room: "we have fallen out for good."

We did not speak to each other until evening. I felt myself in the wrong, was afraid to look at him, and could not busy myself with anything the whole day. Volodya, on the contrary, did his lessons well and chatted and laughed with the girls after dinner as usual.

As soon as a lesson would be over I left the room. I was too afraid, embarrassed, and conscience-stricken to remain alone with my brother. After the evening lesson in history, I took my note-book and started towards the door. As I passed Volodya, in spite of the fact that I wanted to go and make it up with him, I pouted and tried to put on an angry face. Volodya raised his head just at that moment, and with a barely perceptible, good-naturedly derisive smile looked boldly at me. Our eyes met and I knew that he understood me, and also that I realized that he understood me. Yet a feeling stronger than myself made me turn away.

"Nikolenka!" he said, in a perfectly simple tone of voice without the slightest emotion, "you've been angry long enough. Forgive me if I offended you."

151

And he gave me his hand.

All at once something seemed to swell higher and higher in my chest until the pressure almost choked me. That lasted but an instant; then tears came to my eyes and I felt better.

"I'm sorry, Volodya!" I said, grasping his hand.

But Volodya looked at me as though he could not understand at all why there should be tears in my eyes.

Chapter VI

MASHA

However, none of the changes in my views of things was so surprising to me as that which led me to cease to regard one of our maids as a mere servant of the female sex, and to regard her as a woman, on whom my peace and happiness might in some degree depend.

As far back as I can remember anything I remember Masha in our house; and never until the occasion which altered my view of her completely, and which I shall relate presently, did I pay the slightest attention to her. Masha was twenty-five when I was fourteen; she was very pretty. But I am afraid to describe her, afraid lest my fancy should again present to me the enchanting and deceitful picture which existed in it during the period of my passion for her. In order to make no mistake, I shall merely say that her skin was unusually white, she was luxuriantly developed, and was a woman. And I was fourteen years old.

At one of those moments when, lesson-book in hand, you are engrossed in walking up and down the room, trying to step only on cracks in the floor, or in humming some incoherent air, or in smearing the edge of the table with ink, or mechanically repeating some phrase—in a word, at one of those moments when the mind refuses to work and the imagination, assuming the upper hand, seeks impressions—I stepped out of the school-room and went down to the landing without any object whatever.

Some one in slippers was ascending the next flight of stairs. Of course I wanted to know who it was; but the sound of the footsteps suddenly ceased, and I heard Masha's voice:

"Get along with you! What will Marya Ivanovna think if she comes?"

"Oh, but she won't," said Volodya's voice in a whisper, and then I heard a movement, as if Volodya was trying to hold her back.

"Hey! Hands off, you rascal!" and Masha ran past me with her kerchief all on one side and her plump white neck visible beneath it.

I cannot express how amazed I was at this discovery; but my amazement soon gave way to sympathy with Volodya's caper. It was not what he had done that I was surprised at, but how he had come upon the idea that it was pleasant to do it. And involuntarily I began to want to imitate him.

I sometimes spent hours on that landing without thinking of anything, listening with strained attention to the slightest movement, which proceeded from above; but I never could force myself to imitate Volodya, in spite of the fact that I wanted more than anything else in the world to do so. Sometimes I hid behind a door and listened with a guilty feeling of envy and jealousy to the bustle in the maids' room; and the thought occurred to me, what my position would be if I were to go upstairs and, like Volodya, try to kiss Masha? What should I, with my broad nose and my unruly hair, say when she asked me what I wanted? Sometimes I heard Masha say to Volodya, "What a plague! Why do you keep bothering me? Go away, you scamp! Why doesn't Nikolai Petrovich ever come here and play foolish pranks?" She did not know that Nikolai Petrovich was at that moment sitting on the stairs, and would have given anything in the world to be in that scamp Volodya's place.

I was modest by nature, but my modesty was further increased by the conviction of my own ugliness. And I am sure that nothing has such a decisive influence upon a man's course as his personal appearance, and not so much his appearance as his belief in its attractiveness or unattractiveness.

I had too much self-pride to become accustomed to my position, and consoled myself with the assurance that the grapes were sour; that is to say, I endeavoured to despise all the pleasures derived from the pleasing exterior which Volodya enjoyed in my eyes and which I envied with all my soul, and I strained my mind and imagination to find solace in proud solitude.

Chapter VII

SHOT

"My God, powder!" screamed Mimi, gasping with alarm. "What are you doing? Do you want to burn the house down and be the death of us all?"

And with an indescribable expression of firmness Mimi ordered everybody to keep away, walked with long determined strides up to the scattered shot, and, scorning the danger which might result from a premature explosion, she began to stamp it out with her feet. When, in her opinion, the danger was averted, she called Mikhei and ordered him to fling all that *powder* as far away as possible, or, what was better still, into the water; and, proudly smoothing her cap, she betook herself to the drawing-room. "They are well looked after, there's no denying that," she grumbled.

When Papa came from the wing and we accompanied him to Grandmother's room, Mimi was already seated there near the window, gazing threateningly at the door with a certain mysteriously official expression. In her hand was something wrapped in paper. I guessed that it was the shot, and that Grandmamma already knew everything.

In Grandmamma's room, besides Mimi, were Gasha, the maid, who, as was evident from her red and angry face, was very much put out, and Dr. Blumenthal, a small, pock-marked man, who was vainly endeavouring to calm Gasha by making mysterious and pacifying signs to her with his eyes and head.

Grandmamma herself was sitting rather sideways, and laying out her patience, in the *Traveller* pattern, which was always a sign of an extremely unpropitious frame of mind.

"How do you feel today, *maman*? Did you sleep well?" asked Papa, as he respectfully kissed her hand.

"Very well, my dear; I believe you know that I am always well," replied Grandmamma in a tone which seemed to indicate that Papa's question was as misplaced and insulting as was possible. "Well, are you going to give me a clean handkerchief?" she continued, turning to Gasha.

"I have given it to you," replied Gasha, pointing to a snow-white cambric handkerchief which lay on the arm of the chair.

"Take away that dirty thing and give me a clean one, my dear."

Gasha went to the chiffonier, opened a drawer, and slammed it in again with such force that all the glass in the room rattled. Grandmamma glanced threateningly round at all of us, and continued to watch the maid's movements attentively. When the latter gave her what appeared to me to be the same handkerchief, Grandmamma said:

"When will you grind my snuff, my dear?"

"When there's time I'll do it."

"What did you say?"

"I'll do it today."

"If you don't wish to be in my service, my dear, you might have said so; I would have discharged you long ago."

"I shan't cry if you do discharge me," muttered the maid in a low tone.

At that moment the doctor tried to give her a wink, but she looked at him with so much anger and decision that he immediately dropped his eyes and became engrossed in his watch-key.

"You see, my dear," said Grandmamma, turning to Papa when Gasha, still muttering, had left the room, "how people speak to me in my own house."

"If you will permit me, *maman*, I will grind your snuff," said Papa, who was evidently very much embarrassed by this unexpected behaviour.

"No, thank you; she is impudent because she knows that no one but herself knows how to grind snuff as I like it. You know, my dear," Grandmamma went on after a short pause, "your children very nearly set the house on fire today?"

Papa looked at Grandmamma with respectful inquiry.

"Yes, there's what they play with. Show him," she said, turning to Mimi.

Papa took the shot in his hand, and could not refrain from smiling.

"Why, this is shot, *maman*," said he; "it's not at all dangerous."

"I am very much obliged to you, my dear, for teaching me, only I'm too old."

"Nerves, nerves," the doctor whispered.

And Papa immediately turned to us.

"Where did you get that? and how dare you play pranks with such things?"

"It's not them you should ask; ask their *dyadka*," said Grandmamma, pronouncing the word *dyadka* with particular contempt, "what does he look after."

"Voldemar said that Karl Ivanich himself gave him the *powder*," put in Mimi.

"There, see how good he is," continued Grandmamma. "And where is he, that *dyadka*, what's his name? Send him here."

"I gave him leave to go out and pay a visit," said Papa.

"That will not do at all. He ought to be here all the time. The children are yours, not mine, and I have no right to advise you, because you are wiser than I," pursued Grandmamma; "But it does seem time to engage a tutor for them, and not a valet, a German peasant— yes, a stupid peasant, who can teach them nothing but bad manners and Tyrolese songs. Is it really necessary, I ask you, for the children to be able to sing Tyrolese songs? However, nobody thinks of this *now*, and you can do as you please."

The word "now" meant that they had no mother, and called up sad memories in Grandmamma's heart. She dropped her eyes on her snuff-box, with its portrait, and became lost in thought.

"I have been thinking about that for a long time," Papa hastened to say, "and I wanted to ask your advice, *maman*. Shall we ask St. Jérôme, who is now giving them lessons by the day?"

"You will be doing extremely well, my friend," said Grandmamma, no longer in the dissatisfied tone in which she had spoken before. "St. Jérôme is at least a tutor who knows how *des enfants de bonne maison* should behave, and not a paltry valet, who is good for nothing but to take them out for walks."

"I shall speak to him tomorrow," said Papa.

And, in fact, two days after this conversation Karl Ivanich yielded his place to the young French dandy.

Chapter VIII

KARL IVANICH'S HISTORY

Late on the evening which preceded the day when Karl Ivanich was to leave us for ever, he stood beside the bed in his wadded gown and red cap, bending over his trunk, and carefully packing his effects.

Karl Ivanich's attitude towards us had been peculiarly stiff of late: he seemed to avoid all intercourse with us. Now too, when I entered the room, he glanced sullenly at me, and went on with his work. I lay down on my bed, but Karl Ivanich, who had in former times strictly prohibited this, said nothing to me; and the thought that he would never more scold us or check us, that he had nothing to do with us now, was a sharp reminder of the approaching separation. I was sorry that he had ceased to love us, and wanted to express this feeling to him. "Let me help you, Karl Ivanich," I said, going up to him. Karl Ivanich glanced at me and again turned aside; but in the fleeting look which he cast at me I read not the indifference with which I had explained his coldness, but genuine, concentrated grief.

"God sees all, and knows all; and may His holy will be done in all things," he said, drawing himself up to his full height, with a heavy sigh. "Yes, Nikolenka," he went on, noticing the expression of unfeigned sympathy with which I looked at him, "it is my fate to be unhappy from my very infancy to the grave. I have always been repaid with evil for the good I have done to people; and my reward is not here, but yonder," he said, pointing towards heaven. "If only you knew my history and all that I have gone through in this life! I have been a shoemaker, I have been a soldier, I have been a *deserter*, I have been a factory worker, I have been a teacher, and now I am nothing; and, like the Son of God, I have nowhere to lay my head," he concluded, and, closing his eyes, he sank into a chair.

Seeing that Karl Ivanich was in that sensitive state of mind in which he uttered his dearest thoughts for his own satisfaction without heeding the hearer, I seated myself on the bed in silence, and without removing my eyes from his kind face.

"You are not a child, you can understand. I shall tell you my story, and all that I have endured in this life. Some day you will recall the old friend who loved you very much, children."

Karl Ivanich leaned his elbow on the table which stood beside him, took a pinch of snuff, and, rolling his eyes heavenward, began his tale in that peculiar, level, throat voice in which he usually dictated to us.

"I was unhappy even before I was born," he said, with great feeling. *"Das Unglück verfolgte mich schon im Schosse meiner Mutter!"*

As Karl Ivanich related his history to me more than once in exactly the same terms, and always with the very same intonations, I hope to be able to reproduce it almost word for word, with the exception, of course, of the faults of his Russian. Whether it really was his history, or a product of his imagination conceived during his lonely life in our house, or whether he only coloured the real events of his life with fantastic facts, I have not been able to decide to this day. On the one hand, he related his story with too much of that lively feeling and methodical sequence which constitute the chief proofs of veracity to permit one to doubt it; on the other hand, the very profusion of poetic details about his history, tended to raise doubts.

"In my veins flows the noble blood of the Count of Sommerblatt! *In meinen Adern fliesst das edle Blut des Grafen von Sommerblatt!* I was born six weeks after the marriage. My mother's husband (I called him Daddy) was a farmer under Count Sommerblatt. He could never forget my mother's shame, and did not love me. I had a little brother, Johann, and two sisters; but I was a stanger in the midst of my own family! *Ich war ein Fremder in meiner eigenen Familie!* When Johann did anything silly Daddy used to say, 'I never have a moment's peace with that child Karl!' and I was scolded and punished. When my sisters got angry with each other Daddy said, 'Karl will never be an obedient boy!' and I was scolded and punished.

"My good Mamma alone loved me and petted me. She often said to me, 'Karl, come here to my room,' and then she kissed me on the sly. 'Poor, poor Karl!' she said, 'no one loves you, but I would not change you for any one. One thing your mamma begs of you,' she said to me: 'study well, and always be an honourable man, and God will not abandon you! *Trachte nur ein ehrlicher Deutscher zu werden,—sagte sie—und der liebe Gott wird dich nicht verlassen!*' And I tried. When I was fourteen, and could go to communion, Mamma said to Daddy, 'Karl is a big boy now, Gustav; what shall we do with him?' And Daddy said, 'I don't know.' Then Mamma said, 'Let us send him to town to Herr Schultz, and let him be a shoemaker.' And Daddy said, 'Very good,' *'und mein Vater sagte "gut".'* Six years and seven months I lived

160

in town with the master shoemaker, and the master loved me. He said, 'Karl is a good workman, and he shall soon be my *Geselle*.'* But man proposes and God disposes. In 1796 conscription was ordered, and all who were fit for service, from eighteen to twenty-one years of age, had to go to town.

"Papa and brother Johann came to town, and we went together to draw *Loos*** to see who should be a soldier and who should not be a soldier. Johann drew a bad number: he had to become a soldier. I drew a good number: I was not obliged to become a soldier. And Daddy said, 'I had one son, and I must part with him! *Ich hatte einen einzigen Sohn und von diesem muss ich mich trennen!*'

"I took his hand and said, 'Why did you say that, Daddy? Come with me, I'll tell you something.' And Daddy came. Daddy came, and we seated ourselves at a little table in the tavern. 'Give us a couple of *Bier-krug*,'*** I said, and they were brought. We both drank one, and brother Johann drank also.

" 'Daddy,' I said, 'do not say that you had one son, and you must part with him. My heart wants to *leap out* when I hear *that*. Brother Johann shall not go to the army: I will be a soldier. No one needs Karl here, and Karl will be a soldier.'

" 'You're an honest man, Karl,' Daddy said to me, and he kissed me.

"And I became a soldier."

---

* Journeyman.—*Ed.*
** Lots.—*Ed.*
*** Pitchers of beer.—*Ed.*

Chapter IX

CONTINUATION OF THE PRECEDING

"That was a terrible time, Nikolenka," continued Karl Ivanich. "Napoleon was alive then. He wanted to conquer Germany and we defended our country to the last drop of blood!—*und wir vertheidigten unser Vaterland bis auf den letzten Tropfen Blut!*

"I was at Ulm, I was at Austerlitz, I was at Wagram."

"Did you fight too?" I asked, gazing at him in amazement. "Did you also kill men?"

Karl Ivanich immediately eased my mind on that score.

"Once a French Grenadier dropped behind his comrades and fell on the road. I ran up with my gun, and was about to kill him, *aber der Franzose warf sein Gewehr und rief pardon,** and I let him go.

"At Wagram Napoleon chased us to the island, and surrounded us so that there was no escaping anywhere. For three days we had no provisions, and we stood in the water up to our knees.

"The villain would neither take us prisoners nor let us escape. *Und der Bösewicht Napoleon wollte uns nicht gefangen nehmen und auch nicht freilassen!*

"On the fourth day, thank God, we were taken prisoners and led off to a fortress. I had on blue trousers, a uniform of good cloth, fifteen thalers, and a silver watch, a present from my daddy. A French soldier took it all from me. Fortunately, I had three ducats left which Mamma had sewn into my doublet. Nobody found them.

"I did not wish to remain long in the fortress, and decided to escape. Once on a great feast day I told the sergeant who looked after us, 'Herr Sergeant, this is a solemn festival, and I want to observe it. Please fetch

---

* But the Frenchman threw away his gun and cried "Mercy!"—*Ed.*

two bottles of Madeira, and we shall drink them together.' And the sergeant said, 'Very good.' When the sergeant brought the Madeira, and we had drunk a glass each, I took him by the hand and said, 'Herr Sergeant, do you happen to have a father and mother?' He said, 'Yes, Herr Mauer.' 'My father and mother,' said I, 'have not seen me for eight years, and do not know whether I am alive or whether my bones are lying in the damp earth. O Herr Sergeant! I have two ducats, which were in my doublet; take them, and let me go. Be my benefactor, and my mamma will pray to Almighty God for you all her life.'

"The sergeant drank a glass of Madeira, and said, 'Herr Mauer, I love and pity you extremely; but you are a prisoner, and I am a soldier.' I pressed his hand and said, 'Herr Sergeant!' *Ich drückte ihm die Hand und sagte: 'Herr Sergeant!'*

"And the sergeant said, 'You are a poor man, and I will not take your money; but I will help you. When I go to bed, buy a bucket of brandy for the soldiers, and they will sleep. I will not watch you.'

"He was a good man. I bought the bucket of brandy; and when the soldiers were drunk I put on my boots and my old greatcoat and went out of the door. I went to the wall, with the intention of jumping over; but there was water there, and I would not spoil my last remaining clothes. I went to the gate.

"The sentry was marching *auf und ab** with his gun, and he looked at me. *'Qui vive?' sagte er auf einmal,*** and I did not answer. *'Qui vive?'* said he a second time, and I made no answer. *'Qui vive?'* he said for the third time, *and I ran away! I sprang into the water, climbed out on the other side, and ran on.*

---

* Up and down.—*Ed.*
** "Who goes there?" said he all of a sudden.—*Ed.*

"All night I ran along the road; but when it began to dawn I was afraid that they would recognize me, and I hid in the tall rye. Then I knelt down, joined my hands, thanked our heavenly Father for saving me, and fell asleep with a tranquil mind.

"I awoke in the evening, and went on. All at once a great German waggon with two black horses overtook me. In the waggon sat a handsomely-dressed man, who was smoking a pipe and looking at me. I walked slowly, in order that the waggon might pass me; but when I went slowly the waggon went slowly too, and the man stared at me. I walked quicker and so did the waggon, and the man was staring at me all the time. I sat down by the roadside; the man stopped his horses and looked at me. 'Young man,' said he, 'where are you going so late?' I said, 'I am going to Frankfort.' 'Get into my waggon; there's room, and I will take you there. Why have you nothing with you? why is your beard unshaved? and why are your clothes muddy?' he asked me when I had seated myself by him. 'I am a poor man,' I said. 'I want to hire myself somewhere as a workman; and my clothes are muddy because I fell down on the road.' 'You are telling an untruth, young man,' said he; 'the road is dry now.'

"And I remained silent.

" 'Tell me the whole truth,' said the good man to me. 'Who are you, and where have you come from? I like the look of you, and if you are an honest man I shall help you.'

"And I told him all. He said, 'Very good, young man. Come to my rope-factory. I shall give you work, clothes, and money, and you shall live with me.'

"And I said, 'Very well.'

"We went to the rope-factory, and the good man said to his wife, 'Here is a young man who has fought for his country and escaped from captivity; he has neither home,

164

clothes, nor bread. He will live with me. Give him some clean linen and feed him.'

"I lived at the rope-factory for a year and a half, and my master became so fond of me that he would not let me go. I was a handsome man then; I was young, tall, with blue eyes and a Roman nose; and Madame L. (I cannot mention her name), the wife of my master, was a young and pretty woman, and she fell in love with me.

"When she saw me she said, 'Herr Mauer, what does your mamma call you?' I said 'Karlchen.'

"And she said, 'Karlchen, sit here beside me.'

"I sat beside her, and she said, 'Karlchen, kiss me!'

"I kissed her, and she said, 'Karlchen, I love you so much that I cannot endure it any longer,' and she trembled all over."

Here Karl Ivanich made a long pause; and rolling up his kind blue eyes, he rocked his head and began to smile, as people do when under the influence of pleasant reminiscences.

"Yes," he began again, settling himself in his arm-chair and drawing his dressing-gown about him, "I have been through a great deal, both good and bad, in my life; but He is my witness," he said, pointing to a figure of the Saviour, embroidered on canvas, which hung over his bed, "nobody can say that Karl Ivanich has been a dishonest man! I would not repay the kindness Herr L. had shown me with black ingratitude, and I decided to run away from him. In the evening, when all had gone to bed, I wrote a letter to my master, laid it on the table in my room, took my clothes and three thalers, and stepped noiselessly out into the street. No one saw me, and I set out along the road."

Chapter X

CONTINUATION

"I had not seen my mamma for nine years; and I did not know whether she was alive or whether her bones were already lying in the damp earth. I returned to my fatherland. When I reached the town I asked where Gustav Mauer lived, who had been farmer to Count Sommerblatt, and they told me, 'Count Sommerblatt is dead, and Gustav Mauer lives in the main street, and keeps a liquor-shop.' I put on my new vest, a handsome coat (a gift of the manufacturer), brushed my hair well, and went to my dad's liquor-shop. My sister Mariechen was sitting in the shop; she asked me what I wanted. I said, 'May I have a glass of liquor?' and she said, '*Vater*, a young man is asking for a glass of liquor.' And Dad said, 'Give the young man a glass of liquor.' I sat down at the table, drank my glass of liquor, smoked my pipe, and looked at Dad, Mariechen, and Johann, who had also entered the shop. During the conversation Dad said to me, 'You probably know, young man, where our army is now?' I said, 'I have come from the army myself, and it is near Vienna.' 'Our son,' said Dad, 'was a soldier, and it is nine years since he wrote to us, and we do not know whether he is alive or dead. My wife is always weeping for him.' I smoked away at my pipe and said, 'What was your son's name, and where did he serve? Perhaps I know him.' 'His name was Karl Mauer, and he served in the Austrian *Jägers*,' said Papa. He was a tall, handsome man, like you,' said sister Mariechen.

"'I know your Karl,' said I. 'Amalia!' *sagte auf einmal mein Vater,** 'come here; here is a young man who knows our Karl.' *And my dear mamma comes through*

* My father said suddenly.—*Ed.*

166

the rear door. I recognized her at once. 'You know our Karl?' she said, looked at me, turned very pale, and began to tremble. 'Yes, I have seen him,' said I, and did not dare to raise my eyes to her; my heart wanted to *leap.* 'My Karl is alive!' said Mamma, 'Thank God! Where is he, my dear Karl? I should die in peace if I could see him once more, my beloved son; but it is not God's will,' and she began to cry. *I could not bear it.* 'Mamma,' said I, 'I am your Karl,' *and she fell into my arms.*"

Karl Ivanich closed his eyes, and his lips trembled

" '*Mutter!' sagte ich, 'ich bin ihr Sohn, ich bin ihr Karl und sie stürzte mir in die Arme,'* " he repeated, composing himself somewhat and wiping away the big tears which rolled down his cheeks.

"But it was not God's pleasure that I should end my days in my own country. It was my fate to be unhappy. *Das Unglück vervolgte mich überall! ...** I lived in my native land only three months. One Sunday I was in a coffee-house buying a jug of beer, smoking my pipe, and talking *Politik* with my friends, and about the Emperor Franz, about Napoleon and the war, and each one was saying his opinion. Near us sat a strange gentleman, in a grey *Überrock* drinking coffee, and smoking a pipe, and not saying a word. *Er rauchte sein Pfeifchen und schwieg still.* When the night watchman cried ten o'clock I took my hat, paid, and went home. About midnight some one knocked at the door. I woke up and asked, 'Who's there?' '*Macht auf!*'** 'Tell me who you are,' I said, 'and I will open.' *Ich sagte: 'Sagt, wer ihr seid, und ich werde aufmachen.'* 'Macht auf im Namen des Gesetzes!'***I opened. Two soldiers with guns stood at the door, and the stranger in the grey *Überrock* who had been sitting near us in the coffee-house entered the room.

---

* Misfortune pursued me everywhere.—*Ed.*
** Open the door!—*Ed.*
*** Open in the name of the law.—*Ed.*

He was a spy. *Es war ein Spion.* 'Come with me,' said the spy. 'Very good,' said I. I put on my boots and trousers, put on my braces, and walked about the room. I was raging at heart. I said, 'He is a villain.' When I reached the wall where my sword hung, I suddenly seized it, and said, *'You are a spy: defend yourself!'* I gave him *ein Hieb** on the right, *ein Hieb* on the left, *and one on the head. The spy fell!* I seized my *Mantlesack*** and my *Beutel,*** and leaped out of the window. *Ich kam nach Ems;**** there I made the acquaintance of General Sazin. He took a fancy to me, got a passport from the ambassador, and took me to Russia with him to teach his children. When General Sazin died, your mamma called me to her. 'Karl Ivanich,' she said. 'I give my children into your charge; love them, and I will never discharge you; I will make your old age comfortable.' Now she is dead, and all is forgotten. After twenty years' service I must now go out into the street in my old age to seek a crust of dry bread. *God sees it and knows it, and His holy will be done; only I am sorry for you, children!"* Karl Ivanich concluded, drawing me to him by the hand and kissing me on the head.

Chapter XI

BAD MARKS

The year of mourning ended and Grandmamma recovered somewhat from her grief, and began to receive guests now and then, especially children, boys and girls of our own age.

On Lyubochka's birthday, the 13th of December, Princess Kornakova and her daughters, Valakhina and Sone-

* A stroke.—*Ed.*
** Suit-case. Purse.—*Ed.*
*** I went to Ems.—*Ed.*

chka, Ilenka Grap, and the two younger Ivin brothers, arrived before dinner.

Though we could hear talking, laughter, and running about in the drawing-room below, we could not join them until our morning lessons were finished. The time-table in the school-room said: *"Lundi, de 2 à 3, Maître d'Histoire et de Géographie"**; and it was that history teacher whom we were obliged to wait for, listen to, and say good-bye to before we were free. It was twenty minutes past two, but there was still no sign of him even in the street which I watched with a strong desire never to see him at all.

"I don't think Lebedev is coming today," said Volodya, looking up for a moment from Smaragdov's book, out of which he was preparing his lesson.

"I hope to God he won't, because I know nothing. But there he is," I added in a tone of disappointment.

Volodya rose and came to the window.

"No, that is not he; it is some gentleman," said he. "Let's wait until half-past two," he added, stretching himself and scratching his head, as he used to do when resting a minute from his work; "if he has not come by half-past two, we can ask St. Jérôme to put away our note-books."

"Why should he come at all," I said, also stretching and shaking Kaidanov's book above my head with both hands.

For lack of something to do I opened the book at the place of the lesson and began to read it. The lesson was long and difficult. I knew nothing about it, and I realized that I would not succeed in memorizing anything, the more so as I was in that state of nervous irritation in which the mind refuses to concentrate on any subject.

---

* Monday from 2 to 3, history and geography teacher.—*Ed.*

After our last history lesson (which always seemed to me the most stupid and boring of all subjects) Lebedev had complained to St. Jérôme about me and marked me two in my report, which was considered very bad. St. Jérôme told me then that if I got less than three at the next lesson I should be severely punished. Now the next lesson was at hand, and I confess that I felt very much afraid.

I was so carried away with reading over the unlearned lesson that the sound of galoshes being removed in the anteroom caused me a sudden start. I hardly had time to look round before the pock-marked face, so disgusting to me, and the teacher's awkward, only too well-known figure, in its blue coat closely fastened with scholastic buttons, appeared in the doorway.

Slowly he deposited his hat on the window, his note-books on the table, pulled aside the tails of his coat (as though it were a very necessary operation), and seated himself with a puff in his place.

"Now, gentlemen," said he, rubbing one perspiring hand over the other; "let us first review what we saw at the last lesson, and then I shall endeavour to acquaint you with the subsequent events of the Middle Ages."

That meant: Say your lesson.

While Volodya was answering him with the ease and assurance which come of knowing the subject thoroughly, I went aimlessly out on the stairs; and as I was not allowed to go down, it was very natural that I should find myself on the landing without noticing it. But just as I was about to take up my usual *coign of vantage* behind a door, Mimi, who had always been the cause of my misfortunes, suddenly ran against me. "You here?" said she, looking threateningly at me, then at the door of the maids' room, and then at me again.

I felt thoroughly guilty, both because I was not in the school-room and because I was in a place where I had no business to be. So I held my tongue and, hanging my head, exhibited in my person the most touching expression of penitence. "This is too bad!" said Mimi. "What are you doing here?" I remained silent. "No, it won't remain at that," she went on, rapping with her knuckles on the hand-rail; "I shall tell the Countess all about it."

It was five minutes to three by the time I returned to the school-room. The teacher was explaining the following lesson to Volodya as though oblivious of my presence. When he had finished his exposition he began to put his note-books together, and Volodya went into the other room to fetch the lesson-ticket; and the comforting thought occurred to me that all was over and that I had been forgotten.

But all at once the teacher turned to me with a malicious half smile.

"I hope you have learned your lesson, sir," he said, rubbing his hands.

"Yes, sir," I answered.

"Will you tell me something about St. Louis's crusade then," said he, balancing himself in his chair and gazing thoughtfully at his feet. "Tell me first the causes which induced the French King to take the cross," said he, raising his brows and pointing his finger at the ink-bottle. "Then you may explain to me the general characteristics of that expedition," he added, making a movement with his wrist as though endeavouring to catch something. "And, finally, the influence of this crusade upon European states in general," said he, striking the left side of the table with his note-books, "and upon the kingdom of France in particular," he concluded, striking the right side of the table and inclining his head to the right.

I swallowed a few times, coughed, bent my head on one side, and remained silent. Then pecking at a quill which lay upon the table, I began to pluck it to pieces, still remaining silent.

"Give me that quill, please," said the teacher, extending his hand; "it is good for something. Well, sir?"

"Lou—er—King—St. Louis—was—was—er—a good and wise tsar."

"What, sir?"

"A tsar. He made up his mind to go to Jerusalem, and *transferred the reins of government* to his mother."

"What was her name?"

"B—b—lanka."

"What, sir? Bulanka?"*

I laughed in a wry and forced way.

"Hm. Do you know anything else?" he asked.

I had nothing to lose now, so I coughed, and began to say any nonsense that came to my head. The teacher, who sat silently flicking the dust from the table with the quill pen which he had taken away from me, gazed straight past my ear and repeated, "Good, very good, sir." I was conscious that I knew nothing, that I was not expressing myself at all as I should; and it upset me frightfully to see that the teacher did not stop me or correct me.

"Why did he make up his mind to go to Jerusalem?" said he, repeating my words.

"Because—in order to—for the purpose of—because"— I floundered hopelessly and could not say another word; I felt that if that spiteful teacher were to hold his tongue for a whole year and gaze inquiringly at me, I should still not be able to produce another sound. The teacher stared at me for three minutes; then an expression of profound sorrow appeared on his face, and he said in an earnest tone to Volodya, who had just entered the room:

---

* Name for a cream-coloured horse.—*Tr*.

"Give me the record-book, please."

Volodya gave him the book, and carefully laid the ticket beside it.

The teacher opened the book and, cautiously dipping his pen, he put down five, in his beautiful hand, for Volodya, under the head of recitations and behaviour. Then he poised his pen over the column in which my marks were recorded, looked at me, flicked off the ink, and became engrossed in thought.

All at once his hand made an almost imperceptible movement, and there appeared a handsomely shaped one and a full stop; another movement, and in the conduct column stood another one and a full stop.

Carefully closing the record-book, the teacher rose and went to the door as though not noticing my glance, in which despair, entreaty, and reproach were expressed.

"Mikhail Illarionovich," said I.

"No," said he, understanding at once what I wanted to say to him; "that is not the way to study. I will not be paid for nothing."

The teacher put on his galoshes and his camlet cloak and tied his scarf with great care. As if any one could care for anything after what had happened to me! A movement of the pen for him, but the greatest misfortune for me.

"Is the lesson ended?" inquired St. Jérôme, entering the room."

"Yes."

"Was your teacher satisfied with you?"

"Yes," said Volodya.

"What mark did you get?"

"Five."

"And Nicholas?"

I said nothing.

"Four, I think," said Volodya.

He knew that it was necessary to save me, if only for that day. If I were to be punished, let it not be today when there were guests in the house.

"*Voyons, Messieurs*," St. Jérôme had a way prefacing all he said with *voyons, "faites votre toilette et nous descendons.*"

Chapter XII

THE LITTLE KEY

We had hardly got downstairs and greeted our guests when dinner was announced. Papa was in high spirits (his luck was in at cards just then); he presented Lyubochka with a handsome silver service, and after dinner remembered that in his house he also had a bonbonnière which he intended for her.

"Why send a servant? It will be better if you go, Koko," he said to me. "The keys are on the large desk, in the shell, you know. Take them, and with the very largest one open the second drawer on the right. There you will find the box and some sweetmeats in a paper; bring them all here." "And shall I bring you your cigars?" I asked, knowing that he always sent for some after dinner.

"Yes, do, but don't touch anything else," he called after me.

I found the keys where he had said, and was about to open the drawer, when I was stopped by a desire to know what a very small key which hung on the same bunch belonged to.

On the desk, amid a number of various objects, and near the rail, lay an embroidered portfolio with a padlock; I took a fancy to try whether the little key would fit it. My attempt was crowned with complete success: the portfolio opened, and in it I found a whole heap of papers.

Curiosity so strongly urged me to find out what those papers were, that the voice of conscience was stilled, and I set to work to examine what was in the portfolio.

.   .   .   .

The childish sentiment of unquestioning respect towards all my elders, and especially towards Papa, was so strong within me that my mind instinctively refused to draw any conclusions from what I saw. I felt that Papa must live in a sphere of his own, beautiful, inaccessible, and incomprehensible to me, and that any attempt to penetrate the secrets of his life would be a kind of sacrilege on my part.

Therefore the discoveries which I almost involuntarily made in Papa's portfolio left in me no clear impression but only a dim knowledge that I had behaved wrongly. I felt ashamed and uncomfortable.

This feeling made me wish to close the portfolio as quickly as possible, but I was evidently fated to endure every possible kind of misfortune upon that memorable day. Inserting the key in the keyhole of the padlock, I turned it the wrong way; supposing that the lock was closed, I pulled out the key, and—oh, horror! the head of the key came away with my hand. In vain did I endeavour to unite it with the half in the lock, and release it by means of some magic. I was forced at length to resign myself to the frightful thought that I had committed a fresh crime, which must be discovered that very day when Papa returned to his study.

Mimi's complaint, the bad mark, and that little key! Nothing worse could have happened to me. Grandmamma on account of Mimi's complaint, St. Jérôme about the bad mark, Papa about that key—they would all pounce upon me, and not later than that very evening.

"What will become of me? Oh, what have I done?" I said aloud, as I paced the soft carpet of the study. "Ah," I said to myself, as I got the sweetmeats and cigars, *"what must be, will be,"* and I ran into the house.

This fatalistic saying, which I had heard from Nikolai in my childhood, produced a beneficial and temporarily soothing effect upon me at all difficult moments in my life. When I entered the hall I was in a somewhat excited and unnatural yet extremely cheerful mood.

Chapter XIII

THE TRAITRESS

After dinner *petits jeux* began, and I took a most lively part in them. While playing Puss in the Corner I bumped into the Kornakovs' governess, who was playing with us, accidentally stepped on her dress, and tore it. Noticing that it was great satisfaction for all the girls, especially Sonechka, to see the governess retire with a sour face to the maids' room to put a stitch in her dress, I resolved to procure them that pleasure once more. In consequence of this amiable intention, the governess had no sooner returned to the room than I began to gallop round her, and kept up this evolution until I found a favourable opportunity to catch my heel once more in her skirt and tear it. Sonechka and the princesses could hardly restrain their laughter, which very much flattered my vanity; but St. Jérôme, who must have been observing my escapade, came up to me and said with a frown (which I could not endure) that my merriness seemed to be of ill omen, and that if I did not behave he would make me repent of it, even though it was a festive day.

But I was in the state of excitement of a man who has gambled away more than he has in his pocket, and who is afraid to reckon up his accounts, and continues to risk desperate stakes without any hope of redeeming himself, just so as to keep his mind off reality. I smiled impudently and walked away from him.

After the game of Puss in the Corner some one started a game which we called *Lange Nase.** Chairs were placed in two rows facing each other, and the ladies and gentlemen divided into two sides, each choosing partners by turns.

The youngest Princess chose the younger of the Ivin brothers every time; Katenka chose either Volodya or Ilenka; Sonechka took Seryozha every time, and, to my extreme amazement, was not in the least abashed when Seryozha went and seated himself directly opposite her. She laughed with her sweet, ringing laugh, and nodded to him to show that he had guessed right. Nobody ever chose me and it deeply wounded my pride to realize that I was superfluous, *left over*; that they had to say of me every time, "*Who still remains? Yes, Nikolenka; well, take him.*"

When, therefore, it came my turn to guess who had chosen me, I went boldly up either to my sister or to one of the ugly princesses and, unfortunately, was never wrong. Sonechka seemed so absorbed in Seryozha Ivin that for her I just did not exist. I do not know on what grounds I mentally called her a *traitress*, since she had never promised to choose me and not Seryozha; but I was firmly convinced that she had behaved in the most revolting manner.

After the game I noticed that the *traitress*, whom I despised, but from whom, nevertheless, I could not take my eyes, had retired into a corner with Seryozha and Katenka, where they were engaged in some mysterious conversation. I crept up behind the piano in order to discover their secret, and this is what I saw: Katenka was holding a cambric handkerchief by two corners, thus forming a screen between Sonechka's head and Seryozha's. "No, you

---

* Long Nose.—*Ed.*

have lost; now you must pay the forfeit!" said Seryozha. Sonechka stood guiltily before him, her arms hanging beside her, and said, blushing, "No, I have not lost; have I, Mlle. Catherine?" "I like to play fair," replied Katenka; "you have lost your forfeit, my dear."

Katenka had hardly uttered these words when Seryozha bent over Sonechka and kissed her. He kissed her full upon her rosy lips. And Sonechka laughed as though that were nothing, as though it were very jolly. How horrid! Oh, the *artful traitress*!

Chapter XIV

ECLIPSE

I felt a sudden contempt for the female sex in general, and for Sonechka in particular; I began to assure myself that there was nothing jolly about those games, that they were fit for *girls*; and I longed to create an uproar, to do something of such extraordinary boldness that would astonish everybody. An occasion was not long in presenting itself.

St. Jérôme, after talking to Mimi about something, left the room; I could hear his footsteps going upstairs, and then above us, in the direction of the school-room. The thought occurred to me that Mimi had told him where she had seen me during lesson hours, and that he had gone to inspect the register. At that time I did not credit St. Jérôme with any other aim in life than a desire to punish me. I had read somewhere that children between twelve and fourteen years of age, that is to say, those who are in the transition stage of boyhood, are particularly inclined to arson and even murder. In recalling my boyhood, and especially the frame of mind in which I was on that unlucky day, I very clearly appreciate the possibility of the most frightful crime, committed without object or intent to injure, but out of curiosity, out of an instinctive need for activity. There are times when the future presents itself to a man in such sombre colours that he dreads to fix his mental gaze upon it, entirely stops his mind from thinking, and endeavours to persuade himself that the future will never be and that the past has never been. At such moments, when thought does not assess beforehand every decision of the will, and the fleshly instincts remain the sole spring of life, I can understand how a child, by reason of his inexperience, is particularly inclined to such a frame of mind. Then he may set fire to the very house in which his brothers, his father and mother, whom he tenderly loves, are sleeping, without the slightest fear or hesitation, and with a smile of curiosity. Under the influence of the same temporary absence of reflection—almost absence of mind—a peasant lad of seventeen, contemplating the freshly sharpened edge of an axe beside the bench on which his aged father sleeps face downward, suddenly wields the axe, and gazes with stupid curiosity at the blood spurting from the wound in the sleeper's neck; under the influence of the same absence of reflection and instinctive curiosity, a man experiences a certain enjoyment in pausing upon the brink of a precipice and thinking, "What if I should throw myself down?" Or in placing a loaded pistol to his forehead, and wondering, "What if I were to pull the trigger?" Or in thinking as he gazes at some person for whom society universally entertains a peculiar respect, "What if I were to go up to him, take him by the nose, and say, 'Come, my dear fellow, let's go.' "

Under the influence of this kind of internal agitation and absence of reflection, when St. Jérôme came downstairs and told me that I had no right to be there that evening, because I had so ill-behaved and studied so badly, and that I was to go upstairs at once, I stuck out my tongue at him and said that I would not move from where I was.

Surprise and anger for a moment prevented St. Jérôme from uttering a word.

"*C'est bien,*" he said, bearing down upon me; "I have promised to punish you several times already, and your Grandmamma's wish saved you; but now I see that nothing but the birch will make you dutiful, and you fully deserve it today."

He spoke so loud that every one heard what he said. I felt the blood rush to my heart with unusual violence, making it beat so wildly, that the colour fled from my face, and my lips trembled quite involuntarily. I must have looked terrible at that moment, for St. Jérôme, avoiding my glance, came quickly up to me and seized me by the hand; but I no sooner felt the touch of his hand than, beside myself with rage, I tore my hand away and struck him with all my childish strength.

"What has come over you?" said Volodya, approaching, amazed and horrified at my behaviour.

"Let me alone!" I shouted, the tears flowing fast; "not one of you loves me, nor understands how unhappy I am. You are all wicked and disgusting," I added, turning to the whole company in a paroxysm of rage.

But meanwhile St. Jérôme came up to me with a pale, determined face, and before I could adopt a position of defence he gripped both my hands as in a vice with a powerful movement, and dragged me away. My head was whirling with rage. I only remember fighting desperately with head and knees as long as I had any strength left. I remember my nose coming several times in contact with some one's hips, and somebody's coat getting into my mouth, and my being conscious of the presence of some one's feet all around me, and of the smell of dust, and of *violette* with which St. Jérôme perfumed himself.

Five minutes later the garret door closed behind me.

"Vasili!" said *he*, in a revolting, triumphant voice, "bring the birch." . . . .

Chapter XV

REVERIE

Could I at that time imagine that I should survive all the misfortunes which befell me, and that the day would come when I should recall them with composure?

When I remembered what I had done I could not imagine what would become of me, but I had a dim presentiment that I was for ever lost.

At first absolute silence reigned downstairs and around me, or so it seemed to me at least, because of my overpowering inner agitation; but gradually I began to distinguish the different sounds. Vasili came up, and, flinging on the window-ledge something which resembled a broom, he lay down on the chest with a yawn. Below St. Jérôme's loud voice could be heard (he must have been speaking of me), then children's voices, then laughter and running; and a few minutes later everything in the house had again resumed its former course, as though no one knew or thought of me sitting in the dark garret.

I did not cry, but something lay heavy, like a stone, upon my heart. Thoughts and visions flashed before my disturbed imagination; yet the memory of the misfortune which had overtaken me incessantly broke their fanciful chain, and again plunged me into an endless labyrinth of uncertainty as to the fate which awaited me, of terror and despair.

Now it occurred to me that there must exist some cause for the general dislike and even hatred of me. (At that time I was firmly convinced that everybody, from Grandmamma down to Philip the coachman, hated me and found pleasure in my sufferings.) Probably I am not the son of my father and mother, not Volodya's brother, but an unhappy orphan, a foundling, adopted out of charity, I thought; and this absurd idea not only afforded me a certain melancholy comfort, but even appeared quite likely. I rejoiced at the thought that I was unhappy not because I myself was to blame, but because such was my fate from my very birth, and that my lot was similar to that of the unfortunate Karl Ivanich.

"But why conceal this secret any longer, now that I have discovered it?" I said to myself. "Tomorrow I will go to Papa and say to him, 'Papa, in vain do you conceal from me the secret of my birth; I know it.' He will say, 'Well—since you know—sooner or later you would have learned it. You are not my son; but I have adopted you, and if you prove worthy of my love I will never abandon you.' And I shall say to him, 'Papa, although I have no right to call you by that name, and am now doing so for the last time—I have always loved you, and I shall always love you, and I shall never forget that you are my benefactor; but I can no longer remain in your house. No one here loves me, and St. Jérôme has sworn my ruin. Either he or I must leave your house, because I cannot answer for myself. I hate that man to such a degree that I am ready to do anything. I will kill him—that's what I shall say—'Papa, I will kill him.' Papa will begin to entreat me, but I shall wave him aside and say, 'No, my friend, my benefactor, we cannot live together; let me go.' And then I will embrace him, and say in French, '*Oh mon père, oh mon bienfaiteur, donnez moi pour la dernière fois ta bénédiction et que la volonté de Dieu soit faite!*' "* And

---

* O my father! O my benefactor! give me thy blessing for the last time, and God's will be done.—*Ed*.

as I sat on the chest in the dark store-room, I sobbed bitterly at the thought. Then all at once I remembered the shameful punishment in store for me; reality presented itself to me in its true light, and my dreams instantly took flight.

Then I imagined myself already at liberty, far away from home. I enter the Hussars, and go to the war. Enemies bear down upon me from all sides; I brandish my sword, and kill one, then another, and then a third. Finally, exhausted by wounds and fatigue, I fall to the ground and shout "Victory!" The general approaches, and asks, "Where is our saviour?" They point me out to him: he falls on my neck, and shouts, with tears of joy, "Victory!" I recover, and with my arm in a black sling, I stroll along Tverskoi Boulevard. I am a general! I meet the Emperor, and he asks, "Who is this wounded young man?" He is told that it is Nikolai, the hero of renown. The Emperor comes up to me and says, "I thank you. I will do anything you ask of me." I bow respectfully, and, leaning on my sword I say, "I am happy, great Emperor, to have been able to shed my blood for my fatherland, and I would gladly die for it; yet since you are so gracious, allow me to beg one thing of you—permit me to annihilate my enemy, the foreigner, St. Jérôme." I halt threateningly before St. Jérôme, and say to him, "You have caused my misfortune. *A genoux!**" But suddenly the thought occurs to me that the real St. Jérôme may enter at any moment with the birch; and again I see myself, not a general delivering his country, but a very pitiful, weeping creature.

The thought of God comes to me, and I ask Him impudently why He is punishing me. "I have never forgotten my prayers, morning and evening; then why do I suffer?" I can assert without any doubt that the first step towards

---

* On your knees!—*Ed.*

the religious doubts which troubled me during my boyhood was taken then, not because unhappiness incited me to murmuring and unbelief, but because the thought of the injustice of Providence, which entered my mind at that time of spiritual disarray and that whole day of solitude quickly grew and put forth roots, like a pernicious seed which has fallen upon soft earth after rain. Then I fancied that I was going to die, and conjured vivid imaginations of St. Jérôme's bewilderment at finding a lifeless body in the garret instead of me. Recalling Natalya Savishna's tales of how the soul of a dead person does not leave the house for forty days, I imagined myself flying, unseen, through all the rooms of Grandmamma's house, and observing Lyubochka's sincere tears, Grandmamma's grief, and Papa's conversation with St. Jérôme. "He was a fine boy," Papa would say, with tears in his eyes. "Yes," St. Jérôme would reply, "but a terrible scapegrace." "You should respect the dead," Papa would say. "You were the cause of his death; you frightened him; he could not endure the humiliation which you were preparing for him. Away with you, you villain!"

And St. Jérôme would fall on his knees, and weep, and sue for pardon. At the end of the forty days my soul would fly to heaven; there I would see something wonderfully beautiful, white, transparent, and long, and I would feel that it was Mamma. And this white something would surround me, and caress me; but I would feel uneasy as though I did not recognize her. "If it really is you," I would say, "then let me see you more clearly, that I may embrace you." And her voice would answer me, "Here we are all so. I cannot embrace you any better. Do you not feel happy thus?" "Oh yes, I do! But you cannot tickle me, and I cannot kiss your hands." "There is no need to. It is beautiful here as it is," she would say, and I would feel that it really was very beautiful, and we would soar away together, higher and ever higher. Then I would suddenly seem to wake and find myself again on the chest in the dark garret, my cheeks wet with tears, my mind a blank, repeating the words, *"And we soar higher and ever higher."* For a long time I concentrated my strength in an attempt to explain my situation; but all my mind could imagine at the moment was a boundless expanse, impenetrable and dreadful in its gloominess. I endeavoured to resume the delightful dreams of bliss which consciousness of reality had cut short; but, to my amazement, no sooner did I tread the paths of my former reveries than I saw that to continue along them was impossible, nor, what was still more surprising, did it any longer afford me pleasure.

Chapter XVI

NO MEAL WITHOUT GRINDING

I spent the night in the garret, and no one came near me; it was not until the following day, that is to say, on Sunday, that I was taken to a little room adjoining the school-room and again locked in. I began to hope that my punishment would be confined to locking up; and my thoughts, under the influence of sweet, refreshing slumber, of the bright sunlight playing upon the frost patterns on the windows, and the customary noises of the day in the streets, began to grow composed. Nevertheless, my solitude was very oppressive; I wanted to move about, to tell somebody all that was seething in my soul, and there was not a living being near me. My position was all the more unpleasant because, however repulsive it was to me, I could not avoid hearing St. Jérôme whistling gay tunes with perfect tranquillity as he walked about his room. I was perfectly convinced that he did not want to whistle at all, but that he did it solely for the sake of tormenting me.

At two o'clock St. Jérôme and Volodya went downstairs; and Nikolai brought me my dinner, and when I spoke to him about what I had done and what awaited me, he said:

"Pshaw, sir! don't grieve; you can't get meal without grinding."

This saying, which later more than once sustained my firmness of spirit, comforted me somewhat; but the very fact that they had not sent me just bread and water, but a complete dinner, including fancy cakes, gave me much to think about. If they had not sent me the cakes, it would have meant that I was to be punished by locking up; now it turned out that my punishment was still to come and that I had only been isolated from the others because I was a bad influence. While I was busy solving this problem the key turned in the lock of my prison, and St. Jérôme entered with a stern, official countenance.

"Come down and see your grandmother," he said, without looking at me.

I wanted to clean the cuffs of my jacket, which were smeared with chalk, before leaving the room; but St. Jérôme told me that this was quite unnecessary, as though I were already in such a pitiful moral condition that it was not worth while to trouble about my outward appearance.

Katenka, Lyubochka, and Volodya stared at me as St. Jérôme led me through the hall by the hand, with exactly the same expression with which we used to gaze upon the prisoners who were led past our windows every Monday. And when I approached Grandmamma's chair with the intention of kissing her hand, she turned away from me and hid her hand beneath her mantilla.

"Well, my dear," she said, after a fairly long silence, during which she surveyed me from head to foot with such an expression that I did not know where to look or what to do with my hands, "I must say that you prize

my love and are a real consolation for me. Monsieur St.
Jérôme, who, at my request," she added, lingering on
each word, "undertook your education, does not wish
now to remain in my house any longer. And why? Because
of you, my dear. I did hope that you would be grateful for
his care and labour," she continued after a short silence,
and in a tone which showed that her speech had been
prepared beforehand, "and that you would understand the
value of his services; but you, a little boy, dared to raise
your hand against him. Very good! Very good indeed!
I also am beginning to think that you are incapable of
appreciating generous treatment, that other, grosser
methods are what you need. Beg his pardon this instant,"
she added in a tone of stern command, pointing to St. Jérôme; "do you hear?"

I glanced in the direction of Grandmamma's hand, and,
catching sight of St. Jérôme's coat, turned away and did
not stir from the spot; again I began to feel my heart
freezing.

"Well, don't you hear what I say to you?"

I trembled all over, but did not move.

"Koko!" said Grandmamma, who must have perceived
the inward agony which I was suffering. "Koko!" she said
in a tender rather than imperative voice, "is that you?"

"Grandmamma, I will not beg his pardon for anything," I said, and suddenly broke off, feeling that the
tears which were choking me would rush out if I uttered
another word.

"I order you; I ask you. Now then."

"I—I—won't—I can't," I gasped: and the sobs I had so
long contained suddenly burst forth in a flood of despair.

*"C'est ainsi que vous obéissez à votre seconde mère,
c'est ainsi que vous reconnaissez ses bontés,"** said St.
Jérôme in a tragic voice. *"A genoux!"*

---

* Is this the way you obey your second mother? Is this the
way you repay her kindness?—*Ed.*

"My God, if she had seen this!" said Grandmamma, turning from me and wiping away her tears. "If she had seen—all is for the best. No, she could not have borne this sorrow, never."

And Grandmamma wept more and more profusely. I wept also, but I had no intention of begging pardon.

"Tranquillisez-vous au nom du ciel,* M-me la Comtesse," said St. Jérôme.

But Grandmamma did not heed him; she covered her face with her hands, and her sobs soon became hiccoughs and hysterics. Mimi and Gasha rushed into the room with frightened faces and offered her smelling salts, and running and whispering could soon be heard all over the house.

"There's something for you to be proud of," said St. Jérôme, leading me upstairs.

"My God, what have I done? What a wicked boy I am!"

Hardly had St. Jérôme ordered me to my room and gone back to Grandmamma than I ran without knowing what I was doing to the great staircase leading to the street.

I do not remember whether I meant to run away or to drown myself; all I know is that covering my face with my hands so as not to see any one, I rushed blindly down the stairs.

"Where are you going?" suddenly asked a familiar voice. "You're just the one I want, my boy."

I tried to run past; but Papa caught me by the hand and said sternly:

"Oblige me by coming along. How dared you touch the portfolio in my study?" he asked, leading me after him into the little sitting-room. "Well! Why don't you answer?" he added, taking me by the ear.

"I'm sorry," I said; "I don't know what came over me."

---

* "Compose yourself, for heaven's sake."—*Ed.*

"Ah, you don't know what came over you! So you don't know, don't you? You don't know, eh? Really you don't know!" he repeated, giving my ear a pull at each word. "Will you poke your nose where you have no business in future? Will you? Will you?"

My ear hurt terribly, but I did not cry, and the moral feeling I experienced was a pleasant one. No sooner had Papa left hold of my ear than I seized his hand and began to cover it with tears and kisses.

"Beat me again," said I through my tears. "Beat me harder, so that it hurts me; I am a wicked boy, a wretched, miserable boy."

"What's the matter with you?" he said, giving me a slight push.

"No, I won't go," I said, clinging to his coat. "Everybody hates me, I know that; but, for God's sake, listen to me, protect me, or turn me out of the house. I cannot live with him; *he* does all he can to humiliate me. He makes me go on my knees before him. He wants to thrash me. I won't have it; I am not a little boy. I can't endure it; I shall die; I will kill myself. *He* told Grandmamma that I was wicked, and now she is ill, and she will die because of me. I—for God's sake, flog me! Why do they all torture me?"

I was choking with tears. I sat down on the divan, and dropped my head on his knees, sobbing so that it seemed to me that I should die that very minute.

"What are you crying about, you baby?" Papa asked with feeling, bending over me.

"*He* is my tyrant—tormentor. I shall die; nobody loves me!" I could hardly speak, and went into convulsions.

Papa took me in his arms and carried me into the bedroom. I fell asleep. When I awoke it was very late. A single candle was burning near my bed, and our family doctor, Mimi, and Lyubochka were sitting in the room.

189

It was evident from their faces that they feared for my health; but I felt so well and light after my twelve hours' sleep that I could have leapt from the bed had I not been reluctant to shake their belief that I was very ill.

Chapter XVII

HATRED

Yes, it was a feeling of real hatred. Not the hatred they write about in novels and in which I do not believe— hatred which delights in doing evil; but the hatred which inspires you with an insurmountable aversion for a person who nevertheless deserves your respect; which makes his hair, his neck, his walk, the sound of his voice, his every limb, his every motion, repulsive to you, and at the same time attracts you to him by some incomprehensible power and forces you anxiously to watch his slightest acts. This feeling I experienced towards St. Jérôme.

St. Jérôme had been with us for a year and a half. Judging the man now in cold blood, I find that he was a fine Frenchman, but a Frenchman through and through. He was not stupid; he was tolerably well educated, and he conscientiously fulfilled his duties towards us; but he possessed the traits which are typical of his countrymen and are so opposite to the Russian character—fickle egotism, vanity, impudence, and ignorant self-assurance. All this displeased me greatly.

Of course Grandmamma explained to him her views on corporal punishment, and he did not dare to whip us; but in spite of this he often threatened us, especially me, with the birch, and pronounced the word *fouetter** (as if it

_____
* To whip.—*Ed.*

were *fouatter*) in a very repulsive manner, and with an intonation which seemed to indicate that it would afford him the greatest satisfaction to flog me.

I did not fear the pain of punishment at all, never having experienced it; but the mere thought that St. Jérôme might beat me drove me into a state of suppressed rage and despair.

Sometimes Karl Ivanich, in a moment of vexation, had vented his spleen on us with the ruler or his braces, but I recalled this without the slightest anger. Even if Karl Ivanich had struck me at the time of which I am speaking (when I was fourteen), I should have borne it with perfect composure. I loved Karl Ivanich. I could remember him as far back as myself and was accustomed to consider him as one of the family; but St. Jérôme was a haughty, conceited man, for whom I felt no sentiment but that involuntary respect with which all *grown-up* people inspired me. Karl Ivanich was a ridiculous old man, a kind of manservant whom I heartily loved, but placed beneath myself in my childish conception of social status.

St. Jérôme, on the contrary, was a handsome, educated young dandy, who tried to stand on an equal footing with every one.

Karl Ivanich always scolded and punished us coolly. It was evident that he regarded it as a necessary but painful duty. St. Jérôme, on the other hand, liked to flaunt his role of preceptor. It was plain, when he punished us, that he did so more for his own satisfaction than for our good. He was puffed up with his own greatness. His grandiloquent French phrases, which he pronounced with strong emphasis on the last syllable and with circumflex accents, disgusted me beyond words. When Karl Ivanich got angry he said, "Puppets' comedy, mischievous boy, or Spanish fly!" St. Jérôme called us *"mauvais sujet, vilain garnement,"** and the like—names which wounded my pride.

* Scoundrel, wicked scamp.—*Ed.*

191

Karl Ivanich put us on our knees with our faces in a corner; and the punishment consisted merely in the bodily discomfort of the position; St. Jérôme would throw out his chest and shout, with a majestic wave of the hand, and in a tragic voice, "*A genoux, mauvais sujet!*" and make us kneel before him and beg his pardon. The punishment was in the humiliation.

I was not punished, and no one so much as mentioned to me what had happened; yet I could not forget all that I had suffered—the despair, shame, terror, and hatred of those two days. Despite the fact that from that time St. Jérôme seemed to give up all hopes of me, and hardly bothered with me at all, I could not bring myself to treat him with indifference. Every time our eyes met I felt that my look was too openly hostile and I hastened to assume an indifferent air, but then it seemed to me that he understood my hypocrisy, and I blushed and turned away altogether.

In a word, I cannot describe how loathsome it was for me to have anything to do with him.

Chapter XVIII

THE MAIDS' ROOM

I felt more and more lonely, and solitary reflections and observations formed my principal delights. Of the subject of my reflections I shall speak in a succeeding chapter; the chief scene of my observations was the maids' room, where a romance was in progress which interested and moved me profoundly. The heroine of this romance was Masha, of course. She was in love with Vasili, who had known her when she lived out of service, and had promised to marry her at that time. Fate, however, which had parted them five years before and again brought them

192

together in Grandmamma's house, placed a barrier between them in the person of Nikolai (Masha's uncle),
who would not hear of his niece's marriage with Vasili,
whom he called a *dull-witted and dissipated man.*

The effect of this obstacle was to cause the hitherto
cool-headed and indifferent Vasili to fall as passionately
in love with Masha as can only a serf tailor, wearing a
pink shirt and having his hair pomaded.

Although the demonstrations of his love were exceedingly strange and ill-chosen (for instance, when he met
Masha he always tried to cause her pain, and either
pinched her or slapped her or hugged her with such
violence that she could hardly breathe), his affection was
genuine, which was proved by the circumstance that from
the day when Nikolai finally refused him his niece's hand,
Vasili took to drinking from grief, and began to haunt
drinking-houses and create disturbances, in a word, to conduct himself so disgracefully that more than once he was
dealt ignominious chastisement by the police. But this
behaviour and its results made him more deserving in
Masha's eyes and increased her love for him. During
Vasili's detention Masha wept for days together without
drying her eyes, complained of her bitter fate to Gasha
(who took a lively interest in the affairs of the unhappy
lovers); and, scorning the scoldings and beatings of her
uncle, she stole away to the police station on the sly to
visit and comfort her friend.

Be not scornful, reader, of the society to which I am
introducing you. If the chords of love and sympathy have
not grown weak within your soul, sounds to which they
will respond will be found in the maids' room. Whether it
pleases you or not to follow me, I shall betake myself to
the landing from which I could see all that went
on in the maids' room. There is a bench, and on
it the flat-iron, the pasteboard doll with a broken nose,
the little wash-tub, and the hand-basin; there is a win-

dow-sill, upon which are heaped in confusion a lump of black wax, a skein of silk, a bitten, green cucumber and a bonbonnière; there also is the large red table; upon it a brick wrapped in calico lies on a piece of interrupted needlework, and behind it *she* sits in my favourite pink linen dress and blue kerchief, which particularly attracts my attention. She sews, pausing now and then in order to scratch her head with her needle or snuff a candle; and I gaze and think: Why was she not born a lady, with those bright blue eyes, that huge golden braid of hair, and that plump bosom? How it would have become her to sit in the drawing-room in a cap with pink ribbons and a deep red gown, not such as Mimi has, but like the one I saw on Tverskoi Boulevard! She would have embroidered on a frame, and I should have watched her in the mirror; and I would have done whatever she wanted; I would have handed her her mantle and her food myself.

And what a drunken face and disgusting figure that Vasili has in his tight coat, with that dirty pink shirt showing beneath it! At every movement of his body, at every bend of his spine, I seem to perceive the indisputable signs of the revolting punishment which overtook him.

"Oh, Vasya! Again—" exclaimed Masha, sticking her needle into the cushion, but not raising her head to greet Vasili as he entered.

"Yes, what about it? What good can you expect of him?" retorted Vasili. "If only he would settle it somehow! But here are my efforts all wasted, and all through *him*."

"Will you have some tea?" asked Nadezhda, another maid.

"I thank you humbly. And why does your bandit of an uncle hate me? Why? Because I have clothes of my own, because of my pride, because of my gait. Oh, damn it all!" concluded Vasili, with a wave of the hand.

"One must be obedient," said Masha, biting off her thread, "and you are so—"

"Can't stand it any longer, that's why!"

At that moment the door of Grandmamma's room banged and Gasha's grumbling voice could be heard as she came up the stairs.

"There! Try to please her, when she doesn't know herself what she wants. What a cursed life—sheer hard labour! Oh, I wish—the Lord forgive me," she muttered, throwing up her hands.

"My respects, Agafya Mikhailovna," said Vasili, rising to greet her.

"Oh, get away with you! I don't want your respects," she replied grimly, staring at him. "And why do you come here? Is the maids' room a place for men to come to?"

"I wanted to know how you are," said Vasili timidly.

"I shall soon be at my last gasp, that's how I am," shouted Agafya Mikhailovna still more angrily, at the top of her voice.

Vasili laughed.

"There's nothing to laugh at, and if I say that you are to get out of here, you will! Just look at him! Marry her, would he? The filthy rascal! Come on, out you get!"

And Agafya Mikhailovna went stamping to her room, and slammed the door so violently that the windows rattled.

For a while she could be heard behind the partition, abusing everything and everybody, cursing her existence, flinging her effects about, and pulling the ears of her pet cat; finally the door opened just enough for the cat to come flying out, swung by her tail, squalling piteously.

"It seems I'd better come another time for tea," said Vasili in a whisper; "Good-bye, till a better occasion."

"Never mind," said Nadezhda, with a wink, "I'll go and see to the samovar."

"I mean to make an end of it once for all," continued Vasili, sitting down close to Masha as soon as Nadezhda had left the room. "I'll either go straight to the Countess and say, 'This is how things are,' or else—I'll give it all up and run away to the end of the earth, by God I will!"

"And how am I to live here alone?"

"You're the only one I'm sorry for. If it wasn't for you I'd have fled the coop lo-o-ng ago, as sure as God lives."

"Why don't you bring me your shirts to wash, Vasya?" said Masha after a short silence; "see how black this one is," she added, taking hold of the shirt-collar.

At that moment Grandmamma's little bell was heard from below, and Gasha emerged from her chamber.

"What do you want with her now, you villain?" she said, pushing Vasili towards the door as he rose hastily at the sight of her; "you got her in the state she is and you still keep pestering her. I suppose you like to see her cry, you brazen-faced brute! Away with you! Get out of my sight! What did you ever see in him?" she went on, turning to Masha. "Didn't your uncle beat you today because of him? But you will have your own way: 'I won't marry anybody but Vasili Gruskov.' You stupid thing!"

"And I won't either, I don't love anybody, if I'm beaten to death because of him," cried Masha, suddenly bursting into tears.

I gazed long at Masha, who lay on the chest and wiped away her tears with her kerchief; and I did all I could to alter my opinion of Vasili, and tried to find the point of view from which he could appear so attractive to her. But, in spite of my sincere sympathy with her grief, I could not possibly understand how such a charming thing as Masha appeared in my eyes could love Vasili.

"When I grow up," I reflected as I went upstairs to my own quarters, "Petrovskoye will be mine, and Masha and

Vasili will be my serfs. I shall be sitting in the study smoking my pipe, and Masha will go to the kitchen with her flat-iron. I shall say, 'Send Masha to me.' She will come, and there will be no one in the room. Suddenly Vasili will enter, and when he sees Masha he will say, 'I'm lost now!' And Masha will cry; and I shall say, 'Vasili, I know that you love her, and she loves you: here are a thousand rubles for you; marry her; and God grant you happiness.' And then I shall go into the sitting-room. Among the innumerable thoughts and fancies which flash through the mind and imagination leaving no impression, there are others which leave a deep, sensitive furrow, so that, without recalling what you thought about, you remember that it was something pleasant, you feel the effect of the thought and try to reproduce it once again. Such a deep trace did the thought of sacrificing my own feeling for the sake of the happiness which Masha might find in a marriage with Vasili leave in my soul.

Chapter XIX

BOYHOOD

Perhaps people will scarcely believe me when I tell them what were the favourite and most constant subjects of my reflections during my boyhood—so ill-adapted were they to my age and position. But, in my opinion, disparity between a man's position and his moral activity is the surest proof of sincerity.

In the course of the year, during which I led a solitary moral life, concentrated within myself, I was confronted with all the abstract questions concerning the destiny of man, the future life, and the immortality of the soul; and my weak, childish mind endeavoured with all the ardour of inexperience to solve these questions, the formulation of which constitutes the highest stage which the mind of man can attain, but the solution of which is not granted to him.

It seems to me that in each individual, the intellect follows the same path of development as in whole races; that the thoughts which serve as foundation for the various philosophical theories form the inalienable attributes of the mind, but that each man was more or less clearly conscious of them, even before he knew of the philosophical theories.

These thoughts occurred to my mind with such clearness and in such a striking light that I even tried to apply them to life, fancying that I was the *first* to discover such great and useful truths.

Once the thought occurred to me that happiness does not depend upon external conditions, but on our attitude to them; that a man who is accustomed to endure suffering, cannot be unhappy; and, in order to accustom myself to labour, I held Tatishchev's lexicon for five minutes in my outstretched hands, in spite of the dreadful pain, or I went into the garret and scourged my bare back so severely with a rope that tears rose involuntarily to my eyes.

Another time, remembering all of a sudden that death awaited me at any hour, at any moment, I made up my mind, not understanding how people had hitherto failed to grasp it, that man can be happy only by making use of the present and not thinking of the future; and for three days, under the influence of this thought, I neglected my lessons, and did nothing but lie on the bed and enjoy reading a novel and eating gingerbread and honey, which I had bought with the last money I had.

On another occasion, as I stood before the blackboard drawing various figures upon it with chalk, I was suddenly struck by the thought: Why is symmetry pleasing to the eye? What is symmetry?

It is an inborn feeling, I answered. But on what is it founded? Is there symmetry in everything in life? On the contrary, here is life. And I drew an oval figure. After life the soul passes into eternity. And from one side of the oval I drew a line which extended to the very edge of the board. Why is there not another such line on the other side? And, indeed, come to think of it, what kind of eternity is it which has only one side? For we certainly have existed before this life, although we have lost the memory of it.

This reasoning, which appeared to me extremely novel and lucid, and whose thread I can now only catch with difficulty, pleased me exceedingly, and I took a sheet of paper with the idea of committing it to writing; but, in the process, such a mass of thoughts suddenly crowded to my mind that I was obliged to rise and walk about the room. When I approached the window my attention turned to the water horse, which the coachman was harnessing at the moment; and all my thoughts were concentrated upon the solution of the question—into what animal or man will the soul of that horse migrate when it is set free? At that moment Volodya passed through the room; he smiled, when he noticed that I was trying to think out something; and that smile was sufficient to make it clear to me that all I had been thinking about was the most frightful nonsense.

I have related this to me memorable occasion merely for the purpose of giving the reader to understand the nature of my reflections.

But by none of all the philosophical trends was I fascinated so much as by scepticism, which at one time reduced me to a state bordering on madness. I fancied that besides myself nothing and nobody existed in the whole world; that objects were not objects, but images which only appeared when I directed my attention to them; and that as soon as I ceased to think of them those images disappeared.

In a word, I agreed with Schelling in the conviction that it was not objects that existed, but only my relation to them. There were moments when, under the influence of this *fixed idea*, I reached such a stage of derangement that I sometimes glanced quickly in the opposite direction, hoping to surprise nothingness (*néant*) where I was not.

A pitiful, worthless spring of moral action is the mind of man!

My weak mind could not penetrate the impenetrable; but in this labour, which was beyond its strength, I lost one after the other the convictions which, for the happiness of my own life, I never should have dared to touch upon.

From all this arduous moral toil I derived nothing but a subtleness of mind which diminished my strength of will, and a habit of constant moral analysis which destroyed freshness of feeling and clearness of judgement.

Abstract thoughts take shape in consequence of the capacity of man's mind to apprehend the state of his soul at any given moment and transfer it to his memory. My tendency to abstract reasoning developed the perceptive faculties in me to such an unnatural degree that frequently, when I began to think of the simplest sort of thing, I fell into an endless analysis of my thoughts, and no longer considered the question which had occupied me, but thought of what I was thinking about. When I asked myself: What am I thinking of? I replied: I think of what I am thinking. And now what am I thinking of? I think that I am thinking of what I am thinking, and so on. I could not see reason for reasoning.

Nevertheless, the philosophical discoveries which I made were extremely flattering to my self-conceit. I often fancied myself a great man who was discovering new truths for the benefit of mankind, and I gazed upon other mortals with a proud consciousness of my worth; but, strange to say, when I came in contact with those mortals I was shy in the presence of every one of them, and the higher I rated myself in my own opinion the less I was capable of displaying my consciousness of my own merit to others, and I could not even accustom myself not to feel ashamed of my every word and movement, however simple.

Chapter XX

VOLODYA

Yes, the farther I proceed in the description of this period of my life the more painful and difficult does it become for me. Too rarely, amid the memories of this period, do I find moments of the genuine warmth of feeling which so brilliantly and constantly illuminated the beginning of my life. Gladly would I pass as quickly as possible over the desert of boyhood, the sooner to reach that happy time when a truly tender, noble sentiment of friendship lighted up the end of this period and opened up a new one, full of charm and poetry—youth.

I shall not trace my recollections hour by hour; but only cast a quick glance at the principal ones from that time until my association with a remarkable man, who exercised a decided and beneficial influence upon my character and development.

Volodya will enter the university in a few days. Special tutors come to him, and I listen with envy and involuntary respect as he taps the blackboard boldly with the chalk and talks of functions, and sinuses, and co-ordinates, and the like, which seem to me the expression of inaccessible wisdom. At length one Sunday, after dinner, all the teachers and two professors assemble in Grandmamma's room, and in the presence of Papa and several guests they put Volodya through a rehearsal of his university examination, in the course of which Volodya, to Grandmamma's delight, exhibits remarkable learning. Questions on various subjects are also put to me; but I make a very poor show, and the professors evidently endeavour to conceal my ignorance before Grandmamma, which confuses me still more. However, very little attention is paid to me; I am only fifteen, consequently there is still a year in which to prepare for my examination. Volodya comes downstairs only for dinner, and spends whole days and even the evenings over his studies upstairs, not of necessity, but at his own desire. He is extremely vain, and wants not a bare pass, but distinction at his examination.

The day of the first examination arrives at last. Volodya puts on his blue coat with brass buttons, his gold watch, and patent-leather boots; Papa's phaeton is brought up to the door. Nikolai throws aside the apron, and Volodya and St. Jérôme drive off to the university. The girls, especially Katenka, look out of the window at Volodya's fine figure as he gets into the carriage with joyous and rapturous faces; and Papa says, "God grant! God grant!" and Grandmamma, who has also dragged herself to the window, blesses Volodya, with tears in her eyes, until the phaeton disappears round the corner of the lane, and says something in a whisper.

Volodya comes back. All eagerly crowd round him, "Well? Good? What mark?" But his beaming face is an answer in itself. Volodya has received full marks. On the following day he sped on his way with the same anxiety and wishes for success, and was welcomed with the same eagerness and joy. Thus nine days pass. On the tenth day the last and most difficult examination of all awaits him —religious knowledge; we all stand at the window and wait for him with greater impatience than ever. Two o'clock, and still no Volodya.

"Heavens! my dears! here they come! here they come!" screams Lyubochka, with her face glued to the pane.

And sure enough Volodya is sitting beside St. Jérôme in the phaeton, dressed no longer in his blue coat and grey cap, but in student's uniform, with blue embroidered collar, three-cornered hat, and a gilt dagger at his side.

"Oh, if only she were alive now!" Grandmamma shrieks when she sees Volodya in his uniform, and falls into a swoon.

Volodya runs into the vestibule with a beaming face, kisses me, Lyubochka, Mimi, and Katenka, who blushes to her very ears. Volodya is beside himself with joy. And how handsome he looks in his uniform! How well his blue collar suits his scarcely sprouting black whiskers! What a long, slender waist he has, and what a fine gait! On that memorable day all dine in Grandmamma's room. Joy beams from every countenance; and after dinner, at dessert, the butler, with politely majestic but merry countenance, brings in a bottle of champagne wrapped in a napkin. Grandmamma drinks champagne for the first time since Mamma's death; she drinks a whole glass to congratulate Volodya, and she weeps again with joy as she looks at him. Volodya drives out of the court-yard in his own equipage now, receives his acquaintances *in his own apartments*, smokes, goes to balls; and on one occasion I even saw him sharing two bottles of champagne with some guests in his room, and the whole company drinking a toast, with each glass, to some mysterious personages and then disputing as to who would get *le fond de la bouteille*. But he dines regularly at home and spends the afternoon in the sitting-room as before, and is for ever engaged in some mysterious discussion with Katenka; but so far as I can hear—for I do not take part in their conversation—all they talk of is the heroes and heroines of the novels they have read, love and jealousy; I cannot make out what interest they can find in such discussions, or why they smile so delicately and argue so heatedly.

I observe in general that besides the natural friendship between companions of childhood, some strange relations exist between Katenka and Volodya which set them apart from us and bind them to each other in a mysterious way.

Chapter XXI

KATENKA AND LYUBOCHKA

Katenka is now sixteen; she is grown up; the sharpness of figure, the bashfulness and awkwardness of movement peculiar to girls passing from childhood to maidenhood, have made way for the harmonious freshness and grace of a newly-born flower. But she has not changed: the same bright blue eyes and smiling glance, the same small, straight nose forming almost one line with the brow, with its strong nostrils, and the tiny mouth with its bright smile, the dimples on the rosy, transparent cheeks, the same small white hands; and for some reason the expression, a *prim girl*, still fits her peculiarly well. The only new things about her are the way she does her heavy blonde hair into a braid, which she wears in the fashion of grown-up woman, and her young bosom that plainly delights yet shames her.

Although Lyubochka has been brought up and educated with her, she is quite a different girl in every respect.

Lyubochka is rather small of stature, and as a result of the rickets her legs are still crooked and her figure is very ugly. The only pretty thing about her face is her eyes, and they are really very beautiful—large and dark, and with such an indefinably attractive expression of dignity and simplicity that they are bound to attract attention. Lyubochka is natural and simple in everything, whereas Katenka seems to wish to model herself on someone else. Lyubochka's gaze is always straightforward; and sometimes she fixes her great dark eyes on a person and keeps them there so long that she is reproved and told that it is not polite.

Katenka, on the other hand, lowers her eyelashes, screws up her eyes, and says that she is short-sighted, though I know very well that her sight is perfectly good. Lyubochka does not like to make up to strangers; and when anybody begins to kiss her in company she pouts and says that she cannot endure *sentiment*. Katenka, on the contrary, becomes particularly affectionate with Mimi in the presence of guests, and loves to walk arm in arm with some girl in the hall. Lyubochka is easily stirred to laughter; and sometimes in outburst of merriment she waves her hands and runs about the room. Katenka, on the contrary, covers her mouth with her hands or her handkerchief when she begins to laugh. Lyubochka always sits straight, and when she walks she holds her hands by her sides; Katenka puts her head to one side and walks with clasped hands. Lyubochka is always awfully glad when she gets a chance of talking with a grown-up man, and declares that she will certainly marry a Hussar; but Katenka says that all men are horrid, that she will never marry, and becomes quite a different girl when a man speaks to her, as though she were afraid of something. Lyubochka is for ever vexed with Mimi because they lace her up so tight in corsets that she "can't breathe," and she is fond of eating; but Katenka, on the other hand, often thrusts her finger under the point of her bodice and shows us how loose it is on her, and she eats very little. Lyubochka loves to draw heads, but Katenka draws only flowers and butterflies. Lyubochka plays Field's concertos perfectly, and some of Beethoven's sonatas.

Katenka plays variations and waltzes, holds her notes too long, strikes the keys too hard, and uses the pedal incessantly; before beginning to play anything she strikes three arpeggios.

Katenka, I then thought, was much more like an adult, and therefore she pleased me far more.

Chapter XXII

PAPA

Papa has been particularly gay since Volodya entered the university, and comes to dine with Grandmamma much oftener than usual. However, the cause of his cheerfulness, as I heard from Nikolai, lies in the fact that he has won a considerable amount of money lately. Occasionally he comes to see us in the evening before going to his club, sits down to the piano, with us gathering around him, and sings Gipsy songs, tapping out the time with his soft shoes (he cannot bear heels, and never wears them). And you should see the comical rapture of Lyubochka, his favourite, who adores him. Sometimes he comes to the school-room and listens with a stern countenance while I recite my lessons; but I perceive, from his occasional words as he tries to set me right, that he does not know much of what I am learning. Sometimes he gives us a sly wink and makes signs to us when Grandmamma begins to grumble and get angry with everybody without cause. "Well, we got it, children," he says afterwards. On the whole, he has come down somewhat in my eyes from the unapproachable height upon which my childish imagination had placed him. I kiss his large white hand with the same feeling of genuine love and respect; but I already permit myself to think of him, to pass judgement on his acts, and thoughts occur to me which frighten me.

Never shall I forget one incident which roused many such thoughts in me and caused me much moral suffering.

Late one evening, he entered the drawing-room in his black dress-coat and white waistcoat, in order to take Volodya to a ball. The latter was dressing in his room. Grandmother was waiting in her bedroom for Volodya to come and show himself to her (she had a habit of summoning him to her presence before every ball, to inspect him and to bestow upon him her blessing and instructions). Mimi and Katenka were pacing up and down in the hall, which was lighted by one candle only, while Lyubochka was at the piano learning Field's Second Concerto, Mamma's favourite piece.

Never have I met such an intimate likeness between any two persons as existed between my sister and my mother. This likeness was neither in face nor in stature, but in some subtle quality—in the hands, manner of walking, peculiarities of the voice, and certain expressions. When Lyubochka got angry and said, "It won't be allowed for a whole age," she pronounced the words, *a whole age*, which Mamma was also accustomed to use, so that you seemed to hear the length of them in her voice. But the likeness was still more remarkable when she played the piano, in all her ways at the instrument. She adjusted her dress when sitting down in exactly the same way, and turned her pages from above with her left hand, and pounded the keys with her fist in vexation when she could not get a difficult passage right, and said, "Oh, my God!" And she had that same indescribable softness and accuracy of execution, that beautiful Field way, which is so appropriately called *jeu perlé*, and whose charm all the humbug of modern pianists cannot make one forget.

Papa entered the room with swift, short steps, and went up to Lyubochka, who stopped playing when she saw him.

"No, go on playing, Lyuba, go on," he said, making her sit down again: "You know how I love to hear you."

Lyubochka went on playing, and Papa sat opposite her for a long time, supporting his head on his hand; then he gave his shoulders a sudden twitch, rose, and began to walk up and down. Every time he approached the piano, he paused and looked intently at Lyubochka. By his movements and his manner of walking I could see that he was greatly agitated. After walking about the room several times, he paused behind Lyubochka's seat, kissed her black hair, and then, turning away, resumed his pacing. When Lyubochka had finished her piece and went up to him asking: "Do you like it?" he took her head silently in his hands without a word and began to kiss her brow and eyes with such tenderness as I had never seen him display.

"Why, you are weeping!" said Lyubochka, all at once dropping the chain of his watch and fixing her great surprised eyes on his face. "Forgive me, my darling Papa; I had quite forgotten thât was *Mamma's piece.*"

"No, my dear, play it often, will you," he said in a voice trembling with emotion; "if you only knew what good it does me to weep with you."

He kissed her once more, and, endeavouring to overcome his emotion, he twitched his shoulders and went out through the door leading to the corridor and Volodya's room.

"Waldemar! Will you be ready soon?" he cried, stopping half-way along the corridor. At that moment Masha, the maid, passed him, and, seeing the master, she dropped her eyes and tried to avoid him. He stopped her. "Indeed, you look prettier every day," he said, bending over her.

Masha blushed and bowed her head still lower. "Permit me," she whispered.

"Waldemar, are you nearly ready?" repeated Papa, twitching and coughing, when Masha passed and he caught sight of me.

I loved my father; but man's mind does not take counsel of his heart and often harbours thoughts which are insulting to his feelings, too incomprehensible and stern for them. And for all I strove to drive them away, such thoughts kept coming to my mind.

Chapter XXIII

GRANDMAMMA

Grandmamma grew weaker from day to day; her bell, Gasha's grumbling voice, and the slamming of doors were heard more frequently in her room, and she no longer received us in the library in her large easy-chair, but in her bedroom in her high bed with its lace-trimmed pillows. When she greeted us, we noticed a pale, yellowish, shining swelling on her hand, and that oppressive odour in the chamber which I had observed five years before in Mamma's room. The doctor came three times a day, and consulted several times with colleagues. But her character, her haughty and ceremonious ways with all members of the household, particularly with Papa, did not alter in the least; she still protracted her words, raised her brows, and said "my dear" in exactly the same manner as before.

Then for a few days we were not admitted to her; and once in the morning St. Jérôme suggested that I should go for a ride with Lyubochka and Katenka during lesson hours. Although I noticed, as I got into the sleigh, that the street in front of Grandmamma's windows was strewn with straw, and that several people in blue overcoats were standing near our gate, I could not understand why we were being sent out for a ride at this unusual hour. During our whole ride on that day Lyubochka and I were, for some reason, in that particularly cheerful frame of mind when every occurrence, every word, every motion, excites one's laughter.

A pedlar, trotting across the road with his box, made us laugh. Some cabman overtook our sleigh at a gallop, flourishing his reins, and we shouted with laughter. Philip's whip got caught in the runners of the sleigh; he turned around and said, "Bother the thing!"—and we could have died with laughter. Mimi gave us a displeased look and said that only *silly* people laugh for no reason at all; and Lyubochka, her face flushed with suppressed laughter, cast a sidelong glance at me. Our eyes met, and we burst out into such wild laughter that the tears came to our eyes, and we could not contain the bursts of merriment which were suffocating us. Hardly had we quieted down a little when I glanced at Lyubochka, and uttered a mysterious word which had been in fashion for some time among us, and which always provoked laughter; and again we broke out.

Just as we were drawing up at our door I was about to make a very fine grimace at Lyubochka, when suddenly I was startled by the sight of the black lid of a coffin leaning against the door, and the grimace froze on my face.

*"Votre grande-mère est morte!"** said St. Jérôme, coming out to us with a pale face.

During the whole time that Grandmamma's body was in the house I experienced an oppressive fear of death, as if the dead body were alive, and unpleasantly reminding me that I must die some day—a feeling which it is usual, for some reason, to confuse with grief. I did not feel sorry for Grandmamma, and, in fact, although the house was full of mourning visitors, there could hardly be any one who sincerely felt sorry for her, except one individual, whose wild grief greatly surprised me. And that person was Gasha, the maid. She shut herself up in the garret, wept incessantly, cursed herself, tore her hair, refused all

---

* Your grandmother is dead.—*Ed.*

consolation, saying that now her mistress was dead, she only wished to die herself.

I repeat once more that improbability in matters of feeling is a most reliable sign of genuineness.

Although Grandmother was no more with us, reminiscences and references to her still went on in the house. They bore especially on the will which she had made before her death, and the contents of which no one knew, with the exception of her executor, Prince Ivan Ivanich. I observed some excitement among Grandmamma's people, and I frequently overheard remarks as to who would become whose property; and I must confess that I could not help being pleased at the thought that we would inherit something.

At the end of six weeks Nikolai, who was the daily newspaper of our establishment, informed me that Grandmamma had left all her property to Lyubochka intrusting the guardianship until her marriage, not to Papa, but to Prince Ivan Ivanich.

Chapter XXIV

I

Only a few months remain before my entrance to the university. I am studying well. I not only await my teachers without terror, but even find a certain pleasure in my lessons.

I enjoy reciting the lesson I have learned clearly and accurately. I am preparing for the mathematical faculty; and I have chosen it, to tell the truth, simply because of an extraordinary liking for the words, sinuses, tangents, differentials, integrals, and so forth.

I am much shorter of stature than Volodya, broad-shouldered and fleshy, plain as ever, and worried about it as usual. I try to appear original. One thing consoles me: that is, that Papa once said that I had a *sensible phiz*, and I quite believe him.

St. Jérôme is satisfied with me; and I do not hate him any more; indeed, when he occasionally remarks that *with my gifts* and *my intelligence* it is a shame that I do not do this or that, it even seems to me that I like him.

My observation of the maids' room ceased long ago. I am ashamed to hide behind a door, and, moreover, my conviction that Masha loves Vasili has cooled me somewhat, I must confess. Vasili's marriage, the permission for which, at his request, I obtained from Papa, finally cures me of this unhappy passion.

When the newly-wed come, with sweetmeats on a tray, to thank Papa, and Masha in a blue-ribboned cap, kissing each of us on the shoulder, also returns thanks to all of us for something or other, I am conscious only of the rose pomade on her hair, but not of the least emotion.

On the whole, I am beginning gradually to recover from my boyish shortcomings; with the exception, however, of the chief one, which still is to do me much harm in life—my tendency to philosophizing.

Chapter XXV

VOLODYA'S FRIENDS

Although in the company of Volodya's friends I played a part that hurt my pride, I liked sitting in his room when he had visitors and silently watching all that took place there.

The most frequent of all Volodya's guests were an aide-de-camp called Dubkov and a student, Prince Nekhlyudov. Dubkov was a small, muscular, dark-complexioned man, no longer in his first youth, and rather short-legged, but not bad-looking, and always gay. He was one of those limited persons who are particularly agreeable through their very limitations, who are incapable of viewing things from different sides, and who are continually allowing themselves to be carried away with something. The judgement of such people is one-sided and erroneous, yet always open-hearted and captivating. For some reason even their narrow egotism seems pardonable and attractive. Besides this, Dubkov possessed a double charm for Volodya and me—a soldierly appearance and, most of all, the age with which young people are apt to associate respectability—what was called *comme il faut*—which people of our age highly appreciate. Moreover, Dubkov really was what is called a man *comme il faut*. The only thing which I did not like was that Volodya seemed at times to be ashamed, in his presence, of my most innocent acts and, most of all, of my youth.

Nekhlyudov was not handsome: little grey eyes, a low, bumpy forehead, disproportionately long arms and legs, could not be called beautiful features. The only handsome thing about him was his unusually lofty stature, the delicate colouring of his face, and his very fine teeth. But his countenance acquired such a character of originality and energy from his narrow, brilliant eyes and the expression of his smile, which changed from sternness to childish vagueness that it was impossible not to be struck by it.

He appeared to be excessively bashful, for every trifle made him flush up to his very ears; but his shyness was not like mine. The more he reddened the more determination his face expressed. He seemed angry with himself for his weakness.

Although he seemed very friendly with Dubkov and Volodya, it was clearly chance that had brought them together. They were entirely different. Volodya and Dubkov seemed afraid of everything which even resembled serious discussion and feeling; Nekhlyudov, on the contrary, was of an extremely enthusiastic temperament, and often plunged into a discussion of philosophical questions and feelings, heedless of mockery. Volodya and Dubkov were fond of talking about the objects of their love (and they would suddenly fall in love with several, and both with the same persons); Nekhlyudov, on the contrary, always became really angry when they hinted at his love for a certain *red-haired girl.*

Volodya and Dubkov often permitted themselves to make sport of their relatives; Nekhlyudov, on the contrary, could be driven quite beside himself by uncomplimentary allusions to his aunt, for whom he cherished a sort of rapturous reverence. Volodya and Dubkov used to go off somewhere after supper without Nekhlyudov; and they called him a *dainty girl.*

Prince Nekhlyudov impressed me from the first by his conversation as well as by his appearance. But although I found much in his disposition that was common to mine —or perhaps just because of that—the feeling with which he inspired me when I saw him for the first time was anything but agreeable.

I disliked his quick glance, his firm voice, his haughty look, but most of all the utter indifference which he exhibited towards me. Often during a conversation I burned to contradict him and get the better of him in order to punish him for his pride, to show him that I was intelligent, in spite of his disregard for me. But my shyness prevented me.

Chapter XXVI

DISCUSSIONS

When I went to Volodya's room as usual after my evening lessons he was lying with his feet on the divan, leaning on his elbow, reading a French novel. He looked up at me for a second, and then went on reading, a most simple and natural thing to do, and yet it brought the blood to my face. His glance seemed to ask me what I had come for, and the haste with which he lowered his head seemed to indicate a desire to hide from me the meaning of that glance. (This tendency to see a meaning in the simplest movement was characteristic of me at that age.) I walked up to the table and took a book; but before I began to read it, it occurred to me how ridiculous it was not to say anything to each other when we had not seen each other all day.

"Will you be at home this evening?"

"I don't know. Why?"

"I just wondered," said I, and seeing that I could not start a conversation, I took up my book and began to read.

Strangely enough Volodya and I would pass whole hours in silence alone, but the mere presence of a third person, even if he did not speak, sufficed to start the most varied and engrossing of conversations. We felt that we knew each other too well; and knowing a person too well prevents real intimacy as much as knowing him too little.

"Is Volodya at home?" Dubkov's voice was heard asking in the vestibule.

"Yes," said Volodya, lowering his feet and laying his book on the table.

Dubkov and Nekhlyudov entered the room in their coats and hats.

"Are you coming to the theatre?"

"No, I have no time," Volodya replied, turning red.

"What an idea! Do come, please."

"And besides I haven't got a ticket."

"You can get as many tickets as you want at the entrance."

"Wait, I'll come directly," said Volodya, evasively, and he left the room with a twitch of his shoulders.

I knew that Volodya wanted very much to go to the theatre and refused only because he had no money; now he had gone to borrow five rubles from the butler until his next allowance.

"How are you, *Diplomat*?" said Dubkov, giving me his hand.

Volodya's friends called me the diplomat because once, after dinner, my grandmother talked about our future and said that Volodya was to be a soldier and that she hoped to see me a diplomat, in a black dress-coat, and with my hair *à la coq*, which she considered indispensable in the diplomatic profession.

"Where has Volodya gone?" Nekhlyudov asked.

"I don't know," I replied, blushing at the thought that they probably guessed why Volodya had left the room.

"I suppose he has no money, eh? Oh, you *Diplomat*!" he added, interpreting my smile in the affirmative. "Neither have I. Have you, Dubkov?"

"We shall see," answered Dubkov, pulling out his purse, and very carefully feeling a few small coins with his short fingers. "Here's a five-kopek piece, and here's a twenty-kopek piece—pooh!" said he, making a comical gesture with his hand.

At that moment Volodya entered the room.

"Well, shall we go?"

"No."

"How ridiculous you are!" said Nekhlyudov. "Why don't you say that you have no money? Take my ticket if you like."

"But what about you?"

"He will go to his cousins' box," said Dubkov.

"No, I am not going at all."

"Why?"

"Because, as you know, I don't like to sit in a box."

"Why?"

"I don't like it; it makes me feel awkward."

"The same old thing again! I don't understand how

you can feel awkward where every one is glad to have you. It's absurd, *mon cher*."

"What am I to do *si je suis timide*?* I am sure you have never blushed in your life, but I keep blushing at the slightest trifles," he said, blushing indeed as he spoke.

"*Savez-vous d'où vient votre timidité?... d'un excés d'amour propre, mon cher*,"** said Dubkov in a patronizing tone.

"*Excés d'amour propre*, indeed!" said Nekhlyudov, touched to the quick. "On the contrary, it is because I have too little pride; I always feel as though I were being disagreeable, tiresome—"

"Get dressed, Volodya," said Dubkov, seizing him by the shoulders and pulling off his coat. "Ignat, get your master ready!"

"And so it often happens to me—" went on Nekhlyudov.

But Dubkov was no longer listening to him. "Tra-la-la-la," he hummed an air.

"Oh, you won't get away with that," said Nekhlyudov; "I will prove to you that shyness does not proceed from self-love at all."

"You will prove it if you come with us."

"I said that I am not going."

"Well, stay then, and prove it to the *diplomat*; and he shall tell us all about it when we come back."

"I will too," retorted Nekhlyudov, with childish obstinacy; "so hurry up and get back."

"What do you think? am I proud?" he asked, sitting down beside me.

Although I had my opinion on that point, I was so taken aback by this unexpected question that it was some time before I could answer him.

---

* If I am shy.—*Ed*.
** Do you know what your shyness comes from? From excessive pride, my dear chap.—*Ed*.

"Yes, I think so," I said, feeling my voice faltering and my face colouring at the thought that the time had come to show him that *I was intelligent*— "I think that every man is proud, and that everything a man does is done out of pride."

"What is pride, in your opinion?" said Nekhlyudov, smiling somewhat disdainfully, I thought.

"Pride—" said I, "is the conviction that one is better and wiser than anybody else."

"But how can everybody entertain that conviction?"

"I do not know whether it's right or not, but no one confesses to it; now, I am convinced that I am wiser than any one in the world, and I am sure that you are convinced of the same thing."

"No; at least I can say for myself that I have met people whom I have acknowledged to be wiser than myself," said Nekhlyudov.

"Impossible," I answered with conviction.

"Do you really think so?" said Nekhlyudov, looking intently at me.

And then an idea occurred to me, to which I immediately gave utterance.

"I will prove it to you. Why do we love ourselves more than others? Because we consider ourselves better than others, more worthy of love. If we considered others better than ourselves, then we should love them more than ourselves, and that never happens. Even if it does happen, I am right all the same," I added, with an involuntary complacent smile.

Nekhlyudov remained silent for a moment.

"I never suspected that you were so clever!" he said, with such a sweet, good-natured smile that I suddenly felt quite happy.

Praise acts so powerfully not only on the feelings but on the mind of man that under its pleasant influence it seemed to me that I became much cleverer, and ideas occurred to me one after the other with unusual swiftness. From pride we passed, without noticing it, to love; and discussion on this theme seemed inexhaustible. Although our judgements might seem utter nonsense to an uninterested listener—so vague and one-sided were they—they possessed a lofty significance for us. Our souls were so agreeably in harmony that the slightest touch upon any chord in one found an echo in the other. We took pleasure in this mutual echoing of the various chords which we touched in our discussion. It seemed to us that time and words were lacking to express to each other the thoughts which sought utterance.

Chapter XXVII

THE BEGINNING OF FRIENDSHIP

From that time on rather strange but very agreeable relations existed between me and Dmitri Nekhlyudov. In the presence of strangers he paid hardly any attention to me; but as soon as we happened to be alone, we sat in some quiet nook and began to discuss, forgetful of time and everything around us.

We talked of the future life, and of the arts, and of government service, and marriage, and the education of children; and it never entered our heads that all we said was the most frightful nonsense. It never occurred to us, because the nonsense we talked was wise and nice nonsense; and in youth one still prizes wisdom and believes in it. In youth all the powers of the soul are directed towards the future; and that future assumes such varied, vivid, and enchanting forms under the influence of hope— hope founded, not upon the experience of the past, but upon the fancied possibilities of happiness to come—that the mere dreams of future bliss form a genuine happiness at that age, when shared. In the metaphysical discussions which formed one of the chief subjects of our conversation, I loved the moment when thoughts followed each other in ever quicker succession, and, growing ever more abstract, finally attained such a degree of mistiness that you found no means of expressing them, and although you thought you were saying what you meant, you were saying something entirely different. I loved the moment when, soaring higher and higher into the realms of thought, you suddenly grasped all its infiniteness, and confessed the impossibility of proceeding further.

Once during the carnival Nekhludov was so absorbed in various pleasures that, although he came to the house several times a day, he never once spoke to me; and this offended me so much that he again seemed to me a haughty and disagreeable man. I only waited for an opportunity to show him that I did not value his society in the least, and entertained no special affection for him.

On the first occasion after the carnival that he wanted to talk to me, I said that I had lessons to do, and went upstairs; but a quarter of an hour later some one opened the school-room door, and Nekhlyudov entered.

"Am I disturbing you?" he asked.

"No," I replied, although I wanted to say that I really was busy.

"Then why did you leave Volodya's room? We haven't had a talk for a long time. And I have become so used to it that it seems as if something were missing."

My vexation vanished in a moment, and Dmitri again appeared the same kind and charming man as before in my eyes.

"You probably know why I went away," said I.

"Perhaps so," he replied, seating himself beside me. "But though I guess it, I cannot say why, but you can," said he.

"I'll tell you: I went away because I was angry with you—not angry, but vexed. To speak plainly, I am always afraid that you will despise me because I am still so very young."

"Do you know why I have become so intimate with you?" he said, replying to my confession with a good-humoured and sensible smile—"why I love you more than people with whom I am better acquainted and with whom I have more in common? I have just found out. You have a wonderfully rare quality—frankness."

"Yes, I always say just the very things that I am ashamed to acknowledge," I agreed, "but only to those whom I can trust."

"Yes; but in order to trust a person one must be really friendly with him and we are not friends yet, Nicolas. You remember that we discussed friendship; in order to be true friends, it is necessary to trust each other."

"To trust that what I tell you, you will not repeat to any one," said I. "But the most important, the most interesting thoughts are just those which we would not tell each other for anything!"

"And what loathsome thoughts!" he said. "Such thoughts that, had we known we should be forced to acknowledge them, we should never have dared to think them."

"Do you know what has occurred to me, Nicolas?" he added, rising from his chair and rubbing his hands, with a smile. "Let us *do it*, and you will see how beneficial it will be for both of us. Let us give our word to confess everything to each other: we shall know each other, and we shall not be ashamed; but, in order that we may not fear strangers, let us pledge our word *never* to say *anything* to *anybody* about each other. That is what we shall do."

And we actually *did*. What came of it I shall relate hereafter.

Karr said that in every attachment there are two sides: one loves, while the other permits himself to be loved; one kisses, the other offers the cheek. This is perfectly correct; and in our friendship I kissed, and Dmitri offered his cheek; but he was also ready to kiss me. We loved equally, because we knew and valued each other; but this did not prevent his exercising an influence over me, and my submitting to him.

Of course, under the influence of Nekhlyudov, I unconsciously adopted his view, the gist of which consisted in an enthusiastic adoration of the ideal of virtue, and in a belief that man is intended constantly to perfect himself. Then the reformation of all mankind, the annihilation of all human vices and miseries, appeared a practicable thing. It seemed very simple and easy to reform one's self, to acquire all virtues, and be happy.

But God only knows whether these lofty aspirations of youth were ridiculous, and who was to blame that they were not fulfilled.

YOUTH

Chapter I

WHAT I CONSIDER THE BEGINNING OF MY YOUTH

I have said that my friendship with Dmitri revealed to me a new view of life, its aims and bearings. This view consisted essentially in the belief that man's destiny is to strive for moral perfection, and that this perfection is easy, possible, and eternal. But hitherto I had revelled only in the discovery of the new thoughts which sprang from this belief, and in the construction of brilliant plans for a moral and active future; while my life went on in the same petty, confused, and idle fashion.

The virtuous thoughts which I examined in my conversations with my adored friend Dmitri—*wonderful Mitya*, as I called him in a whisper to myself sometimes—still pleased my mind only, but not my feelings. However, the time arrived when these thoughts came into my head with such freshness and force of moral discovery that I was alarmed when I reflected how much time I had wasted; and I wanted to apply these thoughts immediately, that very second, to life, with the firm intention of never being unfaithful to them.

It is from that time I date the beginning of my *youth*. I was then nearly sixteen. Masters continued to give me lessons. St. Jérôme still supervised my studies, and I was forced unwillingly to prepare for the university. Outside my studies, my occupations consisted in solitary, incoherent reveries and meditation; in gymnastic exercises, with a view to making myself the strongest man in the world; in roaming aimlessly through all the rooms, and particularly in the corridor of the maids' room; and in gazing at myself in the mirror, from which last occupation, by the way, I always turned away with an oppressive feeling of despondency and even of repulsion. Not only my appearance was plain, I was convinced, but I could not even comfort myself with the consolations usual in such cases. I could not say that my face was expressive, intellectual, or noble. There was nothing expressive about it; the features were of a homely and ordinary type. My small grey eyes were stupid rather than intelligent, particularly when I looked in the mirror. There was still less of manliness about it. Although I was not small in stature, and was very strong for my age, all my features were soft, flabby, and ill-defined. There was not even anything noble about it; on the contrary, my face resembled rather that of a muzhik, and I had just such big hands and feet; and this seemed to me at that time quite humiliating.

Chapter II

SPRING

In the year when I entered the university Easter fell so late in April that the examinations were set for Quasimodo Week, and I was to take the communion during Passion Week and then finish preparing.

The weather had been soft, warm, and clear for three days after the wet snow which Karl Ivanich had been in the habit of calling *"the son followed the father."* Not a single lump of snow was to be seen in the streets, and the dirty slush had given place to wet, shining pavements and rapid rivulets. The last drops were thawing from the roofs in the sun, the buds were swelling on the trees in the front garden. The path in the court-yard was dry. Near the stables, beyond the frozen heaps of manure, and between the stones about the porch, the moss-like grass was beginning to turn green. It was that particular period of spring which acts most powerfully upon the soul of man—the sun clear, full, brilliant, but not hot, the rivulets and snow-bare places breathing freshness to the air; and the tender blue sky streaked with long transparent clouds. I do not know why, but it seems to me that the influence of this first period of birth of the spring is even more powerful and perceptible in a great city—one sees less, but foresees more. I was standing by the window—through whose double frames the morning sun cast mote-flecked beams upon the floor of the school-room which bored me so intolerably—solving a long algebraic equation on the blackboard. In one hand I held a soft, tattered copy of Franker's *Algebra,* in the other a small piece of chalk, with which I had already smeared both hands, my face, and the elbows of my coat. Nikolai, wearing an apron, and with his sleeves rolled up, was chipping off the putty and pulling the nails out of the windows which opened on the front garden. His occupation, and the noise he made, distracted my attention. Besides, I was in a very evil and dissatisfied state of mind. Nothing would go right with me. I had made a mistake at the beginning of my calculation, so that I had had to begin all over again. I had dropped the chalk twice. I was conscious that my hands and face were dirty. The sponge had disappeared somewhere or other; the noise which Nikolai made was getting on my nerves. I felt like flying into a temper and grumbling at some one. I flung aside the chalk and *Algebra* and began to pace the room. Then I remembered that today I must go to confession, and that I must refrain from anything wrong; and all at once I fell into a peculiar, gentle mood, and approached Nikolai.

"Let me help you, Nikolai," said I, trying to impart the gentlest of tones to my voice. The thought that I was behaving well, stifling my vexation, and helping him, heightened this gentle disposition of mind still further.

The putty was cut away, the nails removed; but although Nikolai tugged at the cross-frame with all his might, it would not yield.

"If the frame comes out immediately now, when we pull together," I thought, "it'll mean that it would be a sin to study more today, so I won't." The frame yielded on one side and came out.

"Where is it to be carried?" said I.

"If you please, I'll manage myself," replied Nikolai, evidently amazed and seemingly displeased with my zeal; "I keep them all in the garret numbered."

"I'll number it," said I, lifting the frame.

It seems to me that if the garret were two versts away, and the window-frame were twice as heavy, I should be very much pleased. I wanted to tire myself out performing this service for Nikolai. When I returned to the room, the tiles and the cones of salt* were already rearranged on the window-sills, and Nikolai had brushed off the sand and torpid flies through the open window. Fresh, sweet air filled the room. With it came also the hum of the city and the twittering of sparrows.

Every object was bathed in light; the room had grown cheerful; the light spring breeze fluttered the leaves of my *Algebra* and Nikolai's hair. I went to the window,

---

* Little cones of salt which are placed between the double windows to absorb dampness. Tiles or little bricks are often added for ornament.—*Tr.*

sat on the ledge, leaned out over the garden, and began to think.

Some new, exceedingly powerful and pleasant sensation penetrated my soul all at once. The wet earth, through which, here and there, bright green spears of grass with yellow stalks pushed their way; the rivulets, sparkling in the sun and whirling little clods of earth and chips of wood along with them and the reddening twigs of the lilac with swollen buds which were nodding just beneath the window; the anxious twittering of the birds thronging this bush; the blackish hedge wet with the melted snow; but chiefly the damp, fragrant air and cheerful sun—spoke to me intelligibly, clearly, of something new and very beautiful, which, though I cannot reproduce it as it told itself to me, I shall endeavour to repeat as I received it. Everything spoke to me of beauty, happiness, and virtue; said that both were easy and possible to me, that one could not exist without the other, and even that beauty, happiness, and virtue are one and the same. "How could I fail to understand this? How wicked I was before! How happy I might have been, and how happy I may be in the future!" I said to myself. "I must become another man quickly, as quickly as possible, this very moment, and begin to live differently." But in spite of this I still sat for a long time in the window, dreaming and doing nothing. Has it ever happened to you in summer to lie down to sleep during the day-time in gloomy, rainy weather, and, waking up at sunset, to open your eyes, to catch sight through the wide square window, under the linen blind which swells and beats its rod against the window-sill, of the shady, purpling side of the linden alley, wet with rain, and the damp garden walks, illuminated by the bright, slanting .ays; to suddenly catch the sound of merry life among the birds in the garden, and to see the insects circling in the opening of the window transparent in the sun, and become conscious of the fragrance of the air after rain, and to think, "How shameful of me to sleep away such an evening!" and then to spring up in haste, in order to go to the garden and rejoice in life? If this has happened to you, then there is a specimen of the powerful feeling which I experienced then.

Chapter III

REVERIES

"Today I shall go to confession, I shall purify myself of all my sins," I thought, "and I shall never commit any more." (Here I recalled all the sins which troubled me most.) "I shall go to church, without fail, every Sunday, and afterwards I shall read the Gospels for a whole hour; and then, out of the twenty-five-ruble note which I shall receive every month when I enter the university, I will be sure to give two and a half rubles (that is one-tenth) to the poor, and in such a manner that no one shall know it—and not to beggars, but I will seek out poor people, an orphan or an old woman, whom no one knows about.

"I shall have a room to myself (probably St. Jérôme's) and I shall take care of it myself, and keep it wonderfully clean; and I shall leave the servant nothing to do for me, for he is a human being like myself. Then I shall walk to the university (and if they give me a droshky, I shall sell it, and give that money also to the poor), and I shall do everything with the greatest precision (what this 'everything' was I had no idea then; but I vividly realized and felt this 'everything' in a sensible, moral, and irreproachable life). I shall prepare my lectures, and even go over the subjects beforehand, so that I shall be at the head of the first course, and write a dissertation; in the second course I shall know everything beforehand, and they may transfer me directly to the third course, so that at eighteen I shall graduate as first candidate, with two gold medals; then I shall sit my examination for the degree of Master, then Doctor, and I shall become the leading scholar in Russia; I may be the most learned man in Europe even. And what afterwards?" I asked myself. But here I remembered that these were dreams—pride, sin, which I should have to tell the priest that evening; and I went back to the beginning of my meditations. "To prepare for my lectures I shall walk out to the Sparrow Hills; there I shall select a spot beneath a tree and read over the lesson. Sometimes I shall take something to eat with me, cheese or patties from Pedotti's, or something. I shall rest, and then I shall read some good book, or sketch landscapes, or play some instrument (I absolutely must learn to play the flute). Then *she* will also go for walks on the Sparrow Hills, and some day she will come up to me and ask who I am. And I shall look at her, oh, so sadly, and say that I am the son of a priest, and that I am happy only here when I am alone, quite, quite alone. Then she will give me her hand and say something, and sit down beside me. Thus we shall go there every day, and we shall become friends, and I shall kiss her. No, that would not be right; on the contrary, from this day forth I shall never more look at a woman. Never, never will I go into the maids' room, I will try not to pass by it even; and in three years I shall be free from guardianship, and I shall marry, without fail. I shall take as much exercise as possible with gymnastics every day, so that when I am twenty I shall be stronger than Rappeau. The first day I will hold half a pood in my outstretched hand for five minutes; on the second day twenty-one pounds; on the third day twenty-two pounds, and so on, so that at last I shall be able to hold four poods in each hand, and I shall be stronger than any man I knew; and when any one dares to insult me, or speak disrespectfully of *her*, I will just take him by the chest, and lift him an arshin or two from the ground with one hand, and only hold him long enough to let him feel my strength, and then I will release him. Yet this isn't right either; oh, it does not matter, I shall not do him any harm, I shall merely show him—"

Let no one reproach me because the dreams of my youth were as childish as those of childhood and boyhood. I am convinced that if I live to extreme old age, and continue my story with the years, I, an old man of seventy, shall be found dreaming dreams just as impossibly childish as those I dream now. I shall dream of some charming Maria, who will love me, a toothless old man, as she loved Mazeppa;* of how my weak-minded son will suddenly become a minister, through some unusual circumstance; or of how a treasure of millions will fall to me all of a sudden. I am convinced that there is no human being or age which is deprived of this beneficent, comforting capacity for dreaming. Yet, save for the one general feature of impossibility—their magical nature— the dreams of each man and of each age in life possess their own distinctive features. During that period of time which I regard as the close of my boyhood and the beginning of my youth, four sentiments formed the foundation of my dreams: love for *her,* an imaginary woman, of whom I thought always in the same strain, and whom I expected to meet somewhere at any moment. This *she* was a little like Sonechka; a little like Masha, Vasili's wife, when she stood washing over the tub; and a little like the woman with pearls round her white neck

---

* An allusion to Pushkin's poem, "Poltava."—*Tr.*

whom I saw in the theatre very long ago in the box next to ours. The second sentiment was love of love. I wanted to have every one know and love me. I wanted to be able to pronounce my name, Nikolai Irtenyev, and have every one, startled by this information, come crowding round and thank me for something. The third feeling was the hope of some remarkable, glorious happiness—so great and firm that it would verge on madness. I was so sure that I should very soon become the greatest and most distinguished man in the world, in consequence of some extraordinary circumstance or other, that I lived in constant, tremulous expectation of something enchantingly blissful. I was always anticipating that it *was about to begin*, and that I would achieve all that man can desire; and I was always hastening about in all directions, supposing that it was already *beginning* in the place where I happened not to be. The fourth and principal feeling was disgust at myself and remorse, but a remorse so mingled with hope of bliss that there was nothing sorrowful about it. It seemed to me so easy and natural to tear myself away from all the past, to do everything anew, to forget everything which had been, and to begin over again my life with all its relations, that the past neither weighed upon nor fettered me. I even took pleasure in detesting the past, and seeing it in more sombre colours than it had. The blacker the circle of memories of the past, the purer and brighter did the pure, bright point of the present and the rainbow hues of the future stand out in relief against it. This voice of remorse, and of passionate desire for perfection, was the chief new spiritual sentiment at that stage of my growth; and this voice it was that provided new principles for my views of myself, of people, and of God's world. Oh kind, consoling voice that in later days—in sorrowful days when the soul silently yielded to the weight of life's

233

falsehood and vice—so often raised a sudden protest against every untruth, exposing the past and pointing to the bright spot of the present and making one love it, and promising good and happiness in the future—oh blessed, comforting voice! Wilt thou one day be silent?

Chapter IV

OUR FAMILY CIRCLE

Papa was seldom at home that spring. But whenever he was, he was extremely gay; he strummed off his favourite pieces on the piano, looked roguishly at us and made jokes about Mimi and all of us; he would say that the Tsarevich of Georgia had seen Mimi out riding, and had fallen so much in love that he had sent a petition to the synod for a divorce, or else that I had been appointed assistant secretary to the ambassador to Vienna—this news he imparted with a perfectly serious face; next, he would frighten Katenka with spiders, which she was afraid of. He was very cordial to our friends Dubkov and Nekhlyudov, and was constantly telling us and visitors his plans for the coming year. Although these plans changed nearly every day, and contradicted each other, they were so attractive that we listened to them eagerly, and Lyubochka stared unblinkingly at Papa's mouth for fear of missing a word. Now his plan would be to leave us in Moscow at the university, and go to Italy with Lyubochka for two years, then to purchase an estate in the Crimea, on the southern shore and go there every summer, or again to move to St. Petersburg with the whole family, and so forth. Yet besides Papa's remarkable gaiety, another change had taken place in him which greatly surprised me. He had got himself some fashionable clothes—an olive-coloured coat, fashionable trousers with boot-straps, and a long overcoat, which became him extremely well—and he was often deliciously perfumed when he went anywhere, particularly to one lady of whom Mimi never spoke except with a sigh, and a look on her face that seemed to say, "Poor orphans! An unfortunate passion. It is well that *she* is no more," and so on. I learned from Nikolai (for Papa never told us about his gambling affairs) that he had been very lucky at cards that winter; he had won an awfully large sum, all of which he had placed in the bank, and did not want to play any more that spring. Probably this was the reason why he was so anxious to go to the country as soon as possible, lest he should not be able to restrain himself. He even decided not to await my entrance to the university and to go with the girls to Petrovskoye immediately after Easter, whither Volodya and I were to follow him later on.

Volodya had been inseparable from Dubkov all winter and even until the spring (but he had cooled greatly towards Dmitri). Their chief pleasures, so far as I could judge from the conversations which I heard, consisted in drinking champagne incessantly, driving in a sleigh past the windows of young ladies with whom they were both in love, and dancing *vis-à-vis*—not at children's balls any more, but at real balls.

This last circumstance caused an estrangement between Volodya and me, in spite of our mutual affection. We were conscious that there was too much difference between a boy who still had tutors and a man who danced at grand balls for us to confide our thoughts to each other. Katenka was already quite grown up and read a great many novels, and the thought that she might soon marry no longer seemed a joke to me; yet though Volodya was also grown up, they did not associate and even seemed to despise each other. Generally, when Katenka was at home, she had nothing to occupy her but novels,

235

and she was bored most of the time; but when men paid calls, she became very lively and charming, made such eyes at them, that I could not in the least understand what she meant by it. Only later, when I learned from her in conversation that the only coquetry permitted to a girl is this coquetry of the eyes, could I explain to myself the strange, unnatural grimaces of the eyes, which did not seem to surprise other people at all. Lyubochka also had begun to wear dresses which were almost long, so that her badly-shaped legs were hardly visible at all; yet she still cried as much as ever. Her dream now was to marry not a Hussar, but a singer or a musician; and accordingly she applied herself to her music with greater diligence than ever. St. Jérôme, who knew that he was to remain in the house only until my examinations were over, had found a situation with some Count, and since then looked upon our household rather disdainfully. He was seldom at home, took to smoking cigarettes, which were then the height of dandyism, and was incessantly whistling merry airs. Mimi became more bitter every day, and, now that we were beginning to grow up, did not seem to expect any good from any one of us.

When I came down to dinner I found only Mimi, Katenka, Lyubochka, and St. Jérôme in the dining-room; Papa was not at home, and Volodya was preparing for his examination with his comrades in his room, and had ordered his dinner to be brought there. Mimi, whom none of us respected, generally sat at the head of the table of late, and dinner lost much of its charm. It was no longer, as in Mamma's and Grandmamma's day, a kind of ceremony which united the whole family at a certain hour and divided the day into two halves. We permitted ourselves to be late, to come in at the second course, to drink wine out of ordinary glasses (St. Jérôme himself set the example on this point), to lounge on our chairs, to leave the table before dinner was over, and similar liberties. From that moment dinner ceased to be, as formerly, a joyous, daily family solemnity.

In the old days, at Petrovskoye, everyone used to come freshly washed and dressed for dinner, to repair to the drawing-room at two o'clock, and sit there chatting merrily while waiting for the appointed hour. Just as the clock in the butler's pantry started to whirr preparatory to striking two, Foka would enter noiselessly, a napkin over his arm, and with a dignified and rather stern countenance. "Dinner is ready!" he would announce in a loud, solemn tone; and all would go to the dining-room, the elder people in front, the young ones behind, with gay, contented faces; their starched skirts rustling, and their shoes squeaking they would seat themselves in their familiar places, talking in low voices.

Again, in Moscow, we would all stand before the table, talking quietly as we waited for Grandmamma. Gavrilo had already gone to announce to her that dinner is served; all at once the door would open, and there would be a faint swish of a dress and the sound of footsteps, and Grandmamma would issue out of her chamber in a cap trimmed with a quaint old lilac bow, smiling or sullen (according to the state of her health). Gavrilo would rush to her chair, the other chairs would scrape and a cold shiver would run down your spine—a forerunner of appetite—you would take your rather dampish, starched napkin, take a bite or two of bread, and rubbing your hands under the table with impatient and joyous greediness, you would gaze at the steaming tureen of soup, which the butler dispenses according to rank, age, and Grandmamma's favour.

Now I no longer experienced any such joy or excitement when I came to dinner.

On the present occasion, the chatter between Mimi, St. Jérôme, and the girls about the frightful shoes which the Russian teacher wore, and Princess Kornakova's flounced dresses, and so on—that chatter which formerly inspired me with a genuine contempt which I did not even try to conceal as far as Lyubochka and Katenka were concerned—failed to ruffle my new and virtuous frame of mind. I was unusually gentle; I listened to them with a peculiarly courteous smile, asked politely for the *kvass* to be passed to me, and agreed with St. Jérôme when he corrected me for a phrase which I had used before dinner, and told me that it was better to say *je puis* than *je peux*. Yet I must confess that it rather displeased me to find that no one took any special notice of my gentleness and amiability. After dinner Lyubochka showed me a paper on which she had written down all her sins; I said that was all very well, but that it would be still better to inscribe one's sins in one's soul, while, as she did it, "it was not the thing."

"Why not?" asked Lyubochka.

"Never mind—that is all right too; you can't understand me." And I went upstairs to my own room, telling St. Jérôme that I was going to study but in reality to spend the time before confession, which was to be in an hour and a half, writing out a list of my duties and occupations for my whole life, and laying out on paper the aim of my life, and the rules by which I was always to act without any deviation.

Chapter V

RULES

I took a sheet of paper, and tried first of all to write out a list of my tasks and duties for the coming year. For this the paper must be ruled; but as I could not find the ruler, I used the Latin dictionary. When I drew the pen along the dictionary, and then moved it back, it appeared that instead of a line I had made a long puddle of ink on the paper; besides, the dictionary was shorter than the paper, and the line curved around its soft corner. I took another piece of paper, and by moving the dictionary I managed to draw the line after a fashion. Dividing my duties into three classes—to myself, to my neighbour, and to God—I began to write down the first; but they turned out to be so numerous, and of so many kinds and subdivisions, that it was necessary to write first, "Rules of Life," and then to set about making a list of them. I took six sheets of paper, sewed them into a book, and wrote at the top "Rules of Life." These words came out in such a crooked scrawl that I pondered for a long while whether I should not write them over; and I worried long as I looked at the tattered list and this shapeless heading. Why does everything which was so beautiful and clean in my soul turn out so repulsive on paper, and in life generally, when I want to put in practice any of the things which I think?

"The priest has arrived; please come downstairs to hear his directions," Nikolai came to announce.

I hid my book in the table, looked in the glass, brushed my hair up, which, in my opinion, gave me a thoughtful look, and went to the sitting-room, where a covered table had been prepared with the images and lighted candles. Papa entered by another door at the same time as myself. The priest, a grey-haired monk with a stern, aged face, gave Papa his blessing. Papa kissed his short, broad, dry hand; I did the same.

"Call Waldemar," said Papa; "where is he? Oh, yes, he is taking the communion at the university."

"He is studying with the Prince," said Katenka, and she looked at Lyubochka. The latter suddenly blushed for some reason, winced pretending that something hurt her, and left the room. I followed her. She paused in the drawing-room, and wrote something else on her paper.

"What, have you committed a fresh sin?" I asked.

"No, nothing of the sort," she replied, turning red.

At that moment we heard Dmitri's voice in the ante-room, as he took leave of Volodya.

"Everything is a temptation to you," said Katenka, entering the room and addressing Lyubochka.

I could not understand what had happened to my sister: she was so embarrassed that tears rose to her eyes, and her embarrassment grew until it became anger at herself and Katenka, who was evidently teasing her.

"One can easily see you are a *foreigner* (nothing could be more insulting to Katenka than to be called 'foreigner,' and that was why Lyubochka did so). Before such a sacrament," she continued with dignity in her voice, "you go and upset me; you ought to understand that this is not a jest at all."

"Do you know what she has written, Nikolenka?" asked Katenka, offended by the word "foreigner." "She has written—"

"I did not expect you to be so spiteful," Lyubochka sputtered out, going away from us. "She leads me into sin, and on purpose, at such a moment. I do not tease you with your feelings and sufferings, do I?"

Chapter VI

CONFESSION

With these and other similar distracting thoughts I returned to the sitting-room when all were assembled there, and the priest, rising, prepared to read the prayer before confession. But as soon as the stern, expressive voice of the monk resounded amid the universal silence, and especially when he addressed us with the words, *"Confess all your sins without shame, concealment or extenuation, and your soul shall be cleansed before God; but if ye conceal aught, so shall ye have greater sin,"* the devout agitation which I had felt on the preceding morning, at the thought of the coming sacrament, returned to me. I even took pleasure in realizing my state, and tried to retain it, putting a stop to all thoughts which occurred to me, and trying to fear something.

Papa was the first to go to confess. He remained for a very long time in Grandmamma's room, and meanwhile all of us in the sitting-room remained silent, or discussed in whispers who should go first. At length the monk's voice was again heard behind the door as he read a prayer, and then Papa's footsteps. The door creaked and he came out, coughing, holding one shoulder higher than the other, as was his wont, and not looking at any of us.

"You go now, Lyuba, and see that you say everything. You are my greatest sinner, you know," said Papa gaily, as he gave her cheek a pinch.

Lyubochka went red and pale by turns, took her list out of her apron and hid it again, and, her head sunk between her shoulders, as though expecting a blow from above, passed through the door. She did not stay long, but when she came out her shoulders were heaving with sobs.

Finally, after pretty Katenka, who came out smiling, my turn came. I entered the half-lighted room with the same dull terror, and a desire deliberately to increase that terror. The priest stood before the lectern, and slowly turned his face towards me.

I did not remain more than five minutes in Grandmamma's room, but when I came out I was happy and, according to my convictions at the time, a perfectly pure, morally changed, and new man. Although all the old surroundings of life struck me unpleasantly, the same rooms, the same furniture, the same face in myself (I should have liked to change my exterior, just as I thought all my interior had been changed)—still, notwithstanding this, I remained in this refreshing frame of mind until I went to bed.

I was already drowsing off, going over in my imagination all the sins of which I had been purified, when all at once I recalled one shameful sin which I had kept back in confession. The words of the prayer before confession came back to me and resounded in my ears without intermission. All my composure vanished in a moment. "And if ye conceal aught, so shall ye have greater sin," I heard incessantly. I saw that I was such a terrible sinner that there was no punishment adequate for me. Long did I toss from side to side as I reflected on my situation, and awaited God's punishment and even sudden death from moment to moment—a thought which threw me into indescribable terror. But suddenly the happy thought occurred to me to go by foot or by cab to the priest at the monastery as soon as it was light: and confess again, and I became calm.

Chapter VII

THE TRIP TO THE MONASTERY

I woke up several times that night, fearing to oversleep, and at six o'clock I was already on my feet. It was hardly light at the windows yet. I put on my clothes and my boots, which lay in a heap and unbrushed by the bed, for Nikolai had not had time to take them away; and without washing or saying my prayers, I went out into the street alone for the first time in my life.

From behind the big, green-roofed house on the other side of the street, the red flush of the dull, cold dawn appeared. A sharp spring morning frost bound the mud and the rivulets, crackled underfoot, and nipped my face and hands.

There was not a single cabman in our street as yet, though I had relied on one in order that I might go there and back the more speedily. Only a few carts were dragging slowly along the Arbat, and a couple of stone-masons passed along the pavement in conversation. After I had gone some thousand paces I began to meet men and women with baskets going to market, or with casks going for water. A pie-seller had come out at the corner; one *kalach*-baker's shop* was open, and at the Arbatsky Gate I came across an old cabman asleep on his blue, worn, patched droshky. Probably still in his sleep he asked me for twenty kopeks to drive me to the monastery and back, but then he suddenly came to; I was about to get in when he lashed his horse with the end of the reins and almost drove away. "My horse wants feeding," he muttered. "I can't take you, sir."

It was with difficulty that I persuaded him to stop by offering him forty kopeks. He pulled up his horse, looked me over carefully, and said, "Get in, sir." I confess that I was rather afraid that he would drive me to some secluded lane and rob me. Catching hold of his tattered coat-collar, his wrinkled neck showing pitifully above his hunched back, I climbed into the blue, curved, rocking seat, and we went rattling down Vozdvizhenka. On the way I observed that the back of the droshky was lined with bits of the greenish material from which the driver's coat was made; and this fact calmed me, for some reason, and I was no longer afraid that he would carry me off to an obscure alley and rob me.

The sun was already quite high, and had gilded the cupolas of the churches brilliantly when we arrived at

---

* *Kalach*, a certain kind of white roll or small loaf.—*Tr.*

the monastery. Frost still lingered in the shade; but along the road flowed swift turbid streams, and the horse splashed along through the thawed slush. On entering the enclosure of the monastery, I inquired of the first person I saw where I could find the priest.

"Yonder is his cell," said the passing monk, pausing for a moment and pointing at a small house with a tiny portico.

"I am extremely obliged," said I.

Then I fell to wondering what all the monks (who at the moment were coming out of the church) must think of me for they all glanced in my direction. I was neither a grown-up nor a child, my face was unwashed, my hair unbrushed, my clothes untidy, and my boots unblacked and muddy. They must be trying to assign me to some class of people—for they stared at me hard enough. And yet I walked on in the direction which the young priest had pointed out to me.

An old man in a black garment, with a thick grey beard, met me in the narrow path which led to the cell and asked what I wanted.

For a moment I wanted to say "Nothing," run back to the carriage, and drive home; but the old man's face inspired confidence, in spite of his contracted brows. I said that I must see the priest, and mentioned his name.

"Come, young sir, I'll show you the way," said he, turning back, and apparently divining at once the reason of my visit. "The father is at matins; he will soon be here."

He opened the door and led me through a clean vestibule and anteroom, over a clean linen floor-covering, into the cell.

"Please wait here," said he, with a kindly, reassuring glance, and went out.

The little room in which I found myself was extremely small, and arranged with great neatness. Its furniture only consisted of a little table covered with oil-cloth, which stood between two double-leafed windows, and upon it two pots of geraniums, a stand supporting the images, and a lamp which swung before them, one arm-chair and two ordinary chairs. In the corner hung a clock its dial adorned with painted flowers, and with its brass weights on chains half unwound; two cassocks hung from nails in the partition, behind which was probably the bed, and which was joined to the ceiling by whitewashed wooden planks.

The windows looked out upon a white wall about two arshins away. Between them and the wall there grew a little bush of lilac. Not a sound from without penetrated to the room, so that the regular tick of the pendulum sounded loud in the silence. As soon as I was alone in this quiet nook, all my former ideas and memories suddenly left my head completely, as if they had never been there, and I became wholly absorbed in an inexpressibly pleasant reverie. That faded nankeen cassock, with its tattered lining, the worn black leather bindings of the books and their brass clasps, the dull green of the plants, the carefully watered earth and well-washed leaves, and the monotonous, intermittent sound of the pendulum in particular, spoke to me distinctly of a new life hitherto unknown to me—a life of solitude, of prayer, of calm, quiet happiness.

"Months pass by, years pass by," I thought. "He is always alone, always calm; he always feels that his conscience is pure in the sight of God, and that his prayers are heard by Him." For half an hour I sat on that chair, trying not to move and not to breathe loudly, in order that I might not disturb that harmony of sounds which were telling me so much. And the pendulum ticked on as before, loudly to the right, more softly to the left.

Chapter VIII

A SECOND CONFESSION

The priest's footsteps aroused me from this reverie.

"Welcome," said he, adjusting his grey hair with his hand. "What can I do for you?"

I asked him to bless me, and kissed his short yellow hand with peculiar satisfaction.

When I explained my petition to him, he made no reply, but went to the icon and began to hear my confession.

When I overcame my shame and told him all that was in my soul and the confession was over, he laid his hands upon my head, and in his quiet, melodious voice he said, "My son, may the blessing of our heavenly Father be upon you, and may He preserve faith, peace, and gentleness within you evermore. Amen."

I was perfectly happy; tears of bliss rose in my throat; I kissed the folds of his fine-cloth cassock, and raised my head. The monk's face was quite calm.

I felt that I was taking delight in the sensation of emotion; and, fearing that I might banish it in some way, I took leave of the priest in haste, and without glancing aside in order not to distract my attention, quitted the enclosure, and seated myself again in the motley and jolting droshky. But the jolts of the equipage, the variety of objects which flashed before my eyes, speedily dissipated that sensation, and I already began to think that the priest was probably thinking by this time that such a fine soul of a young man as I he had never met, and never would meet in all his life, and that there were no others like me. I was convinced of that, and this conviction called forth in me a feeling of cheerfulness of such a nature that it demanded communication to some one.

I wanted dreadfully to talk to some one; but as there was no one at hand except the cabman, I turned to him.

"Well, was I away very long?" I asked.

"Not very, but it was time to feed the horse long ago, I am a night-cabman, you see," he replied, apparently more cheerful now that the sun was up.

"It seemed to me that I was no more than a minute," said I. "And do you know why I went to the monastery?" I added, changing my seat to the hollow nearer the driver.

"Well, it's not my business, is it? I take my passengers wherever they order me," he replied.

"No, but still what do you think?" I insisted.

"Well, probably some one is going to be buried, and you went to buy a place," said he.

"No, my friend; do you know what I went for?"

"I can't know, sir," he repeated.

His voice seemed to me so kind that I decided to relate to him the cause of my journey, and even the feeling which I had experienced, for his edification.

"I will tell you, if you like. You see—"

And I told him everything, and described all my beautiful sentiments. I blush even now at the memory of it.

"Yes, sir," he said incredulously.

And for a long time after that he sat silent and motionless, only now and then adjusting the tail of his coat; it kept escaping from beneath his motley foot which jogged up and down in its big boot on the footboard. I already imagined that he was thinking just the same about me as the priest—that is, that there was not another fine young man like me in the world; but he suddenly turned to me.

"Well, master, that's the sort of thing for you gentlefolks."

"What?" I inquired.

"Just the thing for gentlefolks."

"No, he has not understood me," I thought, but I said nothing more to him until we reached home.

Although the feeling of fervour and devotion did not last the whole way, self-satisfaction in having experienced it did, in spite of the people who dotted the sunlit streets with colour everywhere; but as soon as I reached home that feeling entirely disappeared. I did not have my two twenty-kopek pieces to pay the driver. Gavrilo the butler, to whom I was already indebted, would not lend me any more. Seeing me twice run through the court-yard to get the money, the cabman must have guessed the reason, for he climbed down from his droshky, and, although he had seemed to me so kind, began to talk loudly, with evident hostility towards me, about swindlers who would not pay their fare.

Every one was still asleep in the house, so, except for the servants there was no one from whom I could borrow the forty kopeks. Finally Vasili, under my sacred, most sacred word of honour, in which (as I could see by his face) he had not the slightest faith, but because he loved me and remembered the service which I had rendered him, paid the cabman for me. When I went to dress for church, in order that I might receive the communion with the rest, and it turned out that my new clothes had not yet come, I was highly incensed. Dressing in another suit, I went to communion in a strange mental tumult, and filled with utter distrust of all my finer impulses.

Chapter IX

HOW I PREPARE FOR THE EXAMINATION

On the Friday after Easter, Papa, my sister, Mimi, and Katenka went to the country; so that in all Grandmamma's great house there remained only Volodya, myself, and St. Jérôme. The frame of mind in which I had found myself on the day of confession and when I went to the monastery had completely disappeared, and had left only a dim though agreeable memory, which was more and more submerged by the new impressions of a free life.

The copy-book with the heading, "Rules of Life," had also been tucked away under a pile of roughly written note-books. Although the idea of the possibility of establishing rules for all contingencies of life and of always guiding myself by them pleased me, and seemed very simple and at the same time very grand, and I intended all the same to apply it to life, I seemed to have again forgotten that it was necessary to do this at once, and kept putting it off to some indefinite time. But one fact delighted me; that was that every thought which occurred to me now ranged itself immediately under one of the classifications of my rules and duties—under the head of duty either to my neighbour, to myself, or to God. "Then I will set it down there," I said to myself, "as well as many, many other thoughts which will occur to me later on this subject." I often ask myself now: When was I better and more correct—then, when I believed in the omnipotency of the human intellect, or now that I have lost the faculty of growth, and doubt the power and significance of human reason? And I cannot give myself any positive answer.

The consciousness of freedom, and that spring feeling of expecting something, which I have already mentioned, agitated me to such a degree that I positively could not control myself, and I prepared very badly for my examination. Suppose you are busy in the school-room in the morning, and know that you must work, because tomorrow there is to be an examination on a subject, two whole questions on which you have not read up at all, when all of a sudden a spring perfume wafts in at the window; it seems as though you absolutely must recall something; your hands drop of themselves, your feet begin to move of their own will, and to pace back and forth, and some spring seems to be pressed in your head which sets the whole machine in motion; you feel light-headed, and gay, radiant reveries begin to run through your mind so quickly that you only succeed in catching their radiancy. Thus an hour, two hours, pass unnoticed. Or, you are sitting over your book and concentrating your attention, after a fashion, on what you are reading; and suddenly you hear the sound of a woman's footsteps and the rustle of her dress in the corridor, and everything has escaped your mind, and you just can't sit still, although you know very well that nobody can be passing along that corridor except Gasha, Grandmother's old maid-servant. "Yet suppose it should be *she*?" comes into your mind; "suppose it should begin now, and I miss it?" And darting out into the corridor, you see that it is indeed Gasha; yet you cannot recover control of your head for a long time—the spring has again been pressed, and again the frightful disorder has started. Or, you are sitting alone in the evening, with a tallow candle, in your room; you tear yourself from your book for a moment in order to snuff the candle or to settle in your chair more comfortably—it is dark everywhere, at the doors and in the corners, and it is quiet all over the house; and again it is impossible not to stop and listen to that silence, and not to gaze into that blackness of the open door, and not to remain thus for a long, long time immovable in the same attitude, or not to go downstairs, or walk through all the empty rooms. Often, too, I sat unnoticed for a long time in the hall listening to the sound of the "Nightingale," which Gasha was playing with one finger on the piano, as she sat alone with one tallow candle in the great apartment. And when the moon was bright I could not possibly resist rising from my bed and lying on the window over the garden, and gazing at the lighted roof of the Shaposhnikov house, and the graceful tower of our parish church, and at the night shadows of the hedge and

250

bushes as they lay upon the garden paths. So long did I sit thus that it was ten o'clock in the morning before I could open my eyes.

So that had it not been for the masters who continued to come to me, St. Jérôme, who now and then unwillingly pricked my vanity, and most of all the desire to show myself a capable young fellow in the eyes of my friend Nekhlyudov, that is, to get distinction at the examination, which in his opinion was a matter of great importance—had it not been for this, the spring and liberty would have had the effect of making me forget everything I had known before, and I should not have been able to pass the examination on any account.

Chapter X

THE HISTORY EXAMINATION

On the 16th of April I entered the great hall of the university for the first time, under the protection of St. Jérôme. We drove there in our rather dandified phaeton. I had on a dress-coat for the first time in my life; and all my clothes, down to my linen and stockings, were quite new, and of the very best. When the porter helped me out of my overcoat, and I stood before him in all the beauty of my attire, I was rather ashamed of being so dazzling; but I had no sooner entered the bright hall, with its polished floor, which was filled with people, and seen hundreds of young men in gymnasium uniforms and dress-coats, a few of whom glanced at me with indifference, and the dignified professors at the farther end, walking freely about among the desks or sitting in large arm-chairs, than I was instantly disenchanted in my hope of turning the general attention upon myself, and the expression of my countenance, which at home, and even in the ante-

251

room, had indicated that I possessed that noble and distinguished appearance against my will, changed into an expression of the most excessive timidity, and to some extent of depression. I even fell into the other extreme, and rejoiced greatly when I saw an excessively ugly, untidily dressed gentleman, not yet old but almost entirely grey, sitting on the last bench, at a distance from all the rest. I immediately seated myself beside him, and began to observe the candidates for examination and to draw my conclusions about them. Many and varied were the figures and faces there; but all, according to my opinion at the time, could be easily divided into three classes.

First of all there were those, like myself, attending for examination, in the company of their tutors or parents; and among such I could see the youngest Ivin with the familiar Frost, and Ilenka Grap with his aged father. They all had downy chins, sported prominent linen, and sat quietly without opening the books or copy-books which they had brought with them, and looked with obvious timidity at the professors and the examiners' tables. The second class of candidates were the young men in the gymnasium uniforms, many of whom already shaved. Most of these knew each other, talked loudly, mentioned the professors by their names and patronymics, were already preparing questions, passing their note-books to each other, climbed over the desks, fetched themselves patties and sandwiches, and devoured them then and there, merely bending their heads to the level of the desks. And lastly, there was a third class of candidates, very few in number, however, who were quite old, some attired in dress-coats, but the majority in surtouts, and were without any show of linen. These preserved a serious demeanour, sat by themselves and looked very gloomy. The one who consoled me by being certainly dressed worse than I was belonged to this last class. Leaning forward upon his elbows, and running his fingers through his grey dishevelled hair as he read a book, he had cast at me only a momentary glance—and that not a friendly one—from his glittering eyes, and scowled darkly, thrusting out a shining elbow in my direction, so that I might not come any nearer. The gymnasium students, on the other hand, were too familiar, and I was a little afraid of them. One said, as he thrust a book into my hand, "Give this to that fellow over there." Another said, as he passed me, "'Scuse me, old chap." A third, as he climbed over the desk, leaned on my shoulder as though it had been the bench. All this was outrageous and disagreeable to me. I considered myself superior to these gymnasium students, and thought they had no business to permit themselves such liberties with me. At last they began to call the names out; the gymnasium fellows stepped out boldly, answered well in the majority, and returned cheerfully. Our set were much more timid, and answered worse, it appeared. Of the oldish men, some answered excellently, others very badly indeed. When the name Semenov was called out, my neighbour with the grey hair and glittering eyes rose, jostled me roughly, stepped over my legs, and went up to one of the examiners' tables. It was plain from the professors' faces that he answered well and with assurance. On returning to his place, he took up his note-books and quietly went away without finding out what mark he had got. I had already shuddered several times at the sound of the voice calling out the names, but my turn had not yet come, the list being in alphabetical order, although some names beginning with K had already been called. "Ikonin and Tenyev," shouted some one in the professors' corner all of a sudden. A shiver ran over my back and my hair.

"Whom did they call? Who is Bartenyev," they began to say around me.

"Go, Ikonin, they are calling you; but who is this Bartenyev or Mordenyev?" said a tall, ruddy gymnasiast who stood behind me.

"It must be you," said St. Jérôme.

"My name is Irtenyev," said I to the red-faced gymnasiast. "Did they call for Irtenyev?"

"Yes; why on earth don't you go up? Lord, what a dandy!" he added, not loudly, but so that I heard his words as I left my bench.

In front of me walked Ikonin, a tall young man of five and twenty, who belonged to those whom I classed as oldish candidates. He wore a tight olive coat, a blue satin neckerchief, over which behind hung his long, light hair, cut *à la* muzhik.* His appearance had already caught my attention when we were sitting at the desks. He was rather good-looking and talkative. What especially struck me in him was the queer reddish hair which he had allowed to grow on his throat, and, still more, a strange habit he had of continually unbuttoning his waistcoat and scratching his chest under his shirt.

Three professors were seated at the table to which Ikonin and I went; not one of them answered our greeting. The youngest was shuffling tickets like a pack of cards; the second professor, with a star on his coat, was staring at the gymnasiast, who was rattling off something about Charlemagne, adding "at length" to every word; and the third, an old man, looked at us through his spectacles and pointed to the tickets. I felt that his gaze was directed upon Ikonin and me jointly, and that something in our appearance displeased him (possibly Ikonin's red beard), because as he looked at us again in the same way he made an impatient gesture with his head to us that we should take our tickets quickly. I felt vexed and insulted, in the first place, because no one had returned our greeting, and in the second, because they were evidently classing Ikonin and me in the same category, that of candidates for examination, and were already prejudiced

---

* Cut square all round.—*Tr.*

against me because of Ikonin's red beard. I took my ticket without timidity, and prepared to answer, but the professor directed his gaze at Ikonin. I read my ticket through; I knew it, and while calmly awaiting my turn I observed what was going on before me. Ikonin was not in the least embarrassed, he was even too bold, for as he reached for his ticket, he leaned sideways over the table, shook back his hair, and rapidly read over what was printed on it. He was on the point of opening his mouth to reply, I thought, when the professor with the star, having dismissed the gymnasiast with praise, glanced at him. Ikonin seemed to remember something, and paused. The general silence lasted for a couple of minutes.

"Well?" said the professor with the spectacles.

Ikonin again opened his mouth, but remained silent.

"Come, you are not the only one. Do you mean to answer or not?" asked the young professor, but Ikonin did not even look at him. He stared at the ticket, and did not utter a single word. The professor with the spectacles looked at him through his glasses, and over his glasses, and without his glasses, because he had time to take them off, wipe them carefully, and put them on again. Ikonin never uttered a word. Suddenly a smile spread over his face, he shook back his hair, again turned full broadside to the table, looked at all the professors in turn, then at me, turned, and with a wave of his hands walked jauntily back to his bench. The professors exchanged glances.

"Bless the fellow!" said the young professor, "wants to study at his own expense."

I stepped nearer to the table, but the professors continued to talk almost in undertones among themselves, as though none of them was even aware of my existence. Then I was firmly convinced that all three professors were very much occupied with the question as to whether I would pass the examination, and whether I would come out of it well; but that they were only pretending, for the

255

sake of their dignity, that it was a matter of utter indifference to them and that they did not notice me.

When the professor in spectacles turned indifferently to me, inviting me to answer the questions, I looked him full in the eye and was rather ashamed for him that he should so dissemble before me, and I hesitated somewhat in beginning my answer; but afterwards it became easier and easier, and as the question was from Russian history, which I knew very well, I finished in brilliant style, and even gained confidence to such an extent that, desiring to make the professors feel that I was not Ikonin, and that it was impossible to confound me with him, I proposed to draw a second ticket. But the professor shook his head and said, "That will do, sir," and noted down something in his register. When I returned to the benches I immediately learned from the gymnasiasts, who knew everything, God knows how, that I had got full marks.

Chapter XI

THE MATHEMATICS EXAMINATION

At the succeeding examinations I made many new acquaintances besides Grap, whom I considered unworthy of my acquaintance, and Ivin, who for some reason shunned me. Several already exchanged greetings with me. Ikonin even rejoiced when he saw me, and confided to me that he would be re-examined in history, that the history professor had had a spite against him since the last examination, at which also he had thrown him into confusion. Semenov, who was going to enter the same faculty as I, mathematics, was shy of every one, and until the very end of the examinations he sat silent and alone, always leaning on his elbows, and running his hands through his grey hair. He passed his examinations in excellent style and came out second; a student from the first gymnasium was first. The latter was a tall, thin, extremely pale, dark-complexioned youth, with a neck wrapped in a black neck-cloth, and a forehead covered with pimples. His hands were thin and red, with remarkably long fingers, and nails so bitten that the ends of his fingers seemed to be wound with thread. All this seemed splendid to me, and just as it should be in the case of *the top boy of the gymnasium.* He spoke to everybody exactly like anybody else, and even I made his acquaintance; but it seemed to me that there was something unusually extraordinary and magnetic in his bearing, the movements of his lips, and in his black eyes.

At the mathematics examination, I was called up earlier than usual. I knew the subject pretty well; but there were two questions in algebra which I had contrived in some way to hide from my teacher, and which I knew absolutely nothing about. They were, as I now remember, the theory of combinations, and Newton's binomial theorem. I sat at the desk in the rear, and looked over the two unfamiliar questions; but as I was not accustomed to working in a noisy room, and felt that I would not have enough time, I found it difficult to grasp what I was reading.

"Here he is. This way, Nekhlyudov," said Volodya's familiar voice behind me.

I turned and saw my brother and Dmitri—their coats unbuttoned and their hands waving a greeting to me—threading their way towards me between the benches. It was immediately apparent that they were second-year students and as much at home in the university as in their own houses. The sight of their unbuttoned coats alone expressed disdain for us who were entering, and inspired us with envy and respect. It flattered me very much to think that all around me could see that I was acquainted with two second-year students, and I rose hastily to meet them.

Volodya could not help vaunting his superiority a little.

"Oh, you poor wretch!" said he; "haven't you been examined yet?"

"No."

"What are you reading? Aren't you prepared?"

"Yes; but not quite on two questions. I don't understand them."

"What! this one here?" said Volodya, and began to explain to me Newton's binomial theorem, but so rapidly and in such a confused manner that, reading disbelief in his knowledge in my eyes, he glanced at Dmitri, and probably reading the same in his, he turned red, but went on, nevertheless, to say something which I did not understand.

"No, Volodya, wait; let me go over it with him; perhaps we'll have time enough," said Dmitri, glancing at the professors' corner; and he sat down beside me.

I could immediately see that my friend was in that gentle, complacent mood which he was always in when he was satisfied with himself, and which I specially liked in him. As he knew mathematics well, and spoke clearly, he explained the question so splendidly that I remember it to this day. Scarcely had he finished when St. Jérôme said in a loud whisper, "*A vous*, Nicolas," and I rose and followed Ikonin without having a chance to look over the other question I did not know. I approached the table where the two professors sat, and a gymnasiast was standing before the blackboard. The gymnasiast had boldly announced some formula, breaking his chalk with a tap on the board, and still went on writing, although the professor had already said "Enough!" and ordered us to take our tickets. "Now, what if I get that theory of combinations?" thought I, picking out my ticket with trembling fingers from the soft pile of cut paper. Ikonin took the topmost ticket, without making any choice, with the same bold gesture and sideways lunge of his whole body as in the preceding examination.

"I always have such devilish luck!" he muttered.

I looked at mine.

Oh, horror! It was the theory of combinations.

"What have you got?" asked Ikonin.

I showed him.

"I know that," said he.

"Will you change?"

"No, I don't feel up to it today anyhow," Ikonin barely contrived to whisper, when the professor summoned us to the board.

"Well, all's lost!" I thought. "Instead of the brilliant examination which I dreamed of passing, I shall cover myself with eternal disgrace, even worse than Ikonin." But all at once Ikonin turned to me, right under the professor's eyes, snatched the card from my hand, and gave me his. I glanced at his card. It was Newton's binomial theorem.

The professor was not an old man; and he had a pleasant, sensible expression, to which the extremely prominent lower part of his forehead particularly contributed.

"What is this, gentlemen? Are you exchanging tickets?"

"No, he only gave me his to look at, professor," said Ikonin, inventing—and again the word *professor* was the last one he uttered in that place; and again, as he retired past me, he glanced at the professors, at me, smiled, and shrugged his shoulders, with an expression as much as to say, "What matter!" (I afterwards learned that this was the third year that Ikonin had entered for the examination.)

I answered the question which I had just gone over excellently—even better, as the professor told me, than was required—and received full marks.

Chapter XII

THE LATIN EXAMINATION

All went on fine until my Latin examination. So far the gymnasium boy with his muffled neck was first, Semenov second, and I third. I even began to feel proud, and to think that, in spite of my youth, I was somebody.

From the very first examination everybody had been talking with terror of the Latin professor, who, it appeared, was a brute who took delight in failing young men, especially those who studied at their own expense, and never spoke anything but Latin or Greek. St. Jérôme, who was my tutor in Latin, encouraged me; and it really seemed to me that since I could translate from Cicero and several odes of Horace without a lexicon, and since I knew Zumpt very well indeed, I was no worse prepared than the rest. Yet it proved otherwise. All the morning there was nothing to be heard but tales of the failures of those who preceded me: one had been marked nought; another, one; and still another had been scolded terribly, and had been on the point of getting turned out, and so forth, and so forth. Semenov and the first gymnasiast alone went up and returned with as much composure as usual, each receiving full marks. I already had a presentiment of disaster when I was called up with Ikonin to the little table, facing which the terrible professor sat quite alone. He was a small, thin, yellow man, with long oily hair and a very thoughtful countenance.

He gave Ikonin a volume of Cicero's Orations, and made him translate.

To my great amazement, Ikonin not only read but even translated several lines, with the aid of the professor, who prompted him. Conscious of my superiority over such a feeble rival, I could not help smiling in a rather scornful way, when the question of parsing came up, and Ikonin, as before, sank into stubborn silence. I meant to please the professor by that intelligent, slightly ironical smile; but the effect produced was the opposite.

"You evidently know better, since you smile," said the professor to me in bad Russian. "Well, we shall see. Tell me the answer, then."

I learned afterwards that the Latin professor was Ikonin's protector, and that Ikonin even lived at his house. I lost no time in replying to the question in syntax which had been put to Ikonin, but the professor put on a sad expression and turned away from me.

"Very good, sir; your turn will come; we shall see how much you know," said he, not looking at me, and began to explain to Ikonin what he had questioned him on.

"You may go," he said; and I saw him mark four in the register for Ikonin. "Well," I thought, "he is not nearly as strict as they said." After Ikonin's departure— for at least five minutes, which seemed to me five hours— he arranged his books and cards, blew his nose, adjusted his arm-chair, leaned back in it, and looked round the room, and on all sides except in my direction. But all this dissimulation seemed to him insufficient. He opened a book and pretended to read it, as though I were not there. I stepped up nearer and coughed.

"Ah, yes! You too, of course. Well, translate something," said he, handing me a book. "No; better take this one." He turned over the leaves of a copy of Horace and opened it at a passage which it seemed to me nobody ever could have translated.

"I have not prepared this," said I.

"And you want to recite what you have learned by heart, do you? Very good! No; translate this."

I managed to get the sense of it somehow; but the professor only shook his head at each of my inquiring glances, and merely answered "No," with a sigh. At last he closed his book with such nervous quickness that he pinched his own finger between the leaves. He pulled it out angrily, gave me a question in grammar, and, throwing himself back in his chair, he kept the most malicious silence. I was on the point of answering; but the expression of his countenance fettered my tongue, and everything which I said appeared to me to be wrong.

"That's not it! that's not it at all!" he suddenly broke out with his horrible pronunciation as he briskly changed his position, leaned his elbows on the table, and played with the gold ring which hung loosely on a thin finger of his left hand. "That's not the way, sir, to prepare for a higher educational establishment. All you want is to wear the uniform, with its blue collar, and to get a smattering of knowledge, and you think you can call yourselves students. No, gentlemen; you must be thoroughly grounded in your subject;" and so forth, and so forth.

During the whole of this speech, which was uttered in broken language, I gazed with dull attention at his eyes, which were fixed on the floor. At first the disenchantment of not being third tortured me; then the fear of not passing my examination at all; and, finally, a sense of injustice was added, of wounded vanity and unmerited humiliation. Besides this, contempt for the professor because he was not, in my opinion, a man *comme il faut*—which I discerned by looking at his short, strong, round nails—influenced me still more, and rendered all these feelings poisonous. He glanced at me; and, perceiving my quivering lips and my eyes filled with tears, he must have construed my emotion into a prayer to increase my mark, and he said, as though compassionating me (and before another professor, too, who had come up):

"Very good, sir, although you do not deserve it I will give you a 'pass,' out of consideration for your youth, and in the hope that you will not be so light-headed in the university."

This last phrase, uttered in the presence of the strange professor, who looked at me as if to say, "There, you see, young man!" completed my confusion. For one moment a mist veiled my eyes; the terrible professor, with his table, seemed to me to be sitting somewhere in the far distance, and the wild thought came into my mind, with a terrible one-sided distinctness, "And what if— what will happen if?" But I did not do it, for some reason; but, on the contrary, I bowed to both professors mechanically, with special courtesy, and left the table, smiling slightly, with the same smile, apparently, as Ikonin had exhibited.

This injustice affected me so powerfully at the time that, had I been master of my own actions, I should not have taken any more examinations. I lost all my vanity (since I could not possibly be third), and I let the remaining examinations pass without any exertion, and even without agitation on my part. My average, however, was somewhat over four, but this did not interest me in the least; I made up my mind, and proved it to myself very clearly, that it was bad form to try to be first, and that one ought to be neither too good nor too bad, like Volodya. I meant to keep to this in the university, although I, for the first time, differed from my friend Dmitri on this point.

All I was thinking of was my uniform, my three-cornered hat, my own droshky, my own room, and, above all, my freedom.

Chapter XIII

I AM GROWN UP

And even these thoughts had their charm.

On my return from the last examination in religious knowledge, on the 8th of May, I found at the house a tailor's apprentice from Rosanov's, whom I knew as he had already called to fit my uniform and coat of glossy black cloth, open at the throat, and had marked the lapels with chalk, and who now brought the finished garment with brilliant gilt buttons wrapped in paper.

I put on the garment, and thought it very fine (although St. Jérôme declared that it was loose in the back), and went downstairs with a self-satisfied smile, which spread over my face quite involuntarily, to find Volodya. I was conscious of the glances which the domestics eagerly fixed on me from the anteroom and corridor, though I tried to pretend that I was not. Gavrilo, the butler, overtook me in the hall, congratulated me on my entering the university, handed over to me, by Papa's orders, four twenty-five-ruble bank-notes, and also, by Papa's direction, told me that Kuzma the coachman, a droshky, and the brown horse Beauty, were to be at my exclusive disposal from that day forth. I was so rejoiced at this almost unexpected happiness that I could not manage to appear indifferent before Gavrilo, and in some confusion I said with a sigh the first thing that came into my head, which was that Beauty was a very fine trotter. Glancing at the heads which were thrust out of the doors leading from the anteroom and corridor, I could no longer control myself; and I rushed through the hall in my new coat and shining brass buttons. As I entered Volodya's room I heard the voices of Dubkov and Nekhlyudov, who had come to congratulate me and to propose that we should go somewhere to dine and drink champagne in honour of my entering the university. Dmitri told me that, although he did not care to drink champagne, he would go with us that day in order to drink with me to the beginning of our intimacy. Dubkov declared that I somehow resembled a colonel. Volodya did not congratulate me, but only said very dryly that now we should be able to set out for the country the day after next. It seemed as though, while glad of

264

my entrance, it was rather disagreeable to him that I should now be grown up just like him. St. Jérôme, who had also come to the house, said in a very haughty way that his duties were now at an end, and he did not know whether he had fulfilled them well or ill, but that he had done all he could, and he should go to his Count the next day. In answer to all that was said to me I felt a honeyed, happy, rather foolishly self-satisfied smile play over my face against my will; and I perceived that this smile even communicated itself to all who talked with me.

So there I was, without a tutor; I had a droshky of my own; my name was entered on the register of students; I had a dagger at my belt; the sentries might sometimes salute me. I was grown up, and, I thought, happy.

We decided to dine at the Yar at five o'clock; but as Volodya went off with Dubkov, and Dmitri also disappeared somewhere in his usual fashion, saying that he had an affair to attend to before dinner, I could dispose of two hours as I pleased. I walked about through all the rooms for quite a while, inspecting myself in all the mirrors, now with my coat buttoned, now with it unbuttoned, then with only the upper button fastened; and every way seemed excellent to me. Then, ashamed as I was to exhibit too much joy, I could not refrain from going to the stable and coach-house to inspect Beauty, Kuzma, and the droshky; then I went back and began to wander through the rooms again, looking in the mirrors, counting the money in my pocket, and smiling in the same blissful manner all the while. But before an hour had elapsed I felt rather bored, or sorry that there was no one to see me in that dazzling state; and I longed for movement and activity. In consequence I ordered the droshky to be brought round, and decided that the best thing would be to go to Kuznetsky Most and make some purchases.

I recollected that when Volodya entered the university he had bought himself a lithograph of Victor Adam's horses, some tobacco, and a pipe; and it seemed to me that it was indispensable that I should do the same.

I drove to Kuznetsky Most, with glances turned on me from all sides, with the bright sunlight on my buttons, on the cockade in my hat, and on my dagger, and drew up near Datsiaro's picture shop. I looked around and entered. I did not want to buy Victor Adam's horses, lest I should be accused of aping Volodya; in my eagerness to make my choice as quickly as possible, out of shame at the trouble to which I was putting the polite shopman, I took a water-colour of a woman's head which stood in the window, and paid twenty rubles for it. But after spending twenty rubles I still felt rather conscience-stricken at having troubled the two handsomely-dressed shopmen with such trifles, and yet it seemed as though they looked at me altogether too casually. To let them understand what manner of man I was, I turned my attention to a small silver piece which lay beneath a glass, and learning that it was a *porte-crayon* worth eighteen rubles, I ordered it to be wrapped up, paid for it, and, learning also that good pipes and tobacco were to be had in the adjoining tobacco shop, I bowed politely to the two shopmen and stepped into the street with my picture under my arm. In the neighbouring shop, on whose sign was painted a Negro smoking a cigar, I bought (also out of a desire not to imitate any one) not Zhukov, but Sultan tobacco, a Turkish pipe, and two chubouks, one of linden, the other of rosewood. On emerging from the shop, on my way to my droshky, I saw Semenov walking along the sidewalk at a rapid pace, dressed in civil clothes, and with his head bent down. I was vexed that he did not recognize me. I said in quite a loud tone, "Drive up!" and, seating myself in the droshky, I overtook Semenov.

"How do you do?" I said to him.

"My respects," he answered, pursuing his way.

"Why are you not in uniform?" I inquired.

Semenov halted, screwed up his eyes, and showed his white teeth, as though it hurt him to look at the sun, but in reality to express his indifference towards my droshky and uniform, gazed at me in silence, and walked on.

From Kuznetsky Most I drove to the confectioner's shop on Tverskaya; and though I tried to pretend that it was the newspapers in the shop that interested me principally, I could not restrain myself, and began to devour one cake after another. Despite the shame I felt before some gentlemen who were gazing at me with curiosity from behind their papers, I ate eight cakes, of all the sorts they kept in the shop, with great rapidity.

On arriving home I felt a little touch of heart-burn, but paying no attention to it, I busied myself with examining my purchases. The picture so displeased me that I not only did not have it framed and hung it in my room, as Volodya had done, but I even hid it in a drawer where no one could see it. The pencil-case did not please me either at home. I laid it on the table, comforting myself with the thought that it was made of silver, a thing of worth and extremely useful to a student.

As for the smoking things I resolved to put them into immediate use, and try them.

Having unsealed a quarter-pound package, and carefully filled my Turkish pipe with the reddish-yellow, fine-cut Sultan tobacco, I laid a burning coal upon it, and taking one of my pipe-stems between my third and fourth fingers (a position of the hand which pleased me extremely), I began to smoke.

The odour of the tobacco was very agreeable, but it tasted bitter, and the smoke caught my breath. Yet I forced myself to keep it up for quite a long time, inhaling the smoke, trying to puff it out in rings. The whole room was soon filled with clouds of bluish smoke; the pipe began to bubble, the hot tobacco to leap; I felt a bitterness in my mouth and a slight dizziness in my head; I tried to rise and look at myself in the glass with my pipe, when, to my amazement, I began to stagger, the room whirled round, and as I glanced in the mirror, which I had reached with difficulty, I saw that my face was as white as a sheet. I barely succeeded in dropping upon a divan when I was sensible of such illness and feebleness that, fancying the pipe had been fatal to me, I thought that I was dying. I was seriously alarmed, and wanted to summon assistance and send for the doctor.

But this terror did not last long. I quickly understood where the trouble was; and I lay for a long time on the lounge, weak, with a frightful pain in my head, gazing with dull attention at Bostandzhoglo's coat of arms reproduced upon the quarter-pound package, on the pipe and smoking utensils, and the remains of the confectioner's cakes rolling on the floor, and thought sadly in my disenchantment, "I am surely not grown up yet, if I cannot smoke like other people; and it is plain that I am not destined to hold my pipe, like others, between my middle and my third fingers, to swallow the smoke, and puff it out through my blonde moustache."

When Dmitri called for me at five o'clock he found me in this unpleasant condition. But after I had drunk a glass of water I was nearly well again and ready to go with him.

"What made you want to smoke?" he said, as he gazed upon the traces of my smoking. "It's all nonsense, and a useless waste of money. I have promised myself that I will never smoke. But hurry up—we have to call for Dubkov."

Chapter XIV

HOW VOLODYA AND DUBKOV OCCUPIED THEMSELVES

As soon as Dmitri entered the room I knew by his face, his walk, and by a gesture which was peculiar to him when in a bad humour—a winking of the eyes and a grotesque way of jerking his head to one side—that he was in the cold stubborn frame of mind which came over him when he was displeased with himself, and which always damped my feeling for him. I had lately begun to notice and judge my friend's character, but our friendship had suffered no change in consequence; it was still so youthful and so strong that, from whatever point of view I looked at Dmitri, I could not but perceive his perfection. There were two separate men in him, both of whom were very fine in my eyes. One, whom I warmly loved, was courteous, good, gentle, merry, and conscious of these amiable qualities; when he was in this mood his whole appearance, the sound of his voice, his every movement seemed to say, "I am gentle and virtuous; I enjoy being gentle and virtuous, as all of you can see." The other—I have only now begun to comprehend him and to bow before his grandeur—was cold, stern towards himself and others, proud, religious to fanaticism, and pedantically moral. At the present moment he was that second man.

With the frankness which constituted the indispensable condition of our relations, I told him, when we were in the droshky, that it pained and grieved me to see him in such a heavy, disagreeable frame of mind on a day which was such a happy one to me.

"Surely something has disturbed you; why will you not tell me?" I asked.

"Nikolenka," he replied deliberately, turning his head nervously to one side, his cheek twitching, "since I have given my word not to hide anything from you, you have

269

no cause to suspect me of secrecy. It is impossible to be always in the same mood; and if anything has disturbed me, I cannot even give myself an account of it."

"What a wonderfully frank, honourable character!" I thought, and I said no more to him.

We drove the rest of the way to Dubkov's in silence. Dubkov's quarters were remarkably fine, or it so seemed to me then. There were rugs, pictures, curtains, coloured hangings, portraits, curving arm-chairs everywhere; on the walls hung guns, pistols, tobacco pouches, and some heads of wild animals in cardboard. The sight of this study made me aware who it was that Volodya had been imitating in the adornment of his own room. We found Volodya and Dubkov playing cards. A gentleman whom I did not know (and who must have been of little importance, judging from his humble attitude) was sitting at the table and watching the game with great attention. Dubkov had on a silk dressing-gown and soft shoes. Volodya, in his shirt-sleeves, was sitting opposite him on the sofa; and judging from his flushed face and the dissatisfied, fleeting glance which he gave us as he looked up from the cards, he was very much absorbed in the game. On catching sight of me he turned still redder.

"Come, it's your turn to deal," he said to Dubkov. I saw that it displeased him to let me know that he played cards. But there was no confusion discernible in his glance, which seemed to say to me, "Yes, I'm playing, and you are only surprised at it because you are still young. There is nothing wrong about it—it is even necessary at our age."

I immediately felt and understood this.

Instead of dealing, however, Dubkov rose, shook hands with us, gave us seats, and offered us pipes, which we declined.

"Here is our diplomat then—the hero of the day," said Dubkov. "By heavens, you look awfully like the colonel."

"Hm!" I muttered, as I felt that foolishly self-satisfied smile spreading over my face.

I stood in that awe of Dubkov which only a boy of sixteen can feel for an aide-de-camp of twenty-seven whom all his elders declare to be a very fine young man, who dances and talks French beautifully, and who, though secretly despising my youth, evidently strives to conceal the fact.

But in spite of all my respect for him, I had always, heaven knows why, during the whole period of our acquaintance, found it difficult and awkward to look him in the eye. And I have since observed that there are three classes of people whom it is difficult for me to look in the eye—those who are much worse than myself, those who are much better than myself, and those with whom I cannot make up my mind to mention things that we both know, and who will not mention them to me. I do not know whether Dubkov was better than I or worse; but one thing was certain, that he often lied, without confessing it; that I detected this weakness in him, of course, but could never bring myself to speak of it.

"Let's play one more game," said Volodya, twitching one shoulder like Papa and shuffling the cards.

"There's no getting away from him!" said Dubkov. "We'll play it out later. Oh well, one more hand. Your deal."

While they played I watched their hands. Volodya had a large, handsome hand. He held his thumb apart and bent the other fingers when he held his cards, in a way so much like Papa that at one time it really seemed to me that Volodya held his hands that way on purpose, so as to look the more like a grown-up; but the next moment when I glanced at his face I could see that he was thinking of nothing except his game. Dubkov's hands, on the contrary, were small, plump, bent inwards, and had extremely soft and skilful fingers; just the kind of hands, in fact, which suit rings, and which people have who are inclined to handicraft and are fond of having fine things.

Volodya must have lost, for the gentleman who looked over his cards remarked that Vladimir Petrovich had frightfully bad luck; Dubkov got his pocket-book and noted something down in it, and said, as he showed Volodya what he had written, "Right?"

"Yes," said Volodya, glancing at the note-book with feigned abstraction. "Now let's go."

Volodya drove Dubkov, and Dmitri took me in his phaeton.

"What were they playing?" I inquired of Dmitri.

"Piquet. It's a stupid game, and gambling is a stupid thing any way."

"Do they play for large sums?"

"Not very; but it's not right, all the same."

"And don't you play?"

"No; I have given my word not to; Dubkov can't help playing with anyone he can get hold of, and he usually wins."

"But that surely is not right on his part," said I. "Volodya probably does not play so well as he."

"Of course it's not right; but there's nothing particularly bad about it. Dubkov likes cards, and plays well, but still he's an excellent fellow."

"Well, I had no idea—" said I.

"You must not think ill of him, because he really is a very fine man; and I am very fond of him, and always will be, in spite of his weaknesses."

It seemed to me, for some reason, that just because Dmitri stood up for Dubkov with too much warmth, he no longer loved or respected him, but that he would not confess it, out of obstinacy, and in order that no one might reproach him with fickleness. He was one of those people who love their friends for life, not so much because those friends remain always dear to them, as because, having once taken a liking to a man, even by mistake, they consider it dishonourable to cease to like him.

Chapter XV

MY SUCCESS IS CELEBRATED

Dubkov and Volodya knew all the people at the Yar by name, and every one, from porter to proprietor, showed them the greatest respect. We were immediately conducted to a private room and served with a wonderful dinner, selected by Dubkov from the French menu. A bottle of cool champagne, upon which I tried to look with as much indifference as possible, was already prepared. The dinner passed off very agreeably and merrily, although Dubkov, as was his custom, related the strangest occurrences of doubtful veracity—among others, how his grandmother had shot three robbers, who had attacked her, with a blunderbuss (whereupon I blushed, dropped my eyes, and turned away from him)—and although Volodya was visibly frightened whenever I opened my mouth (which was quite unnecessary, for I did not say anything particularly disgraceful, as far as I can remember). When the champagne was served all congratulated me, and I drank "hands across" with Dubkov and Dmitri, and exchanged kisses with them after which we could address each other "thou." As I did not know to whom the bottle of champagne belonged (it was in common, as they afterwards explained to me), and I wanted to entertain my friends out of my own money, which I kept fingering in my pocket, I stealthily pulled out a ten-ruble note, and, summoning the waiter, gave it to him and told him in a whisper, but in such a manner that they all heard it, to *please to bring another half bottle of champagne.*

Volodya turned red, and began to twitch his shoulder so violently and look at me and at the others in such a fright that I felt sure I had committed a blunder; however the bottle was brought, and we drank it with great satisfaction. Things seemed still to go on merrily. Dubkov lied without intermission, and Volodya, too, told such funny stories, and told them so well—in a way I should have never credited him with, and we laughed a great deal. The character of their wit—that is, Dubkov's and Volodya's—consisted in imitation and exaggeration of the well-known story: "Well, have you been abroad?" says one. "No, I have not," replies the other, "but my brother plays the violin." They had attained such perfection in this sort of comic nonsense that they even related that story thus: "My brother never played the violin either." They replied to every one of each other's questions in this style; and sometimes they tried, without questions, to join two utterly incongruous things—talked this nonsense with sober faces—and it proved extremely laughable. I began to understand the point, and I also tried to tell something funny; but they all looked alarmed, or tried not to look at me while I was speaking, and my story was not a success. Dubkov said, "Well, that's too thick, my dear diplomat"; but I felt so well with the champagne I had drunk, and in the company of these grown-up people, that this remark hardly wounded me at all. Dmitri alone, though he had drunk evenly with us, continued in his calm, serious mood, which put some restraint upon the general merriment.

"Now listen, gentlemen," said Dubkov. "After dinner the diplomat must be taken in hand. Suppose we go to our *aunt*'s? We'll soon settle him there."

"Nekhlyudov won't go," said Volodya.

"The intolerable goody! You're an intolerable goody," said Dubkov, turning to him. "Come with us, and you'll see what a charming lady auntie is."

"I certainly won't go, and what's more I won't let him either," answered Dmitri, turning red.

"Who? the diplomat? Do you want to go, diplomat? Why, look, he beamed all over as soon as we mentioned auntie."

"I don't mean that I won't let him," continued Dmitri, rising from his seat and beginning to pace the room without looking at me, "but I do not advise him nor wish him to go. He is no longer a child, and if he wishes he can go alone without you. But you ought to be ashamed of yourself, Dubkov; what you are doing is not right, and you want others to do the same."

"What's the harm," asked Dubkov, winking at Volodya, "if I invite you all to my aunt's for a cup of tea? Well, if it's not agreeable to you to go with us, then Volodya and I will go. Are you coming, Volodya?"

"Hm, hm!" said Volodya affirmatively. "We'll go there, and then we'll come to my rooms and go on with our piquet."

"Well, do you want to go with them or not?" said Dmitri, coming up to me.

"No," I answered, moving along on the sofa to make room for him beside me, "I do not want to go anyway, and if you advise me not to I won't go on any account."

"No," I added afterwards, "I cannot honestly say that I do not want to go with them; but I am glad that I am not going."

"That's right," he answered. "Live in your own way, and don't dance to any one's piping; that's the best way of all."

This little dispute not only failed to disturb our pleasure, but even heightened it. Dmitri all at once fell into the gentle mood which I loved best—so great was the effect (as I afterwards more than once observed) which the consciousness of a good deed had upon him. He was pleased with himself now for having deterred me from going. He grew unusually gay, ordered another bottle of champagne (which was against his rules), invited a stranger into the room and plied him with wine, sang *Gaudeamus igitur*, requested that all should join in, and proposed to ride to Sokolniki, whereupon Dubkov remarked that it was too sentimental.

"Let's be jolly today," said Dmitri, with a smile; "in honour of his entrance to the university I will get drunk for the first time; can't help it, can I?" This gaiety was rather strangely becoming to Dmitri. He resembled a tutor or a kind father who is satisfied with his children and wishes to please them, and at the same time to show that he can be gay in an honourable and respectable fashion; nevertheless, this unexpected mirth seemed to act infectiously upon us, the more so as each of us had drunk about half a bottle of champagne.

It was in this agreeable frame of mind that I stepped out into the public room to smoke a cigarette which Dubkov had given me.

When I rose from my seat I noticed that my head was swimming a little, and that my feet and my hands were in a natural condition only when I fixed my attention firmly upon them. Otherwise my feet crept off to one side, and my hands described various gestures. I fixed my whole attention upon my limbs, ordered my hands to rise and button my coat and smooth my hair (in the course of which my elbows jerked up fearfully high), and my legs to carry me to the door; which command they complied with, but set themselves down either too hard or too gently, and the left foot in particular stood constantly on its toe. "Where are you going?" someone called out to me. "They'll bring a light directly." I guessed that the voice was Volodya's, and the thought that I had guessed right afforded me satisfaction; I merely smiled in answer, and went on.

Chapter XVI

THE QUARREL

In the public room, at a little table, sat a short, stout gentleman in civil clothes, with a red moustache, eating. Beside him sat a tall, dark-complexioned man without a moustache. They were conversing in French. Their glances confused me, yet I decided for all that to light my cigarette at the candle which stood before them. Looking around to avoid meeting their gaze, I went up to the table and put my cigarette to the flame. When it was fairly alight, I could not help glancing at the gentleman who was dining and found his grey eyes fixed intently and disapprovingly upon me. As I was about to turn away his red moustache moved, and he said in French, "I don't like people to smoke while I am dining, my dear sir."

I muttered some unintelligible reply.

"No, sir, I don't like it," the gentleman with the moustache went on sternly, with a quick glance at the gentleman who had no moustache, as if inviting him to admire the manner in which he was about to settle me. "Nor do I like people who have the impudence, my dear sir, to come and puff their smoke in one's nose; I don't like them at all." I immediately understood that the gentleman was scolding me, and it seemed to me at first that I was very much in the wrong.

"I did not think that it would inconvenience you," said I.

"Well, you did not think you were ill-bred, did you, but I did!" shouted the gentleman.

"What right have you to shout at me like that?" I asked, feeling that he was insulting me, and beginning to get angry myself.

"This much right, that I never permit any one to be insolent to me; and I shall always teach such young

277

fellows like yourself their manners. What's your name, sir, and where do you live?"

I was extremely angry, my lips quivered, and my breath came in gasps. Yet I felt guilty somehow, possibly because I had drunk so much champagne; I did not say anything insulting to the gentleman, but on the contrary my lips uttered my name and our address in the most submissive manner possible.

"My name is Kolpikov, my dear sir; I will trouble you to be more courteous in future. You shall hear from me," (*vous aurez de mes nouvelles*) he concluded, the whole conversation having taken place in French.

I only said, "I shall be delighted," endeavouring to make my voice as firm as possible, turned about, and went back to our room with my cigarette, which had contrived to go out.

I did not mention what had occurred either to my brother or to my friend (the more so as they were engaged in a heated dispute), but sat down alone in a corner to reflect upon this strange happening. The words, "You are ill-bred, sir," (*un mal élevé, Monsieur*) rang in my ears, enraging me more and more. My intoxication was completely gone now, and in considering my behaviour in the matter, the terrible thought struck me that I had behaved like a coward. "What right had he to attack me? Why didn't he say simply that I was annoying him? He must have been in the wrong. Why, then, when he told me that I was ill-bred, did I not say to him, 'He is ill-bred, sir, who permits himself impertinences'; or why did I not simply shout at him, 'Hold your tongue!' That would have been capital. Why did I not challenge him to a duel? No, I did none of these things, but swallowed the insult like a vile coward." "You are ill-bred, sir," rang in my ears incessantly in an exasperating way. "No, I cannot leave it at that," I thought, and I rose firmly resolved to go back to the gentleman and say something dreadful to him, and possibly to strike him over the head with the candlestick, if it should seem suitable. I reflected upon this last intention with the greatest delight, but it was not without great terror that I entered the public room again. Fortunately, Kolpikov was no longer there, but only a waiter, clearing the table. I wanted to tell the waiter what had happened, and to explain to him that I was not at all to blame; but I changed my mind for some reason or other, and returned again to our own room in the most gloomy frame of mind.

"What's the matter with our diplomat?" said Dubkov; "he's probably deciding the fate of Europe now."

"Oh, let me alone," I said crossly, turning away. Then, as I wandered about the room, I began to think for some reason, that Dubkov was not a nice man at all. "And as for his eternal jests, and that nickname 'diplomat,' there was nothing amiable about them. All he was good for was to win money from Volodya, and to go to some aunt of his. And there was nothing pleasing in all that. Everything he said was either lie or something cynical, and he was ever laughing at another's expense. He was simply stupid, and a bad man to boot." I spent five minutes in these reflections, feeling more and more hostile towards Dubkov. For his part, Dubkov paid no attention to me, and this angered me still more. I even got vexed with Volodya and Dmitri because they talked to him.

"Do you know what, gentlemen? We must pour some water over the diplomat," said Dubkov suddenly, glancing at me with what seemed to me to be a mocking and even treacherous smile; "he's in a bad way. By heavens, he's in a bad way!"

"You need to be ducked, you're in a bad way yourself," I retorted, with an evil smile, even forgetting that I had addressed him as *thou*.

This answer must have amazed Dubkov; but he turned

away from me indifferently and continued his conversation with Volodya and Dmitri.

I would have tried to join the conversation, but I felt that I should certainly not be able to dissemble, and I again retreated to my corner, where I remained until our departure.

When we had paid the bill and were putting on our overcoats, Dubkov said to Dmitri, "Well, where are Orestes and Pylades going? Home, probably, to talk about *love*. Now, we'd better go and see our dear auntie; it'll be more entertaining than your sour friendship."

"How dare you talk like that and laugh at us?" I burst out as I went up to him, gesticulating. "How dare you laugh at feelings you don't understand? I won't allow it. Hold your tongue!" I shouted, and fell silent, not knowing what to say next and out of breath with agitation. Dubkov was taken aback at first; then he tried to smile, and take it as a joke; but finally, to my extreme surprise, he got frightened and lowered his eyes.

"I am not laughing at you or your feelings in the least; it's only my way of talking," he said evasively.

"You better not," I shouted; but at the same time I was ashamed of myself and sorry for Dubkov, whose handsome, troubled face betrayed genuine grief.

"What's the matter with you?" asked Volodya and Dmitri together. "Nobody meant to insult you."

"Yes, he did mean to insult me."

"Your brother is such a desperate gentleman," said Dubkov, just as he went out, so that he could not hear what I might say.

Possibly I might have rushed after him and said more impertinent things; but just at that moment the same waiter who had been present at my affair with Kolpikov handed me my coat, and I immediately calmed down, feigning only so much anger in Dmitri's presence as was indispensable in order that my sudden tranquillity might

280

not seem queer. The next day Dubkov and I met in Volodya's room. We did not allude to this affair, yet continued to say "you" to each other; and it was more difficult than ever for us to look each other in the face.

The memory of my quarrel with Kolpikov, who neither on that day nor ever afterwards let me "hear from him," was frightfully oppressive and vivid for many years. I writhed and screamed, full five years later, every time that I recalled that unatoned insult; and comforted myself by remembering with self-satisfaction how manly I had afterwards been in my affair with Dubkov. It was only very much later that I began to regard the matter in quite a different light, and to recall my quarrel with Kolpikov with comical satisfaction, and to repent of the undeserved wound which I had dealt to that *jolly good fellow*, Dubkov.

When I related to Dmitri that same day my encounter with Kolpikov, whose appearance I described to him minutely, he was very much surprised.

"Yes, it's the very same fellow," said he. "Just imagine! That Kolpikov is a well-known scoundrel, a card-sharper, but most of all a coward, who was expelled from his regiment by his comrades because somebody slapped his face and he would not fight. Where did he get his valour?" he added, with a kindly smile, as he glanced at me. "So he didn't say anything more than 'ill-bred'?"

"No," I replied, reddening.

"Well, it's bad, but there's no great harm done," Dmitri said consolingly.

Long afterwards, as I thought this affair over quietly I arrived at the conclusion that it was quite possible that Kolpikov had taken the opportunity of taking his revenge on me in the presence of that clean-shaven, dark-complexioned man for the slap in the face he had received many years ago, just as I immediately revenged myself for his "ill-bred" on the innocent Dubkov.

Chapter XVII

I PREPARE TO PAY SOME CALLS

My first thought on waking the next day was of my adventure with Kolpikov. Again I muttered to myself and ran about the room, but I could do nothing about it; besides, this was the last day I was to spend in Moscow; and by Papa's orders I was to make some calls which he had himself listed for me. Papa's solicitude for us was not so much on the point of morals and learning as on that of worldly connections. On the paper was written in his rapid, pointed hand: "(1) To Prince Ivan Ivanich *without fail*; (2) to the Ivins *without fail*; (3) to Prince Mikhailo; (4) to Princess Nekhlyudova and Madame Valakhina if possible; and, of course, to the curator, the rector, and the professors."

Dmitri dissuaded me from paying these last calls, saying that it not only was not necessary, but would even be improper; but all the rest must be made that day. Of these the first two marked to be paid *without fail*, frightened me particularly. Prince Ivan Ivanich was general-in-chief, an old man, wealthy and alone; and there was I, a student of sixteen, obliged to have direct intercourse with him, which I had a presentiment could not prove at all flattering for me. The Ivins also were wealthy, and their father was an important civil general, who had only been to our home once in Grandmamma's day. After Grandmamma's death, I observed that the youngest Ivin had fought shy of us, and seemed to put on airs. The eldest, as I knew by report, had already completed his law course, and had an appointment in St. Petersburg; the second (Sergei), whom I had once adored, was also in St. Petersburg—a big, fat cadet in the Pages' Corps.

In my youth I not only did not like to associate with people who considered themselves above me; such intercourse was intolerably painful, owing to a constant fear of insult, and the straining of all my mental faculties to prove my independence to such people. But as I was not going to obey Papa's last orders, I felt that I must smooth matters over by complying with the first. I paced my chamber, glancing at my clothes, spread out upon the chairs, and my dagger and hat, and was already preparing to go when old Grap came to congratulate me, bringing Ilenka with him. Father Grap was a Russianized German, intolerably mealy-mouthed and flattering, and very often the worse for drink. He generally came to us simply for the purpose of asking for something; and although Papa sometimes entertained him in his study, he never invited him to dine with us. His humility and persistent begging were so intermingled with a certain superficial good-nature and familiarity with our house that everybody reckoned it as a sort of merit in him that he should be so attached to all of us; but for some reason I never liked him, and when he spoke I always felt ashamed for him.

I was very much displeased at the arrival of these guests, and I made no effort to conceal my displeasure. I had become so accustomed to look down upon Ilenka, and so used to consider that we were in the right in so doing, that it was even disagreeable for me that he should be a student just like me. It struck me, too, that he was rather abashed in my presence by this equality. I greeted them coldly, and did not ask them to sit down, because I was ashamed to, thinking that they might do so without my invitation; and I ordered my carriage to be got ready. Ilenka was a kind, very honourable, and very clever young man, yet he was what is called a man of rather whimsical moods. Some extreme mood was always coming over him, apparently without any reason whatever: now it was a weeping mood, then an inclination to laugh, then to take offence at every trifle. And now, it seemed, he was in this last frame of mind. He said nothing, glanced angrily at me and his father; and only when he was addressed did he smile with the submissive, constrained smile under which he was already accustomed to hide his feelings, and especially the feeling of shame for his father, which he could not help feeling in our presence.

"So, Nikolai Petrovich," said the old man, following me about the room while I dressed, and turning the silver snuff-box which Grandmamma had given him slowly and respectfully between his fat fingers; "as soon as I learned from my son that you had passed an excellent examination—though, of course, your cleverness is known to everyone—I at once came to congratulate you, my dear boy. Why, I carried you on my shoulder, and God sees that I love your folk like relatives; and my Ilenka kept asking me to come and see you. He, too, has already become so used to you."

Meantime Ilenka sat in silence by the window, apparently absorbed in contemplation of my three-cornered hat, and muttering something in an angry undertone.

"Now, I wanted to ask you, Nikolai Petrovich," continued the old man, "did my Ilenka pass a good examination? He says he is going to be in the same faculty as you—so you kindly keep an eye on him, and advise him if need be."

"Why, he did very well," I replied, glancing at Ilenka, who, feeling my glance, blushed and stopped moving his lips.

"And might he spend the day with you?" asked the old man, with a timid smile, as though he were very much afraid of me, yet always keeping so close to me whenever I moved that the fumes of wine and tobacco, in which he was steeped, did not cease for a single second to be perceptible to me. I felt vexed at him for having placed me in such a false position towards his son, as well as at his distracting my attention from what was, to me, a highly important occupation—dressing; but most of all, that ever-present odour of strong brandy so annoyed me that I said, very coldly, that I could not have the pleasure of Ilenka's company because I should not be at home all day.

"Why, you were going to see your sister, weren't you, Father," said Ilenka, smiling, but not looking at me; "and then I have business to attend to." I was still more vexed as well as pricked with compunction, and, in order to smooth over my refusal, I hastened to tell them that I should not be at home because I had to call upon *Prince* Ivan Ivanich, and Princess Kornakova, and Ivin, who held such an influential post, and that I should probably dine with *Princess* Nekhlyudova. I thought that when they learned to what distinguished houses I was going they could make no more claims upon me. When they prepared to depart I invited Ilenka to come again; but Ilenka only muttered something, and smiled with a constrained expression. It was evident that his feet would never cross my threshold again.

After their departure I set out on my round of calls. Volodya, whom I had that morning invited to accompany me, in order that I might not feel quite so shy as when alone, had refused, under the pretext that it would be too sentimental—two loving brothers riding together in a nice little carriage.

Chapter XVIII

THE VALAKHINS

So I set out alone. The first call on my route lay at the Valakhins, in Sivtsev Vrazhek. I had not seen Sonechka for three years, and of course my love for her had long become a thing of the past; yet there still lingered in my soul a lively and touching memory of that past childish love. At times, in the course of those three years, I had remembered her with such force and clearness that I shed tears and felt myself in love again; but this only lasted a few minutes, and had been long in returning.

I knew that Sonechka had been abroad with her mother, where they had remained for two years, and where, it was said, they had been in a carriage accident, and Sonechka's face had been badly cut with the glass, so that she had lost her good looks to a great extent. As I drove to their house I vividly recalled the former Sonechka, and thought of what she would be like this time. After her two years' stay abroad I fancied her extremely tall, with a very fine figure, serious and dignified, but remarkably attractive. My imagination refused to picture her with a face disfigured with scars; on the contrary, having heard somewhere of a passionate lover who remained faithful to his adored one, in spite of her disfigurement by small-pox, I tried to think that I was in love with Sonechka, in order that I might have the merit of remaining true to her in spite of the scars. As a matter of fact, when I drove up to the Valakhins' house I was not in love; but, having stirred up old memories of love, I was well prepared to fall in love, and was very desirous to do so, the more so as I had long felt ashamed when I looked at all my enamoured friends, that I should be left so far behind by them.

The Valakhins lived in a neat little wooden house, approached by a court-yard. The door was opened to me at the sound of the bell, which was then a great rarity in Moscow, by a very small and neatly dressed boy. He either did not understand me or did not want to tell me whether the family were at home; and, leaving me in the dark vestibule, he ran into the still darker corridor.

I remained alone for quite a while in that dark room, in which there was one closed door, besides the one leading to the corridor; and on the one hand I wondered at the gloomy character of the house, and supposed on the other that it must be so with people who had been abroad. After a lapse of five minutes the door to the hall was opened from the inside by the same boy, and he led me to the neatly but not richly furnished drawing-room, into which Sonechka followed me.

She was seventeen. She was short in stature, very thin, and with a yellowish, unhealthy colour in her face. There were no scars visible on her face, and her charming, prominent eyes, and her bright, good-natured, merry smile were the same which I had known and loved in my childhood. I had not expected to find her like this at all, and therefore I could not at once lavish upon her the feelings which I had prepared on the way. She gave me her hand in the English fashion, which was then as much of a rarity as the bell, shook my hand frankly, and offered me a seat beside her on the sofa.

"Oh, how glad I am to see you, my dear Nicolas," she said, gazing into my face with the same genuine expression of pleasure which her words implied. The "my dear Nicolas," I observed, was uttered in a friendly, not in a patronizing, tone. To my amazement, she was more simple, sweet, and natural in her manner after her trip abroad than before. I observed two little scars near her nose and on her forehead; but her wonderful eyes and smile were perfectly true to my recollections, and shone in the old way.

"How you have changed!" said she. "You are quite grown up now. Well, and I—what do you think of me?"

"Ah, I should never have known you," I answered, although at that very time I was thinking that I should have known her anywhere. I again felt myself in that carefree, merry mood in which, five years before, I had danced the "Grandfather" with her at Grandmamma's ball.

"Why, have I grown very ugly?" she asked, shaking her head.

"No, not at all; you have grown a little, you are older," I hastened to reply; "but, on the contrary—you're even—"

"Well, no matter. Do you remember our dances, our games, St. Jérôme, Mme. Dorat." (I did not recollect any Mme. Dorat; she was evidently carried away by the enjoyment of her childish memories, and was confusing them.) "Ah, what a lovely time that was!" she continued; and the same smile, even more beautiful than the one I bore in my memory, and the very same eyes shone before me. While she was speaking I had succeeded in realizing the situation in which I found myself at the present moment, and I decided that at the present moment I was in love. As soon as I had made up my mind about this, that instant my happy, careless mood vanished, a mist seemed to arise before me—veiling even her eyes and smile—I became ashamed of something, and tongue-tied, and blushed.

"Times are different now," she went on with a sigh, raising her brows slightly; "everything seems much worse, and we are worse, aren't we, Nicolas?"

I could not answer, and gazed at her in silence.

"Where are all those Ivins and Kornakovs now? Do you remember?" she continued, looking at my red and frightened face with some curiosity; "that was a grand time!"

And still I could not reply.

The entrance of Madame Valakhina rescued me from this uncomfortable situation for a time. I rose, bowed, and recovered my power of speech; on the other hand a strange change came over Sonechka with her mother's entrance. All her gaiety and friendliness suddenly disappeared, her very smile became different; and all at once, with the exception of her tall stature, she became exactly the young lady returned from abroad whom I had imagined her to be. It seemed as though this change could have no cause, since her mother smiled just as pleasantly, and all her movements expressed as much gentleness, as of old. Valakhina seated herself in a large arm-chair, and indicated to me a place near her. She said something to her daughter in English, and Sonechka immediately left the room, which afforded me some relief. Valakhina inquired after my relatives, my brother, and my father, and then spoke to me of her own sorrow—the loss of her husband—and finally, feeling that there was nothing to say to me, she looked at me in silence, as if to say, "If you will rise now and make your bow and go away you will be doing very well, my dear fellow." But a strange thing happened to me. Sonechka had returned with her work, and seated herself in the corner of the room, so that I felt her glance fixed upon me. While Valakhina was relating the loss of her husband I once more remembered that I was in love, and thought that perhaps the mother guessed it; and I had another fit of shyness so violent that I was unable to move even a single limb in a natural manner. I knew that in order to rise and take my departure I should be obliged to think where to set my foot, what to do with my head, what with my hand; in one word, I felt almost exactly as I had felt the evening before after drinking half a bottle of champagne. I had a presentiment that I would be unable to control myself in all this, and therefore would not be able to rise; and, in fact, I *could not*. Valakhina was probably surprised when she saw my crimson face and my utter immobility; but I decided that it was better to sit still in that stupid pose than to risk rising in an awkward manner and taking my departure. I sat thus for quite a long time, expecting that some unforeseen circumstance would rescue me from that position. This circumstance presented itself in the person of an insignificant young man, who entered the room with the air of a familiar of the house and bowed courteously to me. Valakhina rose, excusing herself on the ground that she had to speak with her *homme d'affaires,* and looked at me with an expression of surprise which said, "If you do mean to go on sitting there for ever you may—I will not drive you out." I made a tremendous effort and rose, but was no longer in a condition to make a bow, and as I went out, accompanied by the compassionate glances of mother and daughter, I knocked against a chair which was not in my way at all; I only ran against it because my whole attention was directed upon not stumbling over the carpet which was under my feet. But once in the open air—after I fidgeted and muttered for a while so loudly that even Kuzma inquired several times, "Yes, sir?"—this feeling disappeared, and I began to meditate quite calmly upon my love for Sonechka, and her attitude to her mother, which struck me as singular. When I afterwards communicated my observations to my father—that Mme. Valakhina and her daughter were not on good terms—he said:

"Yes, she leads the poor girl an awful life with her miserliness; and it's odd enough," he added, with a stronger feeling than he could have for a mere relative. "She used to be such a charming sweet woman! I cannot understand why she is so changed. You did not see any secretary there, did you? What sort of a fashion is it for a Russian lady to have a secretary?" he said, walking away in anger.

"I did see him," said I.

"Well, is he good-looking at least?"

"No, not at all!"

"It's incomprehensible," said Papa, with a cough and an irritable motion of his shoulders.

"Here am I in love, too," I thought as I drove on in my droshky.

Chapter XIX

THE KORNAKOVS

The second call on my way was on the Kornakovs. They lived on the first floor of a large house in the Arbat. The staircase was very showy and clean, but not luxurious—being laid with drugget fixed by polished brass rods; but there were neither flowers nor mirrors. The hall, over whose brightly-polished floor I passed to reach the drawing-room, was also sober, cold, and neatly arranged; everything shone and seemed durable, although not at all new; but neither pictures, curtains, nor any other kind of adornment were anywhere visible. Some of the princesses were in the drawing-room. They were sitting in such precise and idle attitudes that it was obvious that they did not sit so when guests were not expected.

"Mamma will be here immediately," said the eldest of them to me, as she came and sat nearer to me. For a quarter of an hour this Princess engaged me in a very easy conversation, and she did it so skilfully that the conversation never languished for a moment. But it was too evident that she was entertaining me, and therefore she did not please me. Among other things she told me that her brother Stepan, whom they called *Etienne*, and who had been sent to the Junker's School, had already been promoted an officer. When she spoke of her brother, and especially when she mentioned that he had entered the Hussars against his mother's will, she put on a frightened look; and all the princesses, sitting in silence, put on equally frightened faces. When she spoke of Grandmamma's death she assumed a sorrowful look, and all the younger princesses did the same. When she recalled how I had struck St. Jérôme, and how I had been led away, she laughed and showed her bad teeth, and all the princesses laughed and showed their bad teeth.

The Princess entered. She was the same little dried-up woman, with restless eyes, and a habit of looking at somebody else while talking to one. She took me by the hand and raised her hand to my lips, in order that I might kiss it, which I should not otherwise have done, not supposing that it was indispensable.

"How glad I am to see you!" she began, with her usual volubility, glancing at her daughters. "Ah, how like his Mamma he is! Isn't he, *Lise*?"

Lise said I did; though I knew for a fact that I possessed not the slightest resemblance with Mamma.

"And how big you have grown! And my Etienne, you remember, he is your second cousin—no, not your second; but what is he, *Lise*? My mother was Varvara Dmitrievna, daughter of Dmitri Nikolayevich, and your grandmother was Natalya Nikolayevna."

"Then he is our third cousin, Mamma," said the eldest Princess.

"Oh, you are mixing things all up," cried the Princess angrily. "It's not third cousin at all, but *issus de germains* —children of cousins; that's what you and my dear little Etienne are. He's an officer already; did you know? But it's not well in one respect: he has too much liberty. You young people need keeping in hand. Yes, do not be angry with your old aunt for telling you the plain truth. I brought Etienne up strictly, and I think that's the proper way to do.

"Yes, that's the relationship between us," she went on. "Prince Ivan Ivanich was my uncle, and your mother's uncle. So your mamma and I were cousins, not second cousins. Yes, that's it. Now, tell me. Have you been to Prince Ivan's?"

I said that I had not been there yet, but should go that day.

"Ah! how could you!" she exclaimed. "Why, that should have been your very first call. You know that Prince Ivan is just like a father to you. He has no children, so you and my children are his only heirs. You must revere him on account of his age and his position in the world, and everything. I know that you young people of the present generation think nothing of relationship, and do not like old people; but do listen to your old aunt, for I am fond of you, and I was fond of your mamma, and your grandmother too, and I respected her very, very much. You must go without fail. You certainly must."

I said that I certainly would go, and as the call had already lasted long enough, in my opinion, I rose and made a motion to go; but she detained me.

"No, wait a minute. Where is your father, *Lise*? Call him here. He will be so glad to see you," she continued, turning to me.

In a couple of minutes Prince Mikhailo actually entered. He was a short, stout man, very negligently dressed, unshaven, and with an expression of indifference approaching stupidity. He was not at all glad to see me; at all events, he did not say so. But the Princess, of whom he was evidently very much afraid, said to him:

"Waldemar [she had plainly forgotten my name] is very much like his mother, is he not?" and she made such a sign with her eyes that the Prince must have divined her wish, for he came up to me and, with the most apathetic and even dissatisfied expression presented his unshaven cheek to me, which I was forced to kiss.

"You are not dressed yet, though you have to go soon," the Princess began at once to say to him in an angry tone, which was evidently the one she usually adopted with members of her household. "You want to prejudice people against you again, to make people angry with you again!"

"In a moment, in a moment, my dear," said Prince Mikhailo, and departed. I bowed and departed also.

I had heard for the first time that we were heirs of Prince Ivan Ivanich, and the news was an unpleasant surprise for me.

Chapter XX

THE IVINS

Now it distressed me still more to think of that impending, indispensable visit. However, the order of my route took me first to the Ivins. They lived on Tverskoi Boulevard, in a very large handsome house. It was not without nervousness that I drove up to the entrance, at which stood a porter with a staff.

I asked him whether the family was at home.

"Whom do you wish to see, sir? The general's son is at home," said the porter.

"And the general himself?"

"I will inquire. Whom shall I announce?" said the porter, and rang.

A footman's feet showed on the stairs. Somehow I was seized with such a fit of nervousness that I told the footman that he was not to announce me to the general, and that I would go first to the general's son. When I went upstairs, along that great staircase, it seemed to me that I became frightfully small (and not in the figurative, but in the actual sense of the word). I had experienced the same sensation when my droshky drove up to the grand entrance; it had seemed to me that the droshky and the horse and coachman became small. The general's son was lying fast asleep upon a sofa, with an open book before him, when I entered the room. His tutor, Herr Frost, who still remained in the house, followed me into the room with his jaunty step and woke up his pupil. Ivin evinced no especial delight at the sight of me, and I observed that he looked at my eyebrows while he was talking. Although he was very polite, it seemed to me that he was entertaining me exactly as the Princess had done, and that he felt no particular attraction towards me, and did not need my acquaintance, since he probably had his own different circle of acquaintances. All this I imagined, principally because he gazed at my eyebrows. In a word, his attitude to me, however disagreeable it might be to me to confess it, was almost exactly the same as mine to Ilenka. I began to get irritated; I caught every look of Ivin's on the fly, and when his eyes and Frost's met, I translated his question: "And why has he come to see us?"

After talking to me for a short time, Ivin said that his father and mother were at home, and would I not like him to go with me to them?

"I will dress at once," he added, going into another room, although he was perfectly well dressed—in a new coat and a white waistcoat. In a few minutes he came back in his uniform, completely buttoned up, and we went downstairs together. The reception rooms which we passed through were extremely lofty, and apparently very richly furnished; there was marble and gilding, and something wrapped up in muslin, and mirrors. Ivina entered the small room behind the drawing-room through another door at the same time as we did. She received me in a very friendly manner, like a relative, gave me a seat beside her, and inquired with interest about all our family.

Mme. Ivina, of whom I had only caught a couple of fleeting glimpses previous to this, pleased me very much now that I looked at her attentively. She was tall, thin, very white, and seemed always melancholy and exhausted. Her smile was sad, but extremely kind; her eyes were large, weary, and not quite straight, which gave her a still more melancholy and attractive expression. She sat not exactly bent over, but with her whole body limp, and all her movements were languorous. She spoke languidly, and the sound of her voice and her indistinct pronunciation of *r* and *l* were very pleasing. She was not entertaining me. My answers about my relatives evidently afforded her a melancholy interest, as though while listening to me she sadly recalled better days. Her son went off somewhere; she gazed at me in silence for a couple of minutes, and all at once she began to cry. I sat there before her, and could not think of anything whatever to say or do. She went on crying and never looked at me. At first I was sorry for her; then I thought, "Ought I not to comfort her, and how can I?" Finally I became vexed at her for placing me in such an awkward position. "Have I such a pitiful appearance?" I thought; "or is she doing this on purpose to find out how I will behave under the circumstances?"

"It would not do to take leave now—it will seem as though I am running away from her tears," I continued my reflections. I moved about on my chair to remind her of my presence.

"Oh, how foolish of me!" she said, glancing at me and trying to smile; "there are days when one weeps for no reason whatever."

She began to search for her handkerchief beside her on the sofa, and all at once she broke out crying still more.

"Oh, dear! how ridiculous of me to be crying like this! I was so fond of your mother; we were such—friends—and—"

She found her handkerchief, covered her face with it, and went on crying. My position became awkward again, and remained so for quite a while. I felt resentment, but more pity for her. Her tears seemed genuine, and I kept thinking that she was not weeping so much because of my mother as because she was unhappy

296

now, and had known happier days. I do not know how it would have ended had not young Ivin entered and said that old Ivin was ·asking for her. She rose and was on the point of going when Ivin himself entered the room. He was a small, stout, grey-haired gentleman, with thick black brows, perfectly grey close-cut hair, and an extremely stern and firm expression of countenance.

I rose and bowed to him; but Ivin, who had three stars on his green coat, not only did not respond to my greeting, but hardly so much as glanced at me, so that I all at once felt that I was not a human being, but some sort of thing which was not worthy of notice—an arm-chair or a window, or if a human being then one not distinguished in any way from an arm-chair or a window.

"You haven't written to the Countess yet, my dear," he said to his wife in French, with an apathetic but firm expression of countenance.

"Good-bye, Monsieur Irtenyev," said Mme. Ivina to me, inclining her head rather haughtily all at once, and gazing at my eyebrows as her son had done. I bowed once more to her and her husband, and again my salute acted upon the elder Ivin exactly as the opening or shutting of a window would have done. But Ivin the student accompanied me to the door, and told me on the way that he was going to be transferred to the Petersburg university, because his father had received an appointment there (and he mentioned a very important position).

"Well, Papa may like it or not," I muttered to myself as I seated myself in my droshky; "but I will never set foot in that house again. That sniveller cries when she looks at me just as though I were some miserable creature; and that pig of Ivin won't bow to me. I'll give it to him—" How I meant to give it to him I really do not know, but that was the word which occurred to me.

I was often obliged afterwards to endure my father's exhortations, and he said that it was indispensable to *cultivate* this acquaintance, and that I could not require a man in such a position as Ivin's to pay attention to such a boy as myself; but I kept my resolution for a long time.

Chapter XXI

PRINCE IVAN IVANICH

"Now for the last call on Nikitskaya," I said to Kuzma, and we rolled away to Prince Ivan Ivanich's house.

After having gone through several experiences in making calls, I had acquired self-reliance by practice; and now I was about to drive up to the Prince's in a tolerably composed frame of mind, when I suddenly recalled the words of Princess Kornakova about my being his heir; moreover, I caught sight of two carriages waiting at the entrance, and I was overcome by shyness again.

It seemed to me that the old porter who opened the door for me, and the footman who took off my coat, and the three ladies and the two gentlemen whom I found in the drawing-room, and Prince Ivan Ivanich himself in particular, who was sitting on the sofa in a plain coat—it seemed to me that they all looked upon me as an heir, and therefore with ill-will. The Prince was very friendly with me: he kissed me, that is to say, he laid his soft, dry, cold lips against my cheek for a moment, inquired about my occupations and plans, jested with me, asked if I still wrote verses like those which I had written for my grandmother's name-day, and said that I must come and dine with him that day. But the more courteous he was, the more it seemed to me that he wanted to pet me only to prevent my perceiving how disagreeable was to him the thought that I was his heir. He had a habit—arising from the false teeth with which his mouth was filled—of raising his upper lip towards his nose after he had said anything and making a slight noise, as though he were drawing his lip into his nostrils; and when he did this on the present occasion, it seemed to me as though he were saying to himself, "Youngster, youngster, I don't need you to tell me: you are my heir, yes, my heir," and so on.

When we were children we had called Prince Ivan Ivanich "Grandad"; but now, in my capacity of heir, I could not bring my tongue to the phrase, while it seemed to me humiliating to call him "Your Excellency," as one of the other visitors did; so that during the entire conversation I tried not to call him anything at all. But I was embarrassed most of all by the old Princess, who was also one of the Prince's heirs, and lived in his house. During the whole dinner, at which I was seated beside the Princess, I fancied that the Princess did not speak to me because she hated me for being also an heir of the Prince as well as herself; and that the Prince paid no attention to our side of the table because we—the Princess and I—were heirs, and equally repulsive to him.

"Yes, you can't believe how disagreeable it was for me," I said that same evening to Dmitri, desiring to brag to him of my repugnance for the thought that I was his heir (this sentiment seemed very fine to me)—"how disagreeable it was for me to spend two whole hours at the Prince's today. He is a very fine man, and was very polite to me," said I, wishing among other things to impress my friend with the fact that what I said was not in consequence of having felt humiliated before the Prince; "but," I continued, "the thought that they might look upon me as they do upon the Princess who lives in his house, and behaves in such a servile way before him, is frightful. He is a wonderful old man, and extremely kind and delicate with all, but it is painful to see how he *ill-treats* that Princess. This disgusting money spoils all relations!

"Do you know, I think it would be much better to explain myself clearly to the Prince," said I; "to tell him that I revere him as a man, but that I am not thinking of his inheritance, and that I beg him not to leave me anything, and that under that condition only will I go to his house."

Dmitri did not laugh when I told him this; on the contrary, he became thoughtful, and after a silence of several minutes he said to me:

"Do you know what? You are not right. Either you should not suppose at all that people can think of you, as of your Princess; or else if you do suppose it, then you should carry your suppositions further: that is, that you know what people may think of you, but that such thoughts are so far from your intentions that you scorn them, and will do nothing which is founded on them. Now, suppose that they suppose that you suppose this—But, in short," he added, conscious that he was involving himself in his reflections, "it's much better not to suppose at all."

My friend was quite right. It was only later, much later, that I was convinced from my experience of life how harmful it is to think, and how much more injurious to utter, much which seems very noble, but which should remain for ever hidden from all in each one's heart; and how rarely noble words are accompanied by noble deeds. I am convinced that the very fact that a good intention has been announced renders the execution of that good intention more difficult, generally even impossible. But how restrain the utterance of the nobly self-satisfied impulses of youth? One only recollects them afterwards, and mourns over them as over a flower which did not last—which one has plucked ere it had opened, and then finds lying on the ground, crushed and withered.

I, who had but just told my friend Dmitri that money ruined relations, borrowed twenty-five rubles of him,

which he offered me the next morning, before our departure to the country, when I found that I had wasted all
my own money on diverse pictures and pipe stems; and
afterwards I remained in his debt a very long time indeed.

Chapter XXII

AN INTIMATE CONVERSATION WITH MY FRIEND

This conversation arose in the phaeton on the way to
Kuntsevo. Dmitri had dissuaded me from calling on his
mother in the morning; but he came to me after lunch to
carry me off for the whole afternoon, and even to spend
the night at the country-house where his family lived. It
was only when we had emerged from the city and exchanged the dirty, motley streets and the intolerably deafening sound of the pavements for the broad open vista of
the fields and the soft rattle of the wheels on the dusty
road, and the fragrant spring air and the sense of space
enveloped me on all sides—it was only then that I recovered my senses in some degree from the various new impressions and consciousness of freedom which had quite
confused me for the last two days. Dmitri was gentle and
sympathetic, did not adjust his neckerchief with his
head, and did not blink nervously or screw up his eyes.
I was satisfied with the lofty sentiments which I had
communicated to him, in the belief that, in consideration
of them, he had quite forgiven my shameful affair with
Kolpikov, and would not despise me for it; and we conversed in a friendly way of many intimate things which
even friends do not always talk about. Dmitri told me
about his family, whom I did not know as yet—about his
mother, his aunt, his sister, and about the person whom
Volodya and Dubkov considered my friend's passion and
called the *little red-head*. He spoke of his mother with a

certain cool, triumphant praise, as though to forestall any objection on that subject; he expressed enthusiasm with regard to his aunt, but with some condescension; of his sister he said very little, and seemed ashamed to talk to me about her; but as for the *little red-head*, whose real name was Lyubov Sergeyevna, and who was an elderly spinster who lived in the Nekhlyudov's house in some family relation or other, he spoke to me of her with animation.

"Yes, she is a wonderful girl," said he, blushing bashfully, but at the same time looking me boldly in the eye. "She is no longer a young girl—she is even rather old, and not at all pretty; but how stupid, how senseless it is to love beauty! I cannot understand it, it is so stupid (he spoke as if he had just discovered a perfectly new and remarkable truth); but she has such a soul, such a heart, such principles, I am convinced that you will not find another girl like her nowadays." (I do not know why Dmitri had acquired the habit of saying that everything good was rare nowadays; he was fond of repeating this expression, and it seemed to become him.)

"I am only afraid," he continued calmly, after having already annihilated with his condemnation people who had the stupidity to love beauty, "I am afraid that it will take you some time to understand her and learn to know her. She is modest, even reticent; she is not fond of displaying her fine, her wonderful qualities. Mamma, for example, who, as you will see, is a very fine and intelligent woman, has known Lyubov Sergeyevna for several years, and cannot and will not understand her. Even last night—I will tell you why I was out of spirits when you asked me. The day before yesterday Lyubov Sergeyevna wanted me to go with her to Ivan Yakovlevich—you have certainly heard of Ivan Yakovlevich—who is said to be crazy, but in reality is a remarkable man. Lyubov Sergeyevna is very religious, I must tell you, and understands Ivan Yakovlevich perfectly. She frequently goes to see him, talks to him, and gives him money for his poor people, which she has earned herself. She is a wonderful woman, as you will see. Well, so I went with her to Ivan Yakovlevich, and was very grateful to her for having seen that remarkable man. But Mamma never will understand this, and regards it as superstition. Last night I had a quarrel with my mother for the first time in my life, and a rather heated one," he concluded, with a convulsive movement of the neck, as though in memory of the feeling which he had experienced during that quarrel.

"Well, and what do you think? That is, how do you fancy it will turn out? Or do you talk to her of how it is to be, and how your love and friendship will end?" I inquired, wishing to divert him from unpleasant memories.

"You mean to ask whether I think of marrying her?" he inquired, reddening again, but turning and looking me boldly in the face.

"Well," I thought, reassuming myself, "it's quite all right—we are grown up; we two friends are riding in this phaeton and discussing our future life. Any one would enjoy listening to and looking at us now unseen."

"Why not?" he went on, after my answer in the affirmative. "It is my aim, as it is the aim of every right-minded man, to be happy and good, so far as that is possible; and with her, if she will only have it so, I shall be happier and better than with the greatest beauty in the world, as soon as I am entirely independent."

Conversing in this way, we did not notice that we had arrived at Kuntsevo, that the sky had clouded over, and that it was going to rain. The sun stood not very high on the right, above the ancient trees of the Kuntsevo garden, and half of its brilliant red disc was covered with grey, slightly luminous clouds; broken, fiery rays escaped in bursts from the other half and lighted up the old trees of the garden with striking brilliancy as their dense green motionless crowns shone in the illuminated rift of azure sky. The gleam and light of this side of the heavens was strongly contrasted with the heavy purplish cloud before us above the young birches visible on the horizon.

A little farther to the right, behind the bushes and trees, we could already see the multi-coloured roofs of the summer cottages, some of which reflected the brilliant rays of the sun, while some assumed the melancholy character of the other half of the heavens. Below, on the left, the motionless pond gleamed blue, surrounded by pale green willows which stood out darkly against its dull and seemingly swollen surface. Beyond the pond, halfway up the hill, stretched a black steaming field; and the straight line of green which divided it in the middle ran off into the distance and rested on the threatening, lead-coloured horizon. On both sides of the soft road, along which the phaeton rolled with regular motion, luxuriant tangled rye showed a bright green and was already beginning to sprout into stalks here and there. The air was perfectly quiet and exhaled freshness; the verdure of trees, leaves, and rye was motionless and unusually pure and clear. It seemed as though every leaf, every blade of grass, were living its own free, happy, individual life. Beside the road I espied a blackish footpath, which wound amid the dark green rye, now more than quarter grown; and this path, for some reason, reminded me with special vividness of our village; and in consequence of my thoughts of the village, by some strange combination of ideas, it reminded me with special vividness of Sonechka, and that I was in love with her.

In spite of all my friendship for Dmitri, and the pleasure which his frankness afforded me, I did not want to know any more about his feelings and intentions with regard to Lyubov Sergeyevna; but I thought that he should know of my love for Sonechka, which seemed to me love of a much higher type. Yet for some reason I could not make up my mind to tell him directly my ideas of how fine it would be when, having married Sonechka, I should live in the country, and how I should have little children who would crave about the floor and call me Papa, and how delighted I should be when he and his wife, Lyubov Sergeyevna, came to see me in their travelling dress; but instead of all this I pointed at the setting sun. "Look, Dmitri, how charming it is!"

Dmitri said nothing, apparently displeased that I had replied to his confession, which had probably cost him an effort, by directing his attention to nature, towards which he was altogether frigid. Nature affected him very differently from the way it did me; it affected him not so much by its beauty as by its interest; he loved it with his mind rather than with his feelings.

"I am very happy," I said to him after this, paying no heed to the fact that he was evidently occupied with his own thoughts, and was quite indifferent to whatever I might say to him; "I believe I told you about a young lady with whom I was in love when a child; I saw her again today," I continued with enthusiasm, "and now I am decidedly in love with her."

And in spite of the expression of indifference which still lingered on his face I told him about my love and all my plans for future connubial bliss. And, strange to say, no sooner had I minutely described all the strength of my feeling than it began to decrease.

Rain overtook us just after we had entered the birch avenue leading to the villa. I only knew that it was raining because a few drops fell upon my nose and hand, and something pattered on the young, sticky leaves of the birches, whose curling branches drooped motionless and seemed to receive these pure, transparent drops with delight, as was shown by the strong perfume with which they filled the avenue. We descended from the calash in order to reach the house more quickly by running through the garden. But just at the entrance to the house we encountered four ladies, two of whom had some work, the third a book, and the other was approaching at a rapid pace from another direction with a little dog. Dmitri immediately introduced me to his mother, sister, aunt, and Lyubov Sergeyevna. They stopped for a moment, but the rain began to come down faster and faster.

"Let us go to the veranda, and you shall introduce him to us again there," said the one whom I took to be Dmitri's mother; and we went up the steps with the ladies.

Chapter XXIII

THE NEKHLYUDOVS

At first sight, the one who struck me most out of all this company was Lyubov Sergeyevna, who, a lap-dog in her arms, and wearing thick knitted shoes, mounted the steps last of all halting twice to gaze attentively at me, and then kissed her dog. She was anything but good-looking—red-haired, thin, short, and rather one-sided. What rendered her plain face all the plainer was her queer manner of dressing her hair all to one side (one of those coiffures which thin haired women invent for themselves). Try as I would, out of a desire to please my friend, I could not discover a single good feature in her. Even her brown eyes, notwithstanding their good-natured expression, were too small and dull, certainly not pretty; even the hands, which generally reveal character, though not large or badly shaped, were red and rough.

When I followed them on to the veranda each one of the ladies, except Varenka, Dmitri's sister, who only regarded me attentively out of her great, dark-grey eyes, said a few words to me before they resumed their several occupations; Varenka began to read aloud from the book which she held on her knee, using her finger as a marker.

Princess Marya Ivanovna was a tall, stately woman of forty. She might have been given more, judging by the greying curls frankly displayed beneath her cap. But her fresh, delicate face, which was scarcely wrinkled at all, and particularly the lively, merry gleam of her large eyes made her look much younger. Her eyes were brown and wide open; her lips were too thin, and somewhat stern; her nose was sufficiently regular and a little to the left; there were no rings on her large, almost masculine hands, with their slender fingers. She wore a close, dark-blue dress, which fitted tightly to her elegant and still youthful figure, of which she was evidently proud. She sat remarkably upright, and sewed on some garment. When I entered the veranda she took my hand, drew me towards her as though desirous of viewing me more closely, and said, as she looked at me with the same cold, open gaze which her son also possessed, that she had long known me from Dmitri's accounts of me, and that she had invited me to spend a whole day with them in order that she might become better acquainted with me. "Do whatever you like, without minding us in the least, just as we shall put no constraint on ourselves because of you. Walk, read, listen, or sleep, if that amuses you more," she added.

Sophia Ivanovna was an elderly spinster and the Princess's youngest sister, but from her looks she seemed older. She had that peculiar build, full of character, which is only met with in very plump, short old maids who wear corsets. It was as if all her health had risen upwards with such force that it threatened every moment to suffocate her. Her little fat hands could not meet beneath the projecting point of her bodice. The sisters were very much like each other, in spite of the fact that Marya Ivanovna had black hair and dark eyes and Sophia Ivanovna was blonde with large, lively, and at the same time calm, blue eyes (which is a rare combination). They had the same expression, the same nose, and the same lips, only Sophia Ivanovna's nose and lips were a little thicker, and tended towards the right side when she smiled, while the Princess's towards the left. Sophia Ivanovna evidently tried to keep her looks young, judging from her dress and coiffure, and would not have displayed grey curls if she had had any. The way she looked at me and her attitude towards me seemed to me extremely haughty at first, and embarrassed me; while with the Princess, on the other hand, I felt perfectly at my ease. Possibly it was her stoutness, and a certain likeness in her figure to the portrait of Catherine the Great which struck me, that gave her that haughty aspect in my eyes; but I was thoroughly abashed when she said to me, gazing at me intently the while, "The friends of our friends are our friends." I regained my composure, and changed my opinion of her entirely, only when, after uttering these words, she paused a while, and then opened her mouth and sighed heavily. It must have been on account of her stoutness that she had a habit of sighing deeply after every few words, opening her mouth a little, and rolling her large blue eyes. So much amiable good-nature was expressed by this habit, for some reason or other, that after that sigh I lost all fear of her, and she pleased me extremely. Her eyes were charming, her voice melodious and pleasing; even the excessively rounded lines of her form seemed to me at that period of my youth not wholly lacking in beauty.

Lyubov Sergeyevna, as the friend of my friend, would (I supposed) immediately say something extremely friendly and confidential to me, and she even gazed at me quite a long time in silence, as if undecided whether what she meant to say to me were not too friendly; but she only broke the silence in order to inquire in what faculty I was. Then she gazed at me again intently for a while, evidently hesitating whether to utter or not to utter that something confidential and friendly; and I, noticing this doubt, besought her by the expression of my countenance to tell me all; but she said, "They say that very little attention is paid to science in the universities nowadays," and called her little dog Suzette.

Lyubov Sergeyevna talked the whole evening in the same sort of irrelevant, disjointed fragments; but I believed so firmly in Dmitri, and he looked so anxiously first at me and then at her the whole evening with an expression that asked, "Well, what do you think?"—that, as it frequently happens, although I was already convinced in my own soul that there was nothing so very special about Lyubov Sergeyevna, I was far from expressing my thought even to myself.

Finally, the last member of this family, Varenka, was a rather plump girl of sixteen.

The only pretty things about her were her large dark-grey eyes, which had an expression of mingled gaiety and quiet attention and were very much like her aunt's; her very large blonde braid of hair; and her extremely soft and pretty hands.

"I think you are bored, Monsieur Nicolas, not having heard the beginning," said Sophia Ivanovna with her good-natured sigh, turning over some pieces of clothing which she was sewing. The reading had ceased for a moment because Dmitri had gone off somewhere.

"Or perhaps you have read *Rob Roy* before?"

At that time I considered it my duty, if only because I wore a student's uniform, to reply with great intelligence and originality to every question, however simple, put to me by people whom I did not know very well, and regarded such brief, clear answers as "Yes" and "No,"

"Yes, it is tiresome." "Why, it is pleasant," and the like as things to be ashamed of. Glancing at my fashionable new trousers and at the shiny buttons on my coat, I replied that I had not read *Rob Roy,* but that it was very interesting to me to listen to it, because I preferred to read books from the middle instead of from the beginning.

"It is twice as interesting; it starts you guessing what has happened, and what will happen," I added, with a self-satisfied smile.

The Princess began to laugh a kind of unnatural laugh. (I afterwards observed that she had no other laugh).

"Well, probably that is true," she said. "And will you remain here long, Nicolas? You will not take offence if I drop the *monsieur?* When are you going away?"

"I do not know; tomorrow perhaps, but we may stay quite a long time," I replied, though I knew perfectly that we were certain to leave the next day.

"I wish you could remain longer, both for our sakes and for Dmitri's," remarked the Princess, looking away in the distance; "friendship is a wonderful thing at your age."

I felt that they were all looking at me, and waiting to see what I would say, although Varenka pretended to be inspecting her aunt's work. I felt that they were putting me through a kind of examination, and that I must show myself in the best possible light.

"Yes, to me," said I, "Dmitri's friendship is useful; but mine cannot be of any use to him; he is a thousand times better than I." (Dmitri could not hear what I was saying, otherwise I should have been afraid that he would detect the insincerity of my words.)

The Princess laughed again with the unnatural laugh which was natural to her.

"To hear him talk," said she; "*c'est vous qui êtes un petit monstre de perfection.*"

" '*Monstre de perfection*,' that's capital; I must remember that," I thought.

"However, leaving you out of the case, he is a masterhand at that," she went on, lowering her voice (which was particularly agreeable to me), and indicating Lyubov Sergeyevna with her eyes. "He has discovered in our *poor Auntie*" (that was what they called Lyubov Sergeyevna) "whom I have known, with her Suzette, for twenty years, such perfections as I never even suspected. Varya, order them to bring me a glass of water," she added, glancing into the distance again, having probably discovered that it was rather early, or not at all necessary, to initiate me into family affairs; "or, better still, let *him* go. He has nothing to do, and you go on reading. Go straight through that door, my friend, about fifteen paces down the passage, and say in a loud voice, 'Pyotr, bring Marya Ivanovna a glass of water and ice!' " she said to me, and again she laughed lightly with her unnatural laugh.

"She certainly wants to discuss me," I thought, as I left the room; "probably she wants to say that she has observed that I am a very, very intelligent young man." But I had not gone the fifteen steps when fat panting Sophia Ivanovna overtook me with light swift steps.

"*Merci, mon cher*," she said; "I am going there myself; I shall tell him."

Chapter XXIV

LOVE

Sophia Ivanovna, as I afterwards learned, was one of those rare elderly women who, though born for family life, have been denied this happiness, and, in consequence, suddenly make up their minds to pour out all the treasure of love which has been stored up so long and has grown and strengthened in their hearts, upon certain chosen favourites. And the store is so inexhaustible among spinsters of this sort that, although the chosen ones are many, much love still remains, which they pour out upon all around them, on all the good and bad people whom they chance to meet.

There are three kinds of love:—

1) Beautiful love;
2) Self-sacrificing love; and
3) Active love.

I do not speak of the love of a young man for a girl, or hers for him; I fear these sentiments, and I have been so unfortunate in life as never to have seen a single spark of truth in this species of love, but only a lie, in which sensuality, connubial relations, money, a desire to tie or to free one's hands, have to such an extent overlaid the feeling itself that it has been impossible to get to the bottom of it. I am speaking of the love for mankind which, according to the greater or lesser power of soul, concentrates upon one or upon several, or pours itself out upon many; of the love of mother, father, brother, children, for a comrade, friends, fellow-countryman—of love for man.

Beautiful love consists in a love of the beauty of the sentiment itself and its expression. For people who love thus, the object of their affection is lovable only inasmuch as it arouses that agreeable sentiment in the consciousness and expression of which they delight. People who love with beautiful love care very little about reciprocity, as for something which has no influence upon the beauty and pleasure of the sentiment. They frequently change the objects of their love, as their chief aim is simply to have the agreeable feeling of love constantly excited. In order to preserve this pleasing sentiment in themselves, they talk incessantly of their affection in the most elegant terms, both to the object of it and to every

one else, even to those who have no concern whatever
with this love.

In our country, people of a certain class who love
beautifully not only talk about their love to every one,
but inevitably discuss it in French. It is a queer and a
strange thing to say, but I am convinced that there have
been and still are many people of distinguished society,
especially women, whose love for their friends, their hus-
bands, and their children, would be instantly annihilated
if they were but forbidden to speak of it in French.

The second kind of love—*self-sacrificing love*—consists in love of the process of immolating one's self for
the object loved, without any concern whether the beloved
is the better or the worse for that immolation.
"There is nothing so disagreeable that I would not do
it in order to prove my devotion to the whole world, and
to *him* or to *her*." That is the formula of this kind of love.
People who love thus never believe in reciprocity (because it is more meritorious to sacrifice one's self for a
person who does not understand one), and are always
sickly, which also heightens the merit of the sacrifice;
they are constant, for the most part, because it would
be hard for them to lose the merit of those sacrifices which
they have made for the object of their love; they are always ready to die to prove to *him* or to *her* the extent of
their devotion, but they despise the little everyday demonstrations of love which do not require special out-
bursts of self-sacrifice. It makes no difference to them
whether you have eaten or slept well, whether you are
cheery, or whether you are in health, and they do nothing
to procure you those comforts if they are within their
power; but to face bullets, to throw themselves into the
water or into fire, to pine away for love—for these they
are always ready if only the opportunity presents itself.
Moreover, people who are inclined to self-sacrificing love
are always proud of their love, exacting, jealous, dis-

trustful; and, strange to say, they desire danger for its object, that they may rescue him from his misfortune, that they may comfort him—and even vices, that they may reform him.

You are living alone in the country with your wife, who loves you with self-sacrificing love. You are well and calm; you have occupations which you like; your loving wife is so weak that she cannot busy herself with the management of the household, which is confided to the hands of domestics, nor with the children, who are in the hands of nurses, nor with anything which she would love, because she loves nothing but you. She is visibly ill, but not wishing to pain you, she will not mention this to you; she is plainly bored, but for your sake she is ready to be bored all her life. The fact that you are so intently occupied with your affairs (whatever they may be—hunting, books, farming, service) is visibly killing her; she is sure that these occupations are ruining you, but she holds her peace, and suffers. But now you fall ill. Your loving wife forgets her illness for you, and in spite of your entreaties not to torment herself for nothing, she sits by your bedside, and will not leave it; and you feel her sympathetic glance upon you every second, saying, "There! I told you. But now it makes no difference to me, I will not leave you." In the morning you are a little better, and you go to another room. The room is not warmed or tidied up; the soup, which is the only thing you can eat, has not been ordered from the cook; the medicine has not been sent for; but your poor, loving wife, exhausted by her vigil, gazes at you with the same expression of sympathy, walks on tip-toe, and gives the servants confused and unaccustomed orders in a whisper. You want to read; your loving wife tells you with a sigh that she knows you will not listen to her, that you will be angry with her, and she is used to that—but it is better for you not to read. You want to walk across the room; you had better not. You want to speak to a friend who has arrived—talking is not good for you. You have fever again in the night, and you want to be left alone; but your loving wife, pale, haggard, sighing from time to time, sits opposite you in an arm-chair, under the half light of the night-lamp, and arouses in you a feeling of irritation and impatience by her slightest sound or movement. You have a servant who has lived with you for twenty years, to whom you are accustomed, who serves you admirably and satisfactorily because he has slept sufficiently during the day, and, moreover, receives wages for his services; but she will not suffer him to wait upon you. She will do everything with her own weak, unskilled fingers, which you cannot avoid watching with repressed vexation, when those white fingers strive in vain to uncork a phial, to extinguish a candle, to pour out your medicine, or when they cautiously touch you. If you are an impatient, hot-tempered man, and beg her to go away, your irritated ear of a sick person will catch sighing and sobbing outside the door and whispering some nonsense to your man; and finally, if you do not die, your loving wife, who has not slept all the twenty nights you were sick (as she repeats to you incessantly), falls ill, wastes away, suffers, and becomes still less capable of any occupation, and by the time you are in a normal condition expresses her love of self-sacrifice only by shedding around you a kind of benignant dullness which involuntarily communicates itself to you, and to all about you.

The third sort—*active love*—consists in endeavour to satisfy all needs, desires, whims, all vices even, of the object loved. People who love thus always love for life; for the more they love the more they know the object of their love, and the easier it is for them to love—that is, to satisfy his or her desires. Their love is rarely expressed in words; and if expressed, it is not with self-satisfaction, eloquently, but shamefacedly, awkwardly, for they are always afraid that they do not love sufficiently. These people even like the vices of the beloved person because they give them another chance to satisfy his or her wishes. They seek reciprocity, even willingly deceiving themselves, believe in it, and are happy if they have it; but they love all the same even under the opposite conditions, and not only desire happiness for the beloved person, but constantly strive to procure it for him or her by all moral and material, great and small means which are in their power.

And it was this active love for her nephew, for her sister, for Lyubov Sergeyevna, for me even, because Dmitri loved me, which shone in the eyes, in every word and movement, of Sophia Ivanovna.

It was only much later that I appreciated Sophia Ivanovna at her full worth, but even then the question occurred to me: Why did Dmitri, who was trying to understand love in a way totally different from what was usual with young men, and who had always before his eyes this sweet, affectionate Sophia Ivanovna, suddenly take to loving that incomprehensible Lyubov Sergeyevna, and only admit that his aunt also possessed good qualities? Verily it is a true saying that "A prophet is not heeded in his own country." One thing or the other: either there actually is more evil than good in every man, or else man is more receptive to evil than to good. Dmitri had not known Lyubov Sergeyevna long, whereas his aunt's love he had experienced ever since his birth.

Chapter XXV

I BECOME BETTER ACQUAINTED

When I returned to the veranda I found they were not speaking of me at all, as I had supposed; yet Varenka was not reading, and, having laid aside her book, she was engaged in a heated dispute with Dmitri, who was pacing back and forth, settling his neck in his neckerchief, and screwing up his eyes. The subject of their dispute seemed to be some Ivan Yakovlevich and superstition; but it was too heated for its real but unmentioned cause not to be something which concerned the whole family more closely. The Princess and Lyubov Sergeyevna sat silent, listening to every word, evidently desirous at times to take part in the argument, but restraining themselves, and allowing themselves to be represented, the one by Varenka, the other by Dmitri. When I entered, Varenka glanced at me with such an expression of indifference that it was plain that she was deeply interested in the argument and did not mind whether I heard what she said or not. The Princess, who was evidently on Varenka's side, wore the same expression. But Dmitri began to argue with even greater heat in my presence; and Lyubov Sergeyevna seemed excessively frightened at my appearance, and said, not to any one in particular, "Old people are quite right when they say: *"Si jeunesse savait, si vieillesse pouvait."**

But this adage did not put an end to the dispute, and only prompted me to think that Lyubov Sergeyevna and my friend were in the wrong. Although I felt rather awkward at being present at a petty family quarrel, it was nevertheless pleasant to observe the real relations in this family revealed in its progress, and feel that my presence did not prevent their speaking freely.

It often happens that you see a family for years under the same veil of propriety, and the true relations among the members remain a secret to you. (I have even observed that the more impenetrable and ornamental this veil, the coarser are the genuine relations which it conceals from you.) Then it comes to pass one day, quite unexpectedly,

---

* If youth knew, if old age had the power.—*Ed.*

that there arises in this family circle some question, often apparently trivial, concerning some blonde lady, or a visit with the husband's horses; and, without any visible cause, the quarrel grows more and more violent, it becomes impossible to clear up the situation under the cover of the veil, and all at once, to the terror of the wranglers themselves, and to the amazement of those present, all the real, coarse relations are laid bare; the curtain, which no longer covers anything, flutters useless between the warring sides, and only serves to remind you how long you have been deceived by it. Often it is not so painful to dash one's head against the ceiling in full swing as to touch a sore and sensitive spot, though ever so lightly. And such a sore and sensitive spot exists in nearly every family. In the Nekhlyudov family this sensitive spot was Dmitri's strange love for Lyubov Sergeyevna, which aroused in his mother and sister, if not a sense of envy, at least a sentiment of wounded family feeling. That was why the dispute about Ivan Yakovlevich and superstition was of so much importance for all of them.

"You are always trying to see into what other people ridicule and despise," said Varenka, in her melodious voice, pronouncing every letter distinctly. "And you must always try to discover something remarkably fine in it."

"In the first place, only a most *frivolous person* can speak of despising such a remarkable man as Ivan Yakovlevich," retorted Dmitri, with a nervous toss of his head away from his sister; "and in the second place, it is *you* who are trying purposely not to see the good which is under your very eyes."

On rejoining us, Sophia Ivanovna glanced several times in a frightened way now at her nephew, then at her niece, then at me; twice she opened her mouth as though to speak, and sighed heavily.

"Now, please, Varya, go on reading," she said, handing her the book and patting her hand affectionately; "I am

318

very anxious to know whether he ever found her again. (As a matter of fact, the book did not seem to contain a word about any one finding any one else.) And as for you, Mitya, my dear, you had better wrap up your cheek, for the air is fresh, and you will get toothache again," she said to her nephew, notwithstanding the look of displeasure which he cast upon her, probably because she had broken the thread of his argument. The reading was resumed.

This little quarrel did not in the least disturb the family peace and that sensible concord which enveloped the feminine circle.

This circle, to which Princess Marya Ivanovna evidently gave its character and direction, had for me a perfectly novel and attractive tone, of a certain sort of logic, and at the same time of simplicity and elegance. This tone was expressed for me by the beauty, purity, and simplicity of things—the bell, the binding of the book, the arm-chair, the table; and in the upright well-corseted pose of the Princess, in her grey curls brought out into view, and in her way of calling me simply Nicolas and *he* at our first meeting; in their occupations, the reading aloud, the sewing; and in the remarkable whiteness of the ladies' hands. (They all had a common family mark on the hand, which consisted in the soft portion of the palm being of a deep rose hue, and separated sharply from the unusual whiteness of the upper part of the hand.) But this character was expressed most of all in the excellent manner in which all three spoke French and Russian; pronouncing every letter distinctly, and finishing every word and phrase with pedantic accuracy. All this, and in particular the fact that they treated me simply and seriously in this society as a grown-up person, telling me their own thoughts and listening to my opinions (to this I was so little accustomed that, in spite of my shiny buttons and blue facings, I was still afraid of being suddenly asked "Do you think people are going to talk seriously with you? Go and study!") all this resulted in my not feeling the slightest embarrassment in their society. I rose and changed my seat from place to place, and talked with all except Varenka, to whom it still seemed to me improper, for some reason, to speak first.

During the reading, as I listened to her pleasant voice, I glanced now at her, now at the sandy path of the flower-garden, upon which dark round spots of rain were forming, upon the lime-trees, on whose leaves occasional drops of rain still continued to patter from the pale, bluish edge of the thinning thunder-cloud which enveloped us, then at her again, then at the last crimson rays of the setting sun, which enveloped in light the leafy old birches all dripping with rain, and then at Varenka again; and I decided that she was not at all plain, as she had seemed to me at first.

"It's a pity I am already in love," I thought, "and that Varenka is not Sonechka. How nice it would be suddenly to become a member of this family! I should gain a mother, an aunt and a wife all at once." And as meditating thus I glanced at Varenka while she read, and thought that I would magnetize her and make her look at me, Varenka raised her head from her book, glanced at me, and, meeting my eyes, turned away.

"It has not stopped raining yet," she said.

And all at once I experienced a strange sensation. I suddenly recollected that what was now happening to me was an exact repetition of what had happened once before; that then also light rain was falling, and the sun was setting behind the birches, and I was looking at *her,* and she was reading, and I had magnetized her, and she had glanced up, and I had even recollected that this had happened before.

"Is it she? *she*?" I thought. "*Is it beginning?*" But I hastily decided that she was not the *she*, and that it

320

was not beginning yet. "In the first place, she is not good-looking," I thought; "and in the next place, she is simply a young lady, and I have made her acquaintance in the most commonplace manner, while *she* will be re-markable, and I shall meet her somewhere in some un-common place; and, besides, this family only pleases me so much because I have not seen anything yet," I decid-ed. "But of course there are others like this one, and I shall meet many during my life."

Chapter XXVI

I SHOW MYSELF AT MY BEST

At tea-time the reading came to an end; and the ladies engaged in a conversation about persons and circum-stances with which I was unfamiliar, purposely, so it seemed to me, to make me feel, in spite of my cordial re-ception, the difference which existed, both in years and in position, between them and myself. In general con-versation, however, I made up for my former silence, and sought to exhibit my remarkable intelligence and original-ity, which I considered that my uniform specially bound me to do. When the conversation turned on coun-try-houses, I suddenly related how Prince Ivan Ivanich had such a villa near Moscow that people came from London and Paris to see it; that there was a railed en-closure there which was worth three hundred and eighty thousand rubles; and that Prince Ivan Ivanich was a very near relative of mine, that I had dined with him that day, and he had told me that I must be sure and come to spend the whole summer with him at that villa, but that I had refused, because I knew the house very well, since I had been there a number of times, and that all those enclosures and bridges did not interest me at all because I could not bear luxury, especially in the country, and that I liked everything in the country to be like the country. Having uttered this dreadful and complicated lie, I became confused, and turned so red that every one must certainly have perceived that I was lying. Varenka, who handed me a cup of tea at that moment, and Sophia Ivanovna, who had been gazing at me while I was speaking, both turned away from me and began to talk of something else, with an expression which I have often noticed in good people since then, when a very young man begins plainly to lie to their very faces, and which signifies, "Of course we know that he is lying, and why he does it, the poor fellow!"

The reason why I said that Prince Ivan Ivanich had a villa was that I saw no better pretext for mentioning both my relationship to Prince Ivan Ivanich, and the fact that I had dined with him that day; but why did I tell about the railing worth three hundred and eighty thousand rubles, and that I had been to his house so often when I had never been even once, and could not have been, since Prince Ivan Ivanich lived only in Moscow or Naples, which the Nekhlyudovs knew very well? I really cannot account to myself for it. Neither in childhood, nor boyhood, nor afterwards in a riper age, did I ever detect the vice of lying in myself; on the contrary, I have been rather too frank and upright; but during this first period of adolescence a strange desire to lie in the most desperate manner, and without any apparent cause, frequently took possession of me. I say "desperate manner" purposely, because I lied about things where it was extremely easy to find me out. It seems to me that a vainglorious desire to show myself as an entirely different man from what I was, united to the impracticable hope in life of lying so as not to be detected in the lie, was the chief cause of this strange tendency.

After tea, as the rain had stopped and the evening was

clear and calm, the Princess proposed that we go for a walk in the lower garden and admire her favourite spot. Following my rule of always being original, and considering that such clever people as the Princess and myself must stand above banalities of politeness, I replied that I hated walking aimlessly, and if I cared to walk at all, it was quite alone. I did not realize that this was downright rude; it seemed to me then that there was nothing more disgraceful than stale compliments, and nothing more amiable and original than a little discourteous frankness. Nevertheless, quite content with my answer, I went to walk with the rest of the company.

The Princess's favourite spot was at the very bottom of the garden in its depths, on a little bridge which was thrown over a small swamp. The view was extremely restricted, but very melancholy and pleasing. We are so accustomed to confounding art and nature that very frequently those manifestations of nature which we have never encountered in pictures do not strike us as real nature—though real nature they are—and, vice versa, those phenomena which have been too frequently repeated in art seem to us threadbare or in some cases, when too thoroughly penetrated with thought and sentiment alone, seem fantastic. The view from the Princess's favourite place was of this kind. It consisted of a small pond with overgrown banks; directly behind it was a steep hill covered with old spreading trees and bushes, with frequent changes in its many-hued verdure; and at the foot of the hill, drooping over the pond, an old birch, which, partly clinging to the damp bank of the pool with its thick roots, rested its crown upon a tall stately ash-tree, and swung its curling branches over the smooth surface of the pond, in which these dropping boughs and the surrounding greenery were reflected.

"How charming!" said the Princess, shaking her head, and not addressing any one in particular.

"Yes, it is wonderful, but somehow it looks so frightfully like scenery in a theatre," I said, wishing to show that I had an opinion of my own on everything.

The Princess continued to admire the view as though she had not heard my remark, and turning to her sister and Lyubov Sergeyevna she pointed out separate details —the crooked overhanging stump, and the reflection which particularly pleased her. Sophia Ivanovna said that it was all very beautiful, and that her sister was in the habit of passing several hours at a time here; but it was evident that she only said so to please the Princess. I have observed that people who are endowed with the faculty of what I call active love are rarely sensitive to the beauties of nature. Lyubov Sergeyevna also seemed enraptured, asking, among other things, "What does that birch hold on to? will it stand long?" She glanced constantly at her Suzette, who ran back and forth across the bridge on her crooked legs, wagging her tail with an anxious expression, as though for the first time in her life she had chanced not to be in a room. Dmitri began a logical argument with his mother on the point that no view could be very beautiful where the horizon was limited. Varenka said nothing. When I glanced round at her she was standing leaning on the railing of the bridge with her profile towards me, and looking straight in front of her. Something probably interested her deeply, and even touched her; for she was evidently day-dreaming and had no thought for herself or the fact that she was being looked at. Her large eyes were so full of intent observation, of calm, clear thought, her pose was so unaffected, and in spite of her short stature there was so much majesty about her, that I was again struck by what seemed a memory of her, and again I asked myself "Is it not beginning?" And again I answered that I was already in love with Sonechka, and that Varenka was simply a young lady, the sister of my friend. But

I liked her at that moment, and I felt in consequence some vague desire to do or say some little unpleasant thing to her.

"You know, Dmitri," I said to my friend, going nearer to Varenka in order that she might hear what I was about to say, "I think that, even if there were no mosquitoes, there would be nothing beautiful about this place; and now," I added, slapping my forehead and really crushing a mosquito, "it's perfectly dreadful."

"Then you do not care for nature?" said Varenka to me, without turning her head.

"Admiring nature is an idle, useless occupation," I replied, very well satisfied with having uttered my little unpleasantness and having been original. Varenka raised her eyebrows almost imperceptibly for a moment, with an expression of pity, and continued to look straight before her as composedly as ever.

I was vexed with her; but in spite of this, the greyish railing of the bridge with its faded paint, upon which she leaned, the reflection in the dark pond of the drooping stump of the fallen birch, which seemed anxious to join its drooping branches, the odour of the swamp, the feeling of the crushed mosquito upon my forehead, and her attentive gaze and imposing attitude, often rose quite unexpectedly afterwards before my imagination.

Chapter XXVII

DMITRI

When we returned home after our walk Varenka did not wish to sing, as she usually did in the evening; and I had the self-assurance to set it down to my own account, fancying that the cause was what I had said to her on the bridge. The Nekhlyudovs did not have supper, and

went to bed early; and that day, Dmitri, having toothache, as Sophia Ivanovna had predicted, we went
off to his room even earlier than usual. Supposing
that I had done all that my blue collar and my buttons
required of me, and that I had pleased everybody, I was
in an extremely amiable, self-satisfied frame of mind.
Dmitri, on the contrary, was taciturn and morose because of the quarrel and his toothache. He sat down at
the table, got out his copy-books—his diary, and the
book in which he was accustomed every evening to write
down his past and future tasks—and wrote in them for
quite a long time, frowning continually, and touching his
cheek with his hand.

"Oh, leave me alone!" he shouted at the maid who had
been sent by Sophia Ivanovna to inquire how his teeth
were, and whether he did not want to make himself a
fomentation. After that he told me that my bed would be
ready directly, and that he would retire immediately and
went to Lyubov Sergeyevna.

"What a pity that Varenka is not pretty, and not Sonechka!" I meditated when I was left alone in the room.
"How pleasant it would be to come to them and offer her
my hand when I leave the university! I should say, 'Princess, though no longer young and therefore unable to love
passionately, I shall always cherish you like a dear sister.' 'And you I already respect,' I should say to her mother; 'and as for you, Sophia Ivanovna, pray believe that
I esteem you highly.' Then I would ask simply and plainly: 'Will you be my wife?' 'Yes'; and she would give me
her hand, and I would press it, and say, 'My love is not
in words, but in deeds.' Well, the thought struck me, and
what if Dmitri should suddenly fall in love with Lyubochka?"—for Lyubochka is in love with him—and
should wish to marry her? Then one of us would not be
able to marry. And that would be capital, for this is what
I should do. I should immediately notice how things

were, say nothing, but go to Dmitri and say, 'In vain, my friend, have we tried to keep secrets from each other. You know that my love for your sister will end only with my life. Yet I know all—you have deprived me of my best hope, you have rendered me unhappy; but this is the way Nikolai Irtenyev avenges himself for the unhappiness of his whole life—here is my sister,' and I should give him Lyubochka's hand. He would say, 'No, never!' and I should say, 'Prince Nekhlyudov, it is no use trying to outdo me in magnanimity. Not in the whole world is there a more magnanimous man than Nikolai Irtenyev.' Then I should bow and retire. Dmitri and Lyubochka would run after me in tears, and beseech me to accept their sacrifice —and I might consent and be very happy if only I were in love with Varenka." These dreams were so agreeable that I wanted very much to communicate them to my friend; but in spite of our mutual vow of frankness, I felt that for some reason it was physically impossible to do so.

Dmitri returned from Lyubov Sergeyevna, with some drops on his tooth which she had given him, in still greater suffering, and consequently still more gloomy. My bed was not yet ready; and a little boy, Dmitri's servant, came to ask him where I was to sleep.

"Oh, go to the devil!" shouted Dmitri, stamping his foot. "Vaska, Vaska, Vaska!" he cried as soon as the boy was gone, shouting louder each time—"Vaska, lay me out a bed on the floor."

"No; let me sleep on the floor," I said.

"Well, it's no matter. Make it up somewhere," Dmitri went on in the same angry tone. "Here, why don't you do it?"

But Vaska evidently did not understand what was wanted of him, and stood motionless.

"Well, what's the matter with you? D'you hear, go ahead, do as I tell you!" shouted Dmitri, suddenly flying into a kind of fury.

But Vaska, still not understanding, and frightened, stood motionless.

"So you are determined to mur—to drive me mad?" and, springing from his chair, Dmitri flew at Vaska and struck him several blows with his fist upon the head, as he rushed out of the room. Halting at the door, Dmitri glanced at me; and the expression of rage and cruelty which his face had borne for a moment changed into such a gentle, shamefaced, and affectionately childish expression, that I was sorry for him, and much as I wanted to turn away, I could not bring myself to do so. He said nothing, but paced the room for a long time, glancing at me from time to time with the same imploring look; then he took a note-book from the table, wrote something in it, took off his coat, folded it carefully, went to the corner where the icons hung, crossed his large white hands upon his breast, and began to pray. He prayed so long that Vaska had time to fetch a mattress and spread it on the floor, as I directed him in a whisper to do. I undressed and lay down upon the bed thus prepared on the floor; but Dmitri still continued to pray. As I glanced at Dmitri's somewhat bent back, and at the soles of his feet, which were presented to me in a rather submissive way when he prostrated himself on the floor, I loved Dmitri still more than before, and I kept thinking, "Shall I or shall I not tell him what I have been dreaming about our sisters?" Having finished his prayer, Dmitri lay down beside me on the bed; and, supporting himself on his elbow, he looked at me long and silently with a steady affectionate gaze. It was evidently painful for him, but he seemed to be punishing himself. I smiled as I looked at him. He also smiled.

"Why don't you tell me," said he, "that I have acted abominably? Of course, you thought it at once."

"Yes," I answered—although I had been thinking of something else, but it seemed to me that I had really thought it—"yes, it was not nice at all; I did not expect it of you," said I, experiencing a special satisfaction at the moment in addressing him as *thou*. "Well, how are your teeth?" I added.

"Much better. Ah, Nikolenka, my friend," Dmitri broke out so affectionately that tears seemed to stand in his sparkling eyes, "I know, I feel that I am wicked; and God sees how I try to be better, and how I entreat Him to make me better. But what am I to do if I have such a wretched, horrible temper? what am I to do? I try to restrain myself, to reform myself; but all at once it becomes impossible, at all events impossible to me all alone. I need the help and support of someone. Now Lyubov Sergeyevna does understand me and has helped me a great deal in this. I know by my diary that I have improved a great deal during the last year. Ah, Nikolenka, my dear!" he continued with peculiar, unaccustomed affection and a tone that was already calmer after this confession; "how much the influence of a woman like her means! My God! Think how good it will be for me to have a friend like her when I am independent! I am a totally different man with her."

And then Dmitri began to unfold to me his plans for marriage, country life, and constant self-improvement.

"I shall live in the country. You will visit me, perhaps; and you will be married to Sonechka," said he. "Our children will play together. Of course, this all sounds ridiculous, but it may very well come true."

"Of course, why not," said I, smiling, and thinking at the same time that it would be better still if I married his sister.

"I tell you what," said he, after a short silence: "you are only imagining that you are in love with Sonechka, but I can see it's not serious: you do not yet know what the genuine feeling is like."

329

I made no reply, because I almost agreed with him. We remained silent for a while.

"You surely must have noticed that I was in an abominable temper again today and had a nasty quarrel with Varya. I felt very bad about it afterwards, especially because it was in your presence. Although she thinks of many things in a way she should not, she's a splendid girl, and very good when you come to know her more intimately."

His change of the conversation from the statement that I was not in love to praise of his sister rejoiced me greatly, and made me blush; nevertheless, I said nothing to him about his sister, and we went on talking of something else.

Thus we chatted away until the second cock-crow, and the pale dawn was already looking in at the window when Dmitri went to his bed and put out the light.

"Well, now for sleep," he said.

"Yes," I answered, "but just one word more."

"Well?"

"Life is a grand thing, isn't it?"

"Yes, it is," he answered in such a voice that even in the dark I thought I could see the expression of his merry, affectionate eyes and childlike smile.

Chapter XXVIII

IN THE COUNTRY

The next day Volodya and I set off in a post-chaise for the country. As I went over all my Moscow memories in my mind on the way, I remembered Sonechka Valakhina, though not until evening, when we had travelled five stages. "It is strange," I thought, "that I am in love, and yet had quite forgotten about it; I must think of her." And

I did begin to think of her, as one thinks while travelling, incoherently but vividly; and thus I brought myself to such a state that I somehow considered it indispensable to appear sad and thoughtful for two days after our arrival in the country before all the household, and especially in the presence of Katenka, whom I regarded as a great connoisseur in matters of this sort, and to whom I gave a hint of the condition in which I found my heart. But in spite of all my attempts at dissimulation before others and before myself, in spite of my deliberate assumption of all the signs which I had observed in others in an enamoured condition, in the course of those two days I did not constantly bear in mind that I was in love, but remembered it chiefly in the evening; and finally I fell into the new round of country life and occupations so quickly that I quite forgot about my love for Sonechka.

We arrived at Petrovskoye at night; and I was sleeping so soundly that I saw neither the house nor the birch avenue, nor any of the household, who had already retired and had long been asleep. Old Foka, bent, barefooted, and wrapped in a kind of woman's wadded dressing-gown, with a candle in his hand, opened the door to us. He quivered with joy on seeing us, kissed us on the shoulders, hastily gathered up his felt rug, and began to dress himself. I passed through the vestibule and staircase without being thoroughly awake; but in the anteroom the lock of the door, the bolt, the crooked boards, the clothes-press, the ancient candlestick spotted with tallow as of old, the shadow of the cold, bent, recently-lighted tallow candle in the image-lamp, the always dusty double window which was never removed, behind which, as I remembered, there grew a mountain-ash—all this was so familiar, so full of memories, so harmonious within itself, as though united in one thought, that I suddenly felt upon me the caress of this dear old house. "How could we, the house and I," I wondered, "do without each other so long?" and

I ran in haste to see whether the rooms were the same. Everything was the same, only everything had grown smaller, lower, while I taller, heavier and clumsier. But the house received me joyously into its embrace just as I was; and every floor, every window, every step of the stairs, every sound, awakened in me a world of forms, feelings, occurrences of the happy past which would never return. We went to the bedroom of our childhood: all my childish terrors were lurking again in the darkness of the corners and doors. We went into the drawing-room: the same gentle motherly love was diffused over every object in the room. We went to the hall: it seemed as though boisterous, careless childish mirth had lingered in this apartment, and was only waiting to be revived. In the sitting-room whither Foka led us, and where he had made up beds for us, it seemed as if everything—the mirror, the screen, the ancient wooden icon, every bump of the walls covered with white paper—all spoke of suffering, of death, of that which would never exist again.

We lay down, and Foka left us after wishing us good-night.

"It was in this room that Mamma died, wasn't it?" said Volodya.

I did not answer him, and pretended to be asleep. If I had said a word, I should have burst out crying. On awaking next morning I saw Papa still in his dressing-gown and fanciful slippers sitting on Volodya's bed, chatting and laughing with him. He sprang up with a merry bound, came up to me and, slapping me on the back with his large hand, presented his cheek to me and pressed it to my lips.

"Well done, diplomat, thanks," he said in his own peculiar caressing tone, gazing at me with his small, twinkling eyes. "Volodya tells me you got through well, that's grand. You're a fine little fellow when you take a notion not to be stupid. Thanks, my dear boy. Well, we'll have a grand time of it here now, and in the winter, perhaps, we'll move to St. Petersburg; only it's a pity that the hunting is over, I should have liked to give you some amusement in that way. Do you shoot well, Waldemar? There's any quantity of game, and I will go with you myself some day. So, please God, we shall move to St. Petersburg for the winter and you'll see people and make connections. You are grown up now, boys, and I was just telling Waldemar that you now stand on your own feet and my task is over; you can walk alone. But if you want to ask advice please do—I am no longer your daddy, but your friend and comrade and counsellor, wherever I can be of use, and nothing more. How does that fall in with your philosophy, Koko? Well or ill, eh?"

Of course I answered that it fell in with it entirely, and I really thought so. Papa had a peculiarly fascinating, merry, happy expression that day; and these novel relations with me, as with an equal, a companion, made me love him more than ever.

"Now tell me, did you call on all our relatives, and on the Ivins? Did you see the old man? What did he say to you?" he continued to interrogate me. "Did you go to see Prince Ivan Ivanich?"

And we chatted so long before dressing that the sun had already begun to desert the windows of the sitting-room; and Yakov, who was just as old as ever, and twirled his fingers behind his back and always repeated "and again—" entered the room and informed Papa that the calash was ready.

"Where are you going?" I asked Papa.

"Ah, I was forgetting," said Papa, with the usual twitch of his shoulder and cough of vexation. "I promised to go to the Epifanovs' today. Do you remember the Epifanova, *la belle Flamande*? She used to visit your mamma. They are very nice people," and with a self-conscious twitch of his shoulder (so it appeared to me) Papa left the room.

Lyubochka had come to the door several times during our chat and called, "May I come in?" but each time Papa shouted to her through the door that "she really could not, because we were not dressed yet."

"What's the harm? I've seen you in your dressing-gown before."

"You can't see your brothers without their *unmentionables*," he shouted to her, "suppose each of them just knocks at your door, will that be enough for you? Now, boys, go and knock, it is improper for them even to speak to you in such *negligé*."

"Ah, how unbearable you are! At all events, do hurry up and come down to the drawing-room. Mimi is dying to see you!" Lyubochka called from outside.

As soon as Papa went away I put on my student's coat as quickly as possible and went to the drawing-room. Volodya, on the contrary, was in no hurry, and remained upstairs for a long time talking to Yakov about the best places for snipe and woodcock. As I have already said, there was nothing in the world which he dreaded so much as sentimentality as he called it with his brother, sister, or Papa; and avoiding every expression of feeling he fell into the other extreme—coldness—which often hurt the feelings of people who did not understand its cause. In the anteroom I met Papa hurrying to the carriage with short brisk steps. He had on his fashionable new Moscow coat and smelt of scent. When he caught sight of me he nodded gaily, as much as to say, "You see, isn't it fine?" and again I was struck by the expression of happiness in his eyes which I had already observed that morning.

The drawing-room was the same bright, lofty room, with the yellowish English grand piano, and its great open windows, through which the green trees and the

yellowish-red paths of the garden peeped gaily. After kissing Mimi and Lyubochka, I was going up to Katenka
when it suddenly occurred to me that it was not proper
to kiss her; and I stopped short, silent and blushing.
Katenka, who was not at all embarrassed, offered me
her white hand, and congratulated me on my admission to
the university. When Volodya entered, the same thing happened to him at the sight of Katenka. In fact, it was hard
to decide, after having grown up together and having
been in the habit of seeing each other every day during all
that time, how we ought to greet each other now after our
first separation. Katenka blushed far more deeply than all
the rest of us. Volodya suffered no embarrassment, but,
bowing slightly to her, he walked off to Lyubochka, with
whom he talked a little, but not seriously; then he went
off somewhere for a walk.

Chapter XXIX

OUR ATTITUDE TO THE GIRLS

Volodya had such queer views about the girls that he
could interest himself in the questions: were they hungry?
had they slept enough? were they properly dressed? did
they make mistakes in French which he should be ashamed
of before strangers? But he never admitted the idea
that they could think or feel anything human, and still
less did he admit the idea that one could discuss anything
with them. When they chanced to come to him with any
serious question (which, however, they already tried to
avoid), if they asked his opinion about a novel or his
studies at the university, he made a grimace and walked
away in silence, or answered with some mutilated French
phrase, such as *comme ci tri joli,** and the like; or, put-

---

* *Comme c'est très joli.* How nice.—*Tr.*

ting on a serious and purposely stupid face, he uttered some word which had no sense or connection at all with the question, made his eyes dull all at once, and said, *a roll*, or *they have gone away*, or *cabbage*, or something of that sort. When I chanced to repeat to him these words which Lyubochka or Katenka had reported to me, he always said:

"Hm! so you still discuss matters with them? Yes, I see you are still a duffer."

And one needed to hear him to appreciate the profound, invariable contempt which was expressed in this remark. Volodya had been a grown-up person for two years now; he was constantly falling in love with every pretty woman that he met; yet although he saw Katenka every day (she had been wearing long dresses for two years, and grew prettier every day), the possibility of falling in love with her never entered his head. Whether this arose from the prosaic recollections of childhood—the ruler, her frocks, her caprices, were still too fresh in his memory—or from the repugnance which very young people have for everything domestic, or from the general human weakness which, on meeting a good or a very beautiful thing at the beginning of life, leads one to think, "Ah! I shall meet much more like this"—at all events, up to this time Volodya had not looked upon Katenka with a man's eyes.

Volodya was evidently very much bored all that summer. His boredom came from his scorn for us, which, as I have said, he did not attempt to conceal. The expression of his face said constantly, "Oh! how tiresome! there's nobody to talk to." In the morning he would go out shooting or read a book in his room, without dressing until dinner. If Papa was not at home, he even took his book in to that meal, and went on reading without exchanging a syllable with any of us, which made us feel guilty in some way towards him. In the evening too, he would stretch himself on the sofa in the drawing-room and either go to sleep his head propped up on his elbow, or tell us the most impossible stories—at times hardly decent, which made Mimi grow angry and turn red in spots, and us die with laughter; but he never condescended to talk seriously with any member of our family except Papa, or occasionally with me. I quite involuntarily aped my brother in his views about the girls, although I was not so much afraid of sentiment as he was, and my contempt for the girls was far from being so deep and firmly rooted. I even made several attempts that summer, out of lack of amusement, to enter into closer relations with Lyubochka and Katenka and converse with them; but on every occasion I found such an absence of capacity for logical thought, and such ignorance of the simplest, most ordinary things as, for example, what money is, what was studied at the university, what war is, and so on, and such indifference to the explanations of all these things, that these attempts only served to confirm me in my unfavourable opinion of them.

I remember how one evening Lyubochka kept repeating some intolerably tedious passage on the piano. Volodya was lying dozing on the sofa in the drawing-room, and muttering at intervals with a certain malicious irony, but without addressing himself to any one in particular, "Lord! There she pounds away—what a musician, *Beethoven*! (this name he uttered with special irony) that was clever—now once more! That's it," and so on. Katenka and I were still at the tea-table, and I do not remember how Katenka turned the conversation to her favourite topic—love. I was in a mood to philosophize, and I began by loftily defining love as the desire to acquire something that one does not possess, and so forth. But Katenka retorted that, on the contrary, love was not love if a girl contemplated marrying a man for his money, and that in her opinion property was the most worthless of all things, but that the only true love was that which could endure separation (I understood by this that she was hinting at her love for Dubkov). Volodya, who must have overheard our conversation, raised himself on his elbow and cried out interrogatively, *"Katenka, no Russians?"*

"Oh, your eternal nonsense!" said Katenka.

"What? Into a pepper-pot?" Volodya went on, emphasizing each vowel. And I felt that he was quite right.

Apart from the general qualities of intelligence, sensibility, and artistic feeling, there is a private quality which is more or less developed in various circles of society, and especially in families, which I call *understanding*. The essential point of this quality consists in a conventional feeling of proportion, and in an accepted, one-sided view of things. Two individuals of the same circle, or of the same family, who possess this quality can always allow their expression of feeling to reach a certain point beyond which both of them foresee mere phrasing. Both perceive precisely where praise ends and irony begins, where enthusiasm ends and pretence begins; while with people of another understanding it may appear quite otherwise. People of the same understanding view every object in the same ridiculous, beautiful, or repellent light. In order to facilitate this identity of understanding, there arises among people of a certain circle or family a language of its own, certain terms of speech, certain words even, which denote shades of meaning which do not exist for other people. In our family this understanding was developed to the highest degree between Papa and us two brothers. Dubkov also had fitted our little circle pretty well, and *understood*; whereas Dmitri, although much cleverer than he, was stupid in this respect. But in no case was this faculty developed to such a pitch of refinement as between Volodya and myself, who had grown up under identical conditions. Papa was already far behind us, and much that was as clear to us as twice times two are four was incomprehensible to him. For instance, Volodya and I had agreed, God knows why, upon the following words with corresponding meanings: *Raisins* signified a vainglorious desire to show that I had money; a *bump* (the fingers must be joined and special emphasis placed on the two consonants at the same time) signified something fresh, healthy, elegant, but not foppish; a name employed in the plural signified an unreasonable partiality for that person, and so forth. Moreover, the meaning depended on the expression of the face, on the conversation as a whole; so that whatever new expression one of us invented for a new shade of meaning the other understood it exactly in that sense at the first hint. The girls did not have our understanding, and this was the chief cause of our moral solitude, and of the scorn which we felt for them.

Perhaps they had an *understanding* of their own; but it was so unlike ours that where we saw phrasing they saw real feeling; our irony was truth to them, and so forth. I did not understand at the time that they were not to blame for this, and that this lack of comprehension did not prevent them from being very good and clever girls; accordingly I despised them. Having, moreover, hit upon the idea of frankness, and carrying the application of it to extremes in my own case, I accused Lyubochka's quiet, confiding nature of secrecy because she saw no necessity for digging up and examining all her thoughts and spiritual instincts. For example, it seemed to me all sheer make-believe when Lyubochka made the sign of the cross over Papa every night and when she and Katenka wept in the chapel when they attended mass for Mamma, and when Katenka sighed and rolled her eyes when playing the piano; and I asked myself: When did they learn to pretend like grown-up people, and why were they not ashamed of themselves?

Chapter XXX

MY OCCUPATIONS

Nevertheless, that summer brought our young ladies and myself closer together than in other years, because of a passion for music which I developed. That spring a young man, a neighbour, came to see us and had no sooner entered the drawing-room than he began to gaze at the piano and keep edging his chair closer to it as he talked casually with Mimi and Katenka. After discussing the weather and the pleasures of country life for a while, he skilfully led the conversation to piano tuners, to music, to the piano, and ended by saying that he himself played; and indeed he played three waltzes, with Lyubochka, Mimi, and Katenka standing around the piano watching him. This young man never came again; but his playing pleased me extremely, as well as his attitude when at the piano, the way he kept tossing his hair, and in particular the manner in which he took octaves with his left hand, swiftly extending his thumb and little finger over the space of the octave, then slowly drawing them together and again briskly extending them. This graceful gesture of his, his careless pose, the way he tossed his hair, and the attention which our ladies paid to his talent, ended by firing me with the idea of taking up the piano. Having convinced myself, in consequence of this idea, that I had both talent and a passion for music, I set myself to learn. In this respect I behaved like millions of the male and especially the female sex who study without a good teacher, without a real vocation, and without the slightest understanding of what art can give, and of how to set about it to obtain this gift. Music, or rather piano playing, was for me a means of captivating girls through their feelings. With the help of Katenka, who taught me my notes and broke my thick fingers in a little, in which process, by the way, I consumed two months of such zeal that I even exercised my disobedient fourth finger on my knee at dinner and on my pillow in bed, I at once began to play *pieces*, and played them, of course, soulfully, *avec âme*, as even Katenka admitted, but utterly out of time.

The choice of pieces was familiar—waltzes, galops, love-songs (*arranges*), and so forth—all by those pleasing composers of which any man possessed of a little healthy taste will select a little pile for you from the heaps of very beautiful things in the music shops, and say, "These are what you must not play, because nothing worse, more tasteless, and more senseless was ever written on music-paper;" and which, probably for that very reason, you find upon every young Russian lady's piano. It is true, we had the unhappy "Sonate Pathétique," and Beethoven's C minor sonata, which are for ever being massacred by young ladies, and which Lyubochka played in memory of Mamma, and other fine things, which her Moscow teacher had given her; but there were also compositions by this teacher, absurd marches and galops, which Lyubochka played as well. Katenka and I did not like serious things, and our favourites were, above all things, "Le Fou" and the "Nightingale," which Katenka played in such a manner that her fingers were not visible, and I already began to play with much vigour and some continuity. I had adopted the young man's gestures, and often regretted that there were no strangers to see me playing. But Liszt and Kalkbrenner soon proved beyond my powers, and I realized that I could not overtake Katenka. Fancying, in consequence of this, that classical music was easier, and partly for the sake of originality, I all at once came to the conclusion that I liked learned German music and began to go into raptures when Lyubochka played the "Sonate Pathétique," although, to tell the truth, this sonata had long ago palled on me. I began to play Beethoven myself, and to pronounce the name in the German way. But for all this muddle and pretence, as I now recall, there may have been something in the nature of talent in me, for music often affected me even to tears, and the things which pleased me I could manage to pick out upon the piano without notes; so that if any one had then taught me to look upon music as an end, a grace in itself, and not as a means of fascinating girls by the swiftness and sentiment of my playing, I might, perhaps, have actually become quite a good musician.

The perusal of French novels, of which Volodya had brought down a great many, was another of my occupations that summer. At that time *Monte Cristo* and various *Mysteries* had just begun to appear; and I plunged into novels by Sue, Dumas, and Paul de Kock. All the most unnatural personages and occurrences were as alive for me as reality; and I not only did not dare to suspect the author of lying, but the author himself did not even exist for me—living, acting people and adventures appeared before me out of the printed book. Although I had never anywhere met people like those I read about, still I did not for a second doubt that they would *exist* some day.

I discovered in myself all the passions which were described and a likeness to all the characters, heroes and villains of every novel, as a sensitive man finds in himself all the symptoms of all possible diseases when he reads a medical book. What pleased me in these novels was the artful thoughts and fiery sentiments, the genuine characters; the good man was thoroughly good, the bad man as thoroughly bad—exactly as I fancied people were in my early youth. It pleased me very, very much that this was all in French, and that I could remember the magnanimous words uttered by the noble heroes and use them some day when engaged in some noble deed. How many different French phrases I concocted with the aid of those books for Kolpikov, if I should ever encounter him again, and for *her*, when I should at length meet her and declare my love to her! I prepared things to say to them that would kill them on the spot. Upon these novels too I even founded new ideals of the moral worth which I wished to attain. Most of all, I desired to be *"nobel"* in all my deeds and behaviour (I say *nobel* and not *blagorodny*, because the French word has another meaning, which the Germans understood when they adopted the word *nobel*,* and did not confound it with *ehrlich*); next to be *passionate*; and lastly, to be what I already had an inclination to be, as *comme il faut* as possible. I even endeavoured to resemble, in my personal appearance and habits, the heroes who possessed any of these qualities. I remember that in one out of the hundreds of novels which I read that summer there was an excessively passionate hero with thick eyebrows; and I so much desired to be like him externally (I felt myself to be exactly like him spiritually) that, as I examined my eyebrows in the mirror, it occurred to me to clip them a little to make them grow bushier; but when I began to do so I happened to cut away too much in one place. I had to even them down, and when that was accomplished I looked in the glass and beheld myself, to my horror, without any eyebrows, and consequently very ugly indeed. However, I took comfort in the hope that my brows would soon grow thick, like the passionate man's, and was only disturbed as to what our family would say when they should see me without my eyebrows. I got some powder from Volodya, rubbed it on my eyebrows, and set fire to it. Although the powder did not flash up, I was sufficiently like a person who has been burned. No one suspected my trick, and my brows really did grow, much thicker, after I had forgotten all about the passionate man.

---

* *Nobel* means noble, generous. *Ehrlich* signifies honest, honourable, faithful, and so forth.—*Tr.*

Chapter XXXI

COMME IL FAUT

Several times already, in the course of this narrative, I have referred to the idea corresponding to this French title; and now I feel the necessity of devoting a whole chapter to it, for it was one of the most false and pernicious ideas ever engrafted upon me by education and society.

The human race may be divided into several categories —rich and poor, good and bad, soldiers and civilians, clever and stupid, and so on. Each man, however, has his own favourite principle of division according to which he automatically classes each new individual. My chief and favourite principle of division, at the time of which I write, was into people who were *comme il faut*, and people who were *comme il ne faut pas*. The second class was again subdivided into people who were simply not *comme il faut*, and the common people. People who were *comme il faut* I considered worthy of holding equal intercourse with me; as for the second class, I pretended to despise them, but in reality I hated them and entertained towards them a certain sense of personal injury; the third did not exist for me—I scorned them utterly. *This comme il faut-ness* of mine consisted first and chiefly in an excellent knowledge of the French language, and a good pronunciation in particular. A man who did not pronounce French well instantly awakened a feeling of hatred in me. "Why do you want to talk like us when you don't know how?" I asked him mentally, with biting irony. The second condition of *comme il faut* was long, clean, polished finger-nails; a third was a knowledge of how to bow, dance, and converse; a fourth, and very important one, was indifference to everything and the constant expression of a certain elegant, scornful *ennui*. Besides these I had general indications by means of which I decided, without having spoken to a man, to which class he belonged. The chief of these, besides the arrangement of his room, his seal, his handwriting, and his carriage and horses, was his feet. The appropriateness of his boots to his trousers immediately defined the man's status in my eyes. Boots without heels, with pointed toes, and trousers with narrow bottoms, and without footstraps—this was *common*; boots with round, narrow toes and heels, and trousers narrow below with straps surrounding the feet, or wide with straps which arched over the toes like canopies—this was a man of *mauvais genre*; and so on.

It is strange that this idea should have taken such a hold on me who was decidedly disqualified to be *comme il faut*. But perhaps the very reason that it took such deep root in me was because it cost me great efforts to acquire this *comme il faut*. It is fearful to recall how much of my priceless time at the best period of life, sixteen, I wasted to acquire this quality. It all seemed to come easily to every one whom I imitated—Volodya, Dubkov, and the majority of my acquaintances. I gazed at them with envy, and laboured secretly at French, at the art of bowing, without looking at the person I bowed to, at conversation, at dancing, at cultivating indifference and *ennui*, at trimming my finger-nails—when I cut away pieces of flesh with the scissors—and all the while I felt that much yet remained to be done before I should attain my object. But as for my room, my writing-table, my carriage—all these I did not in the least know how to arrange in such a manner that they should be *comme il faut*, although I strove to attend to it in spite of my repugnance to practical matters. Yet all this seemed to come natural to *other* people, just as though things could never have been otherwise. Once, I remember, after arduous and fruitless labour over my nails, I asked Dubkov, whose nails were wonderfully groomed, whether they had long been so, and how he managed it. Dubkov replied, "I have never done anything, as far back as I can remember, to make them so, and I couldn't imagine a gentleman's nails possibly being different." This answer wounded me deeply. I did not then know that one of the chief conditions of being *comme il faut* is secrecy with regard to the labours with which that *comme il faut* is obtained. *Comme il faut* was not only a great merit, in my opinion, a very fine quality, a perfection which I desired to attain, but it was the indispensable condition in life, without which there could be neither happiness, nor glory, nor anything good in the world. I should not have respected a renowned artist, nor a scholar, nor a benefactor of the human race, if he had not been *comme il faut*. The man who was *comme il faut* stood incomparably higher than they; he left it to them to paint pictures, compose music, write books, or do good; he even praised them for doing so, for why should not good be praised, whatever it consisted in? But he could not stand on one level with them: he was *comme il faut*, and they were not, and that was enough. It even seems to me that if we had had a brother, a mother, or a father who was not *comme il faut*, I should have said it was a misfortune for us, but that there could be nothing in common between them and me. But neither the waste of golden time, employed in constant worry to observe all the conditions of *comme if faut* which were so difficult for me and excluded every serious pursuit, nor the hatred and contempt for nine-tenths of the human race, nor the lack of attention for anything fine that lay outside the circle of the *comme il faut*—that was not the chief harm which this idea did me. The chief harm consisted in the conviction that to be *comme il faut* is in itself a position in society; that a man need not exert himself to become either an official or a cartwright, a soldier or a scholar, if he is *comme il faut*; that, having once attained this position, he has fulfilled his vocation,

346

and has even placed himself above the majority of mankind.

At a certain period of adolescence, after many blunders and digressions, every man, as a rule, feels the necessity of taking an active part in social life, selects some branch of industry, and devotes himself to it; but this rarely happens with a man *comme il faut*. I have known, and I still know, many, very many old people, proud, self-confident, sharp in their judgements, who, if the question were put to them in the other world, "Who are you? What did you do there below?" would not be able to return any other answer than, *"Je fus un homme très comme il faut."**

This fate awaited me.

Chapter XXXII

YOUTH

Notwithstanding the confusion of ideas whirling in my head that summer, I was young, innocent, free, and therefore almost happy. Sometimes, and tolerably often too, I rose early. (I slept in the open air on the veranda, and the brilliant, oblique rays of the morning sun awakened me). I dressed quickly, took a towel and a French novel under my arm, and went to bathe in the river, in the shadow of a birch grove, half a verst from the house. Then I stretched myself upon the grass in the shade, raising my eyes now and then from my book to glance at the surface of the river, which showed blue in the shade of the trees as it began to ripple in the morning breeze; at the field of yellowing rye on the opposite shore; at the bright-red morning rays of light as they tinged lower and ever lower the trunks of the beeches, which, hiding one behind

---

* I was a thoroughly genteel man.—*Ed.*

the other, receded into the cool depths of the wood; and I would feel joyously conscious of the same fresh young force of life within myself which breathed forth from nature all around me. When little grey morning clouds filled the sky, and I shivered after my bath, I would often start to walk at random through woods and meadows, joyously wetting my boots through and through in the fresh dew. All the while I indulged in vivid dreams of heroes from the last-read novel and fancied myself now a great soldier, now a minister, then a wonderfully strong man, then a man of passions; and I kept glancing round incessantly, in some trepidation, in the hope of suddenly meeting *her* somewhere in some meadow or behind some tree. Whenever these rambles led me near some peasants at work, all my ignoring of the *common people* did not prevent me from experiencing a powerful, involuntary embarrassment, and from trying to avoid their seeing me. When it had grown hot, but our ladies had not yet made their appearance for tea, I often went into the orchard or the garden to eat of whatever vegetables and fruit were ripe. And this was one of my chief pleasures. Go into the apple orchard, perhaps, plunge into the very midst of a tall, thick, overgrown raspberry bush. Overhead is the hot, clear sky; all around are the pale-green prickly branches of the raspberry bush mingled with weeds. The dark-green nettle, with its thin, flowery crest, stretched gracefully upwards; the claw-like burdock, with its unnatural, prickly, purple flowers, grew rankly above the raspberry bush and higher than your head, and here and there, in company with the nettle, reached even to the luxuriantly-drooping, pale-green boughs of the old apple-tree, high up on which apples, round, shining like ivory, but as yet unripe, mellowed in the heat of the sun. Below, a young raspberry bush, leafless and almost dry, twisted and turned reaching out towards the sun, green, needle-like spears of grass thrust themselves between last years' leaves,

and all, besprinkled with dew, grew green and rich in the
eternal shade, as though they did not know how brightly
the sun was playing upon the apples.

In this thicket it is always damp; it is redolent of dense
and constant shade, of spiders' webs and fallen apples,
which already lie blackening upon the mouldy soil; of
raspberries, and sometimes of the earwigs which you
swallow unwittingly with your berry—after which you eat
another as speedily as possible. As you advance you
frighten the sparrows who always dwell in this thicket;
you hear their anxious twittering and the beating of their
swift, tiny wings against the branches; you hear in one
spot the hum of the wasp, and somewhere on the paths
the footstep of the gardener, of Akim the little fool, and
his perpetual purring to himself; you think to yourself,
"No! neither he nor any one in the world can find me
here." With both hands you pick the juicy berries right
and left from their white, conical stalks, and swallow
them with delight one after the other. Your legs are wet
far above the knee; some frightful nonsense or other keeps
running in your head (you repeat mentally a thousand
times in succession, "A-a-n-d twen-ty-y-y, a-a-n-d
se-e-v-e-en"); the nettles sting your arms and even
your legs through your soaking trousers; the perpen-
dicular rays of the sun, which have penetrated the thicket,
begin to burn your head; your desire to eat has long since
vanished, and you remain sitting in the wild tangle and
listen and look and think, and mechanically go on plucking and eating berries.

At about eleven, when the ladies had usually taken
their tea, and settled down to their work I would go to
the drawing-room. Near the first window, curtained with
an unbleached linen blind, through the chinks of which
the brilliant sun cast such dazzling circles on whatever
came in its way that it hurt the eyes to look at them,
stood the embroidery-frame, over whose white linen the

349

flies promenaded peacefully. At the frame Mimi would be sitting, shaking her head incessantly in an angry manner, and moving from place to place to escape the sun, which, suddenly breaking through somewhere or other, darted a burning streak of light now on her hand, now on her face. Through the other three windows it fell, with the shadows of the frames, in full, brilliant, square patches. Upon one of these, on the unpainted floor of the drawing-room, lay Milka, from ancient habit, pricking up her ears and watching the flies as they walked about over the square of light. Katenka would be sitting on the sofa, knitting or reading, and impatiently waving her white hands, almost transparent in the bright light, or shaking her head, with a frown, in order to drive off the flies which had crawled into her thick golden locks and were buzzing there. Lyubochka either paced back and forth in the room, her hands clasped behind her, waiting until they went into the garden, or played some piece, with every note of which I had long been familiar. I would sit down somewhere and listen to the music or the reading, and wait until I could sit down to the piano myself. After dinner I occasionally condescended to ride on horseback with the girls (I considered walking an exercise unsuitable to my age and position in the world); and our excursions, during which I led them through extraordinary places and ravines, were very pleasant. Sometimes we had adventures in which I displayed great bravery, and the ladies praised my riding and my daring, and regarded me as their protector. In the evening, if there were no visitors, after tea, which we took on the shady veranda, and after a trip with Papa on the business of the estate, I would lie down in my old place on the veranda, and read and dream, as of old, listening to Katenka's and Lyubochka's music. Sometimes, left alone in the drawing-room with Lyubochka playing some ancient music, I would drop my book and, gazing through the open door of the balcony at the curling, drooping boughs of the lofty beeches, upon which the shadows of evening were already falling, and at the pure heavens, in which, if you gazed fixedly, a dusty yellowish spot seemed to appear all at once and vanish again, and listening to the sounds of music from the hall, to the creaking of the gate, the voices of women and the herd returning to the village, I suddenly recalled with great vividness Natalya Savishna, and Mamma, and Karl Ivanich, and for a moment I felt sad. But my soul was so full of life and hope at this period that these memories only brushed me with their wings and fluttered away.

After supper, and sometimes after a night walk in the garden with some one—I was afraid to go along the dark alleys alone—I went off to sleep on the floor of the veranda, which, in spite of the millions of mosquitoes which devoured me, afforded me great pleasure. When the moon was at the full I often spent whole nights sitting on my mattress, gazing at the lights and shadows, listening to the stillness and the noises, dreaming of various subjects, especially of poetic and voluptuous bliss, which then seemed to me to be the highest happiness in life, and grieving because, up to this time, it had been granted to me to imagine it only. Sometimes, no sooner had every one retired, and I had seen the lights in the drawing-room pass to the upper chambers, where feminine voices and the sound of windows opening and shutting would presently be heard, I went to the veranda and paced it, listening eagerly to all the sounds of the house as it lapsed into sleep. So long as there was the smallest, unfounded hope of realizing even a portion of the happiness that I dreamed of, I could not calmly imagine bliss for myself.

At every sound of naked feet, at every cough, sigh, a slight rattling of a window or the rustling of a dress, I would jump up from my bed, stand furtively peering about and listening, and become agitated without any visible cause. But presently the lights disappeared in the upper windows; the sounds of footsteps and conversation gave place to snores; the night-watch-man began to tap upon his board; the garden grew more gloomy, and yet brighter, as the streaks of red light from the windows disappeared; the last candle flitted from the pantry to the anteroom, throwing a strip of light upon the dewy garden; and through the window I could see the bent figure of Foka, on his way to bed, clad in a wrap and with a candle in his hand. I often took a great and agitating delight in creeping over the damp grass in the black shadow of the house, approaching the window of the anteroom and listening with bated breath to the snores of the boy, the groans of Foka, who thought that no one could hear him, and the sound of his aged voice as he recited prayers for a long, long time. At length his last candle was extinguished, the window was slammed to, and I remained quite alone; and glancing all around to see whether there was a white woman anywhere near the clumps of shrubbery or beside my bed, I would hasten to the veranda at a trot. Then I would lay on my bed with my face to the garden and, covering myself as much as possible from the mosquitoes and bats, gazed into the garden, listened to the sounds of the night, and dreamed of love and happiness.

Then everything acquired another meaning for me; and the sight of the ancient birch-trees, their branches on one side showing bright in the moonlight, on the other darken-ing the bushes and the road; and the calm, rich gleam of the pond increasing in brightness like a swelling sound; and the moonlit sparkle of dewdrops upon the flowers in front of the veranda, which threw their graceful shadows across the grey beds; and the cries of snipe beyond the pond; and the voice of a man on the road; and the quiet, almost inaudible scraping of two old birch-trees against each other; and the buzz of a mosquito over my ear and beneath the blanket; and the fall of an apple, which had been caught on the dry bough, upon the dry leaves; and the hops of the frogs which sometimes even got so far as the veranda steps and shone rather mysteriously in the moonlight with their green backs—all this assumed a strange significance for me, the significance of a beauty too great and of endless happiness. And then *she* appeared, with a long black plait of hair, a swelling bosom, always sad and very beautiful, with bare arms and voluptuous embraces. She loved me, and for one moment of her love I sacrificed my whole life. But the moon rose higher and higher, brighter and brighter in the sky; the gorgeous gleam of the pond, swelling like a sound, became clearer and clearer; the shadows grew blacker and blacker, the light more and more transparent; and as I looked upon and listened to it all, something told me that *she*, with her bare arms and fiery embrace, was far, very far from being the whole of happiness, that love for her was far, very far from being all of bliss; and the more I gazed upon the high, full moon, the more and more lofty, the purer and purer, the nearer and nearer to Him, to the source of all beauty and bliss, did true beauty and bliss seem to me; and tears of an unsatisfied but agitated joy rushed to my eyes.

And still I was alone, and still it seemed to me that this mysteriously magnificent nature that seemed to attract the bright disc of the moon and hold it for some reason in a lofty yet uncertain spot in the pale-blue heavens, at the same time filling all immeasurable space, and I, an insignificant worm, already stained with all poor, petty earthly passions, but endowed also with an infinite might of imagination and of love—it seemed to me at such moments as though nature and the moon and I were all one.

Chapter XXXIII

NEIGHBOURS

I had been very much surprised, the first day we were in the country, that Papa should call the Epifanovs fine people, and still more surprised that he should go to their house. There was a lawsuit of long standing between us and the Epifanovs. I had heard Papa rage over this lawsuit many a time when I was a child, storm at the Epifanovs, and summon various people to defend him against them, as I understood it; I had heard Yakov call them our enemies, "evil people"; and I remember how Mamma requested that no mention of these people be made in her house or in her presence.

On these data I had constructed for myself, in my childhood, such a fine and clear idea that the Epifanovs were our *enemies*, who were ready not only to cut Papa's throat or to strangle him, but that of his son also if they could catch him, and that they were *evil people* in the literal sense of the word, that when I beheld Avdotya Vasilyevna Epifanova, *la belle Flamande,* waiting upon Mamma the year she died, it was with difficulty that I could believe that she was one of that family of evil people; and I still retained the basest opinion of that family. Although we often met them in the course of that summer, I continued to be strongly prejudiced against the whole family. In reality, this was what the Epifanovs were. The family consisted of the mother, a widow of fifty but still a fresh and merry old lady, her beautiful daughter Avdotya Vasilyevna, and her stuttering son, Pyotr Vasilyevich, who was a retired lieutenant and a bachelor of very serious disposition.

Anna Dmitrievna Epifanova had lived separated from her husband for twenty years before his death, sometimes in St. Petersburg, where she had relatives, but for the most part in her village of Mytishchi, which was situated at a distance of three versts from us. Such horrors were related in the neighbourhood about her manner of life, that Messalina was an innocent child in comparison with her. In consequence of this, Mamma requested that not even the name of the Epifanova should be mentioned in her house; but speaking entirely without irony, it was impossible to believe even a tenth part of the most malicious of all possible scandals—the scandals of neighbours in the country. But when I knew Anna Dmitrievna, although she had in the house a peasant business manager named Mityusha, always pomaded and curled, and dressed in a coat after the Circassian fashion, who stood behind Anna Dmitrievna's chair at dinner, while she frequently invited her guests in French in his presence to admire his handsome eyes and mouth, there was nothing of the sort which rumour continued to talk about. In fact, it appears that for the last ten years—from the time, indeed, when Anna Dmitrievna had recalled her dutiful son Petrusha from the service—she had entirely changed her manner of life.

Anna Dmitrievna's estate was small, a hundred souls in all, and her expenses during her gay life had been large, so that ten years before this, of course, the mortgages and double mortgages on her estate had fallen due, and its sale by auction was unavoidable. Fancying in these extremities that the trusteeship, the inventory of the estate, the arrival of the judge, and such like unpleasantnesses, arose not so much from her failure to pay the interest as from the fact that she was a woman, Anna Dmitrievna wrote to her son, who was then serving with his regiment, to come to the rescue of his mother in these straits.

Although Pyotr Vasilyevich was doing so well in the service that he hoped soon to be independent, he gave up everything, went on the retired list, and, like a respectful son who considered it as his first duty to comfort his mother's old age (as he wrote with perfect sincerity in his letters), came to the village.

Pyotr Vasilyevich, in spite of his plain features, his awkwardness, and his stutter, was a man of very firm principles and remarkable practical sense. Somehow he kept possession of the property by means of small loans, temporizing, prayers, and promises. Taking over the administration of the estate, Pyotr Vasilyevich donned his father's fur-lined coat, which had been laid up in the store-room, got rid of his horses and carriages, discouraged visitors to Mytishchi, dug drains, increased the arable land, cut down the peasants' allotments, felled his woods and sold them in a business-like way, and got his affairs into order. Pyotr Vasilyevich took a vow, and kept it, that until all the debts were paid he would wear no other clothes than his father's *bekesha* and a canvas coat which he made for himself, and that he would not ride in any other way than in an ordinary cart with the peasants' work-horses. He endeavoured to impose this stoical manner of life upon all the family, in so far as his reverence for his mother, which he considered his duty, permitted. In the drawing-room he stammered and conducted himself in the most obsequious manner towards his mother, fulfilled all her wishes, and scolded people if they did not do what Anna Dmitrievna commanded; but in his own study and in the office he called every one to strict account if a duck had been served at table without his orders, a muzhik had been sent by Anna Dmitrievna to inquire after some neighbour's health, or the peasant girls had been sent to the woods for raspberries instead of weeding the garden.

In the course of three years all the debts had been paid, and Pyotr Vasilyevich returned from a trip to Moscow in new clothes and a *tarantas*. But in spite of this flourishing state of affairs, he still retained the same stoical proclivities, in which he seemed to take a glowing pride before his own family and strangers; and he often said with a stutter, "Any one who really wants to see me will be glad to see me in my sheep-skin coat, and he will also eat my cabbage-soup and gruel—I eat them myself," he added. Every word and movement of his expressed pride, founded upon the consciousness that he had sacrificed himself for his mother and had redeemed the property, and scorn for others because they had done nothing of the sort.

The characters of the mother and daughter were totally unlike his, and they differed from each other in many respects. The mother was one of the most pleasant and cheerful women in society, and always equally good-natured. She really rejoiced in everything that was gay and pleasing. She even possessed, in the highest degree, the capacity of enjoying the sight of young people making merry, which is a trait encountered only in the most good-natured old people. Her daughter, Avdotya Vasilyevna, on the contrary, was of a serious character; or, rather, she possessed that peculiarly indifferent, dreamy disposition, somewhat haughty without any grounds, which unmarried beauties generally possess. Whenever she tried to be gay, her mirth was rather odd, as though she were laughing at herself, at those with whom she spoke, or at all the world, which probably she had no intention of doing. I often wondered what she meant by such remarks as "Yes, I am awfully handsome," or "Of course everybody is in love with me," and so on. Anna Dmitrievna was always active. She had a passion for housekeeping and gardening, for flowers, canaries, and pretty things. Her chambers and garden were neither large nor luxurious; but everything was so clean, so neatly arranged, and everything bore such a general imprint of that daintily light mirth which one hears expressed in a pretty waltz or polka, that the word *toy*, which was often used in commendation by her guests, was particularly suited to Anna Dmitrievna's tidy garden and apartments. And Anna Dmitrievna herself was a toy—small, thin, with a bright complexion, and pretty little hands, always merry, and always becomingly dressed. Only the rather purplish veins which stood out upon her little hands disturbed this general character.

Avdotya Vasilyevna, on the contrary, hardly ever did anything. Not only was she not fond of busying herself with flowers and dainty trifles, but she took little care of her own appearance, and always had to run off to dress when visitors arrived. But when she returned to the room dressed she was remarkably pretty, with the exception of the rather cold and monotonous expression of her eyes and smile peculiar to pretty faces. Her strictly regular and very beautiful face and her stately figure seemed to be constantly saying to you, "You may look at me, if you please."

But for all the mother's liveliness and the daughter's indifferent, dreamy air, something told us that the former had never loved anything either now or in times past except what was pretty and gay, and that Avdotya Vasilyevna was one of those natures which, if they once love, will sacrifice their whole life for the one they love.

Chapter XXXIV

FATHER'S MARRIAGE

Father was forty-eight years old when he took Avdotya Vasilyevna Epifanova for his second wife.

I fancy that when Papa came alone in the spring to the country with the girls he was in that nervously happy and sociable state of mind in which gamblers usually are when they have ceased playing after large winnings. He felt that he still had in store much unexhausted luck, which, if he did not care to squander it on gambling, he might expend upon general success in life. Moreover, it was spring; he was unexpectedly in possession of a good deal of money; he was entirely alone, and bored. In discussing matters with Yakov, and recalling the interminable lawsuit with the Epifanovs and the beautiful Avdotya Vasilyevna, whom he had not seen for a long time, I can fancy him saying to Yakov, "You know what, Yakov Kharlamich, I think it would be better to let that cursed piece of ground go. Eh? What do you think?"

I can imagine Yakov's fingers twirling a negative behind his back at such a question, and how he proved that "we are in the right, *after all*, Pyotr Alexandrovich."

But Papa ordered the calash to be got ready, put on his fashionable olive coat, brushed the remains of his hair, sprinkled his handkerchief with perfume, and in the most cheerful frame of mind, which was inspired in him by the conviction that he was acting with aristocratic distinction, and chiefly by the hope of seeing a pretty woman, he drove off to his neighbour's.

I only know that Papa, at his visit, did not see Pyotr Vasilyevich, who was in the fields, and that he passed an hour or two with the ladies. I can imagine him overflowing with amiability, charming them, as he tapped the floor with his soft boots, whispered, and made eyes. I can imagine, too, how the merry little old woman conceived a sudden tender affection for him, and how animated her cold and beautiful daughter became.

When the maid-servant ran panting to announce to Pyotr Vasilyevich that old Irtenyev himself had come, I can imagine him answering angrily, "Well, what of it? What has he come for?" and how, in consequence of this, he returned home as slowly as possible, and perhaps even turning in to his study, purposely put on his dirty coat, and sent word to the cook not to dare, under any circumstances whatever, make any additions to the dinner, even if the ladies ordered it.

I often saw Papa in Epifanovs' company afterwards,

so that I can form a vivid idea of that first meeting. I can imagine how, in spite of the fact that Papa offered to end that suit peacefully, Pyotr Vasilyevich was morose and resentful because he had sacrificed his career to his mother, and Papa had done nothing of the sort, how he was surprised at nothing; and how Papa, pretending not to see his gloom, was merry and playful, and treated him as a wonderful jester, which at times rather offended Pyotr Vasilyevich, though he could not help yielding to him occasionally against his will. For some reason or other Papa, with his tendency to turn everything into jest, called Pyotr Vasilyevich colonel, and in spite of the fact that Epifanov, reddening with vexation, and stuttering even worse than usual, once remarked in my presence that he "was not a c-c-colonel, but a l-l-lieu-lieutenant," Papa called him colonel again five minutes afterwards.

Lyubochka told me that before our arrival in the village there had been daily meetings with the Epifanovs, and that things had been very lively. Papa, with his faculty for arranging everything with a touch of originality and wit, and at the same time simple and elegant manner, had got up hunting and fishing parties, and a fireworks display at which the Epifanovs had been present. And things would have been jollier still, said Lyubochka, if it had not been for that intolerable Pyotr Vasilyevich, who pouted and stuttered and upset everything.

After our arrival the Epifanovs only came to see us twice and we called on them once. But after the feast of Saint Peter, Papa's name-day, on which the Epifanovs and a lot of others came, our relations with the Epifanovs ceased altogether, father going to see them alone.

During the brief period when I had opportunities of seeing Papa and Dunechka, as her mother called her, together, this is what I noticed about them: Papa was constantly in that happy mood which had struck me on the day of our arrival. He was so gay and young, and full of life and happiness, that his happiness beamed over all around him and involuntarily infected them with the same mood. He never went so much as a step away from Avdotya Vasilyevna when she was in the room and paid her incessantly such sweet compliments that I felt ashamed for him; or he sat gazing at her in silence, and twitched his shoulders in a passionate and self-satisfied sort of way, and coughed; and sometimes even whispered to her smilingly. But he did all this with that joking-like expression peculiar to him in the most serious matters.

Avdotya Vasilyevna seemed to be infected by Papa with happiness, which at this period beamed almost constantly in her great blue eyes, with the exception of the moments when such a fit of shyness suddenly took possession of her that it pained me, who was acquainted with the feeling, and it hurt me to look at her. At such moments she visibly feared every glance and movement; it seemed to her as though every one were staring at her, thinking only of her, and disapproved of everything about her. She glanced timidly at all; the colour coming and going in her face, and she began to talk, boldly and loudly, nonsense for the most part; and she was conscious of it, and conscious that everybody, including Papa, was listening, and then she blushed still more. In such cases Papa did not even notice the nonsense, but went on coughing as passionately as ever, and gazing at her with joyous rapture. I observed that, although Avdotya's fits of shyness came upon her without any cause, they sometimes immediately followed the mention of some young and beautiful woman in Papa's presence. The constant transitions from thoughtfulness to this strange, awkward gaiety of hers of which I have already spoken, the repetition of Papa's favourite words and turns of speech, her way of continuing with other people discussions which had been begun with Papa—all this would have explained to me the relations which existed between Papa and Avdotya Vasilyevna, had the one in question been any one but my own father, and had I been a little older; but I suspected nothing, even when Papa, on receiving in my presence a letter from Pyotr Vasilyevich, was very much put out, and ceased his visits to the Epifanovs until the end of August.

At the end of August Papa again began to visit our neighbours; and on the day before Volodya and I set out for Moscow he informed us that he was going to marry Avdotya Vasilyevna.

Chapter XXXV

HOW WE RECEIVED THE NEWS

Every one in the house knew of the fact the day before it was announced, and was discussing it. Mimi did not leave her room all day, and cried. Katenka sat with her, and only came out to dinner, with an injured expression which she had evidently borrowed from her mother. Lyubochka, on the contrary, was very cheerful, and said at dinner that she knew a splendid secret which she would not tell any one.

"There's nothing splendid in your secret," said Volodya, who did not share her satisfaction. "On the contrary, if you were capable of any serious thought, you would understand that it is very unfortunate." Lyubochka stared at him in amazement and said nothing.

After dinner Volodya wanted to take me by the arm; but fearing probably that this would be too sentimental, he merely touched me on the elbow and motioned me to the hall with a nod.

"Do you know the secret which Lyubochka mentioned?" he asked me, when he had satisfied himself that we were alone.

Volodya and I rarely talked to each other face to face about anything serious, so that when it did happen we felt a kind of mutual awkwardness, and little boys began to dance in our eyes, as Volodya expressed it; but now, in answer to the consternation in my eyes, he continued to stare me steadily and seriously in the face as much as to say, "There's nothing to be alarmed about, but we're brothers all the same, and must consult together upon a weighty family matter." I understood him, and he proceeded:

"Papa is going to marry Epifanova, you know?"

I nodded, because I had already heard about it.

"It's not nice at all," went on Volodya.

"Why?"

"Why?" he replied with vexation; "it will be very pleasant, won't it, to have such a stammering uncle, a colonel, and all those relatives. Yes, and she only seems good now, not a bad sort, but who knows how she'll turn out? Granted that it makes no difference to us, still Lyubochka must soon come out in the world. It's not very pleasant with such a stepmother; she even speaks French badly, and what manners she may give her! She's a fish-wife and nothing more: even if she is good, she's a fish-wife all the same," concluded Volodya, evidently very much pleased with this appellation of "fish-wife."

Strange as it was to me to hear Volodya thus calmly pass judgement on Papa's choice, it struck me that he was right.

"Why is Papa getting married?" I inquired.

"It's a queer story; God only knows. All I know is that Pyotr Vasilyevich persuaded him to marry, and demanded it; that Papa did not wish to, and then he took a fancy to it, out of some kind of chivalry; it's a queer story. I have only just begun to understand Father," Volodya went on (his calling him "Father" instead of "Papa" wounded me deeply): "that he is a very fine man,

363

good and intelligent, but so light-minded and fickle; it's amazing! He can't look at a woman with a cool head. Why, you know that he has not made the acquaintance of any woman without falling in love with her. Even with Mimi, you know."

"What do you mean?"

"I tell you that I recently discovered that he was in love with Mimi when she was young, wrote poetry to her, and there was something between them. Mimi suffers to this day." And Volodya broke into a laugh.

"It can't be so!" I said in amazement.

"But the point is," continued Volodya, becoming serious again, and beginning suddenly to speak in French, "how agreeable such a marriage will be to all our kin! And she'll be sure to have children."

Volodya's sensible view and his foresight startled me so much that I did not know what to answer.

Just then Lyubochka approached us.

"So you know?" she asked, with a happy face.

"Yes," said Volodya; "but I am surprised, Lyubochka. You are no longer a baby, how can you feel glad that Papa is going to marry a piece of trash?"

Lyubochka suddenly looked grave and became thoughtful.

"Oh, Volodya! A piece of trash? How dare you speak so of Avdotya Vasilyevna? If Papa is going to marry her, she cannot be a piece of trash."

"Well, no—that was only my way of putting it; but still—"

"No 'but still' about it," broke in Lyubochka, flaring up. "You have never heard me call the girl you are in love with a piece of trash. How can you say it about Papa and an excellent woman? Don't say that to me even if you are my eldest brother; you must not."

"May I not even express an opinion about—"

"No! not about a father like ours," Lyubochka again

interrupted him. "Mimi may, but not you, my eldest brother."

"Oh, you don't understand anything yet," said Volodya, contemptuously. "Listen. Is it a good thing that some Epifanova, *Dunechka,* should take the place of your dead mother?"

Lyubochka remained silent for a minute, and then tears suddenly came into her eyes.

"I knew that you were conceited, but I did not know that you were so wicked," said she, and left us.

"Into the loaf!" said Volodya, pulling a gravely comical face, and with a dull, stupid look. "Just try to argue with them," he went on, as though reproaching himself for having forgotten himself to such a degree as to condescend to a conversation with Lyubochka.

The weather was bad on the following day, and neither Papa nor the ladies had come down for their tea when I entered the drawing-room. There had been a cold autumnal rain during the night; the remains of the clouds, which had emptied themselves overnight, were still scudding across the sky with the sun's hazy disc, already quite high, showing faintly through them. It was windy, damp, and cold. The door into the garden was open; and pools left by the night's rain were drying on the damp-blackened boards of the porch. The wind was swinging the open door back and forth on its hinges; the paths were damp and muddy; the old birches, with their bare white boughs, the bushes and the grass, the nettles, the currants, the elder, with the pale side of its leaves turned out, struggled each on its own spot and seemed to want to tear themselves from their roots; round yellow leaves flew, twisting and chasing each other, from the lime-tree alley, and, as they became wet through, spread themselves on the wet road and on the damp, dark-green aftermath of the meadow. My thoughts were occupied with my father's second marriage, from the point of view from which Volodya had looked at it. The future of my sister, our future, and even that of my father, promised nothing good to me. I was troubled by the thought that an outsider, a stranger, and, most of all, a *young* woman who had no right to it, should all at once take the place, in many respects—of whom? She was a simple *young* lady, and she was taking the place of my dead mother! My heart was heavy and my father seemed to me more and more guilty. At that moment I heard his voice and Volodya's talking in the butler's pantry. I did not want to see my father just at that moment, and I went away from the door; but Lyubochka came to me, and said that Papa was asking for me.

He was standing in the drawing-room, resting one hand on the piano and looking in my direction impatiently, and at the same time triumphantly. That expression of youth and happiness which I had observed upon his face during all this period was gone. He looked troubled. Volodya was walking about the room with a pipe in his hand. I went up to my father and said good-morning to him.

"Well, my friends," he said with decision, as he raised his head, and in that peculiar, brisk tone in which one speaks of obviously disagreeable things, which it is too late to judge, "you know, I think, that I am going to marry Avdotya Vasilyevna." (He remained silent for a while.) "I never wanted to marry after your mamma, but"—(he paused for a moment)—"but—but it's evidently fate. Dunechka is a dear, kind girl, and no longer very young. I hope you will love her, children; and she already loves you heartily, and she is a good woman. Now," he said, turning to Volodya and me to give us no time to interrupt him, "it's time for you to leave here; but I shall remain until the New Year, when I shall come to Moscow" (again he hesitated) "with my wife and Lyubochka." It pained me to see my father seem so

366

timid and guilty before us, and I stepped up closer to him; but Volodya continued to smoke, and paced the room with drooping head.

"So, my friends, this is what your old man has devised," concluded Papa, and he reddened and coughed, and pressed Volodya's hand and mine. There were tears in his eyes as he spoke; and I observed that the hand which he extended to Volodya, who was at the other end of the room at the moment, trembled a little. The sight of this trembling hand impressed me painfully, and a strange thought occurred to me which upset me still more: the thought came to me that Papa has been in the army in 1812, and had been a brave officer, as was well known. I retained his large, muscular hand, and kissed it. He pressed mine vigorously; and, gulping down his tears, he suddenly took Lyubochka's black head in both hands and began to kiss her on the eyes. Volodya pretended to drop his pipe; and, stooping down, he wiped his eyes with his fist and then left the room, trying to do so unobserved.

Chapter XXXVI

UNIVERSITY

The wedding was to take place in two weeks; but our lectures had begun, and Volodya and I went back to Moscow at the beginning of September. The Nekhlyudovs had also returned from the country. Dmitri (we had promised when we parted to write to each other, and of course we did not write once) immediately came to see me, and we decided that on the following day he would take me to the university for my first lecture.

It was a bright, sunny day.

As soon as I entered the auditorium, I felt my personality disappear in this throng of gay young fellows which undulated noisily through all the doors and corridors in the brilliant sunlight. The sensation of knowing that I was a member of that large company was very pleasant. But very few among all those individuals were known to me, and the acquaintance was limited to a nod of the head and the words, "How are you, Irtenyev?" But all around me they were shaking hands and chatting— words of friendship, smiles, goodwill, jests, showered from all quarters. Everywhere I was conscious of the bond which united all this youthful company, and I felt sadly that this bond had missed me in some way. But this was only a momentary impression. In consequence of this and of the vexation it caused, I even discovered very speedily that, on the contrary, it was a very good thing that I did not belong to this society; that I must have my own little circle of nice people; and I seated myself on the third bench, where sat Count B., Baron Z., Prince R., Ivin, and other gentlemen of that class, of whom I knew only Ivin and the Count. By the way these gentlemen looked at me, I felt that I did not quite belong to their society either. I began to observe all that went on around me. Semenov, with his grey, rumpled hair and his white teeth, and with his coat unbuttoned, sat not far from me, leaning on his elbows, and gnawing at a pen. The gymnasiast who had been first in the examination was sitting upon the first bench, with his neck still wrapped in the black neckcloth, and playing with a silver watch-key upon his satin vest. Ikonin, who had contrived to get into the university, was seated on the highest bench, in blue trousers which completely hid his boots, laughing and shouting that he was on Parnassus. Ilenka, who to my amazement saluted me not only coldly, but even scornfully, as if desirous of reminding me that we were all equal here, seated himself in front of me and, putting up his thin legs upon the bench in a particularly free and easy way (for my benefit, it seemed to me), chatted with another student, and threw occasional glances in my direction.

Ivin's set beside me were talking in French. These gentlemen seemed to be frightfully stupid. Every word of their conversation which I overheard seemed to me not only senseless but incorrect, simply not French at all. *"Ce n'est pas Français,"* I said to myself; while the attitudes, sayings, and behaviour of Semenov, Ilenka, and others, seemed to me ignoble, ungentlemanly, not *comme il faut.*

I did not belong to any set; and, conscious of being isolated and unable to make friends, I grew resentful. One student on the bench in front of me was biting his nails, which were all red with hang-nails; and this seemed so revolting to me that I even moved farther away from him. In my inmost soul, I remember, this first day was a very doleful one for me.

When the professor entered, and there was a general stir and then silence, I remember that I extended my satirical view of things to the professor, and I was surprised that the professor should begin his lecture with an introductory phrase which, in my opinion, had no sense. I wanted the lecture to be so wise from beginning to end that nothing could be cut out nor a single word added to it. Having been undeceived in this respect, I immediately sketched eighteen profiles, joined together in a circle like a wreath, under the heading "First Lecture," in the handsomely bound note-book which I had brought with me, and only moved my hand across the paper now and then so that the professor (who, I was convinced, was paying a great deal of attention to me) might think that I was writing. Having decided, during this same lecture, that it was not necessary to write down everything that every professor said, and that it would even be stupid to do so, I kept to that rule during the whole of my course.

At the succeeding lectures I did not feel my isolation so strongly; I made many acquaintances, shook hands and chatted; yet for some reason or other no real intimacy sprang up between me and my comrades, and I often found myself depressed and only feigning cheerfulness. I could not join the company of Ivin and the aristocrats, as they were called, because, as I now remember, I was rough and churlish with them, and bowed to them only when they bowed to me; and they evidently had very little need of my acquaintance. With most of the others, however, this arose for quite a different reason. As soon as I was conscious that a comrade was beginning to be favourably inclined towards me, I immediately gave him to understand that I dined at Prince Ivan Ivanich's, and that I had a droshky. All this I said simply for the sake of showing myself in a more favourable light, and in order that my comrade might like me more; but almost invariably, on the contrary, I was amazed to see my comrade suddenly adopt a cold and haughty bearing towards me as soon as he heard of my relationship with Prince Ivan Ivanich.

We had among us a student maintained at the expense of the state, Operov, a modest, extremely capable, and industrious young man, who always gave his hand to every one as stiff as a board, without bending his fingers or making any movement with it, so that the jesters among his comrades sometimes shook hands with him in the same way, and called it a plank-way of shaking hands. I almost always sat beside him, and we frequently talked. Operov pleased me particularly by his free opinions about the professors. He defined, in a very clear and categorical manner, the merits and defects of each professor's teaching; and he even ridiculed them sometimes, which produced a particularly strange and startling effect upon me, coming from his very small mouth in his quiet voice. Nevertheless, he carefully took down all the lectures, without exception, in his small hand. We had begun to make friends, and decided to study together. His small, grey, short-sighted eyes had already begun to turn to me with pleasure when I went and took my usual place beside him. But I found it necessary to explain to him once, in the course of conversation, that when my mother was dying she had begged my father not to send us to any state-supported institution, and that all state scholars, though they might be very learned,—well, they are not the right people: "*Ce ne sont pas des gens comme il faut,*" said I, stammering, and conscious that I blushed for some reason or other. Operov said nothing to me; but at subsequent lectures he did not greet me first, did not give me his little board of a hand, did not address me, and when I sat down in my place he bent his head so that it almost seemed to touch his books, and pretended to be absorbed in them. I was surprised at Operov's sudden coldness. But I considered it improper for a young man of good birth to coax the state student Operov; and I left him in peace, although his coolness hurt me, I must confess. Once I arrived earlier than he, and as the lecture was by a popular professor, and the students who were not in the habit of attending lectures had flocked to it, and all the seats were occupied, I sat down in Operov's place, laid my note-books on the desk, and went out. On my return to the auditorium, I was surprised to find my note-books removed to the rear bench, and Operov seated in his own place. I remarked to him that I had laid my books there.

"I know nothing about that," he retorted, suddenly flashing up, without even looking at me.

"I tell you that I placed my books there," I blustered. "Everyone saw me do it," I added, glancing round at the students; but although many of them looked at me with curiosity, no one replied.

"Seats are not booked here; those who come first get them," said Operov, settling himself angrily in his place and glaring indignantly at me.

"That means that you are ill-bred," said I.

Operov seemed to mutter something; it even seemed as though he muttered that "you're a stupid pup," but I certainly did not hear it. And what would have been the good if I had heard it? should we brawl like a couple of *manants*? (I was very fond of the word *manant*, and it served me as an answer and a solution in many a complicated affair.) Perhaps I might have said something more; but just then the door slammed, and the professor, in his blue frock-coat, entered the room with a scrape of his foot and crossed to his desk.

However, when I needed the note-books, before the examinations, Operov, remembering his promise, offered me his, and invited me to study with him.

Chapter XXXVII

AFFAIRS OF THE HEART

Affairs of the heart engrossed my attention a good deal in the course of the winter. I was in love three times. Once I fell passionately in love with a lady of opulent figure who rode in the Freytag riding-school, in consequence of which I went to the school every Tuesday and Friday—the days on which she rode—in order to gaze at her; but on every occasion I was so much afraid that she would see me, that I always stood far away from her and fled directly I thought her likely to approach the spot where I was standing, and turned aside so negligently when she glanced in my direction, that I did not even get a good look at her face, and to this day I do not know whether she was actually pretty or not.

Dubkov, who was acquainted with this lady, once surprised me at the riding-school, hiding behind the footmen and the fur cloaks which they were carrying; and, having learned of my passion from Dmitri, he so frightened me with a proposal to introduce me to this amazon that I rushed away, and the very idea that he had told her about me prevented my ever daring to enter the school again, even as far as the lackeys, for fear of meeting her.

When I was in love with women I did not know, especially married ones, I was overwhelmed with a shyness a thousand times more violent than that which I had experienced in Sonechka's case. I feared more than anything else in the world that the object of my love would discover it, or even my existence. It seemed to me that once she had done so she would feel so insulted that she would never be able to forgive me. And, in fact, if that amazon had known in detail how, when I peeped at her from behind the lackeys, I meditated seizing her and carrying her off to the country, and how I was going to live there with her, and what I was going to do, she would have been justified in feeling greatly insulted. But I could not clearly realize that even if she did know me she would not know all I thought about her, and that therefore there was nothing disgraceful in simply making her acquaintance.

I fell in love with Sonechka again when I saw her with my sister. My second love for her had faded away long ago; but I fell in love for the third time when Lyubochka gave me a volume of poetry which Sonechka had copied, in which many gloomily amorous passages from Lermontov's "Demon" were underlined in red ink, and had flowers laid in to mark them. Recalling how Volodya had kissed his lady-love's little purse the year before, I tried to do the same; and, in fact, when alone in my room in the evening, I fell into reveries and pressed my lips to the flowers as I gazed upon them. I was conscious of a certain agreeably tearful sentiment, and was in love again, or at least fancied I was, for several days.

Finally, I fell in love for the third time that winter with the young lady with whom Volodya was in love, and who visited our house. As I now recall that young lady, there was nothing pretty about her and nothing of that particular beauty which generally pleased me. She was the daughter of a well-known intellectual and learned lady of Moscow; she was small, thin, with long blonde curls after the English fashion, and a transparent profile. Everybody said that this young lady was cleverer and more learned than her mother; but I could form no judgement whatever on this point, for, feeling a kind of craven bashfulness at the thought of her cleverness and learning, I only spoke to her once, and then with inexpressible trepidation. But the ecstasy of Volodya, who was never restrained by the presence of others in the expression of his raptures, was communicated to me with such force that I fell passionately in love with the young woman. As I felt that the news that *two brothers were in love with the same young woman* would not be agreeable to Volodya, I did not mention my love to him. On the other hand, I derived the greatest satisfaction in this sentiment from the fact that our love was so pure that, although its object was one and the same charming being, we should remain friends, and ready, should the emergency occur, to sacrifice ourselves for each other. It appeared, however, that Volodya did not at all share my feeling with regard to the readiness for sacrifice, for he was so violently in love that he intended to give a man who was said to be going to marry her—a real diplomat—a slap in the face and send him a challenge to a duel. It was very agreeable to me to sacrifice my feelings, probably because it cost me no effort, so that I only once addressed to the young lady a very high-flown remark on the worth of classical music; and for all my effort to keep it alive, my love died out the following week.

Chapter XXXVIII

SOCIETY

The fashionable pleasures to which I had dreamed of devoting myself when I entered the university, in imitation of my elder brother, left me quite disappointed that winter. Volodya danced a great deal, Papa also went to balls with his young wife; but they must have considered me still too youthful or unfitted for such pleasures, and no one introduced me in houses where balls were held. In spite of my promise of frankness to Dmitri, I did not speak to any one, even to him, of my desire to go to balls, and of how it pained and vexed me that I was forgotten and evidently regarded as a philosopher, which I pretended to be in consequence.

In the course of the winter, however, Princess Kornakova had an evening party. She herself invited all of us, and me among the rest; and I was to go to a ball for the first time. Volodya came to my room before he set out and wanted to see how I was dressed. This proceeding on his part greatly surprised and puzzled me. It seemed to me that the desire to be well dressed was shameful, and that it was necessary to conceal it; he, on the other hand, considered this desire natural and indispensable to such a degree that he said very frankly that he was afraid I might disgrace myself. He bade me to be sure to put on my patent-leather shoes, and was horrified to see me wear chamois gloves; he arranged my watch in a particular way for me, and carried me off to the hairdresser's in Kuznetsky Most. They curled my hair; Volodya stepped back and viewed me from a distance.

"Well, that's all right; only couldn't you smooth these little tufts?" he said to the hairdresser.

But however much M. Charles smoothed down my tufts with some gummy stuff, they rose the same as ever when I put on my hat; and altogether I looked even worse with curls than before. My only salvation was an affectation of negligence. That alone could give me some kind of appearance.

Volodya, it appears, was of the same opinion, for he begged me to undo the curls; and when I had done so and still did not look well, he would not look at me any more and was silent and depressed all the way to the Kornakovs'.

I entered the Kornakovs' apartments boldly with Volodya; but when the Princess invited me to dance, and I said for some reason or other that I did not dance, in spite of the fact that I had come with the sole idea of dancing a very great deal, I grew timid, and left alone with people whom I did not know, I lapsed into my usual insurmountable and ever-increasing shyness. I remained silent on that spot the whole evening.

During a waltz one of the princesses came up to me, and, with the sort of formal amiability common to all her family, asked me why I was not dancing. I remember how shy I became at this question, but how at the same time, and quite involuntarily, a self-satisfied smile spread over my face, and I began talking such nonsense in pompous French full of parentheses that I am still ashamed to remember it after dozens of years have elapsed. The music must have thus acted upon me, exciting my nerves; I hoped also it would drown the less intelligible things I said. I spoke about high society, about the vanity of people and especially women; and at last I got myself into such a tangle that I stopped short in the middle of a sentence, unable to complete it.

Even the good-mannered Princess became confused and gazed reproachfully at me. I smiled. At that critical moment Volodya, who had noticed that I was speaking with warmth, and probably wanted to know how I was making up for not dancing by my conversation, approached us with Dubkov. Seeing my smiling face and the Princess's frightened mien and overhearing the frightful stuff with which I wound up, he reddened and turned away. The Princess rose and left me. I went on smiling, but in such an agony from the consciousness of my stupidity that I wished the earth could have swallowed me and felt that I must make some movement at any cost and say something to improve my position somehow. I went up to Dubkov and inquired whether he had danced many waltzes with *her*. This I did as though jesting and in a merry mood, but in reality I was imploring help of that very Dubkov to whom I had shouted "Hold your tongue!" during the dinner at the Yar. Dubkov pretended not to hear me and turned aside. I approached Volodya and said with an effort, trying to impart a jesting tone to my voice, "Well, Volodya! aren't you played out yet?" But Volodya looked at me as much as to say "You don't talk like that to me when we are alone," and walked away in silence, evidently fearing that I might continue to attach myself to his person.

"My God! my brother also deserts me!" I thought.

Yet for some reason I had not the strength to take my departure. I stood gloomily where I was till the end of the evening; and only when everyone was leaving the room and crowding into the hall, and the footman helped me on with my coat in such a way as to tilt up my hat, did I laugh drearily through my tears, and say, without addressing any one in particular, *"Comme c'est gracieux!"*

Chapter XXXIX

THE CAROUSE

Although Dmitri's influence had still kept me from giving myself up to the usual students' pleasures, called carouses, that winter saw me once taking part in such a merry-making, and I carried away with me a not quite agreeable impression. This is how it came about.

During a lecture one day at the beginning of the year, Baron Z., a tall blond young man, with a very serious expression and regular features, invited us all to his house to pass a sociable evening with him. All of us meant, of course, all the members of our class who were more or less *comme il faut*; including, of course, neither Grap nor Semenov nor Operov, nor any of the meaner fellows. Volodya smiled contemptuously when he heard that I was going to a first-year students' carouse; but I expected great and remarkable pleasure from this, to me entirely novel mode of spending time, and I was at Baron Z.'s punctually at eight o'clock—the hour indicated.

Baron Z., in a white vest and with his coat unbuttoned, received his guests in the brilliantly lighted hall and drawing-room of the small house in which his parents dwelt: they had allowed him to use the reception rooms for that evening's festivity. In the corridor the heads and dresses of curious maids were visible, and in the pantry the dress of a lady, whom I took to be the Baroness herself, flashed by once.

The guests were twenty in number, and all were students with the exception of Herr Frost, who had come with Ivin, and a tall, ruddy-complexioned gentleman in civilian clothes, who attended to the banquet, and who was known to everybody as a relative of the Baron and a former student at the University of Dorpat. At first the over-brilliant illumination, and the usual formal decoration of the reception rooms, produced a chilling effect upon this youthful company, all of whose members involuntarily hugged the walls, with the exception of a few bold spirits and the ex-Dorpat student, who, his waistcoat already unbuttoned, seemed to be in every room, and in every corner of every room, at one and the same time, and to fill the whole apartment with the sound of his pleasant, resonant and never-silent tenor voice. But the fellows either remained silent or modestly discussed the professors, the sciences, the examinations, and generally serious and uninteresting subjects. Every one, without exception, stared at the door of the supper-room, and involuntarily wore an expression which said "Why, it's time to begin!" I also felt that it was time to begin, and I awaited the *beginning* with impatient joy.

After the footman had handed round tea to the guests, the Dorpat student asked Frost in Russian:

"Do you know how to make punch, Frost?"

"O, *ja!*" replied Frost, wriggling his calves; but the Dorpat student again addressed him in Russian:

"Then get down to it," (he called him *thou*, as a fellow-student at Dorpat), and Frost began to go from the drawing-room to the supper-room and back, with great strides of his curved and muscular legs; and after some walking to and fro, deposited on the table a large soup-tureen, and in it a ten-pound loaf of sugar, supported by three student's daggers laid crosswise. Meanwhile Baron Z. had kept incessantly approaching all the guests, who were assembled in the drawing-room, and saying to all, with an immovably serious face, and in almost the same words, "Come, gentlemen, let us drink like real good comrades, in student fashion. It's a shame we have no good fellowship at all among the members of our course. Unbutton your waistcoat, will you, or take it off —like the others." And, in fact, the Dorpat student, after taking off his coat, and rolling up his white shirt-sleeves above his white elbows, and planting his feet wide apart in a determined fashion, had already set fire to the rum in the soup-tureen.

"Put out the lights, gentlemen!" cried the Dorpat student suddenly, as pleasantly and loudly as if we had all shouted. We all gazed silently at the soup-tureen and at the Dorpat student's white shirt, and all felt that the solemn moment had arrived.

"*Löschen Sie die Lichter aus, Frost!*"* cried the Dorpat student again, having evidently become too much heated. Frost and all the rest of us set about extinguishing the candles. All was dark in the room, only the white sleeves and the hands which lifted the loaf of sugar on the daggers were illuminated by the bluish flame. The Dorpat student's loud tenor was no longer alone, for talking and laughter came from every quarter of the room. Many took off their coats (especially those who had fine and perfectly clean shirts). I did the same, and understood that *it had begun*. Although nothing jolly had happened so far, I was firmly convinced that it would be capital when we had drunk a glass of the beverage which had been prepared.

The concoction was ready. The Dorpat student poured the punch into glasses, spilling a good deal over the table in the process, and shouted, "Now, gentlemen, come along!" And each time we took a full, sticky glass in our hands, the Dorpat student and Frost struck up a German song, in which the exclamation *juchhe* was frequently repeated; we joined in discordantly, began to clink our glasses, to shout something, to praise the punch, and drink the sweet, strong liquor, each with his arm thrust through another's, or just as we stood. There was nothing to wait for now, the carouse was in full swing. I had already drunk a full glass of punch; they poured me an-

---

* Put the lights out.—*Ed.*

other; my temples began to throb, the fire seemed crimson, every one was shouting and laughing around me; but still it not only did not seem jolly, but I was even convinced that I, and every one else, was bored but that we all considered it indispensable, for some reason or other, to pretend that it was very jolly. The only one who could not have been dissimulating was the Dorpat student. He grew constantly redder and more talkative, filled every empty glass, and spilled more and more on the table, which became all sweet and sticky. I do not remember in just what order things occurred, but I recollect that I was awfully fond of Frost and the Dorpat student that evening, that I learned a German song by heart, and kissed them both on their sweet lips. I also recollect that I hated the Dorpat student that same evening, and wanted to throw a chair at him, but refrained. I recollect that, in addition to the consciousness of the insubordination of all my limbs which I had experienced at the Yar, my head ached and swam so that evening that I was awfully afraid I was going to die that very minute. I also recollect that we all sat on the floor, for some reason or other, flourished our arms in imitation of oars, sang *Adown our Mother Volga*, and that meantime I was thinking that it was not at all necessary to do so. Furthermore, I recollect that as I lay on the floor, my one leg hooked around the other, we had a wrestling bout in Gipsy fashion, and I cricked some one's neck, and thought that it would not have happened if he had not been drunk. I remember, too, that we had supper, and drank something else; that I went out into the court-yard to refresh myself, and my head felt cold; and that I noticed when I left that it was dreadfully dark, that the step of my droshky had become steep and slippery, and that it was impossible to hold on to Kuzma, because he had become weak, and swayed about like a rag. But I remember chiefly that in the course of the evening I constantly felt that I was behaving very stupidly in feigning to be very jolly, to be very fond of drinking a great deal, and did not think of being drunk, and all the time I felt that the others were behaving very foolishly in pretending the same. It seemed to me that it was disagreeable for each single one as it was for me; but as each supposed that he alone experienced this disagreeable sensation, he considered himself bound to feign gaiety in order not to interfere with the general jollity. Moreover, strange to say, I felt that I ought to keep up this pretence if only because three bottles of champagne at ten rubles apiece, and ten bottles of rum at four rubles, had been poured into the soup-tureen, which amounted to seventy rubles, besides the supper. I was so fully convinced of all this, that I was very much surprised the next day at the lecture when my comrades who had been at Baron Z.'s not only were not ashamed to mention that they had been there, but talked about the party so that other students could hear. They said that it was a splendid carouse; that the Dorpat fellows were great hands at these things, and that twenty men had drunk forty bottles of rum between them, and that many had been left for dead under the tables. I could not understand why they talked about it, and even lied about themselves.

Chapter XL

MY FRIENDSHIP WITH THE NEKHLYUDOVS

During the winter I saw a great deal not only of Dmitri, who came to our house quite frequently, but of all his family, with whom I began to stand on friendly terms.

The Nekhlyudovs—mother, aunt, and daughter—always spent their evenings at home; and the Princess liked young people to come to see her in the evening, men of the sort whom she described as capable of passing an evening without playing cards or dancing. But there must have been very few such men, for I rarely met any visitors there, though I went there nearly every evening. I became accustomed to the members of this family and to their various dispositions and had already formed a clear idea of their mutual relations. I became accustomed to their rooms and furniture; and when there were no guests I felt myself perfectly at my ease, except on the occasions when I was left alone in the room with Varenka. I could not rid myself of the idea that as she was not a very pretty girl, she would be happy to have me fall in love with her. But even this embarrassment began to wear off. She had such a natural appearance of not caring whether she talked to me, or her brother, or Lyubov Sergeyevna, that I came to look upon her as a person to whom it was not at all either disgraceful or dangerous to show the pleasure which I took in her society. During the whole period of my acquaintance with her she seemed to me sometimes very ugly, again not such a very ugly girl; but never once did I ask myself with regard to her, "Am I in love with her, or not?" I sometimes chanced to talk directly to her, but more frequently I conversed with her by directing my remarks in her presence to Lyubov Sergeyevna or Dmitri, and this last method gave me particular pleasure. I took great satisfaction in talking before her, in listening to her singing, and in the general consciousness of her presence in the room where I was; but the thought of what my relations with Varenka would eventually become and dreams of sacrificing myself for my friend in case he should fall in love with my sister rarely entered my head now. If such ideas and dreams did occur to me, I strove to thrust aside any thought of the future, since I was content with the present.

In spite of this friendship, however, I continued to feel it my imperative duty to conceal from the whole Nekhlyudov society, and from Varenka in particular, my real sentiments and inclinations; I tried always to appear altogether different from what I really was, and such indeed as could never possibly have been. I affected to be soulful; I would go off into raptures, exclamations and passionate gestures when anything pleased me greatly; and at the same time I endeavoured to appear indifferent to every unusual occurrence which I saw, or of which I was told. I tried to appear a malicious scorner who held nothing sacred, and at the same time a keen observer. I tried to appear logical in all my actions, refined and accurate in my life, and at the same time a person who despised all material things. I may safely say that I was much better in reality than the strange being which I affected to be; but represent myself as I would, the Nekhlyudovs liked me and, happily for me as it turned out, did not believe in my dissimulation. Lyubov Sergeyevna alone, who regarded me as a great egoist, a godless and sneering fellow, did not seem to like me, and often quarrelled with me, flew into tempers, and amazed me with her irrelevant and incoherent utterances. But Dmitri still maintained the same strange more than friendly relations with her, and said that no one understood her and that she did him a great deal of good. His friendship with her continued to grieve his family.

Once Varenka, discussing with me this attachment so incomprehensible to them all, explained it thus: "Dmitri is an egoist. He is too proud, and, in spite of all his cleverness, he is very fond of praise and admiration—he loves to be first always; and *aunty*, in the innocence of her soul, finds herself admiring him and has not sufficient tact to conceal this admiration from him, and so she flatters him—and not hypocritically, but sincerely."

I remembered this judgement, and on examining it afterwards I could not but think that Varenka was very clever; and I exalted her in my own opinion with satisfaction in consequence. This sort of exaltation, resulting from the intelligence I had discovered in her, and of other moral qualities, I accomplished with a certain stern moderation, though with satisfaction; and I never went into ecstasies, the highest point of that exaltation. Thus, when Sophia Ivanovna, who never tired of talking of her niece, told me how Varenka, when a child in the country four years before, had given all her clothes and shoes to the peasant children without permission, so that they had to be taken back afterwards, I did not at once accept that fact as worthy of exalting her in my opinion, but even mentally ridiculed her for such an unpractical view of things.

When the Nekhlyudovs had other guests, and among others Volodya and Dubkov, I retired into the background in a self-satisfied way, and with a certain calm consciousness of power, as one of the family, did not talk, and merely listened to what others said. And everything that these others said seemed to me so incredibly stupid that I inwardly wondered how such an intelligent, logical woman as the Princess, and all her equally sensible family, could listen to and answer such rubbish. Had it then occurred to me to compare what others said with what I said myself when I was alone, I should certainly not have felt the least surprise. I should have felt still less surprise if I had believed that the members of our household—Avdotya Vasilyevna, Lyubochka, and Katenka —were just like all other women, and no worse than any others; and if I had recalled the fact that Dubkov, Katenka, and Avdotya Vasilyevna conversed together for whole evenings, laughing merrily; and that, on nearly every occasion, Dubkov, seizing the first suitable word as a pretext, recited, with feeling, the verses, *"Au banquet de* *la vie. infortuné convive*,"* or extracts from "The Demon"; and what nonsense they talked, on the whole, and with how much pleasure, for several hours on end.

When there were visitors, of course, Varenka paid less attention to me than when we were alone; and then there was no music or reading, which I was very fond of listening to. In conversing with visitors she lost what was for me her chief charm—her calm deliberation and simplicity. I remember what a strange surprise her conversations with my brother Volodya about the theatre and the weather were to me. I knew that Volodya avoided and despised commonplaces more than anything else in the world; Varenka also always ridiculed pretended entertaining discussions about the weather, and so forth; then why, when they came together, did they constantly utter the most intolerable absurdities, and that, too, as though they were ashamed of each other? I went into a private rage with Varenka after every such conversation, ridiculed the visitors on the following day, but took still greater pleasure in being alone in the Nekhlyudov family circle.

At all events, I began to take more pleasure in being with Dmitri in his mother's drawing-room than alone face to face with him.

Chapter XLI

MY FRIENDSHIP WITH NEKHLYUDOV

Just at this time my friendship with Dmitri hung by a hair. I had been criticizing him too long not to have discovered that he had failings; and in our early youth we love with passion only, and therefore only perfect people. But as soon as the mist of passion begins to dis-

---

* Unfortunate guest at the banquet of life.—*Ed.*

solve, and of necessity to be pierced by the clear rays of judgement, revealing the object of our passion in its real aspect, with its merits and shortcomings, the shortcomings alone strike us as something unexpected in a vivid and exaggerated manner; the feeling of attraction towards novelty and the hope that it is not utterly impossible in another man encourage us not only to coolness, but to repugnance for the former object of our passion, and we desert it without compunction and hasten forward to seek some new perfection. If this was not precisely what happened to me in my connection with Dmitri, it was because I was bound to him only by an obstinate, pedantic, and intellectual affection, rather than by an affection from the heart, which I would have been ashamed to be false to. We were bound, moreover, by our strange rule of frankness. We were afraid too much that, if we parted, we should leave in each other's power all the intimate secrets which we had confided to each other and of which we were ashamed. Besides, for a long time we had not kept our rule of frankness, as was evident to us; this embarrassed us, and brought about strange relations between us.

Almost every time I went to Dmitri that winter I found with him his university comrade, a student named Bezobyedov, with whom he studied. Bezobyedov was a small, thin, pock-marked man, with very small hands covered with freckles, and a great mass of unkempt red hair. He was always very ragged and dirty; he was uneducated and even studied badly. Dmitri's relations with him were, like his relations with Lyubov Sergeyevna, incomprehensible to me. The sole reason why he could have selected him from among all his comrades, and have become intimate with him, was that there was not a student in the whole university who was uglier in appearance than Bezobyedov. And it must have been precisely for that reason that Dmitri found it agreeable to display friendship for him in defiance of everybody. In his whole intercourse with this student the haughty sentiment was expressed—"No matter who you are, you are all the same to me. If I like him, he's all right."

I was surprised that he did not find it hard to put a constant constraint upon himself, and that the unfortunate Bezobyedov endured his awkward position. This friendship did not please me at all.

Once I went to Dmitri to spend the evening in his mother's drawing-room with him in conversation and listening to Varenka's singing or reading, but Bezobyedov was sitting upstairs. Dmitri replied to me in a sharp tone that he could not come down because he had company, as I could see for myself.

"Besides what is the fun of sitting down there?" he added; "it's much better to stay here and chat." Although the idea of sitting and talking with Bezobyedov for a couple of hours did not appeal to me, I could not bring myself to go to the drawing-room alone; and, vexed at my friend's eccentricity, I sat down in a rocking-chair and began rocking myself in silence. I was very much provoked by Dmitri and Bezobyedov, because they had deprived me of the pleasure of going downstairs. I listened irritably in silence to their conversation, waiting for Bezobyedov to take his departure. "A very pleasant guest to be sitting with," thought I, when the footman brought tea, and Dmitri had to ask Bezobyedov at least five times to take a glass, because the bashful guest considered himself bound to refuse it at first and to say, "Please don't mind me." Dmitri, with a visible effort, engaged his visitor in conversation, into which he made several vain efforts to drag me. I preserved a gloomy silence.

"Why do you try and assume this don't-you-dare-to-think-I'm-bored expression?" I said mentally to Dmitri as I rocked myself silently and regularly in my chair. I fanned the flame of quiet hatred towards my friend within me more and more. "What a fool!" I thought. "He might have spent a delightful evening with his dear relatives, yet he sits here with this beast; and will go on doing so, too, until it is already too late to go down to the drawing-room"; and I glanced at my friend from behind the back of my chair. His hands, his attitude, his neck, and especially the nape of it, and his knees, seemed so repulsive and mortifying that I could have taken great delight at that moment in doing something to him, even something extremely disagreeable.

At length Bezobyedov rose, but Dmitri could not at once part from so pleasant a guest and asked him to stay the night; to which, fortunately, Bezobyedov did not consent, and departed.

After having seen him off, Dmitri returned; and smiling brightly in a self-satisfied way, and rubbing his hands, probably because he had persisted in his purpose, and because he had at last got rid of a bore, he began to pace the room, glancing at me from time to time. He was still more repulsive to me. "How can he go on walking and grinning like that?" I thought.

"Why are you angry?" said he suddenly, halting in front of me.

"I am not in the least angry," I answered, as one always answers on such occasions; "I am only vexed that you should simulate to me, and to Bezobyedov, and to yourself."

"What nonsense! I never simulate to any one."

"I have not forgotten our rule of frankness; I speak openly to you. I am convinced that that Bezobyedov is as intolerable to you as to me, because he is stupid, and God knows what else; but you like to look great in his eyes."

"That's not true, and besides, Bezobyedov is a very fine man to begin with—"

"But I tell you, it is; I will even go so far as to say to you that your friendship with Lyubov Sergeyevna is also founded on the fact that she thinks you a god."

"And I tell you, it isn't."

"I tell you, it is, because I know it by my own experience," I replied with the warmth of suppressed vexation, desirous of disarming him by my frankness. "I have told you, and I repeat it, that it always seems to me that I like people who say pleasant things to me; and when I come to examine the matter well, I see that there is no real attachment."

"No," went on Dmitri, adjusting his neckerchief with an angry motion of the neck; "when I love, neither praise nor blame can change my feelings."

"It is not true. I have confessed to you that when Papa called me a good-for-nothing, I hated him for a while and desired his death, just as you—"

"Speak for yourself. It's a great pity if you are such—"

"On the contrary," I cried, springing from my chair and looking him in the eye with desperate bravery, "what you are saying is not nice; did you not speak to me about my brother? I will not remind you of it, because that would be dishonourable. Did you not speak to me— I will tell you how I understand you now—"

And, burning to wound him even more painfully than he had wounded me, I began to prove to him that he did not love any one, and to tell him everything with which, as it seemed to me, I had a right to reproach him. I was very much pleased at having told him everything, quite forgetting that the only possible purpose of what I said, which was to make him confess the shortcomings with which I charged him, could not be attained at the present moment, when he was excited. But I never said this to him when he was in a state of composure and could acknowledge it.

The dispute already threatened to develop into a quarrel, when Dmitri became silent all at once and went into the next room. I was on the point of following him, talking all the while, but he did not reply to me. I knew that violent passion was in the list of his vices, and that he was trying to overcome it now. I cursed all his plans.

So this was the result of our rule *to tell each other everything that we thought, and never to say anything about each other to any third person.* Carried away by frankness, we had sometimes proceeded to the most shameless confessions, revealing, to our own shame, vague dreams and longings as though they were definite desires and sentiments such as I had just expressed to him, for example; and these confessions not only had not tightened the bond which united us, they had dried up the feeling itself and separated us. And now, all at once, egotism did not permit him to make the most trivial admission; and in the heat of our dispute we made use of the very weapons with which we had previously supplied each other, and which dealt frightfully painful blows.

Chapter XLII

THE STEPMOTHER

Although Papa had not meant to come to Moscow with his wife until after the New Year, he arrived in October, at a season when there was excellent autumn hunting to be had with the dogs. Papa said that he had changed his plan because his case was to be heard in the senate; but Mimi told us that Avdotya Vasilyevna had become so bored in the country, had so frequently spoken of Moscow, and feigned illness, that Papa had decided to comply with her wishes. "She had never loved him, but had only kept buzzing about love in everybody's ears, because she wanted to marry a rich man," said Mimi, sighing thoughtfully, as much as to say, "To think what a *certain person* would have done for him, if he had but known how to prize her."

Yet that *certain person* was unjust to Avdotya Vasil- yevna. Her love for Papa—passionate, devoted love—and self-sacrifice were evident in every word, every look, and every movement. But this love did not in the least pre- vent her cherishing, besides the desire not to leave her husband, a desire for remarkable head-dresses made by Madame Annette, for bonnets with extraordinary blue ostrich feathers, and gowns of blue Venetian velvet, that artistically showed off her fine white arms and bosom, which had hitherto been exhibited to no one except to her husband and dressing-maids. Katenka took her mother's side, of course; while certain odd, jesting relations were established between our stepmother and us from the very day of her arrival. As soon as she alighted from the car- riage Volodya went up, scraping and swaying back and forth, to kiss her hand with a grave face and a dull stupid look, and said, as though he were introducing some one:

"I have the honour to offer my congratulations on the arrival of a dear mamma, and to kiss her hand."

"Ah, my dear son!" said Avdotya Vasilyevna, with her beautiful, monotonous smile.

"And do not forget your second dear son," said I, also approaching to kiss her hand, and involuntarily trying to assume Volodya's expression and tone.

If our stepmother and we had been sure of our mutual attachment, this expression might have indicated scorn of the exhibition of any tokens of affection; if we had already been ill-disposed towards one another, it might have indicated irony, or scorn of hypocrisy, or a desire to conceal our real relations from our father, who was present, and many other thoughts and feelings; but in the present case this expression, which suited Avdotya Vasilyevna's taste extremely well, indicated nothing at all, and only pointed to an utter absence of all relations. I have often observed these false and jesting relations since in other families, whose members foresee that the actual relations will not be quite agreeable; and these relations involuntarily established themselves between us and Avdotya Vasilyevna. We hardly ever departed from them; we were always hypocritically polite to her, spoke French, scraped and bowed, and called her *"chère maman,"* to which she always replied with jests, in the same style, and her beautiful, monotonous smile. Tearful Lyubochka alone, with her crooked legs and innocent prattle, took a liking to our stepmother, and strove very naively, and sometimes awkwardly, to bring her closer to all our family; and in return, the only creature in all the world for whom Avdotya Vasilyevna had a drop of affection, with the exception of her passionate love for Papa, was Lyubochka. Avdotya Vasilyevna even displayed for her a certain ecstatic admiration and a timid respect, which greatly amazed me.

At first Avdotya Vasilyevna was very fond of calling herself a stepmother, and hinting at the evil and unjust way in which children and members of the household always look upon a stepmother, and how difficult her position was in consequence of this. But though she perceived all the unpleasantness of this position, she did nothing to avoid it by, say, caressing this one, or giving presents to another, or forbearing to grumble, which would have been very easy for her, since she was very amiable and not exacting by disposition. Yet, not only did she do none of these things but, on the contrary, foreseeing all the unpleasantness of her position, she prepared herself for defence without having been attacked; and, taking it for granted that all the members of the household wished to use all the means in their power to insult her and make things disagreeable for her, she perceived design in everything, and considered that the most dignified way for her was to suffer in silence; and this attitude of passivity in winning affection won her hostility. Moreover, she was so lacking in that quality of understanding each other almost without words which was developed to such a high degree in our house, and which I have already mentioned, and her habits were so opposed to those which had become rooted in our house, that this alone prejudiced people against her. In our neat, orderly house she always lived as though she had but just arrived; she rose and retired now early, now late; at one time she would come out to dinner, at another she would not; sometimes she had supper, and again she did not. She went about half-dressed the greater part of the time when we had no visitors and was not ashamed to show herself to us, and even to the servants, in a white petticoat, with a shawl thrown around her, and with bare arms. At first this disregard for conventions pleased me; but as a result of it I very soon lost all the respect I had entertained for her. What struck me as even more strange was that there were two totally different women in her, according to whether we had visitors or not: one, in the presence of guests, was a healthy, cold young beauty, elegantly dressed, neither clever nor foolish, but cheerful; the other, when no guests were by, was a depressed, weary woman, no longer young, slovenly, and bored, though affectionate. I often thought, as I looked at her when she returned smiling from making calls, and rosy-faced from the winter cold, happy in the consciousness of her beauty, and went up to the mirror to survey herself as she removed her bonnet; or when she went to the carriage rustling in her rich, low-necked ball-dress, feeling a little bashful, yet proud, before the servants; or at home, when we had little evening gatherings, in a close silk gown, with some delicate lace about her soft neck, she beamed on all sides with her monotonous but beautiful smile—I often thought what those who raved over her would have said if they could have seen her as I did on the evenings when she stayed at home and strayed through the dimly-lighted rooms like a shadow, as she awaited her husband's return from the club, in some sort of a wrap, with unkempt hair? Sometimes she went to the piano and played her one waltz, frowning with the effort; then she would take up a novel and, after reading a few lines out of the middle of it, throw it aside; again, in order not to wake up the servants, she would go to the pantry herself and get a cucumber and cold veal, and eat it standing by the pantry-window; or would wander from room to room aimlessly, both weary and bored. But what above all other things caused estrangement between us was her lack of understanding, which expressed itself chiefly in the peculiar manner of her condescending attention when people talked to her about things of which she had no knowledge. She was not to blame that she had unconsciously acquired a habit of smiling slightly with the lips alone, and bowing her head when she was told things which did not interest her (and nothing except herself and her husband did interest her); but that smile and bow of the head, frequently repeated, were inexpressibly distasteful. Her mirth, too, which seemed to ridicule herself, us, and all the world, was awkward and infected no one; her sensibility was too sugary. But the chief thing of all was that she was not ashamed to talk constantly to every one about her love for Papa. Although she did not lie in the least in saying that her whole life consisted in her love for her husband, and although she proved it with her whole life, yet, according to our views, such ceaseless, unreserved assertion of her affection was disgusting, and we were ashamed for her when she spoke of it before strangers, even more than when she made mistakes in French.

She loved her husband above all in the world; and her husband loved her, especially at first, and when he saw that he was not the only one whom she pleased. The sole aim of her existence was to acquire her husband's love; but it seemed as though she purposely did everything that could be disagreeable to him, and all with the object of showing him the full power of her love, and her readiness to sacrifice herself.

She was fond of dressing up; my father liked to see her a beauty in society, exciting praise and admiration; she sacrificed her love for festivities for father's sake, and grew more and more accustomed to sit at home in a grey blouse. Papa, who had always considered freedom and equality indispensable conditions in family relations, hoped that his beloved Lyubochka and his good young wife would come together in a sincere and friendly way; since Avdotya Vasilyevna was sacrificing herself, she considered it incumbent upon her to show *the real mistress of the house,* as she called Lyubochka, a misplaced respect, which wounded Papa deeply. Father gambled a great deal that winter, and towards the end lost a lot of money; he concealed his gambling matters from all the household, as he always did, not wishing to mix up his play with his family life. Avdotya Vasilyevna sacrificed herself, though sometimes ill, and even towards the end of the winter when she was pregnant, considered it her duty to go to meet Papa with her swinging gait, in her grey blouse and with unkempt hair, at four or five o'clock in the morning when he returned from his club, at times weary and ashamed after his losses.

She inquired, in an absent-minded way, whether he had been lucky at play, and listened, with her condescending attention and little nods of her head as he told her of his doings at the club, and begged her, a hundred times repeated, never to sit up for him. But although his losses and winnings, upon which all Papa's property depended, did not interest her in the least, she was the first to meet him every night when he returned from the club. Moreover, she was urged to go to meet him not by her passion for self-sacrifice alone, but by a certain concealed jealousy from which she suffered exceedingly. No one in the world could convince her that Papa was returning late from the club, and not from some mistress. She tried to read Papa's love secrets in his face; and as she could see nothing there she sighed with a certain luxury of woe and gave herself up to the contemplation of her unhappiness.

As the result of these and many other incessant sacrifices, there grew up in Papa's attitude towards his wife, towards the later months of the winter, during which he lost a great deal, and consequently was out of spirits the greater part of the time, an evident and mingled feeling of *quiet hatred*, of that suppressed repugnance to the object of one's affections which expresses itself in an unconscious eagerness to cause that object every possible sort of petty moral unpleasantnesses.

Chapter XLIII

NEW COMRADES

The winter had passed imperceptibly and the thaw had already begun, and at the university the examination lists were already posted up, when all at once I remembered that I must answer on the eighteen subjects on which I had heard lectures, and not one of which I had listened to, written down, or prepared. Strange that such a plain question, "How am I to pass the examinations?"

should never have once entered my head. But I had been in such a hazy state that whole winter, due to my delight at being grown up and *comme il faut*, that when it did occur to me I compared myself with my comrades, and thought, "They will pass, but most of them are not *comme il faut* yet; so I still have an extra advantage over them, and I must pass." I went to the lectures simply because I had become accustomed to, and because Papa sent me out of the house. Moreover, I had a great many acquaintances, and I often had a jolly time at the university. I loved the noise, the chattering, the laughing in the auditorium; I loved to sit in the back now during lectures and dream of something or other to the monotonous sound of the professor's voice, and to observe my comrades; I liked to run out at times with some one to Matern's, to drink *vodka* and have a snack, and, knowing that I might be reprimanded by the professor for so doing, to enter the auditorium after the professor, creaking the door timidly; I loved to take part in "course versus course" scuffles arranged amid much laughter in the corridors. All this was very jolly.

By the time, however, when everybody had begun to attend the lectures more regularly, and the professor of physics had finished his course, and had taken leave until the examinations came on, the students were busy collecting their note-books and preparing themselves. I also began to think of preparing myself. Operov, to whom I continued to bow, but otherwise was on the coolest of terms, as I have already said, not only offered me his note-books, but invited me to prepare myself from them with him and other students. I thanked him and consented, hoping by this honour entirely to smooth over my former disagreement with him; all I asked was that the gatherings should always be held at my house, as I had fine quarters.

To this they replied that they meant to take turn and turn about—sometimes to meet at one fellow's place, sometimes at another's, as might happen to be the nearest. The first meeting took place at Zukhin's. It was a small room, behind a partition, in a large house on Trubny Boulevard. I was late at the first meeting, and came when they had already begun the reading. The little room was full of smoke from the coarse tobacco which Zukhin used. On the table stood a square bottle of *vodka*, glasses, bread, salt, and a mutton-bone.

Zukhin invited me, without rising, to have a drink of *vodka*, and to take off my coat.

"I expect you are not accustomed to such entertainment," he added.

Everyone was wearing a dirty calico shirt, with a dickey. Trying not to show my scorn for them, I removed my coat and lay down on the sofa with an air of comradeship. Zukhin went on reading aloud, referring now and then to the note-books while the others stopped him to ask questions which he always answered concisely, intelligently, and accurately. I listened for a while, but as I did not understand much, not knowing what had gone before, I asked a question.

"It'll be no good for you to listen, old fellow, if you don't know that," said Zukhin. "I will give you the note-books so that you can read it up by tomorrow."

I was ashamed of my ignorance, and, conscious at the same time of the entire justice of Zukhin's remark, I ceased to listen, and busied myself observing these new associates. According to the classification of men into those who are *comme il faut* and those who are *comme il ne faut pas*, they evidently belonged to the second category, and consequently evoked in me a feeling not only of scorn, but of a certain personal hatred which I experienced for them because, though they were not *comme il faut*, they not only seemed to regard me as their equal, but even patronized me in a good-natured way. This feeling was aroused in me by their feet, their dirty hands with their closely-bitten nails, one long nail on Operov's little finger, their pink shirts, their dickeys, the oaths with which they familiarly addressed one another, the dirty room, and Zukhin's habit of constantly sniffling, pressing one nostril with his finger, and in particular their manner of speaking, of employing and accenting certain words, which seemed to me to be too bookish and disgustingly ungentlemanly. But what aroused my real *comme il faut* hatred was the accent which they placed on certain Russian, and especially on foreign words.

But in spite of their exterior, which at that time was insuperably repugnant to me, I could detect something good about these people; and, envious of the jolly comradeship which united them, I felt attracted to them, and wanted to get better acquainted with them, which was not a difficult thing for me to do. I already knew the gentle and upright Operov. Now, the dashing and remarkably clever Zukhin, who evidently reigned over the circle, pleased me extremely. He was a small, stout, dark-complexioned man, with a somewhat swollen and always shining but extremely intelligent, lively, and independent face. This expression was especially due to his forehead, which was not lofty, but arched over deep black eyes, his short, bristling hair, and his thick black beard, which bore the appearance of never being shaved. He did not seem to think of himself (a thing which always pleased me in people), but it was evident that his mind was never idle. His was one of those expressive countenances which undergo an entire and sudden change in your eyes a few hours after you have seen them for the first time. This is what happened with Zukhin towards the end of the evening. New wrinkles suddenly appeared on his face, his eyes sank still deeper, his smile became different, and his whole face was so changed that it was with difficulty that I would have recognized him.

When the meeting was at an end, Zukhin, the other students, and I drank a glass of *vodka* apiece in order to show our desire to be good comrades, and hardly any remained in the bottle. Zukhin inquired who had a quarter-ruble, that the old woman who served him might be sent for more *vodka*. I offered my money; but Zukhin turned to Operov as though he had not heard me, and Operov, pulling out a little bead purse, gave him the money that was needed.

"See that you don't take too much," said Operov, who did not drink at all himself.

"I should think not," replied Zukhin, sucking the marrow out of the mutton-bone. (I remember thinking at the time that it must be because he ate marrow that he was so clever.) "I should think not," he repeated, smiling slightly, and his smile was such that one noticed it involuntarily, and felt grateful to him for it. "And what's the harm if I do? I bet I can now stand up to any of our dry-as-dusts. Everything is in there already," he added, tapping his head boastfully. "But Semenov is risking to fail, the way he's taken to drink."

Indeed, that same grey-haired Semenov, who had so much delighted me at the first examination by being worse dressed, than I, and who, after having passed second in the entrance examinations, had attended the lectures punctually during his first month as a student, took to drinking hard, and towards the end of the year's course had not put in an appearance at the university at all.

"Where is he?" asked some one.

"I have lost sight of him," went on Zukhin. "The last time we were together we made a night of it at the Lisbon. It turned out magnificently. They say there was some kind of a scandal afterwards. There's a man for you! What fire there is in him! What a mind! It's a pity if he comes to grief; but he certainly will. He isn't the kind of boy to sit still in the university with those outbreaks of his."

After a little further conversation all rose to go, and having agreed to meet at Zukhin's on the following days as his quarters were the nearest to all the rest. When we all emerged into the court-yard I was rather conscience-stricken that they should all be on foot while I alone drove in a droshky; and shamefacedly I proposed to Operov to take him home. Zukhin had come out with us, and, borrowing a silver ruble of Operov, he went off to make a night of it with his friends. As we drove along, Operov told me a great deal about Zukhin's character and manner of life; and when I reached home I did not get to sleep for a long time thinking of the new people with whom I had become acquainted. For a long while as I lay awake I kept wavering between the respect which their learning, simplicity, honesty, and poetry of youth and daring, excited in me, and the distaste which I felt for their ungentlemanly exterior. In spite of all my desire, it was at that time literally impossible for me to associate with them. Our ideas were entirely different. There was an infinitude of shades, which constituted for me all the charm and meaning of life, of which they had not an inkling, and vice versa. But the principal reason why we could not possibly associate was the twenty-ruble cloth of my coat, my droshky, and my fine shirts. This reason had particular weight with me. It seemed to me that I insulted them with the signs of my prosperity. I felt guilty before them; and I could not in any way enter into equal, genuinely friendly relations with them, because I first humbled myself, then rebelled against my undeserved humiliation, becoming self-confident. Yet to such an extent did that powerful poetry of bravery which I felt in Zukhin overwhelm at that time the coarse, vicious side of his character that it did not affect me at all unpleasantly.

For two weeks I went nearly every evening to study at Zukhin's. I studied very little, for, as I have already said, I had lost ground at the start, and not having sufficient grit in me to study alone in order to catch up with them, I only pretended to listen and understand what was read. It seemed to me that my companions divined my pretence; and I observed that they frequently skipped passages which they knew themselves and never asked me.

Every day I became more and more lenient towards the disorder of this circle, I felt drawn towards it, and found much that was poetical in it. My word of honour alone, which I had given to Dmitri, not to go anywhere on a carouse with them, restrained my desire to share their diversions.

Once I thought I would make a display of my knowledge of literature, and particularly of French literature, and so led the conversation to that subject. It turned out, to my amazement, that, although they pronounced titles of foreign books in the Russian fashion, they had read a great deal more than I, that they knew and prized English and even Spanish writers, and Lesage, of whom I had never even heard. Pushkin and Zhukovsky were literature to them (and not, as to me, little books in yellow bindings which I had read and learned as a child). They despised Dumas, Sue, and Féval equally; and passed judgement, Zukhin in particular, upon literature much better and more clearly than I, as I could not but acknowledge. Neither had I any advantage over them in my knowledge of music. Still greater was my amazement to find that Operov played the violin, another of the company the 'cello and the piano; and both played in the university orchestra, knew music very well, and prized it highly. In a word, with the exception of the French and German accent, they knew everything that I attempted to brag about before them much better than I did, and were not

in the least proud of it. I might have boasted of being
a man of the world but, unlike Volodya, I was not one.
What, then, was that height from which I looked down
upon them?—my acquaintance with Prince Ivan Ivanich? my French pronunciation? my droshky? my fine
shirts? my finger-nails? Are not these things all nonsense? the thought would come flitting through my mind
at times, under the influence of envy for the fellowship
and good-natured youthful mirth which I saw before me.
They all called each other *thou*. The simplicity of their
intercourse approached coarseness, but even this rough
exterior could not conceal their fear of hurting one another's feelings. The words *scamp* and *pig*, which were
used by them in an affectionate sense, made me recoil,
and gave me cause for inward ridicule; but these words
did not offend them in the least or prevent their standing
on the most friendly footing with one another. They were
careful and delicate in their dealings with one another,
as only very poor and very young people are. But the
chief point was that I scented something broad and
wild in the character of Zukhin and his adventures at the
Lisbon. I had a suspicion that these carouses must be
something quite different from the sham with burnt
rum and champagne in which I had participated at
Baron Z.'s.

Chapter XLIV

ZUKHIN AND SEMENOV

I do not know to what class of society Zukhin belonged,
but I know that he was from S. gymnasium, had no
money whatever, and apparently was not of gentle birth.
He was eighteen at that time, though he appeared much
older. He was remarkably clever, and particularly quick

at grasping an idea; it was easier for him to embrace the whole of a many-sided subject, to foresee all its branches and the deductions from it, than to examine carefully by means of knowledge the laws by which these deductions are arrived at. He knew that he was clever; he was proud of it, and in consequence of this pride he was uniformly simple and good-natured in his intercourse with every one. He must have suffered much in the course of his life. His fiery, sensitive nature had already succeeded in reflecting in itself love and friendship and business and money. Although in a restricted measure, and in the lower classes of society, there was nothing for which, after having made proof of it, he did not feel either scorn or a certain indifference and inattention, which proceeded from the too great facility with which he acquired everything. Apparently he only grasped at every novelty for the sake of scorning what he had obtained after gaining his object, and his gifted nature always attained its goal, and had a right to be scornful. It was the same thing with the sciences: he studied little, took no notes, yet had a thorough knowledge of mathematics, and it was no vain boast when he said that he could beat the professor. He thought a great deal of what they taught was nonsense; but with his characteristic, unconsciously practical and roguish nature, he immediately fell in with what the professor required, and all the professors liked him. He was outspoken to the authorities, yet the authorities respected him. He not only did not respect or love the sciences, but he even despised those who occupied themselves seriously with what he acquired so easily. The sciences, as he understood them, did not require the tenth part of his gifts; life in his position as a student did not offer anything to which he could devote himself wholly; but, as he said, his fiery, active nature demanded life, and he gave himself up to dissipation of such a kind as his means permitted, and yielded himself with ardour and a desire to exhaust it so far as lay in his power. Now, before the examinations Operov's prediction was fulfilled. He disappeared for a couple of weeks, so that we made our preparations during the last part of the time at another student's rooms. But at the first examination he made his appearance in the hall, pale, haggard, and with trembling hands, and passed brilliantly into the second course.

At the beginning of the course there were eight men in the company of carousers, at whose head stood Zukhin. Ikonin and Semenov were among the number at first. The former left the company because he could not endure the wild dissipation to which they gave themselves over at the beginning of the year; while the second deserted them, because their revelry seemed too trifling to him. At first all the men in our class looked upon them with a kind of horror and related their pranks to each other.

The chief heroes were Zukhin and, towards the end of the year, Semenov. Semenov came to be regarded with a certain terror, and when he appeared at a lecture, which very rarely happened, there was a sensation in the auditorium.

Semenov wound up his career of dissipation, just before the examinations, in the most original and energetic manner, as I myself had occasion to witness thanks to my acquaintance with Zukhin. This is how it was. One evening when we had just assembled at Zukhin's, and Operov, having arranged beside him, in addition to the tallow candle in the candlestick, a tallow candle in a bottle, and with his head bent over the note-books was beginning to read in his shrill voice from his minutely-written notes on physics, the landlady entered the room and informed Zukhin that some one had come with a note for him.

Zukhin left the room but soon returned, looking thoughtful, his head lowered. He was holding a note written on grey wrapping paper and two ten ruble bank-notes.

"Gentlemen! Here is a rather unusual piece of news," he said raising his head and looking at us solemnly, almost gravely. "Got paid for your tutorship?" asked Operov, turning the pages of his note-book. "Let's go on," somebody suggested. "No, gentlemen, not for me," Zukhin went on in the same tone. "I've already told you—an incredible piece of news! Semenov has sent a soldier to bring me these twenty rubles that he had once borrowed from me and writes that if I want to see him I should go to the barracks. Do you realize what that means?" he added, looking at each one of us in turn. We said nothing. "I'm going straight off to him now," continued Zukhin. "Come along, if you like." Everybody immediately pulled on their coats, preparing to go to Semenov. "Won't it be rather awkward," Operov asked in his piping voice, "for the whole lot of us to go and stare at him as if he were some curio." I felt very much as Operov did, particularly as I was but slightly acquainted with Semenov but I was so eager to feel myself a member of the general company and to see Semenov that I didn't comment on this remark.

"Nonsense!" said Zukhin. "What's awkward about all of us going to take leave of a comrade? What does it matter where he is? It's nonsense, really. Why not come, if you feel like it."

We hired a few cabs, took along the soldier and left. The non-commissioned officer on duty didn't want to let us in to the barracks but Zukhin managed to persuade him somehow and the same soldier who brought us the note led us into a large room, dimly lighted by several small night lamps; on bunks that stood on either side sat or lay recruits in their grey greatcoats; all of them had the front part of their heads shaven. What particularly struck me on entering the barracks was its stuffiness and the sound of several hundred persons, cooped together, snoring. We followed our guide and Zukhin who strode confidently ahead of us between the bunks and I shuddered inwardly as I examined each recumbent form, trying to fit it in with my mental image of the awkward, wiry figure of Semenov, with his long, tousled and almost grey hair, pale lips and the grave look of his brilliant eyes. As we reached the farthest corner of the barrack where the hanging end of a guttering wick was flickering in the last little clay pot filled with black oil, Zukhin quickened his pace and then all of a sudden came to a standstill.

"Hello, Semenov," he said to a recruit, shaven like the rest and seated on his bunk, in thick soldier's underwear, a grey greatcoat thrown over his shoulders. He was talking with another recruit and eating something. That was *he,* with his closely cropped head of grey hair and the front of his head bluish from shaving. His face wore, as usual, a grave and energetic expression. I was afraid that my glance might offend him and so I turned aside. Operov seemed to feel the same way, and therefore kept behind; however, the sound of Semenov's voice when he greeted Zukhin and the others in his usual abrupt manner quite reassured us and we hastened to step forward. I offered him my hand, Operov his plank of a hand but Semenov forestalled us and stretched out his swarthy, big hand, saving us from the unpleasant feeling that we were doing him an honour. He spoke, as usual, calmly and reluctantly. "Hello, Zukhin. Thanks for coming. Sit down, gentlemen. You go away, Kudryashka," he said turning to the recruit with whom he had been supping and talking. "We'll finish our talk later on. Come on, sit down. Well? You were surprised, Zukhin? Eh?" "Nothing about you ever surprises me," Zukhin answered, sitting down

408

beside him on the bunk with an expression something like that of a doctor sitting down at his patient's bedside. I would have been more surprised if you had turned up at your exams. Well, tell us where you have been and how it all happened?" "Where?" he said in his rich, strong voice. "In pubs and dives and such places. Go on, sit down, gentlemen. There's plenty of room for all. Take your feet out of the way," he shouted imperatively, with a rapid flash of his white teeth, to the recruit lying to the left of him with his head on his arm and eyes turned on us with idle curiosity. "I was on a spree, of course. It was vile. It was fine too," he continued, the expression of his energetic face changing with every terse sentence. "Heard that story about the merchant? The rascal died. They wanted to expel me. I squandered all the money I had. But that wasn't the worst of it. I'd made no end of debts—nasty ones too. Nothing with which to pay them off. Well, that's all." "But how could such an idea enter your head?" Zukhin asked. "Very simply. I was on a spree at the Yaroslavl, in Stozhenka, you know. I was with a former merchant. He is now a recruiting agent. Says I to him: 'Give me a thousand rubles and I'll enlist.' And I did." "But look, you're a gentleman," Zukhin said. "That's nothing. Kirill Ivanov took care of that." "What Kirill Ivanov?" "The same agent who bought me (his eyes flashed in a very peculiar way—merrily and quizzically—and he seemed to smile as he said this). We got permission from the senate. I went on another spree, paid off my debts and here I am. That's all. Well, it's not bad. They have no right to flog me and I am five rubles to the good.... And who can tell, maybe there'll be a war."

Then he went on telling Zukhin about his odd, incredible adventures, the expression of his energetic face constantly changing, his eyes flashing fiercely.

409

When we could no longer remain at the barracks we took leave of him. He shook hands with each one of us and without getting up to see us out, said: "Come in sometimes, gentlemen. They say we're to be sent off only in a month," and again he gave us that semblance of a smile, peculiar to him. However, Zukhin, after taking several steps, turned back again. As I wanted to see how they would take leave of each other I also stopped. I saw Zukhin take some money out of his pocket and offer them to Semenov, but the latter pushed his hand aside. Then I saw them kiss and heard Zukhin shout rather loudly as he came nearer to us: "Good-bye, old bean! I bet you'll be an officer before I have finished my course." Semenov, who never laughed, answered him with a burst of shrill, unusual laughter that affected me very painfully. We went out.

We walked all the way home. Zukhin kept silent and was constantly sniffling, putting a finger now to one nostril, now to another. He left us when we came home and went on a drinking bout right up to the examinations.

Chapter XLV

I FAIL

At length the day of the first examination—on differential and integral calculus—arrived, but I was still in my hazy state, and had no clear conception of what awaited me. It occurred to me during the evening, after enjoying the society of Zukhin and his comrades, that it was necessary to make some change in my convictions; that there was something about them which was not nice, and not just what it should be; but in the morning, in the light of the sun, I again became *comme il faut*, was very well content with that, and desired no alterations in myself.

410

It was in this frame of mind that I went to the first examination. I seated myself on a bench on the side where the princes, counts, and barons sat, and began to converse with them in French; and, strange as it may seem, the thought never occurred to me that I should presently be called upon to answer questions upon a subject which I knew nothing about. I gazed coolly at those who went up to be examined, and I even permitted myself to make fun of some of them.

"Well, Grap?" I said to Ilenka when he returned from the table. "Did you get frightened?"

"We'll see how you manage," said Ilenka, who had utterly rebelled against my influence from the day he entered the university, did not smile when I spoke to him, and was ill-disposed towards me.

I smiled scornfully at Ilenka's reply, although the doubt which he expressed gave me a momentary shock. But the mist again shrouded this feeling; and I remained so indifferent and absent-minded that I promised to go and lunch with Baron Z. at Matern's as soon as I had been examined (as though this were a most trifling matter). When I was called up with Ikonin, I arranged the skirts of my uniform and stepped up to the examination table with perfect nonchalance.

A slight chill of terror went down my back only when the young professor—the same one who had questioned me at the entrance examination—looked me straight in the face and I touched the note-paper on which the questions were written. Although Ikonin took his ticket with the same swaying of his whole body as during the preceding examinations, he answered after a fashion, though very badly. And I did what he had done at the first examinations; I did even worse; for I took a second card, and made no reply at all. The professor looked me compassionately in the face, and said in a firm but quiet voice—

"You will not pass into the second course, Mr. Irtenyev. You'd do better not present yourself any more for examination. This course must be weeded out. And the same with you, Mr. Ikonin," he added.

Ikonin asked permission to be re-examined, as though it were an alms; but the professor replied that he could not do in two days what he had not done in the course of a year, and that he could not possibly pass. Ikonin begged again in a humble and pitiful manner, but the professor again refused.

"You may go, gentlemen," he said in the same low but firm voice.

It was only then that I could make up my mind to leave the table; and I was ashamed at having, as it were, taken part by my silence in Ikonin's humiliating entreaties. I do not remember how I threaded my way among the students in the hall; what replies I made to their questions; how I passed into the anteroom, and got home. I was offended, humiliated and genuinely unhappy.

For three days I did not leave my room; I saw no one; I found solace in tears, as in my childhood, and wept a great deal. I looked for a pistol, in order that I might shoot myself if I should want to do so very much. I thought that Ilenka Grap would spit in my face when he met me, and that he would be quite right in doing so; that Operov would rejoice at my misfortune, and tell everybody about it; that Kolpikov had been quite correct in insulting me at the Yar; that my stupid speeches to Princess Kornakova could have no other result, and so on, and so on. All the moments of my life which had been torturing to my self-love and hard to bear passed through my mind one after the other; and I tried to blame some one else for my misfortunes. I thought that some one had done this on purpose; I invented a whole intrigue against myself; I grumbled at the professors, at my comrades, at Volodya, at Dmitri, at Papa because he had sent me to the university; I complained of Providence for having allowed me to live to see such disgrace. Finally, conscious of my complete disgrace in the eyes of all who knew me, I begged Papa to let me enter the Hussars, or go to the Caucasus. Papa was displeased with me, but, on seeing my terrible grief, he comforted me by saying that it was not so very bad; that matters might be arranged by my transferring to another faculty. Volodya, too, who did not see anything dreadful in my misfortune, said that I should at least not feel ashamed before my fellow-students in another course.

Our ladies did not understand what it was all about; and would not, or could not, understand what an examination was—what it meant to fail; and only pitied me because they saw my grief.

Dmitri came to see me every day, and was extremely gentle and friendly during this whole period; but, for that very reason, it seemed to me that he had grown cold towards me. It always hurt me and seemed insulting when, coming up to my room, he sat down close to me in silence, with a little of the expression which a doctor wears when he seats himself at the bedside of a very sick man. Sophia Ivanovna and Varenka sent me by him books which I had formerly wanted and wished me to come to see them; but in this very attention I perceived a haughty and insulting condescension towards me who had fallen so very low. At the end of three days I became somewhat composed; but even up to our departure for the country I did not leave the house, and, thinking only of my grief, I wandered idly from room to room, endeavouring to avoid all members of the household.

I thought and thought; and finally, late in the evening, as I was sitting downstairs listening to Avdotya Vasilyevna's waltz, I suddenly sprang up, ran upstairs, got my note-book on which was written "Rules of Life," opened it, and a moment of repentance and moral surge came over me. I wept, but no longer with tears of despair. When I recovered I decided to write out my rules of life again; and I was firmly convinced that I should never henceforth do anything wrong, nor spend a single minute in idleness, nor ever depart from my rules.

Whether this moral impetus lasted long, in what it consisted, and what new laws it imposed upon my moral development, I shall relate in the following and happier half of my youth.

September 24,
Yasnaya Polyana

Printed in the Union of Soviet Socialist Republics.

28 79